Praise for *Halloween Cupcake Murder*

"Don't touch that cupcake—at least, not until Halloween. Amateur sleuths investigate when cupcakes become the weapon of choice in this collection of cozy novellas . . . The three cozy writers successfully exploit the deadly-cupcake theme in entertaining mysteries that will appeal to readers looking for a holiday treat."
—*Library Journal*

"Three different takes on Halloween and cupcakes that range from the historical to the fanciful."
—*Kirkus Reviews*

Published by Kensington Publishing Corp.

HALLOWEEN
CUPCAKE
MURDER

CARLENE O'CONNOR
LIZ IRELAND
CAROL J. PERRY

Kensington Publishing Corp.
www.kensingtonbooks.com

KENSINGTON BOOKS are published by
Kensington Publishing Corp.
900 Third Avenue
New York, NY 10022

All Kensington titles, imprints, and distributed lines are available at
special quantity discounts for bulk purchases for sales promotion,
premiums, fund-raising, educational, or institutional use.

Special book excerpts or customized printings can also be created to fit
specific needs. For details, write or phone the office of the Kensington
Sales Manager: Attn.: Sales Department. Kensington Publishing Corp.,
900 Third Avenue, New York, NY 10022. Phone: 1-800-221-2647.

KENSINGTON and the KENSINGTON COZIES teapot logo Reg
US Pat. & TM Off.

First Kensington Hardcover Edition: September 2023

First Paperback Printing: August 2024
ISBN: 978-1-4967-4027-4

ISBN: 978-1-4967-4028-1 (ebook)

10 9 8 7 6 5 4 3 2 1

Printed in the United States of America

Contents

HALLOWEEN CUPCAKE MURDER

Carlene O'Connor

Chapter One

Tara Meehan strolled down Galway's lively pedestrian street, eager for a morning of Halloween shopping. The air was crisp, and the smell of bacon, yeast, and wood-burning fires filled the air. Tara had that "back to school" feeling. The rain was holding off and the sun was flirting from behind a fluffy cloud. Nearby trees sported orange, red, and yellow leaves. Fall was her favorite season both stateside and here. Her mission was a fun one—purchase anything spooky she could use to either decorate or sell at Renewals, her architectural salvage shop. She had a sense of panic that everyone else was well ahead of her. Pubs had broken out the orange lights and grinning skulls, shop windows featured costumes—apparently sexy nurses and cowboys never went out of style—and even the coffee shops were luring customers in with their Witches' Brew Tea and cinnamon-dusted pumpkin lattes.

Tara had wrongly assumed that Halloween was more of an American thing. But Galway was all-in. Coming up was the big Macnas Halloween parade, the largest free event in Galway, featuring giant creatures, and sculptures, and pyrotechnics, not to mention bespoke costumes both in the parade and among the large and rowdy crowds.

Tara was determined to get into the spirit of things and entice a few tourists into her shop. She was promised the parade would be strange, unpredictable, and utterly mesmerizing. She wanted her shop to be nothing less. Uncle Johnny had recently mentioned that a curiosity shop in town had a recent shipment in, and he'd arranged an invitation for Tara to check it out before the word got out. Being an owner of a shop that sold architectural salvage items in Galway had its perks, priority shopping being one of them.

The little curiosity shop was a few streets away, nestled close to Tara's favorite medieval church. One had to be paying attention to notice it: a wooden sign carved into the shape of a shark with VAL written across it. The glowing eyes of a plastic black cat beckoned from the window. Just mounting the few steps up to the main door gave Tara a thrill. She opened the heavy wooden door and ascended a long flight of stairs. A single door greeted her at the top. The number 13 hung on the door, made of iron and hanging from two rusty nails. This had to be the right place. Tara turned the knob and the door creaked open. She stepped in and the floorboards groaned underneath her, accompanied by the mechanical sounds of a cat yowling.

For a brief moment she wondered if she had accidentally stepped into someone else's private flat. The room was lit only by a single lamp in the corner; she made out an armchair, a sofa, and a coffee table. An old man sat in the chair in the corner. "Welcome, Tara," he said. "I'm afraid me old bones won't allow me to rise quickly."

"No need," Tara said. "Given you know my name, I must be in the right place."

"Are you the curious sort?"

What a funny question. Then again, it was a curiosity shop. "I am."

"Then you're in the right place." He reached up and flipped a switch. With the additional illumination, Tara could see the walls were jammed with shelves and the shelves were jammed with items. In the corner opposite the old man stood a giant grizzly bear, its paws outstretched and its mouth open, flashing large teeth. It couldn't be real, but even its eyes seemed enraged and alive.

"I won her in a poker game," the old man said, gesturing to the bear. "Named her Flora. Isn't she a beaut?"

"I think she's in the right place," Tara said with a laugh. She nearly thought she could hear the bear breathing. "Although I can't help feeling sorry for her."

"She's better off with me than the man she was with. He gave me her and a few fish to boot." He grinned. "There's a man after her but I don't like third wheels."

Tara wasn't going to ask any follow-up questions; she had a feeling that if she did, she would be here all day, and she really needed to start treasure hunting. "I own a little shop in Galway—Renewals," Tara said. "I deal in architectural salvage."

"I know all about you," Val said. "Your Uncle Johnny is always waxing on about his American niece."

"Good old Uncle Johnny," Tara said with a laugh. Moving here from New York City and setting up shop would have been impossible without Uncle Johnny's connections. In Manhattan Tara had been a sought-after interior designer. And although she still advised clients once in a while, she loved running a shop even more.

"Val Sharkey," he said. "Pleased to meet you."

"Likewise." She meant it. She felt an instant kinship with fellow shop owners.

"You'll have to forgive me for not paying a visit to your shop though," Val said. "I don't go outside me door much."

"It looks like you have plenty in here to keep you going," Tara said brightly.

"You'd be surprised," Val said. "The older I get, the less all these things mean to me."

"I can see that too." She wondered if she'd still be manning a shop when she was older. Given she'd only been at it a few years, and still loved it, she had no clue how long it would take for burnout to set in. The thought that the answer could be *never* was delightful.

"What exactly are you looking for?" he asked. "I might be able to help."

"I'm looking for Halloween items."

He grinned. "Pumpkins and skeletons and what-not?"

"Mmmm. Perhaps. But I tend to skew a bit more . . . original?"

"Eyeballs and livers in jars?"

She laughed. "A bit less macabre."

He glanced at the grizzly bear. "But smaller than Flora?"

She laughed. "Yes, much smaller than Flora."

"You wouldn't want her, anyway," he said. "She eats too many fish."

Tara laughed. "I can believe it."

"Do you believe in curses?" he said, his tone suddenly dropping to a lower octave. She waited to see if he would follow it with a smile, or even a raise of an eyebrow. His gaze remained steady.

"No," she said. "I don't believe I do."

"Brilliant!" he said. And this time he did smile. "In that case I have just the thing." He heaved himself from his chair with a groan, then grabbed a nearby cane and hobbled over to the counter. "There's a gentleman who was supposed to pick it up—I've been saving it for him—but he's three days late. Given he didn't pay me a pence for it, I'd say it's yours now."

"I'll take a look," Tara said. He reached the counter, slipped behind it, and ducked down. When he stood back up, he was holding a black slate, like a small chalkboard, only this one was in an oval shape with jagged edges. Tara inched forward as he set it on the counter. A vibrant painting covered the surface, featuring a grand temple, and people in colorful robes making their way toward it. The robes were in almost every color of the rainbow: red, yellow, blue, green, pink. Only the backs of the people were shown, all drawn to the temple, their heads bowed, their robes billowing out behind them. In the background was a hillside, and then a cave. Above the entrance to the cave it read: CAVE OF THE CATS. It certainly was unique. She loved it.

"Do you know what it means?" she asked.

"Why, it's a painting of the first Halloween," he said, with a gleam in his eye. "This is a rendering of the first Samhain Festival."

"The Samhain Festival." Tara knew a little bit about the Gaelic word *Samhain*, pronounced *Sah-win*, and the ancient Celtic tradition that rang in the harvest and welcomed in "the dark half of the year."

"One of my customers was very excited about it," Val said. "This customer offered me five hundred euro."

Tara backed away. "Oh," she said. "That's much more than I want to pay for it."

"Two hundred and fifty euro and it's yours," he said.

Even that was more than she had planned to spend. Then again, there was something compelling about it. It looked old, but the paint was still vibrant. She could see it attracting attention in her store, and if someone wanted it bad enough, perhaps she could get five hundred euro for it. It was possible Val Sharkey was playing her for a fool. *Trick or treat.*

"Are you sure you don't want to wait for the other offer?" On the other hand, maybe he was telling the truth, and in that case she didn't want to take advantage of an elderly man.

"I wouldn't sell it to 'em now if they offered me a thousand euro!"

Tara gazed at the painting. She had never seen anything like it. "Consider it sold."

He grinned, flashing a mouth with few teeth. "Have another go around the place as I wrap it up for ya."

Tara found a few orange candles with ornate holders, and a small ceramic black cat with green eyes. She added it to the pile and set down her credit card. On the counter was a set of pumpkin-carving knives with plastic pumpkins stuck on the end like erasers on a pencil. Val noticed her studying them. "Do you need a set? The box was ruined, so I can give it to you for ten percent off." She nearly laughed. Only ten percent when there was no box. It was hard to imagine someone carrying a fistful of knives down the street. And near Halloween no less. That could cause a stir. *Edward Scissorhands: The Halloween Edition* . . .

He picked one up. The sharp blade gleamed in the light. "How about it?"

She shook her head. "Knowing me, I'd accidentally stab myself on the way home. I'm good, thanks."

"Not a bother." He wrapped her things in festive orange and black tissue paper, then held up a finger and ducked down once more. When he was upright again, he held up a promotional postcard: *Galway Bakes. Grand Opening. Free cupcake!* "Don't tell me you're one of those who don't eat sugar," he said, eyeing her slim figure.

"I do when it's free," she said, plucking the card out of his hand. She had actually been thinking about getting cupcakes for the store for Halloween. What synchronicity! She'd be able to taste the goods before deciding.

"Let me explain what you need to do." He suddenly sounded very serious.

"Okay."

"You need to write an e-mail to this address here." He tapped the e-mail address on the bottom of the flier. *GalwayBakesFreeCupcake.com.*

"Got it."

"I'm not done."

"Okay."

"In the subject of the e-mail you put *Cupcake Winner*." He stared at her until she nodded. "And then in the body of the e-mail you put the number on this postcard." He tapped a number in the corner.

"Lucky number thirteen," she said. "Like the number of your shop."

"Right you are," he said. "You are very observant. That's a quality I admire." He leaned in. "This is the last free cupcake."

"I'm a lucky girl."

He nodded. "Put thirteen and your address in the body of the e-mail. Soon, someone will deliver your free cupcake."

"Great."

"Why don't we do it now?" he said. Before she could insist that she would do it, he was already logging on to the computer on the counter and asking for her address. She gave him the address of the shop. "You won't be needing this now." After he ripped up the flier and tossed it in his bin, he grinned at her. "And good luck."

"I suppose any day you get a free cupcake is lucky."

"Do you know the best way to get rid of snakes?" Val asked.

The non sequitur threw her. She had no idea where he was going with this. "Ask Saint Patrick to drive them out?"

Val threw back his head and laughed. "That," he said. "Or make them chase their own tails." Tara had a feeling there was a long story behind that comment as well, but she really did have to be on her way. "Happy Halloween," he said as he took her credit card. "Wonder which one of us got the trick and which the treat?"

Perhaps, Tara thought on her way back down the narrow stairs with the bag of goodies in her hand, she'd just been played. What did it matter? At least the money was going to a local shop. And she loved the painting. Just as she reached the main door, it swung open and a figure dressed in a black hooded robe and a green face mask towered in the doorway. Although it could be either a man or a woman, Tara guessed the person to be a man. "You startled me," Tara said. The figure did not answer. Instead, he or she lifted the box. A sticker sealed it shut: *Galway Bakes*. It looked like Mr. Sharkey was getting a free cupcake as well.

"I'm looking forward to my cupcake next," she said. The figure stared at her a moment, dark eyes peering out from behind the mask, then quickly stepped to the side, holding the door open. "Thank you," she said as she stepped through. The figure did not reply, but he or she did wait until Tara was on the footpath before the front door slammed shut.

"Okay," Tara said out loud. What a disadvantage, not being able to see someone's facial expressions. Was he or she simply very into his or her role as a . . . what was that costume supposed to be anyway? Perhaps he or she was some poor bakery clerk forced to dress up and deliver Halloween cupcakes. If there was any holiday when you were allowed to be enraged, Tara supposed it might as well be Halloween. Still, she'd be fine with never running into him or her again in her life. Hopefully some chipper employee dressed as a fairy would deliver her cupcake.

It was such a gorgeous day Tara decided to have a walk about before returning to her shop. She headed down the street, inhaling the smell of the bay and a fire that burned nearby, wishing she could bottle this perfect fall day. She soon ducked into a coffee shop. It was decked out for Halloween, with cobwebs and flickering candles in the window, small pumpkins on tables, and a pastry case filled with sugar cookies in the shapes of witches, cats, pumpkins, and ghosts. Once laden with a nice caramel and apple latte, she headed out again, then continued a leisurely walk to the end of the street before looping back around. It was close to an hour later when she found herself passing by Val Sharkey's shop once again. At that moment, her phone rang, and she stopped on the footpath to dig through her handbag. Just as she found her phone, a loud crash sounded from above.

Before she could even mount the steps to Val's shop, someone was barreling down them. Driven more by instinct than logic, Tara ran to the narrow alley between the shop and the building next door and flattened herself against it. Seconds later, the door flew open, hitting the side of the building with a clang. She didn't dare poke her head out to look, but next thing she knew the cloaked man with the mask stood on the footpath in front of her. He began to pace, his cape sweeping the footpath. He looked like the Grim Reaper on the prowl. His back was to her, but all he had to do to spot her would be to turn around. He looked right, then left, then right again. Was Mr. Sharkey okay? Fear kept Tara plastered to the side of the building. He stood for what felt like forever before hurrying down the street and disappearing around a corner. Heart hammering in her chest, Tara counted to thirty before exiting her hiding place and hurrying back into the shop.

Chapter Two

Tara was breathing hard when she flung open the door to the curiosity shop. Utter chaos greeted her. Someone had knocked absolutely every single shelf to the ground. Books and knick-knacks cluttered the floor along with framed prints off the wall. Even a spider plant was face-down, bleeding dirt. Who would do such a thing? "Mr. Sharkey?" Tara called out. Flora was no longer dominating the corner, and it took a few seconds before Tara located the giant grizzly face-down on the floor. She took a few steps toward the counter. That's when she saw a pair of black shoes sticking out.

"Mr. Sharkey?" She hurried toward him. Val Sharkey lay faceup behind the counter, eyes open and unblinking. His mouth was covered in something black and orange—and it wasn't until she saw what was in his hand that she understood what she was looking at. A giant Halloween cupcake was crumbled in his outstretched hand—the top of the cupcake had been ingested—the remainder of it smeared across Val's mouth. Crumbs were scattered all over poor Mr. Sharkey. Tara knelt beside him and, with a trembling hand, tried to feel for a pulse. Zero. Tara was out of her depth, but she was pretty sure he was dead. She felt his wrist. Then his neck. No pulse. His eyes were open and staring. White foam pooled from his lips. Had he been poisoned? She dialed 999, her hands trembling. When the operator answered, the story came out of her in a rush.

"I have emergency services on the way," the operator said. "Make sure you're somewhere safe."

"Detective Sergeant Howard," the tall man standing in front of her said. They stood in the stairwell where Tara had been waiting for them to arrive. He was much younger than she'd imagined a detective sergeant would be; she was used to dealing with Detective Sergeant Gable. Detective Sergeant Howard stood over six feet tall with a head full of wavy black hair and piercing blue eyes. She nearly asked him if he was just dressed up as a detective for Halloween—or was he about to show up at someone's hen party twirling a pair of handcuffs? She suddenly realized he was staring at her, and then she realized she hadn't introduced herself.

"I'm sorry, my mind is racing. I'm Tara Meehan. I own Renewals—a shop in town. I was just here about an hour ago for some Halloween decorations. After I made a purchase"—she held up her bag with the slate painting and other tidbits—"I had a walk-about, then was passing by about an hour later when I heard a terrible crash." She filled him in on the mysterious masked man.

"Let's step back inside," Howard said. "If you think you can?"

"Of course."

They headed back into the shop and stepped over debris until they reached the counter. The detective gestured to the body. "You found him like this?"

"Yes. No. Yes."

"Which is it?"

"The first time I found him in his rocking chair, very much alive." She swallowed hard, understanding that with every word of the truth she spoke, she would become this handsome detective's number one suspect. Except she had no reason at all to murder Val Sharkey, and she wasn't going to psych herself out and start stammering and make herself even more of a target. She went through her entire story, trying not to leave out any details. She half expected him to take the slate painting when she told him about it and the customer that Sharkey claimed would have paid five hundred euro for it.

"It sounds like he was a good salesman," Howard said, with a shake of his head. "Cave of the Cats." It was obvious he thought it was all nonsense. "Halloween. A night where my officers have to be on alert because of people stirring up trouble and scaring themselves silly."

Tara nearly blurted out that he didn't look old enough to attend a Halloween party let alone break one up. "I'm sure it's a crazy night."

He nodded. "Even worse when folks dress up like the Gardaí. It's hard to know the good guys from the bad on Halloween."

Tara was finding it hard to know the good guys from the bad on any given day. "Totally," she said.

"How long was this walk of yours?" the detective asked.

"No more than an hour," Tara said. "And from the looks of the shop, the masked figure spent quite a bit of time tearing the place apart. Do you know any poisons that kill that fast?"

"I'm going to leave all that to the state pathologist," the detective said. As he spoke, Tara's eyes landed on the counter. It had been wiped clean. She tracked the floor around it, but didn't see what she was looking for.

"There were six pumpkin-carving knives on the counter when I left."

"Knives?" He raised an eyebrow.

She nodded. "An entire set. Without the box. Did one of your guards touch them?"

"No." He turned a page in his notebook as guards worked around them, gathering evidence, photographing the scene. "How many knives were there?"

"At least six. They all had plastic pumpkins on them—they were jagged. . . ."

"Are you saying our killer poisoned this man with a cupcake, but on his way out he nicked six pumpkin-carving knives?"

"I'm saying when I left there were pumpkin-carving knives on the counter. Now there are none."

"It seems he could have just stabbed him and be done with it."

"It almost looks as if someone . . . *forced* the cupcake into his mouth," Tara said. Had this killer held one of the pumpkin knives against Val's throat to make him eat it? Perhaps he or she took the knives so that they couldn't lift any fingerprints.

"What's the best description you can give me of the person you passed on the stairwell?"

"The person was taller than me and his or her eyes looked dark in the stairwell—but he—and I think it was a man although I couldn't really tell—he was wearing a hooded cloak and a full green face mask."

"And this mystery man in a green face mask carried a cupcake?"

"He carried a white pastry box that had a sticker that read *Galway Bakes.*"

"Are you sure it wasn't a woman, dressed as an old witch, carrying a poisoned apple?"

"I would laugh at your joke, Detective, but I can't because a man has just been murdered."

He nodded. "Apologies . . . This is my first case where the so-called suspect was a masked man in a hooded cloak."

Tara nodded. "Perhaps it's easier to get away with murder at Halloween."

"Detective Howard?" A guard stood nearby wanting to speak with him. The detective excused himself for a moment. Tara hoped she could go soon; she felt a clawing need to get out of here.

Detective Sergeant Howard returned, his face somber. "You're sure the name of the bakery was Galway Bakes?"

"Absolutely."

"Well," he said. "That's very odd."

"What?"

"There's no pastry box here, there's no flier here, and there's no bakery in Galway under that name."

Tara pointed at the rubbish bin. "He ripped it up and threw it into the bin."

The detective walked over and peered into it. "Empty." He turned to stare at her.

"The killer must have taken it."

The detective frowned. "Why would he do that?"

Tara shrugged. "You can see the cupcake for your-self," she said. "It had to come from somewhere."

"Do you bake?"

"Me?" What was he accusing her of? "Not lately."

"You didn't bring Mr. Sharkey a cupcake, get in an argument—perhaps he was bullying you into a purchase, or perhaps he overcharged you?"

"Let me get this straight. You think I decided to whip up a batch of poisoned cupcakes just in case a defenseless old man might overcharge me? That would make me both psychotic and psychic."

There went that eyebrow again, shooting up. "Are you?"

"No. I am neither."

"You're free to go. But we will be speaking with you again. Don't leave town."

She had questions that she'd planned on asking him. Did Val Sharkey have any known enemies? Would they get CCTV footage from nearby? And why would the killer take the flier and the cupcake box? He or she had no problem leaving the icing and the crumbs. . . . She could feel Detective Sergeant Howard's eyes on her even as she left the building. She reached the footpath, and against her better judgment turned and looked up at the window. Detective Sergeant Howard was gazing out, watching her. She turned and walked away, making sure not to turn around again, knowing if she did, she would see his eyes were still trailing her. Did he really think she was a killer?

He's just doing his job. You were one of the last people to see the victim. His job would be so easy if she was the guilty party. Case closed. He would be the hero detective. She waited until she was out of sight to pull her mobile phone out and google *Galway Bakes.* He was right. There was no such bakery. She had seen the name twice. On the flier and on the cupcake box. If Galway Bakes didn't exist, what was that business about signing her up for a free cupcake? She then googled *poison that kills quickly.* . . . As she sifted through she saw one possible culprit: *cyanide. A rapid-acting, potentially deadly chemical that comes in many forms.* . . .

She would go back to her shop and try to get her mind off poor Mr. Sharkey. One way to do that would be to see what information she could glean about the mysterious slate painting. Her Uncle Johnny, who owned an architectural salvage mill, would be just the person to ask. Was the masked man who entered the shop the same man who had intended on buying her cave painting for five hundred euro? Was he also a killer?

It took a special kind of evil to kill an old man.

Just the sight of her shop filled Tara with relief. Located just off the pedestrianized Shop Street, Renewals was five hundred square feet of hand-selected treasures, and a back patio. She'd painted the walls a lovely shade of mint green that popped against the bamboo floors. Display cabinets featured her hand-picked items, and several antique Guinness advertising signs hung on the walls. White orchids topped surfaces, sculptures stood in every corner, and fireplace accoutrements were set up near the small working fireplace, which was flanked by stone lions. On the mantel, she displayed antique brass and iron candleholders. She'd personally chosen every single item in the shop. Pottery from the 1800s was gathered in one section, vases, tiles, and antique fixtures in another. The cabinet by the register was filled with antique jewelry. A small section of crystal glassware occupied shelves in the middle. Old doorknobs and decorative knockers were laid out on an old wooden barrel with *JAMESON* carved on the side.

On the patio, larger architectural items, such as old wrought-iron gates, were stacked up against the back of the building along with garden sculptures and fountains. She felt awful about Mr. Sharkey, but there was nothing she could do for him. She strung up the orange and white lights she'd purchased, and set the black cat with green eyes on the counter. She wasn't sure what he was made of—her guess was papier-mâché, and someone had done a wonderful job. She was eyeing the walls wondering where she would hang the slate painting when the bell dinged and her favorite publican from the pub across the street stepped in.

"Uncle Tony," she said. "What a lovely surprise." He wasn't her uncle, but as a local at the pub, it was impossible not to call him what everyone else did. He was a jovial older man, thin and short, with a bright smile.

"Hello, pet," he said, taking in the orange and white lights. "It looks like you're getting in the wicked spirit."

"I am indeed."

"Brilliant." He held up a flier. "Then I insist you join in on this." She descended the ladder and took the flier: *Halloween Mystery Tour.* Tara thought it over. It was scheduled for Friday. Then the parade would be on Saturday, and Halloween was Sunday. What a nice, celebratory weekend. The title was overlaid onto a large gilded mirror. It was formatted in wispy black lettering, as if the words were made of smoke. It took her a moment to get it—*smoke and mirrors.* How clever.

"What's this?"

"It's the annual Halloween Mystery Tour. Participating businesses all get to be on the mystery map, and we will also invite the young ones to do a little trick or treating. And with a little luck the people who show up for the tour will also do some shopping. You'll need to have fliers made up featuring your shop—best to distribute them wherever you can. We're hoping for a big crowd, so make sure you have some treats on hand—tricks are optional, pet." He winked. She glanced at the flier, noticing a splotch of orange icing in the corner. She looked at Uncle Tony's hands. His fingernails had orange under them.

"Were you . . . baking something?" Tara asked.

"Pumpkin cookies," he said. "For the Halloween Mystery Tour."

Tara didn't want to be a gossip, but she couldn't help herself. "Do you know Val Sharkey?"

Uncle Tony's face immediately clouded. "Never play poker with the man. He's ruthless."

"How so?"

"He'll make sure you pay him what he's owed, no matter how little and no matter what he has to do to get it."

"That sounds rather ominous."

"He'd take the shirt off your back."

Had Val Sharkey won a game recently to an incredibly poor sport? Someone who couldn't pay?

"How about that mystery tour?" Uncle Tony asked.

"I'm in," Tara said.

Uncle Tony beamed. "I'll bring you some cookies when they're fresh from the cooker."

"That's okay," Tara said quickly. "I think I'm off sweets for the foreseeable future." Just as she was gearing up to tell him about her tragic morning, Uncle Tony was out the door. "The Irish goodbye," she said to the empty space. She'd take the slate painting to Uncle Johnny—given he was her real uncle and not just the publican across the street—and as he knew a thing or three about old items, he would have no choice but to listen to her horror story.

* * *

Irish Revivals was situated by the Galway Bay in an old mill complete with a cast iron wheel. Tara loved it. Johnny sourced items from old churches, estate sales, mansions, and castles. Tara lived on the second floor of the mill in a gorgeous loft space. Uncle Johnny and his now-wife Rose split their time between his cottage and Rose's caravan by the bay. Tara found Johnny in his office, feet propped on the desk, stroking his beard and watching a hurling match on telly. He waved as she walked in without taking his eyes off the screen. She took a seat across from him and waited until he finally wrestled himself away from the game.

"To what do I owe this surprise visit?"

"To this," Tara said, unwrapping the slate painting. "I bought it from the curiosity shop near the old church."

"Val Sharkey's curiosity shop," Uncle Johnny said.

"Yes," Tara said. "I was his last customer. *Ever.*"

Johnny nodded perfunctorily until he actually processed what she said. "What?" he asked, removing his feet from the desk and leaning forward.

Tara filled him in on the morning, the painting, the mysterious stranger, and discovering him dead behind the counter, covered and smeared with a cupcake. "Pumpkin-carving knives were stolen too," Tara said. *What is the killer going to do with them? Did he take them, thinking he'd go after me?* The image of the cloaked man pacing the footpath, scanning each direction, filled her with dread. She could have been stabbed in an alley by a pumpkin-carving knife.

Johnny rubbed his face and turned off the game. "Death follows you around, doesn't it?" he said. "Don't tell Rose."

"Don't tell Rose what?" Rose appeared in the doorway, wearing a red velvet cape, her long black hair flowing down. Tara couldn't help but stare. Rose wasn't trying on a Halloween outfit, this was her usual attire for reading tarot cards. But she reminded Tara of one of the participants in the cave painting, making her way steadily to the temple, awaiting the Samhain Festival. "What were the two of ye on about?" she asked again, placing her hands on her hips.

"I was just saying you're wearing your lovely red cape and it suits ya." Johnny grinned.

Rose didn't reply. She was staring at the slate painting. "Is that . . ." She took a step forward and pointed. "Cave of the Cats?"

"You know this painting?" Tara asked.

"No," Rose said. "I know that cave. It's in Roscommon. Oweynagat Cave . . ." Her voice drifted off. She looked troubled. Even Uncle leaned in.

"And?" Tara and Uncle Johnny said in stereo.

"It's a terrifying cave," Rose said. "Technically a souterrain."

"Why is it terrifying?" is all Tara could think to say.

"Why?" Rose repeated. "Because that, my dear, is no ordinary cave. On one night a year, October thirty-first to be exact, the Cave of the Cats is a portal to the Underworld."

Chapter Three

"A portal to the Underworld?" Tara repeated. "You mean . . . evil spirits?"

Rose's eyes danced with excitement as she fixed them on Tara. "During the Samhain Festival it wasn't just any evil spirits. We're dealing with the real thing here. Monsters. Fairies. Demons." Rose bent down, tapping the painting with a long red fingernail. "If only this painting could talk. Who knows what sacrifices it has seen?"

"Right, so," Uncle Johnny said, thumping his feet back on the desk and turning the telly back on. "Demons and ritual sacrifices. Do you mind taking this girl talk elsewhere?"

Rose seared Johnny with a look. "If you aren't interested in the ancient ways of Ireland, what are you doing with me, like?"

Uncle Johnny laughed, then muted the telly and crossed his arms. "Go on, so."

"Does this cave still exist?" Tara interjected.

"Of course. In fact, it's been put forth for consideration as one of UNESCO's World Heritage sights. It's in Roscommon. Rathcroghan to be exact," Rose said. "During the Samhain Festival, in Celtic times, many participants dressed as monsters so that the demons wouldn't drag them into the Underworld. Animal sacrifices, chanting, and costumed pagans. This is the true start of Halloween."

"Bet ya didn't know that, did ya, Yank?" Uncle Johnny said jovially.

"Honestly, no," Tara said. "I had no idea."

"Lucky for all the little children of the world, the costumed pagans are now appeased with candy instead of sacrifices," Uncle Johnny said.

A look flickered over Rose's face as she studied Tara. "Your aura is tinged with fear. Did something *violent* happen this morning?"

Tara took a step back. She had gone back and forth on whether Rose was truly psychic or putting on a good act, but this time she was on the nose. She told Rose about her morning. Rose began to pace. "Tell me again," she said. "Everything you can remember."

Tara repeated the story from the top. Her visit to the shop. Her chitchat with Val. The abandoned slate painting. All the way up until her exit when she saw a person with a hooded cloak and green face mask run into the shop. It felt like a relief to get the story out again, especially the traumatic moment where she discovered Mr. Sharkey dead behind the counter, the ravaged cupcake smeared around his lips.

"Could the rumors be true?" Rose said, as she

left the office and began to pace the main floor of the mill. Tara hurried after her, and so did Uncle Johnny. It seemed he was now hooked on their "girl talk." "Do they really exist?" Rose said.

"Do who really exist?" Tara asked. Rose looked as if she was debating whether or not to say more. "Please," Tara said. "It could be important."

Rose came to a stop and whirled around. "The Samhain Six."

"The Samhain Six," Tara repeated.

Rose nodded. "There's a rumor about a secret group of men and women who live and breathe for the Samhain Festival. They hold their clandestine meetings somewhere in Galway. This year is a Blood Moon and there's talk of some kind of big celebration planned for the thirty-first. And it won't be here in Galway while tourists and locals enjoy the parade and the pub crawls and the haunted houses. No. It will be in the dead of night in Rothcroghan near the Cave of the Cats." She tapped her lips with her red nail. "What did Val Sharkey get himself messed up in?"

Tara lost herself in the image of the full moon, heavy and tinged with red, hanging over this mythical cave. "Can they really get close to the site?"

Rose nodded. "You wouldn't know it to see it. To most people it would look like a typical farmer's field with paddocks. But it's open to the public. It's a limestone cave—a souterrain that dates somewhere between the seventh and twelfth century. But if it becomes a heritage site, and if they can excavate the land . . . why, it would be a sensation. As it should be. The royal site of ancient Connaught, including the temple featured in your painting? It could attract as many visitors as the Cliffs of Moher."

"Be careful what you wish for," Uncle Johnny said. "If that site becomes a tourist destination they'll have the sugar-fueled spectacle of American Halloween parading all over the place." He shook his head, disgusted. "That would send the demons back to the Underworld." He howled with laughter until another searing look from Rose shut his gob.

Tara took steady breaths. "Do you think . . . the Samhain Six would want this painting?"

"Want it?" Rose said, eyeing the painting. "If I were you I'd hide that painting away and never let it see the light of day."

"You would?"

"I would indeed. If the Samhain Six exist? They wouldn't just want it. They'd kill for it."

Tara took her time walking from the salvage mill to her shop. She stopped by the Galway Bay to calm herself by the rippling waters, then soaked in the smell of ale and yeasty bread as she passed all the restaurants and shops, and took a moment to throw a euro into the hat of a talented busker. She loved living in a walkable city close to water with everything you could imagine in its lively downtown: shopping, pubs, restaurants, plenty of buskers, and in between medieval churches and dwellings. Galway was a college town, which also ensured it was diverse. Tara felt grateful to live here. By the time she arrived at her shop and went to unlock the door, she made a startling discovery. The door was ajar. Given the horrific morning she'd had, she hesitated. What if someone was hiding in wait?

She was suddenly aware of the weight of the cave painting in her bag. Had someone come for it? Was it one of the Samhain Six? Or had she allowed Rose's superstitions to run away with her? If she called the guards because her door was ajar and nothing was out of place, would she get in trouble?

"Are you going to just stand there?" a male voice said from behind.

Tara whirled around to find Danny O'Donnell standing behind her with a big grin on his handsome face. Her on-again off-again love. He was tall, with tints of green in his hazel eyes and hair the color of sand. He'd been in Australia for the past month, and his hair looked even lighter. Sunkissed. She was thrilled to see him, but caught off guard. He held up a stuffed kangaroo. She took it and tucked it under her arm. Then, she kissed and hugged him, before gently shoving him. "What did you do that for?" He tapped the stuffed kangaroo. "Check his pocket." Danny grinned. Was it jewelry? If so, it certainly wouldn't be a ring. Danny O'Donnell was full of charm, but his commitment-gene was running on fumes. But as much as she thought about giving him an ultimatum, she wasn't ready to have him walk out of her life. And she had plenty to keep her busy. And now it would seem, she would not only be busy, she'd be constantly looking over her shoulder for a figure in a cloak and a green mask. "Check his pocket," Danny said again, pointing to the stuffed kangaroo.

"In a minute," Tara said. "Did you open my door?"

His grin quickly faded. "Why would I open your door?"

"I need to call the guards, I think someone broke in." She pointed to the door. "It was ajar when I arrived. But I closed and locked it."

"Let's see." Danny strode past her, entering into the shop.

"Danny," she yelled. "Wait." It was too late; he'd already bulldozed his way in in typical Danny O'Donnell fashion. She hurried after him, half expecting and dreading the place to be tossed. Instead, it was empty. Except for one thing. Sitting on the counter was a giant cupcake.

"Mystery solved," Danny said dramatically. "A ghoul has broken in to ply you with sweets." He went to grab it.

"Don't touch that!"

Danny withdrew his hand as if he'd been slapped. "Don't come between Tara Meehan and her sweet tooth. Got it."

Tara set the kangaroo on the counter, far away from the cupcake. "You don't understand." She crept up to the cupcake." No box. No name. Was this the free cupcake that Val signed her up for? "I saw a dead man eat the same cupcake."

Danny whirled around and arched an eyebrow. "I think you buried the lead?" Tara couldn't think. Her brain was stuck between gears. "You saw a dead man eat a cupcake?" he asked. "*Dead men don't eat cupcakes.*" He tilted his head. "I think that's a brilliant title for a film, don't you? *Dead Men Don't*

Eat Cupcakes starring Tom Cruise." He grinned. "Or me. They can pay me in cupcakes."

"I normally would be all over this cupcake," Tara said. "But I saw poor Val Sharkey right after he was murdered—poisoned, I believe, by a cupcake just like this—and the killer, for some reason, smashed a cupcake all over him."

Danny backed away from the counter. "This is not quite the welcome home I was expecting," he said. "Do you have any whiskey?"

"Only the bottle you left the last time you were here."

Danny retrieved the bottle from the shelf and rummaged around until he found a couple of glasses. "Now," he said, once they each had a glass. "Once more, please. From the beginning." And so Tara told her tale again. When she was finished, Danny drained his glass. "Things have gone insane since I left the country."

"It was awful," Tara said. "Val Sharkey sold me a painting that Rose thinks belongs to a secret cult."

"Of course she does," Danny said. "I wouldn't give that more than a pinch of salt."

"Normally I would agree with you."

"I wouldn't say that now," Danny said, flashing a grin. "You love to disagree."

"I saw a cloaked and masked man enter the shop with this cupcake, then run away, and less than an hour later, when I went back upstairs, Val Sharkey was dead."

Danny leaned down so he could stare closely at the cupcake on the counter. "Instead of cloak and daggers, you saw a cloak and cupcakes?" He stood up, then downed his whiskey.

"Should I call the guards?" Tara asked, eyeing the cupcake on the counter.

"And tell them—what? Someone broke in to give you a Halloween cupcake?"

"You see my dilemma." She began to pace. "But if it turns out that Mr. Sharkey was poisoned by a cupcake, and the same day, I suddenly have a cupcake on my counter—from a bakery that doesn't even exist nonetheless, then don't you think they'd want to take the cupcake into evidence?"

"I'll take a bite. Just get ready to call nine-nine-nine." Danny headed for the cupcake.

Tara darted in front of him. "Not a chance. If you don't mind, that's my cupcake and I'll figure out what if anything I should do about it."

Danny shrugged. "Throw it in the bin."

"Isn't that throwing away evidence?"

"By all means, call nine-nine-nine and report the cupcake." Danny fell into the Queen Anne chair in the corner. "Put it on speaker. This I've got to hear." Tara dialed 999, but did not put it on speaker. Danny didn't need to hear what was being said; he could see her face turn five shades of red. "That bad?" he said when she hung up.

"I'll wrap it up and put it in the fridge and see if Detective Howard eventually wants it."

"As evidence?" Danny asked. "Or a midday treat?"

She sighed. No one was going to take her seriously as long as there were cupcakes involved. They were interrupted by the sound of lightning and thunder followed by an evil laugh. Danny raised an eyebrow.

"It's my new doorbell," Tara said.

"You're joking me."

"I'm on the Halloween Mystery Tour this year," Tara explained. "It's festive."

She pushed the intercom button. Uncle Tony's voice greeted her. She buzzed him in, then hurrying, threw cling film around her cupcake and placed it in her mini fridge. As an afterthought, she grabbed a yellow sticky note, drew a skull and crossbones, and stuck it over the cupcake.

"I added Renewals to the fliers I made up for the Halloween Mystery Tour," Uncle Tony said when he walked in. "I figured, since we were a hop, skip, and a jump from each other we could go halfsies."

"Certainly," Tara said. Uncle Tony placed the fliers on the counter. "Do you want cash?" Tara asked.

He grinned. "You know me like me own daughter." He placed his hand on his heart. "Forty euro. There's five hundred fliers there and I paid up for the gloss."

She examined the flier. It was the same smoke and mirror image, but this time the name of Tara's shop had been added below Tony's pub, along with their addresses and a line that read: HALLOWEEN SALES AND SURPRISES! She told him she loved it, then before she could talk herself out of it, she blurted out what she really wanted to ask. "Did you leave a cupcake on my counter just a bit ago?"

Uncle Tony frowned. "Was I supposed to?"

"No."

"Then no."

Her phone rang, startling all of them, making her jump. "Renewals. Tara Meehan speaking."

"I have passed the torch," a male voice said.

"What torch?" Someone was taking the piss. Was it an early Halloween prank?

"Such a sweet offering. The answer is within." There was a click and the phone went dead.

"Who was that?" Danny asked. "You look befuddled."

"Just a prank call," Tara said. *Such a sweet offering* . . . Was he referring to the cupcake?

"Make sure you distribute the fliers," Uncle Tony said. "And if you do bake some Halloween cupcakes, save one for me." Tara and Danny watched him go.

"I take it you didn't tell him about the murder?" Danny asked.

"I didn't get the chance," Tara said. "Do you want to see the mysterious slate painting?"

"Another time," Danny said, planting a kiss on her cheek. "I have to get to an auction."

"I'm jealous." Tara loved the salvage auctions, but she was up to her plastic eyeballs in Halloween preparation.

"Don't forget to check Roo's pocket." He pulled her in for a kiss and then was out the door. She would check Roo's pocket. *The answer is within.* But first she wanted to check the cupcake.

Chapter Four

After contacting her friend Breanna, who was clerk at the Galway Garda Station, and Breanna reluctantly admitting that they'd all laughed at Tara for reporting an unidentified cupcake, Tara decided there would be no harm in cutting into the cupcake—she would still save every scrap in case the guards decided to take her seriously. She had CCTV cameras in her shop, but a recent rainstorm had interfered with the service and the cameras hadn't been on since. Otherwise she might have been able to identify who snuck in with the treat. Had she left the door unlocked this morning? She could have sworn she'd locked it, but it hadn't been forced or messed with that she could see. It seemed she was in such a state to take the painting to Uncle Johnny that she'd been careless. Before dealing with the cupcake, she checked the pocket of the kangaroo. Instead of a jewelry box she found a note: *I love Tara Meehan. I like your couch. Can I move in?*

She laughed and shook her head. Danny, Danny, Danny. Did he really want to move into her loft or was he joking? Did she want him to move in? Would he really settle down? Or would he use it like a crash pad? She'd have to mull on that when she could focus.

On to the cupcake. She retrieved it from the fridge and carried it over to the counter. The voice from the strange phone call came rushing back to her. *I have passed the torch. The answer is within.* She studied the icing. It was orange and red and twisting upward. Like a torch. She was probably being ridiculous. She spread a napkin out and split the cupcake in two. Nothing. Just a normal cupcake. But she might as well finish the job. She continued to shred it. On one of the last chunks, something tumbled out and clinked onto the countertop. She found herself staring at a large bronze key. "Holy cupcake," she said, even though no one was around to hear. What in the world?

The key looked old, but what did she know? She wished Danny, or Rose, or Uncle Johnny, or Breanna, or Uncle Tony, or anyone at all, was here to witness this. Why were all the bizarre things happening to her when she was alone? What was she supposed to do now? Who had given her the cupcake with the key and why? And what did it open? Did Val Sharkey arrange this when he "ordered" her a cupcake? Was this because she bought the painting? Maybe that's why it cost five hundred euro—maybe it was some kind of code, for the *real* item, something worth five hundred euro, something that you needed a big bronze key to open.

No one except Uncle Johnny, Rose, and Danny knew that she had the painting. Only Danny knew about the cupcake. She scrolled through the call log on her phone to see if she could identify the mysterious man who called. *Such a sweet offering. The answer is within.* Unknown caller. *Nothing creepy about that.*

She stared at the destroyed cupcake on the counter. And then it hit her. Val had also received a cupcake. Someone had destroyed it and rained the crumbs down on his dead body. Why? Were they looking for *this*? She twirled the key in her hand. Val had been so eager to fill out the e-mail for Tara to get a free cupcake. Was this why? Was he trying to pass on the key? Would the guards believe her now? She wrapped the crumbled cupcake back in the cling film, and this time placed it in the freezer. She stowed the bronze key in the safe along with the cave painting.

Roscommon was only a few hours north. Maybe she could get a group together to visit the site of this cave. Or was that asking for trouble? She'd speak to Danny or Uncle Johnny about it when she got the chance. She still had to decorate her shop for Halloween. She would also speak to Breanna. It didn't hurt to have a friend at the garda station, especially one who took payment in bags of crisps. Maybe she could learn a little about the Val Sharkey investigation, and more intriguingly, the Samhain Six.

* * *

It was a little after three o'clock when a tall and slim woman entered her shop.

"Welcome," Tara said cheerfully. She had just finished her decorations, and if she did say so herself, they were sublime. Fall leaves hung from the ceiling, a string of orange lights glowed around the circumference of the room, plastic pumpkins dotted a few corners, and the papier-mâché black cat sat atop the counter. It was beginning to look a lot like Halloween.

The woman stood blinking for a moment, and then said: "Have you received the torch?"

Tara felt a tingle up her spine. "Cave of the Cats," she blurted out before she could think it through.

The woman stared, then nodded. "Was there"—she gulped—"anything inside?"

If this woman wasn't sure whether or not the key was inside, and Val's had been crushed like someone was enraged . . . then perhaps she was simply guessing. Was this some kind of bizarre cakewalk where the prize was passed around? Would Tara be safer in admitting she had the key or lying about it? "What do you mean?" Tara would play dumb. It was often the safest way to go.

"I'm one of the Samhain Six," the woman said.

"I see," Tara replied as a tingle of excitement fluttered through her. "How can I help you?"

"Come to our next meeting," the woman said. "But tell no one. If you breathe a word of our gathering to *anyone*, this will be all over." Before Tara could ask any questions about this meeting, the

woman laid a flier on her counter and left the
shop as quietly as she'd arrived. Tara approached
the flier, her stomach already beginning to knot.
She stared at a familiar name: *Galway Bakes*. The
nonexistent bakery. This time she had an address.
Tara turned the flier over. *FRIDAY 7 P.M. SHARP.
SECOND FLOOR.*

Friday. The meeting was tomorrow night.

Tara expected them to do what any boyfriend,
uncle, or wife of an uncle should do when a lost
soul was debating on a possibly foolish course of
action—talk her out of it, tell her no way, insist she
was crazy for even *thinking* about attending a meeting of a secret cult near Halloween in a nonexistent
bakery after a man had been allegedly murdered
with a cupcake. *Run away.* That was what a loving
boyfriend and family would do. They would talk
some sense into her. It was Friday morning, and
they were all seated on the back patio of the salvage mill with blueberry scones and coffee for
Tara, and Barry's Tea for the rest of them. Hound,
their collective Irish wolfhound, was stretched out
on the warm bricks, snoozing away as if he'd par-
tied all night with the college kids.

"You have to go!" Rose said. "You'll never get another invitation like it in your life."

"You only live once," Uncle Johnny said. "You'll
be grand."

She turned to Danny, thinking he'd be the rea-
sonable one. "That's gas," he said. "During the
Halloween season no less."

"What if they want to poison me?" Tara said.

"Simple," Danny said. "Don't ingest or touch anything."

"Don't touch anything?"

He shrugged. "Wear gloves."

"I feel none of you are taking Mr. Sharkey's murder seriously."

"Val Sharkey had a list of enemies," Uncle Johnny said. "The shop was just a front for much shadier dealings."

"What?" This was news to her.

"Gambling," Uncle Johnny said. "He took under-the-table bets. Do you really think he supported himself by selling eyeballs fermenting in jars?"

She hadn't actually *seen* eyeballs fermenting in jars; she would have purchased one for her shop. "You're serious?"

"As a heart attack," Uncle Johnny said.

"But what about the cupcake someone left on my counter—the painting, the key?"

"It's the Samhain Six," Rose said. "But chances are they're a harmless group of nerds, not diabolical killers." Rose threw a few tarot cards down on the patio table, her go-to when making any kind of decision. "Page of Wands—he marks your journey into a new world. Three of Cups—it's somewhat of a creative endeavor . . . and . . . there you have it. The Empress! Chances are you shall attend this meeting and live!"

"Very reassuring that I at least have a chance at living," Tara said.

Danny laughed. "We'll go with you."

Tara shook her head. "I was warned to come alone. It's all very hush-hush."

"If you truly believe you'll be murdered, then

leave a trail in case we need to locate your dead body." Danny maintained a faux-somber expression, until he finally recognized that she was truly worried. "I'll track you," he said. "Via your phone."

"What if they make me leave the phone in a bowl?"

"In a bowl?" he said, arching an eyebrow. "What movies are you watching?"

"It could happen." Tara shoved the scone in her mouth. If this was her last day on earth, she was going to finish the whole thing for once. She silently apologized to the gulls at the bay.

"If they make you put your phone in a bowl, I will track that bowl to the ends of the earth!" Danny thrust his index finger into the air. Uncle Johnny howled with laughter. Rose rolled her eyes.

"You know what? Forget it. I don't have time to get involved with some crazy group. It's enough to know that Mr. Sharkey probably died at the hands of an unhappy gambler. I have the Halloween Mystery Tour to prepare for." Tara stood, feeling angry and foolish at the same time.

"I could go in your place," Rose said. "Pretend to be you."

"That's the last thing I need," Tara said. "I'm just going to forget about all this nonsense." She kissed Danny, hugged Uncle Johnny, and gave a smile and a nod to Rose, who normally did not like to be touched—she said doing so would cause extra energy to accumulate on her aura. She turned to Rose and glanced at the tarot cards. "Would you be willing to be a reader at my shop during the Halloween Mystery Tour? I could pay you."

"Halloween is my best night," Rose said.

"This is the day before Halloween," Tara said.

"Halloween *weekend* is my best weekend," Rose said. "Don't be cheeky."

"You could redirect your clients to my shop, and given the traffic that will come through, it would probably double your readings and potential future clients."

Rose tapped a long red fingernail against her lips as she considered it. "I like to do readings outside under the moon, but with adequate lighting."

"I'll set you up on my patio, which I've already strung with orange lights."

Rose stuck out her hand for a shake. "My fee is five hundred euro."

What was happening? Here it was only a day later and someone else was trying to get five hundred euro out of her. Was this some kind of cosmic joke? "Are you serious?"

Rose grinned. "As a heart attack."

"I'll pay if you both stop saying 'heart attack,'" Tara said. "But then I keep whatever I charge the clients, including the tips."

Rose tilted her head and considered it. "You make your five hundred euro back and then we split the remainder fifty-fifty."

"And if I don't make my five hundred euro back?"

Rose clicked her fingernails together. "It's your loss."

"Five hundred euro and if we make over that we split it sixty-forty." Rose was a strong negotiator, but Tara had learned a thing or three from Uncle Johnny.

"Fine," Rose said. "But only because you're related to this teddy bear." She punched Uncle Johnny on the shoulder.

"You're welcome," Uncle Johnny said, flashing Tara his signature grin. "And make it fifty-fifty," he said, looping an arm around Rose. "I have to look after my wife."

Tara sighed. There was no use squabbling over money. Rose would be a fantastic draw to the shop. "It's a date," Tara said. Halloween was next Sunday, but the celebrating would begin in earnest on Friday with the Halloween Mystery Tour and then Saturday evening with the parade. Hopefully she'd live long enough to see it. For despite what she told them, there was no way she was going to miss this secret meeting.

Chapter Five

Tara googled the walking directions to Galway Bakes. Although she was nervous, she had texted Danny the address and told him to come looking for her if she didn't check in with him by seven fifteen. Tara decided to go straight from the mill, and she was just in time to see the sun sinking into the Galway Bay and spreading its light over the surface of the water, making it sparkle. It was sweater weather—or jumpers as they said in Ireland. Today the skies had been clear of rain, and there was a joyous atmosphere on the streets. Not as many folks as there would be next week for Halloween, but those who were around carried the energy of a celebratory mood.

Tara would find Galway Bakes and then look for an inconspicuous place to hide and watch who went in and out before deciding whether or not she felt safe walking in. As she ventured further away from the pedestrian street, and the shops and pubs fell away, the mood grew less celebratory. Just ahead was the spookiest house she'd ever seen. The top of the house featured a gable painted black, with a hideous gargoyle hanging off it and hovering over the footpath. Shutters lined all six windows, three vertical ones on each side, bookending the windows like hideous fake eyelashes. Everything that was in black—the gable, the shutters, the door—looked as if they had been freshly painted. They *gleamed*. But the rest of the house looked positively ancient, the body of the house was caked with a depressing gray with chipped-off bits, and broken stone steps led up to a massive black door. The most startling bit—aside from the gargoyle hunching over her from above—were the bars. Iron bars covered every single window and the front door. Tara was used to seeing bars in New York, but in Galway? It was unheard of. This place was screaming *GET OUT*.

"You made it." Tara let out a frightened yelp and whirled around to see the tall and slim woman who had invited her to the meeting. Tara's plans to stake the place out and run if she felt any twinge of danger had been thwarted. She could still run, but her options were narrowing. Tara's heart beat rapidly as she studied the woman in the remaining light of the day. She pegged her to be in her late twenties, at least a decade younger than her. But she purported herself as older; maybe it was the sharp pantsuit and briefcase, and the stiff manner in which she held herself.

"I didn't catch your name the other day," Tara said.

The woman stuck her hand out. "I'm Lucy. Lucy Gilroy."

Tara shook her hand. "Tara Meehan."

"I do hope you'll explain how you were chosen," Lucy said. "We're all dying to hear."

Chosen? Had she been chosen? Instead of answering, she flashed what probably came off as a pained smile. Lucy strode past her and opened the door, gesturing for Tara to walk through. *And she was never seen again.* Tara stepped into the foyer, and then followed Lucy as she made her way into a large dining area. Up front stood a dusty pastry case, and the remnants of a kitchen could be seen through a pass-through window. Tara could clearly see that it *used* to be a bakery. Chairs were set up in a circle and in the middle sat a wooden table with a tray of cupcakes, all with the same orange torches as the one left at her shop. But otherwise the house was empty. An old brick fireplace looked naked and abandoned, devoid of wood or a mantel. The windows were bare apart from the iron bars and a thick layer of grime, rendering them opaque. Cobwebs hung in corners, and unlike her decorations at the shop, these were real webs with real spiders spinning their traps. This place didn't just feel like Halloween, this place was Halloween.

"We're the first," Lucy said, unwrapping her scarf and removing her coat. She hung both up in a nearby closet, then waited to see if Tara wanted to hang anything. Tara wore a leather jacket over her jumper, which she had already tossed on the back of a chair.

"No thank you," Tara said. Lucy stared at the

jacket so intensely that Tara finally had to ask, "Is that alright?"

"Well," Lucy said, as she tucked a stray blond hair behind her ear. "We tend to keep our coats hung up."

"I appreciate that, but I may have to run at the last minute, and I'd rather keep my coat. I can wear it if the sight of it draped across a chair is bothering you?"

"Don't be silly," Lucy said, although she continued to stare at the coat. Did Lucy Gilroy think Tara had the bronze key in her coat and she planned on searching it? "Listen," Lucy said. "I don't have much time."

"You're dying?" Tara blurted out.

"What?" Lucy sounded horrified.

"You said you don't have much time."

"Before the others show up," Lucy hissed. She shut the closet door and leaned against it. "Joe," she whispered.

"Joe?" Tara whispered back.

Lucy nodded. Then put a finger up to her lips. "Shhh."

Tara waited. Lucy looked around again, then approached Tara. She leaned in and whispered in her ear, "Don't believe a word he says."

"What are you whispering about?" a male voice called out.

Lucy gasped and spun around. "Professor Ferris!" she said. "You startled me."

Tara stayed back as they chatted. Professor Ferris wore plaid pants, a brown blazer, and a top hat. Did they all go around daily looking as if they were dressed for Halloween? Aside from his outfit, he was handsome in a quirky way—wavy brown hair and hazel eyes.

"Lucy, Lucy, Lucy," Professor Ferris said. "What do I have to do to get you to call me Quinn?" He waited for an answer. She stared at him, blushing slightly. "Do you want me down on me knees?" Lucy turned three shades of red as Quinn dropped to one knee and placed his hands in prayer-position.

"Fine," Lucy said, her face now blazing red. "Quinn. This is Tara Meehan."

His head whipped around, and he rose. "Well, well, well," he said. "The newest addition." He looked her over. "I'm finally no longer the 'baby' of the group."

"I'm not quite sure about that," Tara said. "I'm not here to become a member." Coming here had been a mistake. She saw that now. She had no explanations for why she was here—except for the truth, and every cell in her body was telling her to lie through her teeth.

Quinn rubbed his hands together. "Then I have my work cut out for me, do I?"

"I honestly don't know," Tara said.

Quinn studied her, then nodded. "What was Lucy whispering into your ear as I walked in? Was it about me?"

"I'm afraid I was warning her about Joe Cross," Lucy said.

"Don't let him 'Cross' you," Quinn said, then laughed. He ambled up to the table and hovered over the cupcakes.

"Do you know who brought the cupcakes?" Tara asked, taking a step forward. She could not let anyone eat them. Not until they knew everything she knew. Then, if they wished to take their lives into their own hands over a cupcake, so be it.

"That would be Joe Cross," Lucy said, staring at her a bit intensely, as if Tara had forgotten the warning. "His family used to own the bakery." She pointed toward the kitchen. "Cooker still works. He makes a batch for every meeting."

Was Joe Cross their killer? Quinn continued to stare at the cupcakes. "You shouldn't eat them," Tara said.

"You don't have to worry about that," Quinn said. "I'm a diabetic. But I can still look, can't I?"

"Sounds like torture to me," Tara said.

"You learn to enjoy what you can," Quinn said.

"I hope you'll offer a bit more of an explanation," Lucy said. "What do you know about Joe's cupcakes?"

"Is it possible to get rid of those cupcakes before anyone else comes in?" Tara asked.

"You're the special guest," Quinn said, flashing Tara a grin. "Do what you like with them."

Special guest? Tara was starting to feel like the sacrificial lamb. At least it wasn't yet Halloween and they weren't standing in front of the Cave of the Cats.

Her thoughts were interrupted by the sound of a door opening, accompanied by women's laughter and footsteps. Seconds later, two women entered, arm in arm, big smiles on their faces. They were both dark-haired; one with a long and straight style, the other's piled on top of her head.

"May I introduce Hannah Dailey and Ella Boggan." Hannah had the long straight hair and Ella the pile on top of her head. "Hannah is our resident spiritualist and Ella is our photographer." Lucy placed her hand on her heart. "I am a seamstress and am in charge of our robes."

Their robes. Like the robes worn by the people in the slate painting?

"She's being modest," Professor Quinn said. "She's the founder of the Samhain Six." Lucy gave a bow of thanks as Quinn alone applauded her.

"New member," Ella said. "Welcome to our deserted bakery. Get it? Deserted. Dessert?" She threw her head back and cackled. It was such a good cackle Tara wanted to ask if she could record it—it would be fun to play the sound for Halloween, have it go off anytime anyone entered the shop.

Ella stepped up to the cupcakes, talking to them like they were her children. "Hello, you sweet lot." She whipped out a camera and began taking pictures of them. "Almost too pretty to eat," she said. "I love the burning flame on top." She stopped taking pictures and reached for one.

"Wait," Tara said.

As if the word had cast a spell on her and frozen her in time, Ella's hand stayed exactly where it was—hovering over a cupcake.

"She's worried about Joe's cupcakes," Lucy said. "She thinks we should chuck them out even though she won't tell us why." Lucy fluttered her fake eyelashes.

"We're only a week out from Halloween," Tara said. "I think we should all be careful."

Ella stepped forward and she cast a concerned gaze over Tara. "Because of what happened to Val Sharkey?" she said. "Is that why you're worried?"

"Aren't you?" Tara shot back. "Or do members of your group get murdered often?"

"He wasn't technically a member," Lucy said. "Just a prospective donor."

"Murdered?" Quinn said. He gravitated toward the cupcakes and stared down at them. "Murdered?"

"What do you know about Val Sharkey's death?" Hannah said. "We heard he was killed during a robbery."

"It was such a shock," Lucy said. "We're all very torn up." Tara took in the group. They all stared back, faces expressionless. None of them looked torn up.

"What does a resident spiritualist do?" Tara asked.

"A resident spiritualist gets to the bottom of all sorts of things," Hannah said. "So why don't you tell me what you know about Val Sharkey's murder?"

"I know he had a cupcake that looked just like these delivered shortly before he died," Tara said.

Ella yelped and stepped away from the cupcakes.

"You touch it, you eat it," a male voice called out. Tara's head whipped around. A tall man stood in the doorway. He had a shaved head and blue eyes. He wore a dark trench coat. Had this been the man she'd seen hurrying up the steps to Val's shop? Tara had perceived the masked figure's eyes as being dark, but given the lighting in the stairwell had been dim, it could be any of them.

"Joe," Lucy said. "Tara, this is Joe Cross. He's an archeologist."

"What a fascinating job," Tara said. She meant it. Who hadn't dreamed of being an archeologist?

"This is his house," Lucy said. "His grandparents used to run the bakery." She cleared her throat. "And he made the cupcakes."

Joe Cross stepped up to the cupcakes, picked up the exact one Ella had touched, and brought it to her. "Eat it," he said.

"Thanks." Ella took the cupcake, but her eyes flew to Tara. Tara shook her head.

"Problem?" Joe said as a lazy smile took over his face. "Does our esteemed guest not like cupcakes?"

"She says Val received one of your cupcakes before he died," Quinn said.

"And how would she know something like that?" Joe's right eyebrow formed a perfect arc.

"Because I was there when someone delivered it," Tara asked. "Any clue as to who that was?"

"Me?" Joe Cross said. Tara took a step back. Was he clarifying her question or confirming it was him? Joe stared at her for a long moment, as if he was trying to work something out.

Once more they were interrupted by the door. It creaked open, then shut with a bang. Heavy footsteps sounded before a large man appeared. "We're getting a storm, lads. I can feel it in me bones." The man was frowning until he spied the cupcakes. He whipped off his scarf and headed toward them.

"Careful, Riley," Quinn Ferris said to the man as he reached for one. "Our special guest thinks Joe is trying to poison everyone."

Riley stuffed the cupcake in his mouth, then

turned to Tara. "Delicious," he said, spraying crumbs. Tara felt as if she held her breath as she waited to see if he would start choking or keel over. He noticed her staring and stuck out his hand.

"Riley Enright," he said. They shook hands.

"Tara Meehan."

"Well, Ms. Meehan," Riley said. "How did you get so unlucky?"

"Pardon?"

"To get stuck with us?" Crumbs flew from his mouth as he spoke.

"And this is Riley, our intrepid reporter," Lucy said. "Riley, would you like us to call an ambulance just in case?"

"Nah," he said, taking a second cupcake. "If it's my time, I'm going out on a sugar high."

They all took their seats, leaving the one at the top of the circle for Tara. She walked to the chair slowly, having absolutely no idea anymore why she even came.

"You received the torch, did you not?" Joe Cross said, staring at Tara.

"If the torch is icing on a cupcake, I did."

Joe nodded. "Did you bring it?"

Did he mean the key? They all seemed to know about the key. "Of course not."

For a moment he looked angry, but then just as quickly it faded and he grinned. "Smart." He tapped his forehead with his index finger.

"I don't know who delivered my cupcake," Tara said. "But shortly before it arrived an unidentified caller phoned me and said 'I have passed the torch.'"

"Val nominated you," Joe said. "He must have

arranged the cupcake to be delivered before he died."

"Before he was *murdered*," Tara said.

"Yes," Joe said. "Grizzly business."

For a moment she wondered if he was making a pun about the grizzly bear. She stared at him. He stared back, tilting his head in a question. She looked away.

"I don't know why Mr. Sharkey would nominate me for anything," Tara said. His first words to her came roaring back: *Are you the curious sort?* Had that been some kind of interview? "And I don't really have time to be part of any groups."

"We hope we can change your mind," Lucy explained. "At least stay with us until October thirty-first."

"Halloween," Tara said.

"I bet she thought Halloween was American," Quinn said with a wink.

"Guilty," Tara admitted. "But I've since learned the origins stem from the Samhain Festival, and Irish immigrants brought the tradition to the United States in the eighteen hundreds."

Professor Quinn Ferris clapped loudly and slowly.

"Don't be fooled," Hannah said. "He still wants to give his lecture."

Quinn lifted a briefcase. "I have slides."

Riley suddenly started coughing. He leaned over, his entire body shaking. Seconds later, he slid to the ground, convulsing. Tara jumped up along with Hannah and Ella. As soon as they reached him, he stopped convulsing, then sat straight up.

"Trick or treat!" Riley yelled.

Ella was startled for a moment, but then grinned, shaking her finger at Riley like he'd been a naughty child. Hannah shook her head but laughed. Lucy remained in her seat, wearing a grim expression. Quinn rolled his eyes and Joe Cross seemed to be studying Tara.

She could feel herself getting worked up; her heart was beating, and she was shaking. Legs feeling wobbly, she headed for her leather jacket. She lifted it, and without another word walked away from this group. She didn't care who they were or what they called themselves. A member of their group was murdered and Riley Enright thought it would be hilarious to fake an attack. She would not be a part of whatever this was. A gust of wind threw the door back as she opened it, and she didn't even try to stop it from slamming shut behind her.

Chapter Six

It was the next evening at closing time when Breanna walked into Renewals with a pile of shiny clothing draped over her arm. Tara was thrilled to see her. It had been a busy day preparing for the Halloween Mystery Tour. After she'd fled the meeting at the abandoned bakery, she'd been expecting one or all of the members of the Samhain Six to show up unannounced. There had been no sign of them, but it was still making Tara jittery. This year she'd be happy when Halloween—normally her favorite holiday—was safely behind her.

"What's that?" Tara asked, gesturing to the pile of clothing.

"You said you didn't have a Halloween costume," Breanna said. "We're going to solve that."

Tara groaned. "I'm a host," she said. "Do hosts really need to dress up?"

"Absolutely."

"Then I'm going to need a drink." Tara headed for Danny's whiskey stash.

"And crisps," Breanna said.

"But no cupcakes."

Breanna set the costumes on a Queen Anne chair in the corner. "Speaking of which . . ." She let the rest linger.

"Is there word on Val Sharkey?" Tara asked eagerly.

Breanna nodded. "You're probably going to be officially interviewed soon."

"I wish I could be more helpful," Tara said. "He was wearing a mask."

"Halloween," Breanna said with a sigh. "You'd be surprised how many nefarious people take advantage of the holiday to commit crimes."

It was genius. And evil. "Uncle Johnny said Mr. Sharkey was a gambler."

"True," Breanna said. "And apparently a very good one. A lot of people owed him money."

Tara knew that look on Breanna's face. She had gossip to spill. "Anyone I know?" Tara asked lightly.

"We found a ledger of Val's. He kept meticulous records of who owed him. One of the names on the list is Lucy Gilroy." Tara had already filled Breanna in on her visit from Lucy Gilroy and the Samhain Six.

Interesting. "How much does she owe?"

"Unfortunately, he didn't write that bit down. But if he was hounding her for it and she couldn't pay . . ."

"It's a motive for murder," Tara said.

Breanna nodded, then lifted a red cape from the pile of clothing and jiggled it. "How about this? You could be a vampire, or Little Red Riding Hood."

"Or . . . maybe Little Red Riding Hood just became a vampire."

"I knew there was a reason I loved ya to bits. Brilliant."

Tara poured the whiskey. "But let's see what else you brought."

"Do you want the bad news now or later?" Breanna asked.

Tara pointed to the red cape. "That's not the bad news?"

"Hilarious." Breanna set the cape down and commandeered the whiskey bottle from Tara. She poured a double and thrust it at her. "Drink."

"This must be really bad," Tara said. She downed the shot, then sat down. "Hit me."

"I could get in a lot of trouble telling you this, so you didn't hear it from me."

"Got it."

"The guards are considering you as a person of interest."

Tara flew out of her chair. "Me?"

Breanna nodded. "They only have your word that you saw a masked man enter with a cupcake. There's no such bakery as Galway Bakes."

"It's an abandoned creepy house. I can take them there."

"You're on CCTV entering the shop." Breanna pursed her lips. "Tara. No one else is seen on the video."

"What?"

"I really shouldn't be telling you this."

"You have to."

"You're seen entering the shop. Chatting with him. Making a purchase. Leaving. And then the tape goes haywire. When it comes back on, you're seen entering the shop again about an hour later."

"That's proof. The killer doctored the tape!" Which also meant the killer had seen her return. Maybe he had been looking for her when she saw him pacing in front of the shop loaded up with pumpkin-carving knives.

Breanna nodded sympathetically, but then her forehead creased with worry. "The guards think *you* could have doctored the tapes."

"That's insane!" Tara wouldn't even know how. "I can't even get my own security cameras to work."

"Why did you go back into the shop?"

"I bought a coffee, and when I walked past his shop again my phone rang. I was fumbling through my handbag so I could answer it." She paused. "That's when I noticed the door to the shop was open. I had a strange feeling."

"Don't say that to the guards, it will make you sound woo woo."

"I meant it. I wouldn't even know how to doctor a CCTV tape."

"I believe you. I'm just trying to explain how the guards might see it."

"Might see it? Or that's exactly how they see it?"

"When you're called in to talk to them"—she hesitated—"it wouldn't hurt to have a solicitor."

"I see."

"I'm so sorry. But you did call them and report *another* suspicious cupcake from Galway Bakes."

"I had no choice."

"Unfortunately, they're just not taking your theories seriously."

That would change once they got the toxicology reports. But how long would that take? "Not only did someone leave a Halloween cupcake on my counter, it had an antique key hidden inside."

Breanna's eyebrow shot up. "A key?"

Tara held up a finger, then retrieved the key from the safe behind her counter. She dangled it. "Apparently, Val Sharkey passed the torch to me."

"Passed the torch?" Breanna opened a bag of crisps. "Maybe you should take a holiday."

"Won't that look like I'm running away?" Tara placed the key back in the safe and shut the door.

"Maybe you should run away." Breanna continued to crunch.

"Do they really think I did this?" Tara shook her head. "Why would I kill Val Sharkey?"

"He could be seen as a competitor."

"That's ridiculous."

"Don't shoot the messenger." She grimaced. "Don't poison me either."

"I don't even know where to get cyanide," Tara said.

"Cyanide?" Breanna froze with a chip en route to her mouth.

"I googled. It's one of the only poisons that would have killed him that fast, and can be found pretty readily." Where was she going to get a solicitor and how was she going to afford him or her? "I want to tell the guards everything. I'll bring them the slate painting, and the key—they should know about the Samhain Six. They're up to something. Something to do with the Cave of the Cats on Halloween."

Breanna stopped eating crisps altogether, which usually only happened once the bag was gone. Apparently, Tara was ruining her potato-chip buzz. "What do you mean? What are they up to?"

"That's what I need to find out."

Breanna wagged her finger. "No. Absolutely not."

"But you just said I'm a person of interest."

"I said that so that you'll proceed with caution when you talk to the guards. Not so you can go playing Sherlock Holmes." Breanna held up the red cape. "But you could be Sherlock Holmes for Halloween." She jiggled the cape. "Or Charlotte Holmes. His estranged wife who's been locked in a bell tower their entire life and she's the real genius behind solving all his cases." She grinned. "Or whatever spin you want to put on it."

Tara squinted. "Sherlock Holmes didn't wear a red cape."

"Maybe he did for Halloween," Breanna said. "Use your imagination."

Tara began to pace. "I know the location of Galway Bakes. I left the meeting when one of them pulled a nasty prank." What if Riley Enright, the reporter, was also the killer? It would make sense that he had no qualms joking about a man's murder this soon.

Breanna folded the cape. "At this point, I truly think it's best to just get ahead of this. Tell the guards absolutely everything."

"When they call me in for an interview, I'll come clean," Tara said.

Breanna rifled through the costumes. "Maybe you should wear this." She held up a white dress. "You could be an angel, or throw some red paint on it and be the Bride of Frankenstein."

"I do like how you always present me with choices." Tara squinted. "What are you dressing up as?"

Breanna shrugged. "If nothing else, I'll just wear a mask." She plucked a mask from out of her handbag and put it on. For a moment Tara was convinced she was on one of those hidden camera shows. This had to be a joke. Another inappropriate one at that. It wasn't just that it was *any* green mask. It was *the* green mask. The one worn by the mysterious man she'd passed on the steps. "What?" Breanna said. "You look like you've seen a ghost."

"Where did you get that mask?"

"At the pub," Breanna said. "Uncle Tony was giving them away." She pulled it off her face and rested it on top of her head. "Scary?"

"It's the exact mask the mysterious stranger was wearing," Tara said. How many had Uncle Tony given away? And even if he knew every single person who had one—which she highly doubted—someone could have promptly tossed the mask and the man on the stairs had plucked it off the footpath. But she would still have a word with Uncle Tony. Would he let her look through CCTV footage? Although . . . that was a job for the guards and she didn't want to be seen as interfering. "Do you think you could get someone in your station to pull CCTV footage from Uncle Tony's pub? I might recognize the man—or woman—at least she is taller than me. Dark eyes . . ."

"Slim," Breanna said.

"Not really," Tara said. "But he was wearing a bulky cloak."

"I meant your chances of identifying a masked man on grainy pub footage. *Slim.*"

"But it's the exact mask. It has to mean something, right?"

Breanna took off the mask. "I'll talk with someone at the station. See if they think you should come in. Hold off on getting a solicitor. I'll let them know about the mask and see what shakes out in a day or so."

"Whatever you think is best. If they're focused on me, the real killer could slip away."

"You need foghorns and smoke machines and skeletons flying across the room," Breanna said, turning back to the much more pleasant topic of Halloween decorations.

"I think you're confusing me with a Broadway play."

Breanna laughed. "There's so much to look forward to this year. The Halloween Mystery Tour on Friday, and the parade will be after sunset on Saturday, but then what will there be on Sunday, the real Halloween? Pubs, I suppose. Oh! And there's the haunted house this year—I'm definitely going to that."

Did the Samhain Six plan on going to Rathcroghan on Halloween? And then what? Wait to see if ancient beasts came out of the cave?

A sudden knock on the door startled Tara. "The sign says closed," Tara said, as she headed for the door. And even though she normally loved welcoming visitors, something about this knock put her on edge. Ever since Val Sharkey had dropped dead, all she could think was: *What now?*

Chapter Seven

Riley Enright's large frame filled the doorway. When Tara approached he removed his hat and clutched it to his chest, then teased down a strand of hair. "I'm sorry," she said. "We're closed."

"I came to apologize," he said. "If you'll only give me a minute of your time." He sounded sincere, and given Breanna was in the shop, Tara decided to let him in.

"My friend from the garda station is visiting, but you're welcome to join us for a minute."

He followed Tara into the shop. Breanna had put her mask back on, and Riley came to a dead stop when he saw her. His mouth dropped open. "Is something wrong?" Tara asked.

Breanna whipped off the mask and grinned. Riley's face was unreadable. Then he threw his head back and laughed. "Riley Enright," he said, thrusting out his hand for a shake.

"Breanna Cunningham," she said. "Pleased to meet ya."

"You as well, Garda."

Tara lasered her with a look. *Play along.*

"I'm not a garda, just a clerk at the station."

So much for playing along. "She's friends with a lot of guards though," Tara said. "And detectives."

"Friends in low places," Riley said with a wink. Then he opened his arms, swinging his hat around. "I apologize. I do have a rough sense of humor. I forget that it's not always welcome."

"It's gas," Breanna said with a grin.

"I'm afraid my behavior the other night was out of bounds. I meant no disrespect to Val—in fact, he and I were quite close. And even though it may have seemed in poor taste, I can't help but think Val would have been laughing the loudest and the longest."

"It's your group. I honestly shouldn't have come," Tara said. "But apology accepted."

"Thank you." He glanced at Breanna before continuing. "Is there any chance we could try it again? Val chose you for some reason. And we'd like to see if maybe you're a fit."

"This sounds intriguing," Breanna said. "But I'm afraid I must run. Text me when you want to visit Uncle Tony and I'll come along for the ride."

"Lovely woman," Riley said, watching her go.

Tara thought about telling him that Breanna was single, and always looking, but she wasn't sure how she felt about Riley yet.

Tara turned to Riley. "I do accept your apology, but there was no need."

"It was in poor taste and I scared you off, and

really that's the last thing any of us wanted." He chewed on his lip and crunched his hat in his hand. "It's been a very nail-biting time, I'm afraid. And although I'm sure one can argue there's never really a good time to die, Val's timing is particularly bad."

He was acting as if Val had something to do with the timing. "I don't think Mr. Sharkey planned on dying either," Tara said. "I'm sure he'd be just as upset as you are."

"Did you decide?" Riley asked.

"When I'm going to die?"

Riley frowned. "I was referring to your costume." Riley gestured to the pile on the Queen Anne chair. He lifted the white dress in one hand and the red cape in the other. "Angel?" he said, lifting the white one higher. "Or devil?" He lowered the white one and raised the red cape. Tara found herself wondering why Lucy Gilroy had warned her against Joe Cross when it was clearly this was the man who was unstable.

"What can I do for you, Mr. Enright?"

"You missed my slide show on Oweynagat and the remarkable archeological site at Rathcroghan."

"I know a bit of the history."

"Did you know that buried beneath that field, spread out over two square miles, are two hundred and forty archeological sites that go back fifty-five hundred years?"

"I do." She sort of did.

"Burial mounds, ring forts, standing stones, Iron Age rituals—and of course, Oweynagat, the Cave of the Cats—the gate to the underworld."

"It's remarkable." It truly was. But she had a feeling Riley Enright wasn't standing in front of her just to educate her on this ancient site.

"Cliffs of Moher—do you know how many visitors they get each year?"

"A million?" Irish folks loved quizzing her. She usually failed.

"Spot on—maybe a bit more than a million. But this remarkable site? Only twenty-two thousand. Imagine if we could only achieve UNESCO World Heritage!" His eyes sparkled with excitement. "As long as we can prevent it from becoming some gimmicky American Halloween attraction—because I assure you, it couldn't be further from that." He seemed to suddenly remember she was American as he reddened. "No offense."

"None taken."

He looked around the shop. "I'm looking for a painting."

"I sell architectural salvage."

"I believe you acquired this painting recently."

"You're the one," Tara said.

Riley took a step back. "Pardon?"

"Did you tell Val Sharkey you would purchase a slate painting from him for five hundred euro?"

He gulped. "Of course not." He began to blink rapidly. "That's too much for my blood."

He was lying. Not many paintings were done on slate. He didn't react to this or ask any follow-up questions. He was the mysterious man who had been after the painting. Had he killed for it? "Everything I have for sale is in the shop. If you don't see it, it's not for sale."

"I know we got off on the wrong foot. And I've apologized. But that painting wasn't Val's to sell."

"You seem more upset over this painting than you do over his murder," Tara said.

"It's not that. The truth is, and perhaps you will find this equally appalling, but the truth is, I'm just not surprised."

"Why is that?"

"I don't want to speak ill of the dead. But Val recently procured a few objects that should not have been given to him at all."

"I'm afraid I don't know anything about that."

"Among these objects was a rare painting. Claimed it was a painting of the first Halloween, or Samhain Festival. It's quite old. And quite valuable." He studied Tara carefully. "And as you mentioned, it was painted on a piece of slate."

Tara wondered if Riley could see her heart pounding through her chest. "How valuable?" Tara asked, making sure her voice stayed calm.

Riley threw his arms open. "I don't have a clue. Tens of thousands? Knowing these ancient Celtic types—maybe even more." He shook his head. "Art is a funny thing. I'm not in the business. But whatever the amount, it's quite dear."

And yet he never followed through with the purchase. Why? "If you're not an art collector, what is your interest in this painting?"

He placed his hand on his heart. "It's not for me personally. I would donate all the funds to a documentary we are making about Oweynagat. We're committed to doing all we can to make sure the ancient site gets the recognition it deserves."

"I believe the Irish government is pursuing the same goal. Wouldn't they have a better chance?"

"My dear. All monumental efforts throughout history come from the average man. We, the Samhain Six, are average men and women. But we are determined to do our part."

"I admire the goal. I'm not sure how I can help." She wasn't just going to hand the painting over to this man. If everything he said was true, she would give it to the group—but she didn't yet trust any of them. One of them could be a killer.

Riley took a step forward. "Why did you visit Val's shop the other day?"

"I wanted to decorate my shop for the Halloween Mystery Tour." She gestured to her decorations. He glanced around, but if he was impressed he didn't show it.

"We've all received our cupcakes and . . . well, we didn't get what was promised. You received the last cupcake." He stared at her.

"I hardly see how a painting could fit in a cupcake," Tara said. "But I still have it, if you'd like to see it."

Riley frowned. "The cupcake?"

"Yes. It crumbled all over, but I wrapped it in cling film. I was saving it for the guards."

"Because you're worried it's poisoned?"

"Yes." *Cyanide. She'd be dead within the hour.*

"And there was nothing . . . unusual about the cupcake?"

"Whatever do you mean?"

"Maybe the killer has it," Riley mumbled.

They knew there was a key. *What does the key have*

to do with the painting? Tara put that aside for a moment. Val hid this key in a cupcake. The group knew one of them would receive a cupcake with something in it. She wasn't sure if they knew exactly what it was. But he'd arranged to have a cupcake delivered to all of them. And now they were perplexed that none of them had confessed to receiving anything. And now they were all going to be focused on Tara. "I'm sorry I can't be of more help," Tara said. Val had to have done what he did for a very good reason. And she wasn't going to make a move until she knew what that reason was.

"Our group is going to meet at the Cave of the Cats on Halloween, and if anything supernatural occurs, I'll be there to document it."

"That sounds exciting," Tara said. She meant it. "How long has your group been together?"

"It's only been a few years. Val wasn't a member per se, but about six months ago he took an interest in funding our documentary about Cave of the Cats. Shortly after that, Lucy snagged Professor Quinn." He beamed. "We finally have the perfect group—an opportunity to make history—to make a real difference."

Tara thought it over. Lucy was the founder of the group, and a seamstress for their costumes. According to Breanna she was in debt to Val. By how much? Joe Cross owned the space that hosted their meetings, and he was an archeologist. Hannah was a spiritualist. Ella a photographer. Riley a reporter. So where did Val fit in to the Samhain Six? What did he bring to the table? It had to be his "donation." The slate painting. But Val Sharkey did not seem like a volunteering/donating type of guy. What made him want to get involved with this lot? "You said Val received objects acquired under dubious circumstances. What exactly are those circumstances?"

"You're very clever," Riley said. "But I'm afraid I cannot divulge that information." He cleared this throat.

"Protecting your sources?"

"Spot on." He shrugged. "Comes with the territory." His eyes traveled around the shop. "What would make the article exciting is if we could find that painting."

"What was it you were expecting to find in the cupcake?" Tara asked. "It can't possibly be the painting."

"A key," Riley said. "Perhaps it goes to a safe that holds the painting."

He was lying. Otherwise he wouldn't have asked her if she had the painting, and he wouldn't be eyeing her shop like he was playing a solo game of Where's Waldo? "Did Val Sharkey have any enemies?" Tara asked.

"Some people are so stubborn they insist on doing everything themselves," Riley said. "That's a very dangerous kind of person to be." The doorbell sounded, sending the cackling laugh throughout the room. Riley startled, then laughed. "Festive."

Tara headed for the door, wondering why someone would ring the bell when the sign said OPEN. A postman stood outside with a large envelope. "Need a signature," he said.

Tara signed for the envelope, thanked him, and

returned to the shop. Riley was busy nosing around the shelves. She saw him glance at her safe more than once. She was going to have to find another hiding place for the painting and the key. Given she already had the painting—what treasure did the key unlock? Tara set the envelope on the counter, noting that the return address was a local solicitor's office. What did a solicitor want with her? She wanted Riley to leave. He picked up an old doorknob, with a porcelain surface and blue flowers painted on it. "Found just the thing," he said. He ambled up to the counter, and just as his eyes slid to the envelope, she turned it facedown.

"That will be forty euro," she said. "I hope you know just the right door for that beautiful knob."

"Believe me," he said. "I'll find it."

"And then all you'll need is a key," Tara said lightly.

He stared at her. "Exactly. That's exactly what I need."

"I'm sorry that we lost the key long ago. You'll have to look elsewhere."

He tipped his hat. "I understand if you want nothing to do with us. But if anything ever happens to me—look no further than Hannah Dailey."

"Hannah?" Tara said. "The spiritualist?"

"Spiritualist, me arse. Witch maybe. Definitely a shrew. A few days ago Val Sharkey confided in me that he thought she was a fake. She makes a load of money doing readings, and cleanses, and blessings—and it's all based on lies." Had Val confronted her? Called her a liar? Threatened to "out" her? Could Hannah Dailey be their killer?

"Does Hannah make her living doing all this?"

"She owns one of those Call a Psychic businesses. I bet she makes a fortune. And she wouldn't take too kindly to having her reputation ruined, or being shut down."

"Wait. Are you writing a secret exposé about Hannah Dailey?"

He gave her a long look, then a lazy smile. "If I was, darling, and I told you, then it wouldn't be very secret, now, would it?"

Would Rose know anything about Hannah? It couldn't hurt to ask.

"It's been lovely chatting with you," Riley said. He shoved a business card at her. She finally took it. "If anyone gives you a hard time, about anything, don't hesitate to call." He paused. "And I don't want to come across as pushy, but if you could find it in yourself to join us in Roscommon on Halloween—I can't promise any demons, but it's likely to be a night to remember."

"Why is everyone so insistent I join?" Tara was genuinely curious.

"Val was going to fund us. Now he's passed the torch to you. We may not know why, but there you have it. I suppose we're a little superstitious, but if any group is allowed to be, it would be us." Another tip of the hat and this time he was gone.

Tara waited until he was well and gone to open the envelope. It was an official-looking letter from an executor of Val Sharkey's estate. Tara read through it, totally perplexed. It said he had an urgent matter to discuss with her and asked her to make an appointment with his office. First the key and now this? Thank goodness she followed her instincts and did not open the envelope in front of the annoying reporter. The lawyer worked downtown; she'd even be able to walk. She picked up the phone to make an appointment, feeling butterflies in her stomach as she dialed, wondering if this was the start of something good, or something very very bad.

Chapter Eight

Tara sat across from the solicitor in his very organized office, feeling her anxiety grow as he pulled out a sheet of paper. He appeared to be in his late sixties with salt-and-pepper hair slicked back and a light rust-colored suit that was perfect for fall.

"May I ask you a question?" The solicitor eagerly leaned forward.

"Of course."

"How long have you known Val Sharkey?"

Tara shook her head. "I wouldn't say I knew him at all. I only met him one time."

He fussed with a stack of papers on his desk. "You're lucky to have such a generous uncle."

"Uncle Johnny?" Tara wanted to slap his hand, stop him from futzing with the papers on his desk and talk to her. "What does he have to do with any of this?"

"You really don't know?"

"The only reason I'm here is because you sent me a letter."

He nibbled on his bottom lip before catching himself. Then he smoothed down his already flattened hair and resumed fussing with papers on his desk before letting out a sigh. "Val Sharkey has left you his entire estate."

"What?" Tara sat up straight. There had to be a mistake.

"There's not much. His shop. And the items within. He doesn't own the shop, but his lease is paid for the next four months. His debts will be paid off by his bank account, but I wouldn't say they're considerable. You should get a nice check. It will take several months to sort it out, but in the meantime you are permitted to go through the space and his items—I understand you own a shop and you sell secondhand things as well?"

"I'm more of an architectural salvage shop. But between myself and my Uncle Johnny I think we could take it on." She hesitated. "But I must admit, I'm terribly confused. When did Val Sharkey name me as the beneficiary of his will?"

The solicitor turned the pages of the will. "Three months ago . . ."

"Three months ago?" Tara was already shaking her head. "That's not possible."

"Apparently, he owed your Uncle Johnny from a bet they made a ways back. Val called Johnny and expressed a concern about his group. That one of them was harassing him over a recently acquired item, but he wouldn't say which one. He thought they were all trying to get "his fortune." He told

Johnny he'd leave *him* his estate. Johnny suggested he leave it to you instead."

"I see." And yet Val didn't say a word about it when Tara came into the shop, not to mention Uncle Johnny. "Do you think Val Sharkey was of sound mind?"

"He was when he drew up that will. That's what matters."

"Are you saying lately he wasn't of sound mind?"

"He had become erratic. He truly thought someone was after him."

"It seems he was right." She hesitated. "Did he have any idea who it might be?"

The solicitor hesitated. "He did a bit of gambling with wealthy men. One of them was the owner of Cue Chemicals."

"Cue Chemicals," she repeated. "I've never heard of them."

"Why would ya? Anyhoo, he did take a lot of money off the CEO of Cue Chemicals in a poker game, but there's no way he's our culprit."

"Why is that?"

"Because he passed away last month."

"Was there . . . foul play involved?"

The lawyer shook his head. "He'd been sick for quite some time."

"Did he die owing Val money?"

"According to Val he paid in full." Another dead end. Did Val keep any kind of journal? Write any letters? Maybe she'd be able to find something in his shop. Her shop now. It was surreal.

"Perhaps you might not want to announce that you're his beneficiary until . . ."

"His killer is caught," Tara said.

The solicitor nodded. "And although I wouldn't advise removing anything until the dust clears, as I said, you are free to go through his inventory at the shop."

"Have the guards finished processing it?"

"They have." He slid an envelope across the table. "The key to the shop."

Another key. She glanced in the envelope. This one was nothing like the bronze key she'd found in the cupcake. Did it fit something inside the shop? "Thank you."

The solicitor shrugged. "I'm not sure whether to say congratulations, or I'm sorry."

"It's the thought that counts," Tara said.

"Good luck to ya!" the solicitor said with a large, pasted-on grin and boosted voice. As she left his office she swore she could hear an add-on: "You're going to need it."

Tara had just left the solicitor's office and was headed to Uncle Tony's pub. She needed lunch and she wanted to see about that green mask. And if anyone had the goods on Val Sharkey, it would be Uncle Tony. He was Old Stock in Galway and he'd seen and heard everything. The biggest problem was that most publicans didn't talk outside school, so if she wanted Uncle Tony to spill the beans on Val Sharkey—and more importantly anyone he might have crossed paths with—she was going to have to finesse it. She was just about to enter the pub when she heard voices behind her.

"There you are," a female voice said. "Tara?"

She whirled around to find Hannah Dailey and

Ella Boggan trailing her. "Hey," Tara said. "How are you?" The two were smiling as if this was a happy run-in. But Tara didn't buy it. First Riley, now these two.

"We're grand, we're grand," Hannah sang.

"I can't believe we ran into ya," Ella said. "We were on our way to your shop."

"Just to have a look," Hannah said.

"How sweet," Tara said. "Rose will be happy to help you." Rose was watching the shop for Tara, and probably advertising her tarot readings to any victims who wandered in.

"Rose?" Hannah said.

"One of my employees," Tara said. She genuinely wanted Rose's take on these two. "And my uncle's wife." She made eye contact with Hannah. "I think you and Rose have a lot in common. She's a psychic."

Hannah nibbled her lip. "We were actually hoping to have a chat with you."

Ella nodded. "We weren't able to speak freely in the meeting—and then you ran out—and we're so sorry about Riley."

"He's a right eejit," Hannah said.

"Honestly, I'm about to have lunch and I'm starved," Tara said. "I'm going to Uncle Tony's pub."

"Do you mind if we join you?" Ella said. "The kind of talk we need to have with ya goes better with a pint."

"Or six," Hannah added.

Tara was torn. Part of her wanted nothing to do with this group. Then again, if she wanted to learn anything useful, she was going to have to chat with them.

"Why not," Tara said, as a million answers to that question swam in her mind. "The more the scarier."

"Don't you mean merrier?" Ella said.

"Right," Tara said. "Sorry, I have Halloween on my mind."

Hannah laughed. "Good," she said. "I was hoping it wasn't because of who I am."

"Who you are?" Tara said.

Hannah nodded. "Lucy calls me a spiritualist because she's afraid of the stigma."

"She's a witch," Ella said. "Literally." She grinned. "Now, how often do you get to say that about your bestie without a slap to the face?"

Uncle Tony's pub, a traditional Irish pub near the bay, had been decorated to the hilt. It now looked more like a haunted house. He had a replica of Frankenstein standing at the door, and it wasn't until you passed the mannequin that it moved. Its eyes lit up green, and smoke came out of its nostrils. Next came the sound of thunder and lightning, followed by an evil laugh. Inside, there were pumpkins, and orange and black lights, and a broom dancing across the floor as if by magic. In reality, Tara could see it had been attached to the top of a robo-vacuum. Ella laughed and clapped her hands. "There's your ride home," she teased Hannah.

Carved pumpkins sat on the bar and the standing tables. Hannah shuddered. "I can't help thinking of poor Mr. Sharkey."

Tara studied Hannah. Had details of the stolen pumpkin-carving knife been leaked? She was staring at a carved pumpkin as she said it. "I know," Tara said. "It's been traumatic."

Hannah gasped. "I nearly forgot you were there when he was murdered," she said. "I'm so sorry." Hannah was already making her way to a table.

"I'm going to sit at the bar," Tara said. "Sorry, it's my habit."

"No worries," Ella said, grabbing Hannah's elbow and swinging her around. "Wherever you'd like."

Once they were seated at the bar, they were immediately greeted by a female bartender in a green face mask. She was holding three identical ones. "Would you like a disguise?" she said.

"What are you supposed to be, like?" Ella asked. "Are ya from outer space?"

"Nah," she answered playfully. "But most of my customers are."

Hannah and Ella grabbed for a mask, and Tara reluctantly took the third. "How long have you been giving these out?"

"All month," the bartender said. "Uncle Tony accidentally had them ship a hundred instead of ten for the staff."

A hundred masks. It would be impossible for the guards to trace it. Nor was it out of the question that someone had bought one in a shop or ordered the same mask online. This was a dead end. "Is Uncle Tony in?" Tara asked hopefully.

"He's off today, love. He'll be back in tomorrow. Now, what can I get ye?"

"Three pints, and three shots of Jameson," Hannah said.

The bartender nodded and walked away before Tara could protest. "I'm just going to have a mineral."

"No worries," Hannah said. "But you'll probably change your mind when you hear what we've got to say."

Chapter Nine

"Val recently procured an item from a prominent customer," Hannah said.

"And you suspect someone was trying to get the object back?" Tara guessed.

"What?" Hannah said, crinkling her nose, reminding Tara briefly of *Bewitched*. "No."

"Why did you guess that?" Ella asked.

Tara hesitated. She didn't know whom to trust in this group, but perhaps letting them bounce off each other like pinballs was a way to get to the truth. "Riley Enright came to see me. He wanted to apologize—and he told me that he believed Val Sharkey had recently been given something that the gifter had no right to give." As Tara spoke, something else occurred to her. Did Riley Enright know that Val had left her his entire estate? Did they all know? Was that the reason for their sudden interest in her?

"Interesting," Hannah said, twirling a strand of blond hair in her finger.

"We've nothing to do with any of that," Ella said. "But one of the items is cursed and we need to return it to the Cave of the Cats by midnight on Halloween."

That was an interesting development. *Cursed.* "What kind of item?" Tara asked.

"It's a painting of the very first Samhain Festival," Hannah said. "We believe it belongs in the souterrain." She hesitated. "Furthermore, we believe any person who hangs on to it without the intention of returning it to the cave will be in grave danger."

"Cursed," Ella repeated.

Cursed. Grave danger. The image of a line of graves flashed in front of Tara. She wasn't falling for this, but she wanted to see what else they would come up with. Ireland had numerous souterrains, a French word simply meaning underground. These early Christian passageways often led to one or more chambers. Ancient inhabitants used them to store corn or other such provisions, or as a place to retreat in times of danger. Some scholars dated them between 500 and 1200 AD. Some say monks brought the idea to Ireland from Europe. They were man-made and Tara was fascinated by the subject. But in all her readings and discussions, no one had ever mentioned anyone in modern days keeping items in them, and she was pretty sure Ella and Hannah had pegged her as naive. What was becoming apparent was that someone wanted this painting very badly. Maybe she should get it evaluated. Uncle Johnny knew all the experts. There had to be one they could trust.

"That's why Val Sharkey is dead," Ella said. "He wouldn't heed our warnings."

Perhaps it was these two he'd feared. "This is all very interesting," Tara said. "But I don't believe in curses."

"We heard about the curse from an expert," Ella said.

"An expert on curses?" Tara wished Rose were here to fight this battle.

"Professor Quinn," Hannah said. "He's an expert on Celtic mythology, and yes, the curses that stem from the ancient rituals of the Samhain Festival."

"That's all very interesting, but how do you think I can help you?" Tara said.

"I told you she wasn't going to cooperate." Hannah crossed her arms and stared down the length of the bar.

Ella leaned in. "Please don't lie to us," she said. "We know you have the slate painting."

How could they know? They were fishing, plain and simple. Did they know what the bronze key was for? "If this is about the cupcake," Tara said, "as I told Riley Enright—yes, I received a cupcake. If you'd like to go see it, it's all crumbled, wrapped in cling film and in my freezer."

"What?" Hannah said. "Why?"

"Because I thought it might be poisoned."

"Why is it all crumbled?" Ella asked, as if horrified someone would do that to a cupcake.

This time Tara would tell the truth. "Because a

man called me shortly after the cupcake magically appeared on my counter. He told me *the answer is within.*"

"And you thought he meant within the cupcake?" Ella asked.

"I thought it couldn't hurt to check."

"And?" Hannah said.

"Crumbs." Tara made steady eye contact. "Nothing but crumbs." She studied their faces. They weren't sure whether to believe her. "Riley had a theory," Tara said. "What if the killer has—well, whatever it is that all of you seem to think was in the cupcake."

"The killer?" Ella said.

Tara's story had hit the news this morning. She wouldn't be telling them anything they couldn't easily find out. "I passed a cloaked and masked person on the stairwell the morning Val Sharkey was killed. He or she was carrying a pastry box with a sticker that read *Galway Bakes.* When I found Mr. Sharkey's body, a cupcake was crumbled all over him. It was as if someone had torn it apart, in a frenzied rage."

"But if they were so enraged, that means they *didn't* find anything inside the cupcake," Ella pointed out.

"Not necessarily," Tara said. "Perhaps this person was enraged at the lengths they had to go to get it."

"I know you have the painting," Hannah said. "And I'd bet me life on the fact that you have the winning cupcake."

"What exactly would I have won?" Tara asked.

Hannah leaned in. "I'm guessing you did get

the prize, you just don't know what to do with it, is that it?"

Tara hoped her expression didn't give herself away. "I didn't get anything in the cupcake," she insisted. "But your question is interesting. There are only so many objects that can fit inside a cupcake. I'm assuming it's a piece of jewelry or a coin, or a small note. Why wouldn't I know what to do with it?"

Hannah and Ella exchanged a look. "The killer does have it then," Ella said.

"You said Riley Enright approached you," Hannah said.

"That's correct."

"And now us," Ella said. "Anyone else?"

Tara knew what they were getting at. The killer would have no reason to approach Tara about whatever was in the cupcake if they had the item. However, given that Tara was lying, she wasn't going to throw the other members of their group under the bus any more than she already had. "I haven't had any other visits," she said.

They finished their lunch and pints and headed for the exit where they had an awkward goodbye. "Watch your back," Hannah said as she fumbled in her handbag for a set of keys.

"If the killer has whatever is in the cupcake, why would I need to do that?" Tara replied.

"Good point," Hannah said. "I guess you'll only need to watch your back if you're lying." With that warning, Ella and Hannah headed off, and as they did, something tumbled out of Hannah's coat pocket. Tara jogged to reach it, and tried calling out for Hannah, but she and Ella had already disappeared into a crowd of shoppers, and Tara's voice was drowned out by a nearby busker. She picked up some kind of doll—its body was soft—along with a calling card. The calling card was Ella's, and it looked hand painted:

ELLA BOGGAN
PAINTER/PHOTOGRAPHER

Ella, it turns out, wasn't just a photographer, she was an artist. Her style looked familiar, the colors and strokes just like those in the slate painting. Was Ella the artist of the slate painting? If so, there was nothing ancient about the painting, and Tara saw no reason not to give it back. But not until she knew the whole story. Was Ella's painting the item Val Sharkey shouldn't have been given? The doll, Tara realized with a shock, looked like Val Sharkey. Little pins were sticking out of him. It seemed Hannah Dailey, the spiritualist, had made Val into a voodoo doll.

"Val Sharkey really left you his entire estate?" Uncle Johnny was chuffed to bits over the news. "He said he was going to, but I thought he was only messing." He, Rose, and Danny sat on the patio of the salvage mill enjoying a drink. They were just the three people whose help Tara wanted to enlist.

"Yes, and although I cannot remove anything at this time, I am permitted to enter and inventory items. I would like all of your help." Tara held up the bronze key. "Your mission, if you choose to accept it, is to find out what this opens."

* * *

It was even eerier standing in the little curiosity shop the third time around. The absence of Val felt like a living, breathing thing. The items already collecting dust, the remains of the police tape, the splotch of blood on the carpet behind the counter, the grizzly bear still facedown on the carpet.

"That's the bear Val won in a poker game!" Uncle Johnny exclaimed. "That was pretty recent. He crowed about that, boyo."

"There are no bears in Ireland," Danny said.

"He won it from a big executive," Uncle Johnny said. "And I mean big. This man headed up Cue Chemicals."

"Cue Chemicals?" Tara said. "The solicitor mentioned that too."

"Val Sharkey certainly crowed about it. But I heard this exec had a son who was none too happy about the amount his father had to fork over."

"The solicitor mentioned that this executive passed away some months ago," Tara said. Which meant he wasn't the killer. But what about the son? She stared at the facedown bear. "Should we give him a lift up?"

"The executive?" Uncle Johnny said. "If so, we're going to need Rose's help. The man is six feet under."

Tara laughed; she was used to Uncle Johnny's humor by now. "It is the perfect time of year for a séance."

"Let's get the bear up," Danny said. "I can't stand to see a man down."

Danny and Johnny took either side of the grizzly

and, audibly groaning, heaved him up. "He's heavier than I thought," Danny said. "But then again, he's American." The grizzly seemed to be watching them from behind his glassy dark eyes.

"I don't even know where to start," Tara said.

"We should look for an old safe," Danny said.

"That key isn't to a safe," Uncle Johnny said. "Val always tinkered with locks. He could have turned anything into a safe."

"Let's divide and conquer," Tara said. "I'm going to take the counter and the area behind the counter."

Rose was already enthralled with the left side of the store and said she'd cover that area.

"I'll take the right side," Uncle Johnny said.

"I guess that leaves me in the middle," Danny said.

Tara headed for the counter. She'd nearly forgotten about the pumpkin-carving knives. Was there any rhyme or reason why the killer had taken them? She hoped he or she didn't have nefarious plans for them.

Val's counter was relatively messy. There were invoices, catalogues, a jar of coins, and the cash register. It was an antique one, quite beautiful. She had no idea how to open it and wondered if the guards checked it. She'd have a nose around and then ask Johnny if he knew how to work it.

A ledger sat on the counter. On top of it was a sticky note. In large letters someone had written: *NOBODY LIKES A THIRD WHEEL!!!*

What was that all about? Tara had spent time looking at Val's counter, and this note had not been there. Had he written it while his murderer stood right in front of him? Had Val Sharkey been involved in some kind of love-triangle? Tara didn't want to be ageist, but he hardly seemed like a Romeo. Was this some kind of awkward friendship he was referring to?

"I found the jar of eyeballs!" Danny said, holding up a jar filled with liquid and something resembling eyeballs. "Can I keep them?"

"Save something for your birthday," Uncle Johnny said, as he swiped the jar out of his hands. "This baby is mine."

Joe Cross looked surprised to see Tara standing at his door. Nevertheless, he invited her in. Tara followed him into the dining room where they'd held their meeting. The chairs were still arranged in a circle. "Are you here with questions about a recently acquired painting?" Joe asked.

"No. I'm here about the cupcakes."

Joe raised an eyebrow. "I take it as a compliment, however I didn't make a batch today. I only make them for special occasions."

"And recently Val Sharkey visited you while you were making a batch."

Joe nodded. "That's true. Our big celebration at the Cave of the Cats is coming up. I was making a batch for our meeting when he burst in. I didn't know he had dropped something into the batter until it was too late—they were already in the oven."

Tara believed him. She had been thinking about this a lot. She'd become convinced that Val had dropped the key into the cupcake batter in the heat of a moment. Once it was done, he needed an explanation. "What was his demeanor?"

Joe tilted his head. "Funny you should ask. He was out of breath and seemed a bit out of sorts."

"Do you think someone could have been chasing him?"

"Chasing him?"

Tara had to trust one of them. And if she was right—the killer could not be Joe Cross, because it wasn't possible for Joe to be baking cupcakes and chasing Val Sharkey through Galway at the same time. "I believe Val dropped that key into your cupcake batter as a last-minute attempt to hide it from someone who was chasing him."

Joe's mouth dropped open. "He was out of breath, and he did burst in here without warning."

"And Val wasn't usually the type to 'go for a jog,' was he?"

"Not at all." Joe began to pace. "I wish he would have confided in me."

Tara was pondering Joe's words when her eyes landed on a green mask on a nearby shelf. She snatched it up. "Do you know who delivered the cupcakes?"

Joe's shoulders slumped. "I suppose I can tell you since I've already told the guards. I delivered them. You passed me on the stairwell."

"Did you deliver mine as well?"

He nodded. "And I called you to say, *I have passed the torch. The answer is within.*" He held up his hand. "And before you ask—no, I do not know whose cupcake had something—if anything—inside it."

If Joe was telling the truth, which Tara was inclined to think he was, then the real killer must have entered the shop just as Joe left, but just before Tara passed by the shop again. "Why did you dress up to deliver the cupcakes?"

"It was Val's idea. He thought it would be mysterious and festive." He rubbed his face with both hands. "I know I have to tell the guards that it was me you saw on the stairwell. But Val was very much alive when I left him."

The man she'd seen pacing the footpath had been dressed identical to Joe. But it was an easy costume to get a hold of—a dark cloak and the mask that Uncle Tony's pub had been handing out by the dozens. But this killer knew that Joe had been dressing like this to deliver the cupcakes. If the killer wasn't Joe, then he or she was someone who knew how Joe dressed to deliver the cupcakes. Val Sharkey would have mistaken the killer for Joe Cross. Val would have had no reason not to bite into the cupcake.

But if Val was being chased, and he didn't want to lose the bronze key—she saw how dropping it into the batter would get rid of it for the moment, but how did he control who received the "winning" cupcake? "Did Val give any kind of instructions about which cupcake to deliver to whom?"

Joe was already nodding. "He insisted on boxing and numbering them himself." He frowned. "But the numbers weren't chronological. They were just random if you ask me."

"Was Val's cupcake number thirteen?"

Joe looked startled. "How did you know?" He caught himself, then laughed. "Because I delivered it to you."

Had the killer made it known he was visiting Val that morning? Perhaps he had even threatened him. Was that why Val had seemed in such a rush to send *her* the final cupcake?

Tara thought of something else. If she was given Val's cupcake, number thirteen, then that meant the cupcake found crushed and smeared on Val had been the *killer's* cupcake. Not that that would help solve the crime. She didn't have to be a gambler to bet that most of the suspects had already ingested their alibis.

Chapter Ten

"**H**ow do I look?" Tara twirled around in her witch outfit—a black dress and cape, as dark as her long black hair. She'd put on heavy eye makeup, which made her light blue eyes pop.

"That's class," Breanna said. She was dressed as an angel. "We're like opposite worlds."

It was finally here, the Halloween Mystery Tour. The shop looked fantastic. Tara had added some carved pumpkins, a gorgeous flower arrangement of orange and black roses, and some haystacks and a fire pit to the back patio.

Tara had a punch bowl with nonalcoholic Witches' Brew—there were plenty of other places for folks to get their drink on—and Breanna had made cupcakes with orange torches out of icing so Tara could trust them and "get over her trauma." Given Tara had already eaten two, it seemed to be working.

Tara had also invited the members of the Samhain Six to attend. She'd had the slate painting evaluated and it was neither old, nor valuable. She had been taken by Val, who had most likely teamed up with Ella Boggan to create the painting and sell it to Riley Enright for five hundred euro. Tara intended on presenting the Samhain Six with the slate painting and let them do what they wished with it for Halloween. Uncle Johnny had come up with a second part to that plan, only Tara had no idea whether or not to follow through with it.

"What's the plan?" Breanna said. "I'll give ya my opinion."

"He says he can find another bronze key that resembles the one in my cupcake. He thinks I should give it to them as well."

Breanna frowned. "To what end?"

"We believe once the killer has the key, he or she will sneak into the shop to see where it fits."

"How will you know to whom to give the key? And what if the killer murders someone else to get his grubby hands on it?"

"That's the rub," Tara said. She was only going to slip the key to someone if she suspected he or she was the killer.

"Are you zeroing in on someone?" Breanna asked.

"I have thoughts floating around my poor head. I just haven't snatched any of them out of the air yet. I'm like a kid with a glass jar, waiting to catch a lightning bug."

"You're a what with a what trying to do what?"

Lost in translation. "Never mind."

Breanna didn't press her. "Are you going to tell them the painting isn't valuable?"

"No. Why ruin it for them? Especially if they plan on placing it in the Cave of the Cats on Halloween."

"You're a good sport, Tara Meehan. And this way—if there is a curse—you should be well clear of it."

Here it was, moments before the doors would be opening for the Halloween Mystery Tour. Tara was having fun in her witch costume, and she'd stolen Hound (her Uncle's Irish wolfhound) to be her companion for the evening. Customers loved Hound, and he loved taking over the back patio. Hound wasn't much for costumes, but he tolerated an orange bandana around his neck, accentuated with black cats, pumpkins, and ghosts. Rose swept in an hour after Tara hoped she would arrive, but she proved worth the wait.

Out on the patio Rose set up her station, a pop-up tent in a gorgeous crimson color, complete with lights, a witch's cauldron that emitted billows of faux steam, and a glittering crystal ball.

"Wouldn't it be something," Tara said, "if everyone's fortune advised them to buy something from the shop?"

"That would be something, alright," Rose said. "Would I get a cut?"

Tara laughed. "You witch," she said.

"Back at ya," Rose replied. Then she shooed Tara away so she could prepare for her readings.

Tara unlocked the door, and immediately two figures entered in bear costumes. They were well made—thick brown fur, large paws with claws, and two giant bear heads. Tara was starting to worry that they'd knock things off her counters with those massive paws. Suddenly, one of the bears grabbed her and wrapped his arms around her. She screamed and began to push on the fur, getting some inadvertently in her mouth. She was still screaming and pounding on the bear with her fists when the other bear doubled over in laughter. Realization dawned on her.

"Danny!" she said. She pounded on his furry chest as he shook with laughter.

He whipped his bear head off, still laughing. "Uncle Johnny!" Tara turned to admonish him.

He whipped off his bear head and winked. "Hot," he said. "Too hot."

"Where did you get those?"

"We ordered them special from the States," Uncle Johnny said. "Paid for overnight shipping. All of Val Sharkey's old poker pals ordered them too."

"In honor of Val," Danny said. "His last big win."

"I got that," Tara said. "Just don't touch anything in my shop with those big paws."

"This is the one night of the year I get to call you a witch, is it?" Danny asked.

"And yet I have to grin and bear you all year long," Tara replied.

"Let's go to Uncle Tony's," Johnny said. "If I'm going to sweat this much, I need to hydrate."

Danny leaned in and gave her a kiss. He glanced out at Rose, who was barely visible behind a wall of steam. "You feeling okay here without me?"

"I'll be grand," Tara said.

Danny glanced at the cupcakes on the counter. "Where did you get those?"

"Breanna made them," Tara said. "Have one."

Danny patted his stomach. "Better save room for a pint."

"We'll be right across the way if you need us," Johnny said.

The door opened and a group of costumed revelers entered. There was a Spiderman, a ballerina, a sexy nurse, and a rock star. Tara's shop was small, so Breanna had agreed to stay and only admit ten at a time. Chatter and laughter filled the room, and Tara enjoyed interacting with her guests as they marveled at each other's costumes, fussed over the cupcakes, and gravitated to the patio to pet Hound and get a reading from Rose. Once the cupcakes ran out, Tara had bags of candy. It wasn't long before she was ringing up the first purchase of the night from a man dressed as Sherlock Holmes. He bought ten Spanish tiles. "Where were you the morning Val Sharkey was murdered?" Holmes said when she handed him the bag of tiles. It took a minute to realize the man was Joe Cross.

"Given the circumstances, I don't find that funny," Tara said. "But now that you've asked me—where were you, Joe?"

Joe took the large pipe out of his mouth. "You weren't fooled for a second, were you?"

"It's a nice costume, but no," Tara said.

"There's a rumor that you inherited Val's shop," Joe said. "And you were the last person to see him alive." He tucked the pipe into his coat pocket. "Is that why you were questioning me the other day? To throw me off *your* scent?"

"No."

Joe arched an eyebrow. "Why would Val Sharkey leave his entire estate to you?"

She didn't need to explain herself to anyone. Some questions were best left unanswered. "I plan on giving the slate painting to Lucy and your group," Tara said. "Along with the bronze key."

"I knew it." He leaned in. "Give it to me."

"I will present it to the group," Tara said. "Did you not receive the invite?"

"Your shop, tonight at ten p.m."

"Correct." The mystery tour would be over by then and Uncle Johnny and Danny would return before ten so that she wouldn't be alone. She wasn't so keen on the other part of the plan, Danny and Johnny following the person who ended up with the key.

Joe Cross tilted his head and stared at her. "Do you know what the key opens?"

"No," she said. "Do you?"

"I haven't a clue."

"If anyone can figure it out, it's your group," Tara said.

"I just can't figure out why Val sent it to you," Joe continued. "Especially if you don't even know what to do with it."

"You just said you wouldn't know what to do with it either."

"Touché."

"If you do know where the key fits, we could help each other out."

"It's too bad I don't know then."

A scream was heard on the back patio. Everyone turned to see the woman dressed as a nurse running from Rose's tent, tears streaming down her face. It took a minute for Tara to realize it was Lucy Gilroy. She entered the shop and made a beeline for the exit.

"Lucy," Joe Cross said. Lucy stopped at the door, then whirled around.

"He's cursed us all," she said. "We're doomed."

"I'm giving you the slate painting," Tara said. What had Rose done? These readings were supposed to be fun, not terrorizing. Tara had paid her five hundred euro and now everyone in her shop was startled. She should have known better.

"Give it to me now," Lucy demanded.

"Lucy," Joe said. "Calm down."

"I will not. I don't trust her."

"No one is asking you to trust me," Tara said. "I'll be presenting you the painting after this event. When Hannah and Ella are present."

"I'm the one who started the Samhain Six," Lucy said. "Not Hannah or Ella."

"Did you owe Val Sharkey money?"

Lucy froze. "I did," she said after a moment. "How did you know?"

"Val kept a ledger," Tara said. "Only next to your name there's no amount."

Lucy laughed. "Perhaps he had a sense of shame after all."

"May I ask how much?" Tara kept her tone light, not wanting to upset her.

"One euro," Lucy said, holding up one finger. "I owed Val Sharkey one euro."

If that was true, there went her motive for murder.

Joe turned to Lucy. "Let's take a walk," he said. He gave a nod to Tara. "I'm sorry."

"Are you apologizing for me?" Lucy said.

Joe ignored her question and looped his arm through Lucy's as he guided her to the door. "We'll see you at ten."

"Unless the curse comes true and I'm already dead," Lucy Gilroy could be heard saying as Joe Cross dragged her out the door.

Chapter Eleven

Rose was not at all contrite about spooking Lucy Gilroy. "I had to tell the truth," she said. "There's a darkness hanging over her."

"They have a big night coming up," Tara said. "They're filming a mock ritual at the Cave of the Cats on Halloween Eve."

Rose was packing up to go home, putting her cards away, and blowing out candles. "I almost forgot," she said, entering the shop. She held up a bronze key. It looked identical to the one Tara had found in her cupcake.

"How will we make sure the killer is the one who gets the key?" Tara asked.

"Murderers are like lovers," Rose said. "When you find the right one, you'll know." She patted Tara on the back and left without another word.

It was five minutes until meeting time when Tara received an unexpected text:

We've changed the meeting place. Riverbank to say a prayer for Val Sharkey. Galway Cathedral. Bring a candle.

"No," Danny said. He'd just returned to the shop and she had shown him the text. "Never let them take you to a second location."

"They're not kidnapping me," Tara said. "It's a meeting that I arranged."

"Then they shouldn't be changing the location at the last minute."

"I'm going," Tara said. "But you can come with me."

"Now you're talking." Danny was always up for a secret adventure. It was one of the check marks in the "Things Tara Loved about Danny O'Donnell" column. It helped distract her from the "Things Tara Can't Stand about Danny O'Donnell" column.

"Let's go," she said. "We're already late." She headed for the door.

"I thought we were taking your broom," Danny yelled after her.

The impressive Galway Cathedral, situated near the River Corrib, sat on the site of the old city prison, and it was one of the last great stone cathedrals built in Europe. A Renaissance style was evident in the dome and pillars, and other features included mosaics and rose windows, and the stained glass was stunning. Tara loved the old cathedral, even if she wasn't a frequent visitor. The dome was

an iconic part of Galway City's skyline. A faded
plaque was embedded into a section of the car
park, and every time Tara visited she gravitated toward it. She and Danny were early, and this time
their Halloween costumes were that of a nun and a
priest. Danny had paid three hundred euro to a
couple of drunk lads in the pub to get the costumes. Tara was just praying that no one in the
Samhain Six would be the wiser, let alone any nuns
or priests within the cathedral. But given there
were no structures to hide behind, hopefully they
could get close enough to the group to eavesdrop
without alarming them. Tara stood over the plaque
dedicated to the old prison. She always read it whenever she visited, and today she was joined by Danny
as she thought of all those people from long ago:

THIS MARKS THE BURIAL PLACE
OF ALL WHO DIED
OR WERE EXECUTED
IN
THE OLD GAOL OF GALWAY
(1810–1939)
ON WHICH SITE
THE CATHEDRAL NOW STANDS
ETERNAL REST GRANT UNTO THEM O'LORD

Tara took a moment to honor the past. Humans, no matter what time period in history, had
always faced deep sorrows. Every human suffered.
It made Tara want to work that much harder to appreciate the joys.

"They're here," Danny said. She turned to see
the members of the group emerging from two

cars. As requested in the text, several of them were holding candles. But instead of making their way to the church, the group turned to make their way to the river.

"I hope we can get close enough," Tara said.

"We'll be subtle," Danny said. "No sudden moves." Although the car park was wide open, trees and stone walls were visible near the river, providing plenty of places to hide behind. They slowly followed the group, keeping a wide distance. The group stopped near the bank and tried to light candles, but they kept blowing out in the wind.

"Amateurs," Danny said as they ducked behind a tree with overgrown hedges surrounding it.

Hannah and Ella stood together while Lucy Gilroy paced the embankment. Joe Cross was looking at his watch, and then the car park, and Tara had the feeling he was waiting for her. Riley Enright and Ferris Quinn each stood apart and slightly outside the group, like bookends in need of books. They were all a little quirky, but which one was a killer? The seamstress? The photographer? The professor? The archeologist? The spiritualist? Or the reporter?

"I don't think she's coming," Joe said.

"Why did we have to meet here?" Ella whined.

"To light a candle for Val," Lucy snapped. "He loved this cathedral."

Several of them crossed themselves as they eyed each other. "What if Tara Meehan killed Val?" Joe Cross said. "She's the one who inherits his estate."

"Really?" Ferris said.

"What do you mean she inherits the estate?"

Hannah said. "She said she'd only met Val that once."

"Is that why she has no problem giving us the slate painting?" Lucy said. "Because she gets everything else?"

"Val was free to leave his estate to whomever he chose," Riley said. "We can still be thankful she's giving the painting."

"She also received the key," Joe said. "She finally admitted it to me." Tara waited for him to add that she said she would give them that as well, but he didn't. Did he plan on telling them or was he trying to get the key for himself? Had she been wrong about Val being followed? Had he been running to the bakery that day to give Joe Cross the key but in the last minute slipped it into the batter?

"Does she know what the key opens?" Hannah asked.

"Do you?" Joe shot back.

"Why would I?" Hannah put her hands on her hips.

"Because you're into all that premonition stuff," Riley said. "And I think you should really play that up on Halloween."

Tara slipped off her nun's costume and handed it to Danny. She removed the slate painting from a canvas bag she'd slung over her shoulder. Then she removed the bronze key that Johnny had sourced.

"Here," Danny said. He grabbed the key, and to Tara's surprise, he'd been hiding one of her cupcakes underneath his black robe. He dipped the key into the cupcake, then handed her the smudged key.

"Weirdo," she said.

"Now it's legit." He shoved the cupcake into his mouth.

"Sorry I'm late," Tara said. She succeeded in startling the group, especially Hannah; the one who should have seen it coming let out a yelp.

"Do you have the painting?" Lucy asked, striding over to her.

Tara held out the bag. "It's right here."

Lucy snatched it and the group gathered to have a look. "Thank heavens," Lucy said.

"This will make a great prop for our big night," Riley said.

"It's hardly a prop," Lucy said.

"Actually, it is," Tara said. "I had it evaluated."

Ella looked her up and down. "Of course you did."

"Evaluating objects for value is my current line of work," Tara said. "I'm afraid that is not an ancient painting, and it holds no considerable value." Tara turned to Ella. "But you knew that, didn't you, Ella?"

Ella's eyes widened. "Me?"

"Are you not the artist?"

"I knew it!" Riley said. "I knew Val was trying to trick me."

Ella sighed. "Fine. I did the painting and Val tried to sell it to Riley for five hundred euro."

"Why?" Riley said. "That's not nice."

"Because all of us chipped in for this documentary but you!" Ella said.

"I am donating my valuable reporting time," Riley said.

"Value is in the eye of the beholder," Hannah said. "It's still a painting that depicts the first ever Samhain Festival and I think it's a smart move to place it in the cave."

"I had something else for this group," Tara said. "Only I'm not sure whom I should give it to." She held up the bronze key. "It's the key from my cupcake." Joe reached for it. "This key is worthless," Tara said. "Unless one of you knows what it opens."

"You own the estate," Riley said. "Why don't you just have a look around his things?"

"When the guards are finished processing the scene, that's what I'll do." She had decided she couldn't in good conscience let the killer go after another person. She would keep the key. She would be expecting a confrontation, and she would make sure she wasn't alone to deal with it. She took her time to look over each member. "But what do you think it opens? You must have some ideas." One by one they looked at Riley Enright. He sighed.

"I have a source," he said, "that claims Val Sharkey won a ton of money in a poker game. But it turns out, the player who paid out paid Val Sharkey with a family treasure that was worth ten times his debt. The family wanted it back."

"Is this the Cue Chemicals family?" Tara asked.

Riley stepped forward. "Who told you that? I will neither confirm nor deny."

Tara was dying to know the details.

"What treasure did Val receive?" Danny asked.

"Ten coins," Riley said. "The rich exec thought Val should have them because the fish depicted on one side of the coin reminded him of a shark." He looked at Tara as if waiting to see if that meant something to her.

"Okay," Tara said.

"It's a 1943 florin." Tara remembered her first visit to the shop. The giant grizzly bear and what Val told her: *Named her Flora . . .*

"There's a harp on one side and a fish on the other," Riley continued. Tara recalled Val's words: *He gave me to her and a few fish to boot. . . .*

"Only thirty-five are in circulation and this yoke had ten. Val was owed about ten thousand euro and he ended up with approximately ninety-two thousand euro."

"Why would Val give the florin over to any of you?" Tara asked. Once again Val's own words floated back to her: *Do you know the best way to get rid of snakes? . . . Make them chase their own tails. . . .* He'd been messing with the killer, trying to drive him mad. Only this time, Val Sharkey went too far.

"He didn't give them to us, did he?" Lucy said. "He was stringing us along."

"But why did he pretend he was going to?" *Because the killer was breathing down his neck . . .* The more they talked, the clearer things were starting to become for Tara. She nearly had her lightning bug in the jar.

"He said it was to help bring attention to the Cave of the Cats," Ella said. "With Joe's help we wanted to do a fully fleshed documentary and help it become a UNESCO World Heritage site."

"Val didn't have children," Hannah said. "He said we were the closest he had to family."

"Apparently he was telling the truth," Quinn said. "No one treats you worse than family."

Lucy sighed. "Deirdre of the Sorrows, right, Professor?"

"Quite right," Professor Quinn said.

Tara knew a little of the Irish tale. The woman whose beauty was predicted to bring sorrow and war upon the country.

"Let's all give our prayers to Val," Hannah said. They spread out along the river.

Tara stood next to Ferris Quinn. *Deirdre of the Sorrows* . . . Lucky for Tara she knew a bit about the old tale. "What a horrific death Deirdre of the Sorrows had," Tara said, staring at the river.

"Indeed," Quinn said. He followed Tara's gaze. "Rivers have taken many lives," he said. "It's a tale as old as time."

Tara nodded, then slipped Ferris Quinn the key. "You're the only one I can trust," she said. "It's yours."

"You trust me?" Ferris was surprised. "Why?"

"Because you're the newest member of the group. They're all deeply embedded." She lowered her voice. *"Corrupt."*

"Indeed. You made the right choice."

"A professor of Celtic mythology would want what's best for the ancient site."

"You won't be sorry," Ferris said.

He was right. She wouldn't be sorry. But hopefully, he would be.

Chapter Twelve

"We'll set the trap," Johnny said. "Then we'll wait." It was Saturday morning, the day of the parade and the morning before Halloween. They were standing in Sharkey's. Last night Tara had given the key to the killer. She was pretty sure she came across as believable. Val's murder was never about the slate painting, it was all about ten little coins. The 1943 florin. A hundred thousand euro inheritance that Val had won in a poker game from an executive of a chemical company, and the son was not going to stand for it. When the solicitor said the name of the chemical company, she thought it was *Cue*. It wasn't. It was Q. *Quinn*. Ferris Quinn was the heir of Q Chemicals.

Tara had been mulling through her first meeting with Val. When she had arrived at his shop that morning, Val Sharkey knew someone was after his florin. And that someone was following Val Sharkey shortly before his murder. In order to dodge him, Val ran to Galway Bakes. He dropped a key into a batch of cupcakes that was about to slide into the oven. Tara was pretty sure Ferris followed him right into the bakery and saw him do it. And decided to play Val's game. He claimed to want to join their group. But he needed a cover. This is when he became a professor of Celtic mythology.

But when they all received their cupcakes and none of them had received a key, he knew he had been played. And this time when he confronted Val, it was with a deadly cupcake.

Val had remained stubborn, and when he realized what was about to happen to him, he jotted down the note—*Nobody likes a third wheel!!!* He must have been afraid that if the killer saw his name written out, he would have taken the note.

Third wheel . . . Ferris wheel. Cue Chemicals . . . Q Chemicals. But the final clue had dropped at the riverbank. Deirdre of the Sorrows. She hadn't drowned herself in a river—she bashed her own head against a rock. Any professor of mythology would have known that. Ferris not only had easy access to cyanide, he had the motive. He was after his father's florins. If only Val had given them over. No amount of money was worth one's life. And Ferris was a diabetic. Of course he didn't eat his cupcake. Instead, he gave it a deadly little tweak and regifted it. None of it was hard evidence, but Tara knew he was the killer.

And now, they waited to catch Ferris Quinn in action. Ferris had no clue the florins were hidden in the giant grizzly or he would have already ripped it open. Hopefully he would believe that it was in the safe that Tara, Uncle Johnny, and Danny had set on the counter. Meanwhile, guards were hiding in the back storeroom. Inside the safe, Danny had rigged a bomb of sorts. But this one was made of goo. When the safe opened, there would be an explosion of nontoxic slime—that would coat the thief's face, and give the guards time to run out and cuff him before he could make his escape.

"Time for you three to leave," one of the guards said, as he flicked off the lights. "Do you need a torch to exit?"

"We do if you don't want us breaking our necks," Uncle Johnny said. Just then, the unmistakable sound of a creaking door came from downstairs.

"It's too late," Tara said. "He's here."

They all piled into the storeroom. It soon became apparent that at least one of them wasn't a fan of deodorant. Tara held her breath, and although it felt like forever, soon they heard footsteps. Whoever it was either had a torch of his or her own, or perhaps he or she was using the light from their phone, but they could see the light and shadows bouncing along the floor. As the sound drew closer, it sounded to Tara as if there were two sets of footsteps approaching the antique safe. Tara hoped Danny's slime experiment would work. It was a shame to put one's special talent to waste. Tara felt Danny squeeze her hand as they heard the key slip into the lock, then the click as it turned and the groan as it opened.

The pop came first, and then the sound of not one but two people screaming. "What is that?" they heard a female say.

"It's in my eyes," a male said.

"Is it poison?" the female screeched. "Are we going to die?"

The guards shoved open the door and flooded the shop with light. "Don't move," a guard yelled. "This is An Garda Síochána and you are under arrest. You are not obliged to say anything. . . ."

As they read out their statement, Tara, Johnny, and Danny slipped out of the room. It was easy to identify Joe Cross and Lucy Gilroy even with green slime on their faces. The other guard had handed them towels to wipe their faces and assured them that it was nontoxic slime and they were not going to die. Tara couldn't believe her eyes. Had she been wrong all along?

"We're only guilty of breaking and entering," Joe said.

"Not even that," Lucy said. "We were given a key."

"Professor Quinn gave you the key," Tara said. He must have done some googling of his own. When he realized Deirdre of the Sorrows had not died by drowning, he'd set up Joe and Lucy to take the fall.

"He said he nicked it off you," Lucy said.

"I gave it to him," Tara said. "I think he's our killer."

"This is why you leave detecting to us," a guard replied. "We've got our killers right here."

"No," Joe said. "Tara—you're right. It's not us!"

"Tell that to your solicitor," the guard said as he cuffed Joe and Lucy.

"Help us," Lucy said to Tara. "Please."

"I'll do my best."

Tara would have to find another way to prove Ferris was the killer. But how? He was on to her now. And the guards were going to waste time focusing on Joe and Lucy.

"Don't worry," the guard said to Tara as they escorted Lucy Gilroy and Joe Cross out of the building. "We'll get a confession out of them before sundown."

The sun was sinking into the Galway Bay which meant it was nearly time for the Halloween parade. By the time the clock struck midnight, it would officially be Halloween. Tomorrow the Samhain Six—now four—would gather at the Oweynagat Cave. Tara had agreed to join. And when Val's estate was settled, she'd donate a significant amount to their documentary. She set about closing early; she was going to attend the parade with Danny. He said he had a "spooky question" for her, and a few surprises lined up for tonight. It was also lining up to be a full moon, and Tara had agreed to put her witch costume back on for this evening. She quickly donned the hat and black dress, then added a bit of makeup—green eyeshadow and ruby-red lips. Danny arrived early, trussed up in the ridiculous bear suit.

"You're going to be hot," Tara said as she came out. Danny-the-bear shrugged. "Ready?"

He nodded.

"I'm really looking forward to this," Tara said. "I need to get my mind off murder." Danny took her hand and they headed outside. The parade had kicked off, and what a vibrant spectacle. Large sculptures and characters marched by—a giant monster puppet on strings with incredible detail, a band all dressed as zombies, a float of a haunted house, and thousands of people in costume in the audience as well as in the parade itself. The crowd thrummed with excitement and the drums vibrated in Tara's chest. To her surprise, Danny pulled her through the crowd on the footpath and into the parade itself, and before she knew what was happening she was being jostled to the left by the monstrous puppet and sidestepping a zombie trumpet player on her right. Danny was squeezing her hand hard—too hard, and when she tried to pull it back—he yanked her to him.

That's when she knew it wasn't Danny. It was a monster, only this time a real one. "Help," she yelled. But it was way too loud. Her screams were drowned out by the chaotic stew of noise. He put his arm around her throat, and that's when she saw the pumpkin-carving knife. It was Ferris Quinn. He began to pull her through the parade, to the other side of the street and down an alley. Tara's handbag thumped on her side. Would she be able to reach in with one hand and grab her mobile phone? Not without him noticing and knocking it out of her clumsy grip. He pulled her into a nearby alley. A lone man was leaning against a wall, smoking.

"Help!" she yelled again. The man looked away. The bear pulled harder. "Ferris!" she said. "I know it's you."

He came to a dead stop. She had to be careful, he had already killed once. Before he could deny it was him, she reached quickly with her free hand

and whipped off the bear head. Startled, Ferris dropped her hand and the pumpkin-carving knife clattered to the ground. "Help!" Tara yelled again as she kicked the knife away. A door to the back of a pub flew open and several lads barreled out. "He's attacking me," Tara yelled. The lads advanced toward Ferris. He glared at Tara, then he ran. Tara watched as the lads overtook him and brought him down to the ground.

"Let me go, let me go!"

Tara caught up. The lads continued to hold him as he thrashed on the ground. "I'm calling the guards," Tara said. She pressed Record on her phone. "Your father is the executive of Q Chemicals. You're not a professor. You wanted your florin back."

Ferris Quinn snarled. "Who do you think you are? A guard? I'll just deny it."

"You were the last to join the Samhain Six. You told them you were a Celtic scholar, yet you didn't even know the story of Deirdre of the Sorrows."

"Lying about what one does for a living doesn't make one a killer."

"No. But you had the motive and access to cyanide. I'm sure there is some method of accounting for chemicals at the company, even if it is the heir who took it."

"I just want what's mine. Where's my florin?"

"They were eaten by a bear."

"Liar!"

"What do giant grizzly bears eat, Ferris?" She leaned down. "They eat little *fishies*."

Ferris's eyes bulged as understanding dawned.

He pleaded with the lads still holding him down. "Let me go and I'll split the treasure with you."

The lads looked at each other.

"He murdered Val Sharkey to get it," Tara said. "He wouldn't hesitate to murder both of you."

The lads held him tighter.

Ferris stopped struggling. "Tricks," he said. "All I got for Halloween this year were tricks."

Chapter Thirteen

It looked like any other gorgeous field in Ireland. The remaining members of the Samhain Six stood with candles and told stories of the ancient site as Riley Enright filmed. Above them hung a fat yellow moon. They had been asked *not* to place the slate painting into the Oweynagat Cave, and instead they were going to hang it in their meeting space at Galway Bakes. Tara did get to enter the Cave of the Cats, and she couldn't help but feel a tingle of wonder as she traversed the underground space. And when they emerged aboveground, and the moon shone down on them, she could feel the ancient history and awe of land.

"I can't believe we didn't vet Ferris," Ella said. "We were so excited that he specialized in Celtic mythology, we simply believed him."

"All's well that ends well," Hannah said. "I guess there was a lesson in it for us all—we didn't need to add anything extra to this sacred space to bring attention to it. It's magical just the way it is."

Lucy Gilroy and Joe Cross had been released and the courts would have to sort out the breaking and entering, but they had been disinvited to this evening's gathering.

"We should have kept it simple from the beginning," Ella said. "But cheers to us, and another Samhain Eve!"

"Keep up the quest for UNESCO World Heritage status," Tara said. "It is a special place."

She turned to where Danny O'Donnell was waiting for her. They walked hand in hand farther down the field.

"I have two surprises for you," Danny said.

"Only two?" He gave her the side-eye and she laughed. "Only messing."

"First surprise—we were cleaning up Val's shop after the break-in, and you'll never guess what we found."

"Ten 1943 florins," Tara said.

Danny sighed. "You always guess it right." He crossed his arms. "Do you know where we found them?"

"In the giant grizzly bear?"

"You knew!" he said. "How?"

"Val liked puns. What does a bear eat?"

"I know what he does in the woods," Danny said.

"Fish," Tara said, shaking her head. "And the bear was the other item he won from the late Mr. Quinn. What better way to give someone something you don't want to give up than to hide them in a giant bear?"

Danny nodded. "When we were moving him

around we found a loose patch of fur, and under-neath was a little lock. Our key opened it and the coins spilled out."

"If the pair of ye hadn't been groaning so loud when you lifted the bear, we probably would have discovered that earlier," Tara said.

"Well, thanks to you, at least his killer has been caught." Before she knew what was happening, Danny was down on one knee.

"Danny?" she said.

"I can't think of a better setting to do this. In a spot where they once offered sacrifices to appease the demons—"

"Maybe you should skip right to the question," Tara said.

Danny laughed. "You get me," he said. "And I promise my wandering days are over."

"What if I want to wander with you?"

"Then a-wandering we will go. Tara Meehan, Ms. America. Will you marry this Irish fool?" He opened the box to reveal a gorgeous antique dia-mond ring. It sparkled under the light of the fat yellow moon. She loved it.

Tara knelt next to him. "Danny O'Donnell. No one tries my patience or makes me laugh like you do. I love Galway, I love my shop, and I love you."

A barn owl screeched in the distance, making them jump. "Hurry and answer," he said. "Before we remember this night for something other than this proposal."

"It's just like you to propose on the spookiest day of the year," Tara chided.

"Hey," Danny said. "Nothing frightens me more

than commitment. Except the thought of losing you."

"You'll never lose me."

"Is that a yes, Ms. America?" Danny asked.

"Yes," Tara said. "On this All Hallows' Eve, I say yes."

"I think you got the trick and I got the treat," Danny said as he slipped the ring on her finger.

"Kiss me before I change my mind." They kissed near the ancient site that held so much mystery and history. They kissed by the Cave of the Cats. They kissed underneath the gorgeous full moon, on this All Hallows' Eve, in the spot of the very first Halloween, and not a single monster, demon, or ghoul came forth to stop them.

MRS. CLAUS AND THE CANDY CORN CAPER

Liz Ireland

Chapter One

Santaland isn't exactly a hotbed of crime. We have our share of troubles, but until just lately the *Christmastown Herald*'s biggest story of the year featured an elf finding a potato shaped like a walrus in his greenhouse. So when a robbery occurred the week of Halloween, it was banner headline news. That the theft involved a large candy corn shipment might seem trivial anywhere else, but in Santaland candy is serious business.

Christmastown, where the theft occurred, was on edge. Elves contemplated locking their cottage doors at night, and rumors had started to circulate of shady characters in snowy alleys peddling street corn. Meanwhile, confectioners struggled to catch up with consumer demand for a product, candy corn, that had been unknown to them mere weeks before.

"What do you think, Mrs. Claus?" asked Dash, the owner of Dash's Candy and Nut Shoppe. He puffed up with pride as he slid a decorative red-and-green tray of his latest creation toward me. The confection was supposed to be candy corn, but Dash had molded the candy into tiny ears of corn. The shape reminded me of the corn-on-the-cob holders that had appeared on my grand-mother's table every summer.

"That's *not quite* how candy corn usually looks," I said carefully.

Dash's Candy and Nut Shoppe was my favorite confectionary in Christmastown. I loved the mixed smells of chocolate and roasting nuts. The chocolates and fudge lay in trays behind glass cabinets, and the nuts and candies were contained in wide jars sitting atop aged oak counters. I was as famil-iar with all the offerings here as I was with the snowdrop designs in the floor tiles and the Christ-mas tunes that played softly from ceiling speakers all year long. The last thing I wanted was to tee off the owner and have my Frequent Fudger card re-voked.

Besides, candy corn was such a novelty in Santa-land, his mistake was understandable. "Although I'm sure it's very tasty," I added.

Despite my effort to be diplomatic, Dash's face went red to the tips of his large elf ears. "What's wrong? It's candy, shaped like corn."

My elf friend Juniper, who'd come with me, lifted on the tapered, curly toes of her booties and asked eagerly, "May I try some, Dash?"

"Of course." He pushed the tray forward again.

"Traditional candy corn is triangle shaped and

usually is tricolored—yellow, orange, and just a tip of white," I explained. In Santaland I was supposed to be something of a Halloween authority, since I was American by birth and helped bring the holiday here. "Candy corn pieces are shaped like kernels of corn, not the whole ear."

"Aha! I have my slogan." He arced his hands in front of us as if imagining his words on a flashing Times Square billboard. *"Dash's Artisan Candy Corn Gives You a Full-Cob Experience."*

"Um—"

"It's delicious," Juniper interrupted as she reached for a second piece and nibbled at the tip of the ear.

Of course I had to sample a bite myself. And it *was* very good. Like real candy corn, although slightly more grainy and with a hint . . . "Is that cardamom?"

Dash folded his arms. "Sorry. Trade secret."

"These will be a smash," Juniper gushed. "You're a candy corn hero, Dash."

He beamed in triumph at me before natural modesty took over. "Under the circumstances, of course, the most important thing is to get as much candy corn into production as possible. But I want mine to be special."

The "circumstances" were that Santaland was suffering a candy corn shortage mere days away from our Halloween carnival, which this year included multiple music acts, a haunted ice castle, and a Halloween bake-off. I'd been given the honor of naming the bake-off's theme ingredient, so I was the one who'd chosen candy corn. What could be more Halloweeny than that?

Aside from pumpkin, of course. Pumpkin had seemed too obvious.

The trouble was, celebrating Halloween was still a recent thing in Santaland. A relative newcomer myself, I hadn't realized that candy corn was unknown here. We'd had to send off for examples via Santaland Parcel Express—SPEX—but when the shipment arrived, it had been stolen from the SPEX office.

The bell over the door tinkled, and Deputy Ollie entered the store, a dusting of snow on his blue constabulary uniform tunic, which always struck me as half English bobby, half Keystone Kop. His eyes held that desperate look I'd seen on the faces of baking enthusiasts all over town. As soon as he saw Dash's sample tray, he zipped over.

"Is that candy corn?"

"Yes," Dash said, at the same time I muttered, "Sort of."

Ollie, naturally, was all-in for the bake-off. The aroma of fresh baked goods always wafted from the little cottage that housed the Christmastown Constabulary. Thanks to Ollie, Christmastown criminals were the best fed miscreants in the world.

"This is *authentic*, whole-ear candy corn." Dash shot me a look, daring me to contradict him.

"I'll take a pound," Ollie said without even tasting it.

A pound sounded like a lot, but it was hard to perfect a bake-off recipe when the main ingredient was so scarce.

"Maybe we should change the theme ingredient to pumpkin," I said.

The three elves looked up at me as if I'd lost my mind.

"You can't change sleds halfway down the hill," Dash argued. "Halloween is three days away, and I've just made ten batches of my authentic whole-ear candy corn."

"Besides, pumpkins are so last year," Juniper pointed out.

The previous year, when Santaland had celebrated Halloween for the very first time, the whole country had developed pumpkin mania, thanks to Castle Kringle's chief gardener and grounds-keeper, Salty. He was doing hayrides around his pumpkin patch greenhouse again this year, but now the excitement was all about the candy corn bake-off and the haunted ice castle.

"Ten batches?" I asked Dash.

He nodded.

"I'll take a pound too," I said, capitulating. Even if Dash's was all wrong, shape-wise, candy corn *was* scarce. My mother-in-law, Pamela, the dowager Mrs. Claus, was spearheading Castle Kringle's bake-off entry, so my bringing her some candy corn should please her.

Pamela would be happier about my purchase than my husband, Nick, would be; he was perhaps the only person in Santaland who hadn't caught candy corn fever. It made sense that Santa Claus would be unimpressed by such a Halloween-centric candy, but one taste during a summer visit to Oregon had left him especially revolted. "That's sickening," he'd declared.

I'd nodded enthusiastically. "It's been giving

people stomachaches every Halloween for one hundred years."

"I just don't understand this so-called holiday," he'd grumbled.

Nick's lack of love for trick-or-treat time made him an outlier in the North Pole now. This might only be the second year Halloween was celebrated in Santaland, but the elves were pulling out all the stops, replacing our year-round Christmas decorations with orange-and-black bunting and wreaths. Festive sparkly cobwebs festooned downtown light poles, and jack-o'-lanterns blazed on every doorstep. Elf children were impatient to try out their costumes, so that it wasn't uncommon to bump into a little Frankenstein, witch, or snow monster on the bustling town streets.

While Dash measured out our candy corn, I asked Ollie, "Has there been any progress in finding out who was behind the candy corn theft?"

Any mention of solving an actual crime made the deputy look like a reindeer trapped in the sleigh lights. "Um, no. But Unc's on it."

"Unc" was Constable Crinkles, Santaland's number one lawman. Aside from Ollie, he was the only lawman.

The SPEX office had been broken into after hours. *Broken into,* meaning the culprit had walked right in. Filbert, who worked at SPEX, hadn't locked up. "No one's ever robbed us before," he'd said. "Whoever heard of such a thing?"

He had a point. Property crimes were uncommon in Christmastown. That's why Crinkles and Ollie had so much time to devote to the bake-off.

They were the Maytag repairmen of crime fighters.

Juniper and I left Ollie and Dash talking. By unspoken agreement, we headed toward Peppermint Pond. The library, where Juniper was due for her librarian shift in a half hour, was in the opposite direction, but these days everyone in Christmastown wandered by the park to look at the progress of the Halloween carnival's haunted ice castle—a gloriously strange and very North Pole–like update on the traditional haunted house.

"And to think," Juniper said with awe as we stopped to survey the structure, "just two weeks ago that was nothing but a snow-covered field."

Now there was a castle of white-blue ice rising up between Peppermint Pond and the park's sled hill. A holiday atmosphere pervaded the scene. An accordion-playing elf serenaded the worker elves with "Jolly Old Saint Nicholas," close to where Gert's Pretzel Stand was parked. Nearby, two young elves were tossing snowballs at each other. Next to where Juniper and I stood, Pumblechook the snowman stood in a velvet stovepipe hat, a fixed pebble smile on his white face, and, oddly, a handwritten sign around his neck reading *Let's Not Lose Our Heads.*

I had to ask, "What does that mean?" I nodded at his sign.

In a measured but cheerful tone, he said, "Snowmen need heads."

"Very true," Juniper said.

Snowmen were peculiar. You never knew what was going on in their icy brains.

When the castle in the park was finished, the two towers with crenellated tops would flank a square that formed the main building; as yet only one tower was completed, but the second was rising rapidly. All the ice bricks for the castle were being fashioned from the ice of Peppermint Pond itself. In an all-elves-on-deck effort, a crew of volunteers cut blocks from the frozen pond and piled them to be shaped into bricks, buttresses, gargoyles, and other architectural ornaments by sculptor elves. I spotted several elves from Castle Kringle working around the pond, as well as Christmastown's apothecary. Even Sugar, one of the elves from the Silver Bell Bakery, was hefting ice blocks with large tongs like a longshoreman over to the ice sculptors.

Ice sculpting was a revered art in Santaland, and for the castle these artisans were pulling out all the stops. They had fashioned an elaborate arched entrance complete with a fake drawbridge, and the ice castle's cornices featured gargoyles that looked like crystal rivals to those found on Notre Dame Cathedral.

"Looks like they'll be done in plenty of time for Halloween," I observed. The organizers of the carnival would need a day to set up the inside with decorations, booths, and all the scary features to scare and delight young elves. Close by, a pavilion would be set up for the candy corn bake-off. Already, elves were twining orange and white fairy lights in the trees around the pond.

Having satisfied our curiosity, Juniper and I turned our steps toward the library. A light snow fell, making Christmastown look more than usual like a picture postcard. The city sat at the foot of Sugarplum Mountain, where Castle Kringle was located. Festival Boulevard, the village's main thoroughfare, was lined with half-timbered buildings two and three stories high, and the elves didn't stint on the colorful paint for the doors, shutters, and trim. Wreaths with tiny pumpkins and cobwebs hung on every door, and orange twinkle lights outlined leaded glass windows, replacing the customary red, green, and white ones. One business had a ghost hanging from its awning that let out spooky moans as we passed. Two twenty-something elves wearing pumpkin caps stopped to laugh at it, and then continued on in front of us, their mittened hands joined.

Juniper was silent for half a block, then said, "Maybe I should take up baking. The candy corn bake-off might take my mind off being single."

Where had that come from? "You're not single, exactly. You've always got Smudge."

She shot me a look. "We are *not* a couple."

Juniper had suffered a run of bad boyfriends. Smudge had been at the beginning of that run, but what had come after him had been so disastrous that he was now looking pretty good in comparison. As I'd gotten to know Smudge through playing percussion in the Santaland Concert Band together, I'd even started to like him. He was just a little . . . dour. Smudgy.

As I started to put in a positive word for our band mate, I realized I was talking to air.

I turned around. Juniper, who'd halted several feet behind me, pointed across the street. "Will you look at that?"

I followed her gaze to a line of elves stretching across the block. A new sign in cherry-red and white lettering swung on a pole sticking out of an old half-timbered building. *Chestnut's Cake Emporium.*

My jaw dropped. "*The* Chestnut?"

"It's got to be," Juniper said.

Like magnets to a fridge door, we zipped across the street. Sure enough, Chestnut could be seen through the plate glass of the new establishment, handing a bright red cake box to a customer.

I was flabbergasted. Chestnut was—or had been—the cake baker extraordinaire at the Silver Bell Bakery, located just across Festival Boulevard on the opposite corner. For years, everyone had gone to the Silver Bell Bakery to buy their cakes. Even Castle Kringle, my home, which had a host of elf bakers working in its kitchen, sometimes sent out for a Chestnut-made cake from Silver Bell's on special occasions. They were that good.

And now Chestnut had gone into business for himself. Right across the street from the Silver Bell Bakery.

"Poor Bell," I said. "She's lost her best employee."

In unison, our heads turned in the direction we'd just come from. No line stretched in front of the Silver Bell Bakery. In fact, the well-known storefront now exuded a dated, almost shabby air compared to Chestnut's clean, bright storefront. Bell was apparently aware of the contrast, because she was straightening the plates of sugar cookies and lackluster pies in the window. There was a notable absence of cakes on display. Her blunt-cut blond bob stuck out like bristles beneath her sagging elf cap. What was most noteworthy about her appearance, however, were her sharp, dark eyes, which were fixed on the lineup across the street. Even thirty feet away and through the window, I could detect the resentment in those eyes.

Then, startlingly, Bell's gaze fixed on Juniper and me. We both froze. We'd been about to join the queue for Chestnut's—natural curiosity and a desire to sample Chestnut's cakes were an irresistible combination. The years of being faithful Silver Bell Bakery customers meant nothing in the face of that cake craving—until the moment Bell's disapproving glare fell on us.

We both hesitated and then turned away from the crowd.

"I'd better get to the library," Juniper said uncomfortably.

We both tore ourselves away before we could become bakery traitors.

Still, I should have known from Bell's glare that the candy corn shortage would be the least of Santaland's troubles this Halloween.

Chapter Two

I was giving myself a final once-over in the mirror at my dressing table the next morning when someone pounded on the thick arched door to our bedroom. I'd barely said "come in" before Butterbean the footman tumbled through the doorway, followed by the castle steward, Jingles, bearing a coffee tray. Both were dressed in the new castle livery—red-and-green tunics and caps. Jingles, who was half elf, half human, towered several inches over his elf minion, but Butterbean's rubber ball exuberance could overpower anyone.

If Butterbean's red face was anything to go by, something big had happened.

"There's been a—"

"*I'll* tell it," Jingles insisted. But he didn't get the chance.

"Murder!" Butterbean punctuated the exclamation with an emphatic hop.

Jingles banged the coffee tray down on the cleared space of my dressing table, somehow managing not to spill a drop despite his annoyance at being beaten to the punch, gossip-wise. "No one knows it's murder yet."

No amount of warning not to jump to conclusions would sink through Butterbean's elf cap. "Killed by candy corn!"

"What?" Nick, my husband, strode out from his dressing room.

In his everyday red wool suit with white trim, he appeared impressively Santalike. I'd met Nick several years ago while he was on vacation in Oregon, staying at the inn I ran there in a coastal town called Cloudberry Bay. I'd had no idea of his true identity until, after a whirlwind holiday romance, he proposed marriage. His transformation into Father Christmas would never be something I took for granted.

The sight of the revered suit quieted Butterbean more effectively than any scolding from Jingles could have.

"Who died?" Nick asked.

"Wink Jollyflake," Jingles answered, standing at attention.

"The elf from the Silver Bell Bakery?" I asked.

"Wink started working at Chestnut's Cake Emporium," Butterbean said.

"Chestnut and Wink *both* defected from the Silver Bell Bakery? No wonder Bell was glaring across the street yesterday at Chestnut's Cake Emporium."

Jingles didn't miss the significance of the remark. "Was she?"

Butterbean gasped. "Rival bakery murder!"

Nick shot a cautionary look at us all. "You just said no one was sure it was murder."

Jingles opened his mouth, but Butterbean, emboldened, piped up, "What else could it have been? Wink was found lying on the floor of the bakery when Chestnut opened the shop early this morning, and on the table next to him was a half-eaten candy corn cupcake." The little round elf lifted on his toes. "Elves are saying the candy corn itself was poisoned."

"This is all hearsay and speculation," Jingles said.

It was hard not to laugh. If hearsay and speculation had a king, Jingles would wear the crown.

"I'll need to visit the Jollyflakes." Nick frowned thoughtfully. "Wink used to have a job at the Candy Cane Factory."

Interesting. The Candy Cane Factory was considered one of the best places to work in Santaland. Elves hired there tended to stay on from youth till retirement. Apparently Wink was an elf with a mind to follow his own ambitions.

Was. Now Wink was gone. I'd only glimpsed him a few times when I'd stopped at the Silver Bell Bakery, but Wink had always seemed friendly. "I should visit the Jollyflake family, too," I said.

Nick put his hand on my shoulder. "We'll stop by the new cake shop first and speak with Constable Crinkles. He'll probably still be there."

I looked over at Jingles, expecting him to regret not being able to go, or at least for him to insist that I tell him what I discovered as soon as I got back. But he was already hustling Butterbean out of the room as if he had better things to do than investigate a possible murder.

The first thing that struck me about Chestnut's Cake Emporium was the heavenly smell. Combined aromas of butter, sugar, chocolate, and vanilla hung in the air as I stepped across the threshold into the sparkling interior. The freshly painted red walls contrasted with the white stone counter where a cash register and a glass case stood ready to greet customers. Or at least, they would have on a normal day. The glass case was empty.

Three white bistro tables sat between the plate glass window looking onto Festival Boulevard and the white service counter, but most of the shop's square footage was dedicated to the business of cake baking. Beyond the cash register counter, gleaming stainless-steel tables held stand mixers and milky white glass mixing bowls at the ready. Utensil holders the size of Ming vases blossomed with spatulas, wooden spoons, and whisks. Most impressively, on one side of the work space, massive metal hoppers marked *Flour, Sugar,* and *Icing Sugar* hung overhead like space satellites. I gaped up at them, amazed. Chestnut could store enough ingredients in those bins to last through Armageddon.

Viewing all of the work area from the front of the store, I was in awe. But when, following Nick, I stepped around the white customer counter to the back, my enchantment died. Next to the first stain-less-steel table, Wink lay facedown on the white tile floor. A large pool of liquid surrounded the body, and the sight caused me to suck in a shocked breath. Was that blood?

On second glance, the liquid on the floor appeared to be cocoa and, curiously, water. Only a few drops of blood were visible. The cocoa could be explained by a broken mug on the ground. Wink must have been fortifying himself with a cup of cocoa as he worked late. But where did all that water come from?

Constable Crinkles greeted Nick and me in his usual tight blue uniform that stretched across his substantial belly like a woolen sausage casing. He scratched the place where the strap of his tall policeman's hat dug into his multiple chins.

"We're waiting on Doc Honeytree," he informed us.

As Christmastown's oldest physician, Doc also served as coroner when needed. But who was the "we" Crinkles referred to? Ollie didn't seem to be with him.

"Where's Ollie?" I asked.

Crinkles sighed. "He's recused himself from the investigation."

I'd never heard of a deputy constable recusing himself. "What for?"

"Too much conflict of interest," the constable explained, "what with the bake-off and all. It wouldn't be fair if he discovered too much about what Chestnut was planning for his entry."

So a murder case was taking a backseat to the candy corn bake-off?

Not that I should jump to the conclusion that this *was* murder. After all, maybe there was no mystery here. Though elves were generally long-lived, coronaries weren't unheard of. Wink could have just died while he was working late. That water, though . . .

"Why would all this water be here?" I asked the constable.

He looked as baffled as I was. "Maybe he spilled something?"

The sinks were nowhere near where Wink had fallen, and I didn't see any container on the counter that would have held water. Just one partially eaten cupcake on a plate—that already infamous candy corn cupcake Butterbean had mentioned.

"There's no broken glass nearby," I said. "Did Chestnut pick up anything at all when he came in, like a pitcher or broken glass that this water could have spilled from?"

Crinkles shook his head. "He swore it was just like this when he came in this morning. I haven't moved anything, either. I don't want to disturb the scene before Doc arrives to examine the body. He was assisting at a reindeer birth this morning."

"The water might have been from making cocoa," I said, "but I don't see a kettle sitting out."

Crinkles and Nick gaped at me as if I'd just said something bizarre.

"What?" I asked.

"Who makes cocoa with *water*?" Crinkles asked.

"Instant cocoa?" I blurted out before I could think twice. From the horror on Crinkles' face, I'd just spoken sacrilege.

"Elves don't use water with cocoa," he said. "Milk's

what makes cocoa nutritious." His lips turned down in a frown. "Well, that and the chocolate."

Chestnut came in from the back, tucking his phone into the pocket of his apron. Nick and I hadn't realized the shop owner was on the premises, and his appearance was startling. Chestnut was a changed elf. Normally he looked starched and immaculate in a white coat—more like a doctor of cake-ology than a mere baker. Today his dark eyes were filled with worry, his white coat looked stained and wrinkly, and his white chef's hat drooped like a collapsed soufflé.

"I just called Wink's family," he said despondently. "He has a widowed mother and a brother. I told them I'd lost the best assistant a baker could hope for."

"I'm sorry," I said.

He lifted his arms and dropped them again. "Wink seemed fine yesterday." I got a sense from his tone that this was not the first time he'd spoken those words aloud. "Last night he said he was going to stay late and work on the Halloween bake-off cupcake." He nodded toward the plate on the counter.

The cupcake in question was a tricolored sponge cake—yellow, orange, and white—covered with chocolate icing and sprinkled with traditional candy corn.

Not from Dash's, I registered with relief. If this was a case of candy corn poisoning, I didn't want my favorite confectioner implicated.

"We argued about the chocolate icing." As Chestnut studied the half-eaten specimen, he spoke in a voice heavy with regret. "I thought it should be vanilla icing dyed orange. I should have trusted Wink's instinct—maybe he wouldn't have felt the need to stay late and make a cupcake to convince me he was right." He sank onto a stool. "If only I'd been more open to frosting options, he might still be alive."

Just then, the bell over the door tinkled and old, wizened Doc Honeytree shuffled in. The long-tailed black suit the elderly elf always wore made him look like an undertaker, but the stethoscope around his neck and the worn black leather bag in his hand spoke to his real profession.

"Sorry to be so late, but I had to help deliver a new Cupid youngster," he said, adjusting the Coke bottle glasses that made me wonder how he managed to see anything. "Even for a late-year birth, the newborn seems like a future sleigh puller. I hurried back as—" Just then, his gaze fell on Wink. "Oh dear. What happened here?"

"That's what *I* was wondering," Crinkles said.

"All the elves at the castle are saying Wink was poisoned," I told them.

Chestnut sputtered in protest at the idea, while Doc Honeytree harrumphed. "Tittle-tattle," Doc said. "I never heed it."

"What else could have killed him if not poison?" I asked.

With effort, the doctor crouched down to the floor and examined Wink more closely. "Big bump on the head here. He might have slipped in that puddle of water and hit his head right there on that steel counter. Or someone could have delivered a fatal blow with a pipe or some such thing. Or maybe the elves are right and he ate that cupcake and fell because it had poison in it. In that case the bump would just be by-the-by."

"The cupcake wasn't poisoned," Chestnut asserted. "How could it have been? Wink made it himself."

Crinkles sucked in a breath. "Suicide by cupcake!"

That sounded crazy, but I supposed even the unlikeliest scenarios couldn't be dismissed out of hand. "Wink made the entire cupcake by himself?" I asked Chestnut.

He bit his lip before confessing, "I prepared the batter last night."

"Where did you get the candy corn?" I asked.

"At the Santaland Sweet Shop."

I didn't like that candy maker as well as Dash's Candy and Nut Shoppe, but I never suspected them of being killers.

"If word gets around that there was a cupcake poisoning here," Chestnut said plaintively, "my business will die before it's had a chance to get off the ground."

So much for his grief over losing the best cake assistant ever. Self-interest and financial survival were already kicking in.

Not that I blamed him for worrying about the fiscal prospects of his new business. The only elves lined up outside Chestnut's Cake Emporium now were curious rubberneckers. Meanwhile, across the street elves were heading into the Silver Bell Bakery.

Doc Honeytree creaked back up to his feet. "I'll have to take samples of the cupcake and everything else and run tests," he said. "Results should take a day—I'll put my nephew on it right away."

"Your nephew?" I'd never heard of Doc's having a nephew.

"He just finished his medical training in the Farthest Frozen Reaches," Doc explained. "His father, my youngest brother, was the black sheep of the Honeytree family. As a youth my brother turned rebellious, ran away to the Farthest Frozen Reaches, and fell in love with a wild elf. Algid's mother."

Algid? What kind of name was that?

A wild elf name, I guessed. The Farthest Frozen Reaches was the wilderness to the north, beyond the boundaries of the Christmas Tree Forest that ribboned through and around Santaland. The Reaches was a wild land—the only part visible from the Christmastown environs were the formidable, craggy peaks of Mount Myrrh. Inhospitable, unbelievably cold, and dangerous, it was a place of ferocious beasts—abominable snow monsters, snow leopards, and polar bears. A lawless land of renegade elves, lone miners, and exiled criminals. And, occasionally, just normal elves like Doc's brother, who wanted to take a walk on the very wild side. Wild elves were elves that were born and raised in that cold, forbidding land.

"Algid prefers microscopes and test tubes to house calls," Doc said. "This poison investigation will be right up his alley."

"It couldn't have been poison," Chestnut insisted, growing more agitated. "Like Doc said, it was probably just an accident. He slipped and fell. You have to explain that to everyone, or I'll be ruined."

Nick put a calming hand on the elf's shoulder. "Don't worry. The truth will come out."

The assurance didn't seem to pacify the baker.

I hoped this was just a tragic accident, too. But in case it wasn't, I wanted to lend a hand to find out who did this. Halloween was a holiday I'd introduced to Santaland, and candy corn was the theme ingredient I'd personally picked. If there really *was* a crazed candy corn killer on the loose, we needed to find him, fast, before he could strike again.

Chapter Three

The Jollyflake family lived in Tinkertown, Christmastown's industrial sister city and the location of all of Santa's Workshops and factories. Most of the worker elves resided in the neighborhoods of compact cottages that surrounded the factories and warehouses. The trip over took about twenty minutes in Nick's everyday sleigh with a four-reindeer team.

Visiting the bereaved was never easy. Sometimes I worried that having Santa and Mrs. Claus appear on the doorstep at such a difficult time could be considered intrusive. But the moment she opened the door and looked up at Nick and me, Mrs. Jollyflake, Wink's mother, seemed grateful that we were there. She was already dressed in mourning, from her black silk elf cap to her best black booties with large buckles and sedately curling toes.

With tears in her eyes, Mrs. Jollyflake accepted the decorative tin of fruitcake I'd brought. It was the customary condolence gift in Santaland, and by the end of today she would no doubt amass a pile of them in her kitchen, but she made a fuss over it and kept hold of the tin even as she introduced us to Wink's brother, Chuckle, and led us into the parlor. As in many working-class elf homes, the front room of the cottage was a formal salon for greeting guests and showing off family treasures. The Jollyflakes had especially fine china figurines of Santa's sleigh and the nine reindeer prancing across their mantelpiece. A fire was blazing behind the grate, leading me to assume that we were far from the first guests she'd received this morning.

She set the fruitcake on a glass-covered coffee table and invited me to join her on a settee upholstered in white fabric embroidered with cranberries. I sat, landing with more of a thump than I was expecting. I always forgot how hard it was to situate myself gracefully on elf furniture. It was like an adult sitting in an elementary school classroom.

Nick settled on a chair opposite us. Though he was taller than me and also looked unnaturally large in the elf cottage, he appeared at ease. A benefit of being to the North Pole manner born.

Chuckle, who had dark red hair peeking out from his cap, remained standing.

"This is so kind of you." Mrs. Jollyflake nodded at the fruitcake tin and lifted a black hanky to her eyes. "Wink always admired the fruitcakes from Castle Kringle. In his opinion, no other fruitcake held a candle to them. One time he made himself sick eating a whole cake to figure out if there was a secret ingredient." She blew her nose. "That was my Wink. There wasn't another elf in Santaland as dedicated to cake as he was."

"From what I've heard, he was a valued employee at the cake emporium," I said.

She nodded, refolding her handkerchief. "He felt he'd hit the big time when Chestnut picked him to work with him when he opened his own shop. He idolized Chestnut. But mark my words, in time Wink Jollyflake would have been a name to contend with in the cake world."

We could all only hope our parents spoke of us with the same pride. Nick noticed this, too. "Wink was very fortunate to be surrounded by such supportive loved ones."

Mrs. Jollyflake drew up abruptly. Her entire demeanor changed. "He wasn't always so lucky."

Chuckle, who had been quiet up till now, let out a sputter of exasperation. "Mama, please."

"I can't help it, Chuckle. Where *is* she? Everyone has heard about my poor boy by now, but his own girlfriend can't even be bothered to bring a lousy fruitcake?"

"They broke up," her son reminded her.

In answering, she looked at me, not Chuckle. "For six years Dandy Redball and my Wink were together, and then she just up and dumped him. Of course, *I* could see what she was from the very beginning. I also know there are no coincidences in this life. They broke up after all that time together, and then mere weeks later my younger son is dead?"

Chuckle pulled off his cap and ran a hand through

his hair. "You're making it sound like Dandy did something sinister. She's not—"

His mother cut him off. "The fire's low, Chuckle. Why don't you go get us some more wood from the pile."

"But Dandy's really—"

"Go, Chuckle." Mrs. Jollyflake's face was so stern, I felt squirmy even though I wasn't the one she was barking commands at.

Nick stood. "Let me give you a hand." He steered Chuckle toward the door.

As soon as she heard the back door close behind them, Mrs. Jollyflake scooted forward on the settee, her eyes bright and clear now.

"Don't listen to Chuckle. He's as in thrall to Dandy and her no-good brother, Fir, as Wink ever was. But Chuckle's more easily influenced than Wink. After he started hanging around those Redballs, I'd notice grog on his breath when he came home at night. He started calling himself Chuck, like a tough guy."

Juvenile delinquency, Santaland style.

A flame sparked in her blue eyes. "I heard that you're good at figuring things out. I already told Constable Crinkles about Wink's trouble with Dandy, but he didn't seem to think it was significant. They're saying he was poisoned—by this candy corn stuff. And where has Dandy worked for nearly a decade?" She folded her arms. "The Candy Cane Factory."

It might have seemed significant, except for one problem. "The Candy Cane Factory doesn't make candy corn." Not to mention, a lot of the elves in Tinkertown worked at the Candy Cane Factory, and they weren't all master confectioners. The Candy Cane Factory was a warehouse complex where the candy was made, yes, but candy canes were also wrapped and packaged there. The factory hired all sorts of workers—office clerks, warehouse people, drivers, even chemists.

"Dandy knows how to make candy," Mrs. Jollyflake said, "and she's also been a taste tester. She told Wink that she was instrumental in upping the plant's mint-to-syrup ratio." She leaned back, shaking her head. "Always bragging on herself, that one."

It did sound as if Dandy's work might have given her the skill to experiment with making candy corn at home and slip a little cyanide into candy syrup. *If* Wink was poisoned. The verdict would be out on that until Algid Honeytree finished his testing.

Mrs. Jollyflake took my hands in hers. "Please, Mrs. Claus. I need you to get to the bottom of what happened to my boy."

I hesitated. I was there in my official capacity as Mrs. Claus. I probably shouldn't be making promises to investigate behind Constable Crinkles' back.

On the other hand, it was hard to deny a grieving mother's request. And I had to be honest with myself: If there was a suspicious death in Christmastown, it would be on my mind until the cause of it was discovered. I might not have been born Mrs. Claus, but I was born nosy.

The sound of the back door opening spurred me to make a decision before Nick and Chuckle came back into the room.

"I'll see what I can find out," I promised Mrs. Jollyflake.

She squeezed my hands. "Thank you, Mrs. Claus."

Nick and Chuckle returned with armfuls of wood. Chuckle threw several logs on the already roaring fire while Nick arranged his neatly in the log holder by the mantel. After that, it was time to say our goodbyes. Chuckle showed us out. At the door, he darted a glance back toward the parlor and then slipped onto the tiny porch with us, snicking the cottage door closed behind him.

"Please don't pay any attention to Mama," he said, keeping his voice low. "She's distraught, and she never liked Dandy or her family. But Dandy and Fir are my friends, and I know neither of them would dream of hurting Wink."

"Of course," Nick said. He was halfway down the porch before he realized I wasn't following.

"How long were Dandy and Wink engaged?" I asked.

"About six years."

That seemed like a long time. A breakup after a six-year engagement was bound to gin up murderous thoughts at some point.

"Did Dandy break up with Wink, or was it the other way around?"

"It was Dandy. Their relationship had been strained ever since Wink took the job at the Silver Bell Bakery. He hadn't been there all that long, you know. Just a few months."

"And when did the breakup happen?"

"A few weeks ago, after he agreed to go work with Chestnut. Dandy always thought he should have stayed at the Candy Cane Factory, where we all met. It's a better job, and she was assuming that they'd be starting a family soon."

"So she was ready to start a family with him, but broke up because he took a job at a bakery? That's a pretty extreme reaction to a job change."

"It wasn't just a job to Wink, though. Cake was Wink's obsession. He'd stay up late trying new recipes, and never wanted to do anything on weekends but bake. Then one day Dandy discovered he'd spent a chunk of their savings on expensive bakeware and appliances without telling her. She just got fed up."

I was fairly certain this wasn't the whole picture, but as a survivor of a contentious first marriage, I knew the straw-versus-camel's back quotient didn't always seem logical from an outsider's perspective. Of course, the final straw for me was discovering that my husband had been a cheater.

Had there been a final straw for Dandy, too? Something more significant than high-end kitchenware?

"I just don't want the constable bothering Dandy and her brother," Chuckle said.

"Even if Doc declares that Wink was murdered?" I asked. "Surely you'd want to find out who killed your brother in that case."

"But I know it wasn't Dandy."

Nick cleared his throat. An elderly elf couple bearing a fruitcake tin had turned into the cottage's walkway. Nick and I said our goodbyes to Chuckle and sidled out of the way to make room for the Jollyflakes' next visitors.

"That was peculiar," I said when Nick and I were settled back in the sleigh. The reindeer team, who had been cooling their hooves during our condolence call, were impatient to get moving again. Nick thanked them for waiting and urged them forward, and we headed to the main snow path leading back to Christmastown.

"Did you notice how Chuckle seemed more concerned about Dandy than what's happened to his brother?"

"Grief affects everyone differently," Nick said.

But did it make a guy overprotective of his brother's ex-girlfriend? I was willing to admit that Mrs. Jollyflake was pointing the finger of blame at Dandy based on pure animosity, but wasn't it just as odd for Chuckle to extend a blanket exoneration toward Dandy before anyone really knew what had happened to Wink?

Could there have been some bad blood between the brothers? Mrs. Jollyflake exhibited a noted preference for her younger son over Chuckle. Maybe fraternal resentment had led Chuckle to covet Wink's fiancée. That coveting might have really been what had broken up the engagement.

Could it have also led to murder?

Chapter Four

When we got back to Christmastown, Nick stopped the sleigh in front of Municipal Hall, where I had a meeting to attend. The building, which overlooked the park by Peppermint Pond, now had the best view of the haunted ice castle. The workers had finished the construction of the second tower and now an array of elves were busy stringing lights around the structure. I couldn't wait to view it lit in orange and see what spooky touches the organizers had planned.

I leaned over and kissed Nick, overwhelmed with love for my magical home, and for him. I wasn't normally big on PDAs, but there's something about a guy in a Santa suit.

Pumblechook the snowman, who was still standing nearby with his odd sign, snorted. "Hey—get a room, you two."

Nick and I laughed.

Given all that had happened of a criminal or suspicious nature lately in Santaland, I wasn't expecting to see Constable Crinkles at the meeting of the Christmastown Events Committee. True, Crinkles was supposed to advise us on the law-and-order aspects of large gatherings like the Halloween carnival, but with a candy corn thief and a rumored killer on the loose, I assumed the constabulary had bigger fish to fry. When I walked into the conference room on the second floor of Municipal Hall, however, there he sat at the long conference table, positioned strategically near the platter of Puffy's All-Day Donuts.

I just had time to swing by the sideboard table holding a hot cider urn and the ubiquitous eggnog pitcher before the meeting started. I poured a mug of cider, grabbed a plate, and took the place next to Mrs. Firlog, the mayor's wife and this year's committee chair. Also at the table were Mayor Firlog, recording secretary Hope Dovebright, symphony conductor Nippy Goldmitt, and Red Candler, who as the owner of the Santaland Sweet Shop represented the business community on the council.

I flicked a glance at Puffy's platter and noted to my annoyance that Crinkles had bogarted all the Christmastown creams. The cream-filled and chocolate-glazed donuts were Puffy's equivalent to a Boston cream pie. I ended up grabbing a cherry bismarck topped with enough powdered sugar to smother a moose.

I squirmed to adjust to my short chair. "It's nice to see a platter of baked goods without pumpkins or candy corn involved. Although I guess it's harder to integrate candy corn into donuts."

"Oh no." Red set me straight on that score. "Puffy's hard at work on a candy corn donut for the bake-off. He's ordered three pounds of my candy corn. I have two candy makers working overtime to fill all the orders. Halloween's been great for business—at least until this morning. What happens next is anybody's guess. If someone's poisoning candy corn . . ." He shook his head ominously.

"I wonder if Chestnut will be able to open back up again," Nippy said. "Poisoned cupcakes aren't a good way to launch a business."

Crinkles' mouth was full, so I felt the need to insert a correction. "It's not yet certain what killed Wink."

"That half-eaten cupcake, though," Mrs. Firlog said.

"Wink was also drinking cocoa," I pointed out. "It's easier to poison a drink than a cake. And Doc Honeytree still hasn't ruled out natural causes."

"Doc's got his nephew doing tests on everything Wink ate," Crinkles said after gulping down a bite of his Christmastown cream. "He'll figure it out. Kid's a genius, according to Doc."

Mrs. Firlog cleared her throat. She was an elf of a certain age, with graying hair piled high and the look of a pouter pigeon in her linen smock. "Maybe we should start the meeting. Murder or no murder, we need to go over final plans for the Halloween carnival."

"The symphony is all set to play in the band shell outside the haunted ice castle," Nippy said. "We have a forty-minute program."

To that, I added, "They'll be followed by the

Santaland Concert Band, and the Swingin' Santas are all set to play outside the haunted ice castle after we're done. For Halloween they've volunteered to appear in costume and change their name to the Groovin' Ghoulies."

Everyone approved. The Swingin' Santas were always a hit.

"Before we move on to the subject of overflow carnival sleigh parking, we need to address the issue of the headless snowman," the mayor announced. "My office is already getting complaints."

I scanned the faces around the table. "Headless snowman?"

Hope tapped her pen impatiently. "There's going to be a headless snowman outside the haunted ice castle," she explained to me. "It's just one."

"Some of the other snowmen are objecting," the mayor said.

Pumblechook's sign made sense now. I hadn't heard about this. "How are you going to find a headless snowman?"

"Durdles has volunteered," Hope said brightly.

Red's lips twisted down. "Some snowmen will do anything for a laugh."

"That's why some of the snowmen are objecting." The mayor sniffed dismissively. "They think it's dangerous and exploitive or something."

I nearly choked on my cider. "Well, he *is* going to be without a head." Snowmen who fell apart could be reassembled, but that always came with risks.

"Please, his head will be right there on the ground next to him," Hope said. "We'll put it back when the night's over."

"Do you have to behead an existing snowman, though?" I asked. "Couldn't we just make a new headless snowman especially for the event?"

All the elves around the table gaped at me as if I were a monster. I shifted self-consciously.

"Just build a snowman willy-nilly in order to have something to stick in a Halloween carnival?" Mayor Firlog asked, his voice looping up incredulously.

"And what would we tell the poor snowman once we put a head on him?" Hope asked me. "That he was created as some kind of gag?"

"No." I nodded. "I see the problem."

Snowman ethics could get tricky.

Mayor Firlog's brow scrunched. "What's so scary about a headless snowman anyway? Not like it could actually hurt anybody."

I snorted. "Unless the victim is frozen in fear, like in old horror movies."

Eyes around the table stared blankly at me—yet another reminder that I was from a different world. I attempted to explain that characters in classic black-and-white horror movies were often unable to escape the slow-moving blob, or the amorphous monster (aka a man under a carpet remnant) as in *The Creeping Terror,* or any number of shambling zombies.

"Zombies!" Crinkles said, shuddering. "I'd freeze in fear, too."

"It's fiction, Constable," I reminded him.

Crinkles took offense. "Headless snowmen are real, and I don't care what anybody says, they *are* terrifying." He blinked and started to look shaky, as if there were one in the conference room with us now. "Or just imagine—a snowman zombie." His blue-wool-clad body rippled in a shudder.

"Ice zombies!" Red said, seeming to relish the idea—or to relish scaring Crinkles.

"Ice zombies aren't a thing." I looked around the table. "Are they?"

"You never know what's lurking up in the Farthest Frozen Reaches," Crinkles told me.

Hope cleared her throat impatiently. "Well, this is just going to be one plain old headless snowman."

"If Durdles wants to do it, I don't see why we should object," Mrs. Firlog said. "Is everyone agreed?"

Hands darted up around the table, except for the constable's. He was so upset about ice zombies he'd had to set down his half-eaten donut. "I know it's Halloween, but does everything have to be so darn scary?"

Before anyone could respond, the door opened and my sister-in-law, Lucia, strode in, followed by her best friend, a reindeer named Quasar. As soon as she appeared, the elf men leapt to their feet. Lucia was almost as tall as Nick, wore her thick blond hair in a long braid down her back, and dressed in well-worn boots, woolen pants, and a quilted vest jacket.

Gazes then turned to Quasar. Reindeer in the corridors of Municipal Hall weren't unheard of, but the ones who did appear there tended to be the leaders of the great herds—the Blitzens, the Prancers, the Comets. Quasar, though clearly a Rudolph descendant, was born with a malfunctioning nose and one slightly short leg, which gave him a shambling gait. He hadn't yet started to shed his antlers for the winter, though, and their full growth made him look more impressive than he usually did by Christmas. He often knocked things over with them, but the elves in the room didn't know that. Their startled, slightly distasteful looks probably had more to do with the strong musky odor that now permeated the room.

In fairness to Quasar, the source of that musky odor was just as likely to be Lucia as him. Lucia resided at Castle Kringle, but her days were spent with the reindeer herds.

"What are you doing here?" I asked her.

Lucia approached the empty seat at the head of the table opposite Mrs. Firlog. "I'm here on behalf of the Society for the Benefit of Misfit Reindeer," Lucia said. "We've got an idea for a Halloween carnival ride."

"But we already have our concessions set up around the haunted ice castle," Mrs. Firlog said, flipping through the pages on her clipboard. "I'm afraid that the Society for the Benefit of Misfit Reindeer isn't on our list."

"This is last minute, but we wouldn't interrupt your plans. We could use the other side of Peppermint Pond from the haunted ice castle . . . and maybe a few city blocks."

"What do you have in mind?" Mrs. Firlog asked.

"Quasar's Runaway Sleigh Ride," Lucia announced.

"I-I won't really run away with anyone," Quasar explained, his nose fizzling nervously.

"The ride'll be a hit with the kids," Lucia said. "And adults, too."

"This is irregular," Mayor Firlog said. "How can we close streets when the city is going to be packed?"

"The biggest crowds will be around the park, where the haunted ice castle is. We just need a street or two—Quasar will hop over a rooftop and bump the sleigh down for a few blocks of breakneck fun. I've rigged out a sleigh for the occasion with seat belts and padding. The riders will be as safe as Santa on Christmas Eve."

That analogy gave me no comfort. I still quailed inside at seeing Nick fly off in his huge sleigh on the big night. But Lucia's sales pitch seemed to satisfy everyone else. And then she sealed the deal with an enticing offer.

"Just to prove how safe it is, and how fun, we want to treat the council to a sample runaway sleigh ride. Quasar and I set up a test path just outside town."

A collective squeal went up. If there was anything elves loved—other than candy, carbs, and year-round Christmas carols—it was a sleigh ride. Around the table, eyes lit with childlike excitement.

"Permission granted," Mrs. Firlog said, not even bothering with a vote. She smacked her gavel on the table. "Meeting adjourned to sample Quasar's Runaway Sleigh Ride."

Forget overflow sleigh parking or whatever else was on the meeting's agenda; a mad dash for the door ensued. I barely had time to grab Crinkles by the coat sleeve. "You're going sleigh riding?"

His eyes widened. "Why not?"

"What about the candy corn theft? And the suspicious death?"

"Can't do anything about Wink until I hear back from Doc Honeytree. And as for the candy corn theft"—he scratched his head under the bill of his cap—"we've had no new leads on that."

"But shouldn't you be out looking?"

He cast a longing gaze through the doorway and down the hall, where the council members were retreating behind Lucia for their sleigh ride.

"Sorry, April. I'm a member of this council and an officer of the law—I need to make sure that sleigh ride's safe for the children."

He pulled free and scrambled away to catch up with the others.

I did not follow my fellow council members. I'd experienced enough reindeer and sleigh flight to know I preferred the boring safety of solid ground. More importantly, I'd agreed to meet Juniper for coffee. We had a lot to catch up on.

Chapter Five

By the time I arrived at the We Three Beans coffeehouse, Juniper had already claimed a quiet corner table. As quiet as the low-ceilinged room could manage. Speakers blared out a Halloween mix. Just waiting for my double latte, I was treated to an all-café sing-along to "Monster Mash." Whenever elves came together to socialize, there was singing—usually Christmas carols, although ever since Trumpet, the owner of We Three Beans, had found this mix album of Halloween hits on Elf Bay, it was in rotation all during October. Between endless repetitions of "Monster Mash" and the number of pumpkin spice eggnog lattes I saw elves ordering, I sometimes regretted introducing Santalanders to Halloween.

I carried my coffee over to Juniper in the corner.

"Something the matter?" she asked, pushing her pumpkin muffin toward me to share.

"I just came from the events committee meeting." I took a sip of my coffee. Heaven. "Crinkles was there, and I can tell he's not seriously considering Wink's death as a murder, and it doesn't sound like he's even investigating the candy corn heist, either."

"You'd think if any crime would hit home for Crinkles, it would be a theft involving sugary foods," Juniper said. "So I guess he has no idea about who poisoned Wink?"

"*If* he was poisoned. Doc Honeytree still hasn't declared the cause of death."

"Good gravy—Doc Honeytree's as slow as syrup in January."

I reached over and took a bit of Juniper's pumpkin muffin. Like all the baked goods Trumpet served, it was delicious. I mentally took back my bad words about pumpkin spice everything. "Maybe not this time. Doc Honeytree has his nephew-assistant working on it."

"Doc has a nephew? Since when?"

I shrugged. "Doc said he just finished his medical training in the Farthest Frozen Reaches."

"Doc's nephew is also a doctor?" She sat up straighter, and I couldn't miss the glint in her eye. "How did I not know this? Is he good looking?"

"I don't know. I've never seen him."

"How old is he?"

"No idea."

"You didn't ask?"

I laughed. "I was preoccupied with a suspicious

death, not whether Doc Honeytree's nephew has boyfriend potential."

"Some friend you are," she said.

"He has an odd name," I said, trying to remember. "Sounds like Algae."

"Algid?"

"That's it. It's a weird name, isn't it? It sounds foreign."

Juniper laughed. "It's English, April. A synonym for *cold*."

"Oh."

"A doctor from the Farthest Frozen Reaches . . ." She smiled dreamily. "Sounds like he could be brainy *and* rugged."

"Doc told me that Algid's more interested in research than anything else. I hope this means that he'll nudge along the investigation into Wink's cause of death."

Juniper put down her mug. "If you really want to see what's going on, why don't you go to Doc Honeytree's and give him a nudge yourself?"

It wasn't a bad idea, especially in light of the promise I'd made to Mrs. Jollyflake to find out what happened to Wink.

"And I'll go with you," Juniper added with a smile.

Doc Honeytree's combination home-office-surgery was located on the brow of the hill of Bow Street, in a neighborhood where the houses were set apart from each other and more modern in character. Modern, in that they looked like nineteenth-century Americana more than a medieval German village, which was what downtown Christmastown seemed to be patterned after. Of course, this being Santaland, the elf owners painted their homes in eye-popping hues. Doc Honeytree's place, a three-story house set apart from the others, was a bloodred crimson, with a white door and shutters. It was conspicuous enough that it was never hard to find the doctor's castle in an emergency, even if you failed to notice the sign by the street announcing *Doctor Jubilation Honeytree, Physician and Surgeon.*

We walked up to the door, which had a large brass walrus head in the center, and I gave it a firm knock.

As we waited for someone to answer, Juniper performed a not-so-subtle appearance check in the doorknob's brass plate, fluffing the curls pillowing below her elf hat.

No one answered, though.

"That's strange. Usually Nurse Cinnamon is here." She knocked again.

We were about to give up when the sound of footsteps finally echoed from inside. When the heavy door finally creaked open, Juniper and I both jumped back. We hadn't expected to come face-to-face with a large rat.

But it wasn't just the beady red eyes of the white rodent that startled us. The rat perched on the shoulder of a lab-coated young man with skin so pale that it was hard to believe he'd ever seen sunlight at all. His gray eyes reinforced that vampiric impression, as did his hair, which was blond, technically, but so wispy and close to the color of his skin that it disappeared on his scalp.

I swallowed, collecting myself. "Dr. Algid, I presume?"

His head tilted, lizard-like, as did the rat's. "And I presume you're *not* from the undertakers."

Juniper gulped. "Don't be absurd. This is Mrs. Claus. We're here to talk to Doc Honeytree."

"My uncle was called out to Tinkertown," Algid said. "There was an accident at the Wrapping Works."

The Wrapping Works was a three-story workshop with a Rube Goldberg network of conveyer belts carrying toys and other gifts from one job station to another: boxing, wrapping and taping, and bows. Watching it all working was amazing, but remembering all the blades and belts everywhere, I could understand the dangers, too.

"I hope it's nothing too serious," I said.

"Serious enough that he took Nurse Cinnamon instead of me." Reading our confusion, he explained, "I don't mind blood, but I find pain . . . disturbing."

Juniper and I exchanged side-eyed glances.

"Well. Sorry we missed Doc Honeytree," Juniper piped up. "April here was just curious if there was any news about Wink, but if it's not a good time, then—"

She was already taking my arm to tug me back down the porch steps. Apparently she'd seen enough of Algid to know a grand passion for him wasn't written in the stars.

"Oh, I've got news," he said.

I dug in my heels before Juniper could pull me away. "What?"

Algid's skeletal hand beckoned us inside. "Come in—I'll explain."

Juniper looked about as eager to enter the house now as she would be to walk into the lair of an abominable snow monster, so I kept hold of her arm to prevent her from bolting. I was determined to hear him out, but I'd prefer not to go into the house alone.

With trepidation, we crossed the threshold. We were both being silly. This was just the doctor's house. Every elf in Santaland came here at some point to get a cut stitched, an illness tended to, or a broken bone set.

But Algid led us past what was clearly the doctor's office and opened a door further down a dark hallway.

"Where are we going?" I asked.

"Down to the basement, where my lab is." He blinked. "It's also where my uncle does the autopsies."

Juniper sent me a "no way" look, but there was no way I wasn't going to try to find out what Algid knew.

"After you," I told Algid.

I followed the ghoulish elf, and Juniper reluctantly traipsed after me down the rickety wooden stairs to the basement.

The rat turned on his master's shoulder so that he looked up at us, his spooky eyes gleaming, as we descended.

"What's your friend's name?" I asked.

"This is Newton," he said. "Excuse him for staring. He's awkward around strangers."

He's not the only one. I tried to laugh. "I thought maybe he was just aloof and judgy."

"Oh, he's that, too. Newton has very strong opinions—we get in some pretty heated arguments."

Okay. Nothing odd about that.

In the basement, Algid made a ta-da gesture with his arms at the laboratory. The floor was cement that had been painted over several times; now, from treading of feet over the years, the various grays, black, and even red showed through in a speckled pattern. The walls were white, but that did little to brighten the room, which was lit only by two ancient incandescent bulbs hanging from the ceiling and an industrial-looking lamp on a worktable. Two long granite-topped worktables held various hot plates, beakers, and vials containing heaven-only-knew what. It reminded me of a mad scientist's lab in a classic horror movie.

"I never knew this was down here," Juniper said. "How—" She gulped at the sight of a sheet-covered form lying on top of a wheeled steel table. "Is that . . . Wink?"

"Yes." Algid clasped his hands together. "Just waiting for the undertakers now."

Juniper and I edged away.

"I'm assuming you'd like to see my findings on Wink's blood and the various samples my uncle brought from the scene of the crime," Algid said.

Interesting choice of words. "You don't think it was an accident, then?"

"Oh no. Not likely." He took a clipboard off his desk where he'd scrawled the results of the day's experiments in tiny, cramped writing. "Wink's blood contained no toxins, and neither did the candy or the beverages that were sampled."

The candy makers and bakers would be relieved to hear that.

"What about the water that was on the floor?" I asked.

He shrugged. "Only water."

Juniper thought about that. "So he could have just had a heart attack or something?"

"Oh no. He was murdered, all right. But not by poison." Algid headed toward the stainless-steel table, but Juniper and I froze in place.

"Just tell us," I said before he could whisk off the sheet. I'd already seen Wink, and I didn't think Juniper was up to it.

He stopped, disappointed. "Oh. I forget that some are squeamish about dead bodies. So odd."

"*We're* odd?" Juniper muttered under her breath.

I directed a subtle shake of my head her way. I didn't want to do anything to make our ghoulish host clam up—I was already worried that it would occur to him that he shouldn't be releasing this information to us before telling his uncle, or Constable Crinkles, so the Jollyflakes could be informed.

"The subject has a goose-egg-sized lump on the back of his head," Algid said.

"We noticed that at the cake emporium. Your uncle thought he might have hit his head as he fell."

Algid lifted a hand in an aha gesture. "I considered that. But then I went to the cake shop and made a diagram of where the table was, and how Wink was lying on the floor when he was discovered. If he'd hit the back of his head as he fell, there's no way he could have ended up facedown. It would have required him to do a three-quarter turn and then take two steps. That would have been an almost acrobatic death. It defies physical logic."

Before I could work through the falling scenarios that he'd already imagined, he added, "And there's one other reason I suspect this was in no way a natural death. I think I saw his killer."

Juniper and I both sucked in our breath. "You saw him? When?"

Algid backpedaled. "I *heard* the killer, I should say. I was walking late at night—Newton and I are night owls—and the sound of raised voices about a block ahead made me stop. It sounded like two elves arguing."

Juniper crossed her arms. "How did you know they were elves?"

His eyes narrowed. "They weren't deep voices."

I'd never thought about it before, but the timbre of elves' voices did differ from humans'.

"My instinct was to turn around," he continued, "but when I peered around the corner, that elf"— he jabbed a thumb toward the unfortunate Wink—"was standing in the middle of Festival Boulevard, dazed, watching the elf he'd just been arguing with walk away."

"When was this?" I asked.

"Night before last."

A little of the tension sagged out of me. "But Wink was killed last night."

"Maybe the other elf came back last night to finish the argument. Unless you think this Wink character had arguments with different elves every night." Algid snuffled out a laugh. "Wouldn't surprise me, actually. Wink wasn't at all friendly when I tried to help him. I asked him if everything was all right, and he just scowled at me and told me to go away. And when I told him I didn't feel comfortable leaving him in the middle of the street, he insulted me."

"What did he say?" Juniper and I asked in unison.

"He said, *Go away, Rat Boy.* I had Newton with me." He crooked his head to indicate his albino friend.

"You walk with your pet rat at night?" Juniper asked.

"Of course. Newton's good company."

She tilted her head, considering. "I have a rabbit. I never thought of taking him walking with me."

Newton's whiskers twitched and he seemed to squeak in Algid's ear.

Algid's thin lips quirked into a smile. "Rabbits *aren't* the brightest."

Who was he talking to?

Juniper's face reddened. Before a rats-versus-rabbits squabble could break out, I asked him, "Did you see the other elf?"

"Just from the back. It was snowing pretty hard. Whoever it was wore a parka with the hood pulled up." His mouth twisted into a sneer. "These Santa-landers react to every little flurry like it's a blizzard. They should spend a few weeks in the Farthest Frozen Reaches." He nodded his head at the draped form on the steel table. "He was all bundled up that evening, too."

"You're sure it was Wink."

"Oh yes, it was him all right." His lips flattened. "After he called me Rat Boy, I got a good look at him. I remember elves who insult me."

"What was their argument about?"

"I don't recall the actual words so much as the tone, you know?" He concentrated. "I caught a few snippets—something about betrayal, or cheating. *I never meant to cheat you.* That's the last thing this Wink character yelled after the other one."

I couldn't help remembering Wink's mother's accusations against his ex-girlfriend, Dandy. "Did he say *I didn't mean to cheat you,* or *I didn't mean to cheat on you?*"

He frowned in concentration and then shook his head. "I couldn't swear to either. And like I said, after he yelled it, Wink just stood there watching the other elf walk away. He was so still, I was worried he'd been hurt. That was the only reason I approached him at all."

Cheating. "Was the other elf male, or female?"

He considered. "Female, I think. I couldn't swear to it—when voices are raised, it's sometimes hard to tell. And she would have been on the tall side." He looked up at me, making me feel self-conscious about my height. "Tall for an elf, I mean."

"Taller than me?" Juniper asked.

"Oh yes," he said. "You're very squat."

At that point, I figured it would be best to hustle red-faced Juniper out of there as soon as possible.

Chapter Six

"**S**quat!"

Juniper was so incensed that I was forced—forced, mind you—to take her to Tea-piphany for a therapeutic cup of tea and my sister-in-law Tiffany's decadent specialty, the Tower of Scones. Nothing blotted out life's irritations as effectively as scones with clotted cream.

Tiffany ran the teahouse in addition to her other job, teaching figure skating. Business was so good, though, it was hard to believe the tea shop had ever been planned as just a sideline. Pouring tea and delivering our scone tower, Tiffany moved with the efficiency and power of the junior champion figure skater she'd once been, and her long hair bobbed behind her in a Kristi Yamaguchi ponytail.

"Something wrong?" she asked us.

Juniper's face was set in an uncharacteristic scowl. "What would you do if someone called you squat?"

"I'd deck him." Tiffany set the teapot down. "I'm assuming this was a him."

"More like an it," Juniper fumed. "I wouldn't get close enough to that ghoul to touch him. Imagine looking like an amoeba in elf form and having the crust to criticize someone's looks."

"Doc Honeytree's nephew," I explained to Tiffany. "Algid."

"I'd just as soon go out with his pet rat," Juniper said.

"Newton actually seemed the more sensitive of the two," I agreed.

Juniper took a bite out of an iced pumpkin spice scone. "I'm not so sure about that. Did you notice how upset he still was over Wink calling him Rat Boy?" She looked up at Tiffany and explained, "He answered the door with an arctic ice rat on his shoulder. Wouldn't that give you the willies?"

Something clicked in Tiffany's expression. "I know who you're talking about. Shifty eyes, skin the color of tapioca, carries a rat around with him?"

"There can't be two of them in Christmastown," Juniper said.

"Odd character," Tiffany said. "He takes his tea without sugar."

"He would." Juniper's mouth curled down in a disgusted frown, as if she'd heard that he drank blood.

I was less concerned with Algid than with the information he'd given me. A blow to the head . . . an assailant who'd felt cheated, or cheated on . . . a female elf in a parka.

If that last detail could be believed, we could

scratch Chuckle Jollyflake off the suspect list. But could Chuckle's anxiousness at the possibility of Crinkles questioning Dandy have been because of something he knew about her? Maybe Wink's mother was correct to point the finger of blame at Dandy Redball.

While I was distracted, Smudge came into the tea shop. It seemed like an odd coincidence—a cozy tea shop with floral centerpieces and lace cloths didn't strike me as one of the black-clad drummer's hangouts. But then I saw Juniper glance at him as if she'd been expecting him, and I realized she must have texted him after we left Doc's house. He pulled up a chair and wedged himself in the empty aisle spot between me and Juniper. "Who are you talking about?"

Juniper got him up to speed on Algid Honeytree.

Smudge smirked. "Sounds almost like one of those ice zombies everyone's talking about."

I frowned. "Who's talking about ice zombies?"

"Everybody," he said. "Constable Crinkles was warning folks about them. Now Sparkletoe's Mercantile already has an ax display in the window—anti-zombie weaponry."

I laughed. In Christmastown, gossip spread faster than ivy tendrils. "The constable's scared himself into believing his own made-up story, and now he's busy panicking the rest of the city."

Smudge shook his head. "As if we didn't have enough to worry about with a candy corn killer at large."

"There is no candy corn killer," I said. "Algid told us the candy corn wasn't poisoned."

"He was so creepy," Juniper told Smudge. "I'm not sure I believe anything he said."

"We can't ignore his testimony just because we don't like his looks or his manner," I said. "He's the only witness to the argument between Wink and the elf who might have come back the next night to kill him."

"That's what I mean." Juniper folded her hands in her lap. "Algid was the only one who witnessed that argument. What if *he* had something to do with all this?"

"I think you might be letting his calling you *squat* prejudice your opinion," I said.

Smudge drew back, outraged. "He called you that?"

Juniper recounted our dealings with Algid this morning in more detail. Smudge took her side one hundred percent. "That jerk can go climb a Christmas tree."

She regarded Smudge with something approaching admiration.

"I still don't think Algid would lie about his experiments," I said. "Doc Honeytree will surely review his findings. And what about the explanation of how Wink fell? I found that convincing."

Juniper bit her lip, thinking. "I wish Constable Crinkles was working harder to figure out who stole the candy corn. Can it really be a coincidence that these two things happened at once?"

"It *would* all be less confusing if we at least knew who had stolen that candy corn," Smudge said. "That way we could at least eliminate one element."

We?

Juniper brightened. "You're right. How should we start?"

Smudge shrugged, as if he tracked down criminals all the time. "It's just a matter of logic and deduction, right?"

"Right," Juniper chimed.

I was tempted to laugh at this squabbling elf duo's transformation into Tommy and Tuppence, but maybe Juniper was on to something. Could it be purely coincidence that the largest heist in Christmastown history and a suspicious murder both happened in the same week?

"I bet I get to the bottom of that heist before Crinkles finds a single clue," Smudge said. "I'll start this afternoon."

"We have band rehearsal this afternoon," Juniper reminded him.

We all three groaned. Normally, we loved rehearsals with the Santaland Concert Band, but there was so much going on now.

A movement outside the tea shop window caught my eye. I spotted Chestnut weaving down the street, cap askew, holding a three-tiered cake carrier. He didn't look at all well.

I hopped to my feet. "I have to run," I told Juniper and Smudge. "I'll meet you at band rehearsal."

They looked startled but not entirely displeased to be left on their own.

On the way out, I asked Tiffany to put our table's bill on my tab. She nodded in agreement. "Be careful out there," she said with a wink. "Don't go chasing any ice zombies."

Chestnut was walking like a zombie. Hunched

in a black overcoat, he shambled unsteadily down the sidewalk. Where had he come from, and where was he going?

I hurried my steps to keep up with him. This shouldn't have been hard, since I was more than half a foot taller. Elves' short legs move quickly, though, and their lower center of gravity helps with balance. After two years in Santaland, I still skittered and slipped crossing ice-packed streets.

"Chestnut!" I had to call out his name several times before he finally turned around. I closed the distance between us.

Up close, his appearance was even more concerning. His eyes were bloodshot, the pointy tips of his ears were as red as Santa's coat, and the smell of grog wafted off him.

I nodded down at his cake carrier. "Looks like you've been baking."

"Stress baking at home," he explained. "I couldn't stay at the store today."

As if our conversation were at an end, he turned away from me and sped toward Festival Boulevard.

I scrambled after him. "Where are you going?"

"To the bakery. There's something I have to do." He sighed. "It's so unfair. My dream had finally come true—my own shop, and success. Now everyone's saying I poisoned that cupcake that killed Wink."

"Then everyone's wrong," I told him firmly. "You should go back home and sleep off the grog. Things will look better tomorrow. Soon elves will forget about Wink's death and remember that you're the best cake maker in Christmastown."

He stopped, sucking in deep breaths. I assumed

that my advice was sinking in, but then he shook his head, and the mittened hand that wasn't holding the cake cover balled into a fist. "Then why are all the elves lined up at the Silver Bell Bakery?"

I followed his gaze. Sure enough, the line at Bell's was two deep down the block. Chestnut, nearly apoplectic, plunged into the middle of the street and headed toward his rival's storefront.

Then, in the middle of the wide road, he dropped to one knee, commando-style, and removed the cake carrier's cover, revealing a pyramid of cupcakes that he set on the ground next to him as if he were stockpiling ammunition. He picked up a cherry cupcake and lobbed it like a grenade at the Silver Bell Bakery. "I am the master cake artist!" His declaration sounded like a battle cry. The first throw made a direct hit on Bell's sign.

Several more volleys followed in quick succession. The bewildered elves lined up in front of Bell's scattered under the barrage. Chestnut had a surprisingly strong throwing arm, and the cupcakes flew fast and furiously. Elves screamed and ducked, and a few threw themselves to the sidewalk and covered their heads with their hands, as if there was shrapnel flying instead of cake. Cupcake debris littered the sidewalk and Bell's plate glass window.

Chestnut unfastened the second cake cover and unleashed another bombardment—chocolate cupcakes this time. "Justice for Wink!"

What was he talking about? I tugged on his arm. "Stop! You aren't helping your cause."

"I don't care!" He yanked his arm out of my grasp.

His next grenade, a chocolate cupcake with delicious-looking ganache icing, scored a direct hit on the bakery's Open sign. *What a waste,* I couldn't help thinking.

Bell rushed out, planting herself arms akimbo in front of her shop. Elves who had been pinned to the sidewalk took this stand-off as an opportunity to scramble out of the line of fire.

"I've called the constable!" Bell yelled out, looking more bristly than ever.

"Good—I'll tell him what you did," Chestnut shot back.

"What *I* did? Are you crazy?"

She had to ask?

"You killed Wink," Chestnut shouted at her. *"You* poisoned that cupcake."

He removed the last cake carrier's cover, revealing a full-sized snowball cake. It was my all-time favorite—delicious, nutty, toasted coconut over fondant icing and a moist white cake with just a hint of rum. I watched in horror as he lifted it on one palm, holding it aloft to lob at Bell.

This was too much. I grabbed his throwing arm. "Think about what you're doing! This isn't just an assault and a crime against property, it's a crime against cake."

Chestnut hesitated.

"No one poisoned Wink," I told him. "The candy corn cupcake contained no poison."

"Who says?"

"Algid—Doc Honeytree's nephew. He thinks Wink was killed by a blow to the head."

Chestnut froze. "Not a cupcake?"

"No."

It wasn't ethical of me to be announcing the doctor's findings this way, right in the middle of Christmastown, when I wasn't certain Crinkles had informed the Jollyflakes yet. I hoped the constable would understand. The information did seem to have a soothing effect. Chestnut lowered the cake, and I took it from him.

"I never would have hurt Wink," he said. "He was my right-hand elf."

"I know."

From the distance, the sound of the constabulary snowmobile's siren rent the air.

"I'm going to have you arrested!" Bell yelled from across the street at us.

As the siren grew louder, Chestnut's eyes grew frantic. Before I could react, he turned on his heel and took off running.

"Wait!" I called after him. But his bandy legs were already speeding him down the middle of the street. I sighed. The idiot. Running from the police was usually the worst thing to do.

Crinkles appeared on his snowmobile, and Bell darted toward him.

"It's Chestnut," she said. "He went crazy and attacked my shop!" She pointed down the street in the direction Chestnut had just run. With a salute, Crinkles put on his flashing lights, turned on the siren again, and sped after the fleeing baker.

Chapter Seven

Inside the bakery, Bell had to take a moment to recover. Her assistant, Sugar, had flipped the Closed sign in the window. All the customers had fled during Chestnut's cupcake attack anyway.

My nerves were so frazzled that I downed the fortifying mug of eggnog Sugar handed me. Usually I found eggnog a little nauseating, but Sugar had laced it with brandy, cutting the gluey consistency.

Bell knocked hers back. "Did you hear what he called me?" she asked. "Murderer!"

"The stress of finding Wink this morning must have gotten to him," I said.

"Hmph." Bell folded her arms. "Sheer deflection, if you ask me. The first thing someone with a guilty conscience does is try to point the finger of blame at someone else."

Sugar shook her head. Bell's helper, now that I got a good look at her, looked around the same age as her boss, that is to say, around forty-five or fifty. They were wearing matching silver aprons over light green tunics, with the bells and ribbons logo of the store on the bib of the apron. Side by side, Bell and Sugar looked more like sisters than employer-employee.

"It was like he just snapped," Sugar said. "He was never like that when he worked here."

"He snapped, all right." Bell drummed her fingers. "But that shouldn't let him off the hook. He's calculating that folks will think I'm so jealous of his fancy new store that I would do a diabolical thing like hurting Wink. Accusing someone without proof is almost as evil as the murder itself."

She was right, yet I couldn't forget her glaring across the street at Chestnut's Cake Emporium, and the anger and betrayal in her eyes when she'd spotted me considering getting in line. And I was just an occasional customer of hers. How much angrier must she have felt toward Wink, her employee who'd defected along with Chestnut?

Could Bell have been the elf in the parka Algid had seen arguing with Wink in the middle of the night?

"Did you ever have words with Wink about his leaving?" I asked.

She poured herself some more eggnog. "When Chestnut announced that he was going to open his own shop and take Wink with him, I admit it— that hurt. I'd taught them everything about the bakery business and nurtured their talents, and there Chestnut was, announcing that he was opening a shop right across the street from mine. Sure, I was upset, and I told them so."

"But what about more recently? In the past few days, say."

"Until today, I hadn't spoken to Chestnut in weeks, or Wink, either."

"You didn't talk to Wink late on the night before he died?"

She blinked in confusion. "No . . ."

The front door banged shut. Through the glass front, we watched Sugar begin clearing up the cake-splattered snow with a shovel and a pail.

"Frankly, I didn't care if I never spoke to Chestnut or Wink ever again," Bell continued. "My employees were always more than just workers to me, Mrs. Claus. I like to think we're family here at the Silver Bell Bakery. But even though he did betray me by defecting to Chestnut's store, there's no one more upset about what happened to Wink than I am."

If Bell was sincere and she really had considered Chestnut and Wink to be family, wouldn't that make their defection all the more painful and any violence toward them easier to justify to herself?

My imagination was off and running with this Bell-as-culprit theory. I had to remind myself that here, now, Bell was the victim.

"I'm sorry this happened to you," I said.

She was not soothed. "I won't be attacked and accused. And I won't rest easy until whoever's responsible for what happened to Wink is exiled to the darkest corner of the Farthest Frozen Reaches."

The door opened and Crinkles bustled in, puffing as if he'd just run a marathon. "We got him!" From the pride in his voice, you'd think he'd just collared Al Capone instead of a cupcake-lobbing baker. "Ollie is taking him back to the constabulary now."

"Good," Bell said. "In my opinion, you've got Wink's killer, as well."

Crinkle's eyes bulged. "Really, who?"

"Chestnut," Bell said, enunciating the name as she would to someone half deaf, or half witted.

The constable rocked back on his heels, overwhelmed by his own achievement. "That's the fastest I've ever caught a killer."

I pinned my gaze on him. "Constable, can I speak to you outside?"

"Of course," he said.

Out on the sidewalk, I buried my hands in my coat pockets and gave him the bad news. "I don't think Chestnut killed Wink."

He frowned. "Why not? It would have been easy for him to poison something Wink ate. Piece of cake, in fact." He chortled at his own joke. "He even admitted to preparing the lethal cupcake batter."

"Algid said Wink wasn't poisoned."

"What?" Crinkles' face fell. "Doc Honeytree didn't say anything to me."

"Doc's been tending to an emergency in Tinkertown this afternoon. What's more, Algid said he overheard Wink having a loud fight with a woman the night before."

"Why haven't I heard any of this?"

That's what happens when you go sleigh riding instead of conducting an investigation.

His mouth twisted. "Well! A *female* elf. That's almost half of Santaland. How am I supposed to narrow down *that* suspect list?"

"You could start by talking to Bell—she's harboring some strong resentments against both Chestnut and Wink."

A look of dread crossed his face as he glanced back at the bakery. I half expected him to dig his curly-toed booty into the ground and whine, "Do I *have* to?"

Instead, he muttered, "I guess you're right."

Belatedly, Bell's words from earlier echoed in my head: *Accusing someone without proof is almost as wicked as the murder itself.* Had I just done something wicked?

But I didn't actually accuse Bell. I'd just told Crinkles he should question her. He should be questioning a lot of people.

Crinkles shuffled reluctantly back inside and I was close on his heels when Sugar called out my name, waylaying me. She'd moved on from shoveling to wiping icing off the bakery's window. Her expression was apprehensive as she flicked a glance inside. "Is Crinkles here to arrest Bell?"

I drew back. "No, of course not. Why would he be?"

Her expression didn't give anything away. "I was just worried. . . ."

"As a matter of fact," I said, "he was half convinced by Bell that Chestnut killed Wink."

"But that's all wrong!" Sugar tossed her cleaning cloth in the bucket. "Completely wrong! Chestnut would never hurt Wink."

"Do you know someone who might have?"

I could tell that she regretted having said anything. Which of course made me all the more curious about what she knew. Especially when she flicked an anxious glance toward the bakery's interior.

"Do you think Bell could have had anything to do with Wink's death?" I asked.

Quickly—almost too quickly—she gave her head a frantic shake. "I didn't say that." She stopped, then looked down at the snow. "I mean, sure, she does have a ferocious temper. . . ."

I was beginning to wonder if that was a trait that all bakers shared.

"Bell's been really mad these past weeks, ever since she found out about Chestnut's shop, and his taking Wink with him. But that's understandable, right? I know she feels cheated. But it's been hard to watch."

Sugar had had a front row seat to Bell's resentment. I felt sorry for her.

"Didn't I see you at Peppermint Pond, moving ice blocks?" I asked.

She nodded. "The city called for volunteers."

Sugar was a helper—one of those citizens that communities depended on—that employers depended on. A worker bee, not a queen bee.

A word Sugar had used earlier snagged in my brain. *Cheated.*

That was the word Algid had mentioned overhearing during the late-night argument.

"Do you know if Bell had spoken to either Chestnut or Wink recently?" I asked.

"She told me she'd given Chestnut a piece of her mind."

"When?"

She thought back. "I'm not sure when the conversation occurred. She told me about it"—she bit her lip—"yesterday."

Now that was interesting. Bell had lied to me. What else was she lying about?

"I've been working for Bell for almost a decade," Sugar said. "Longer than Chestnut, and certainly longer than Wink. But I don't want to stay here if Bell's . . . unstable."

Was she? I kept reminding myself not to let my suspicions run away from me. With a former co-worker murdered, though, I could see why Sugar would be nervous.

Crinkles emerged from the bakery. I wasn't sure if he'd gotten any answers out of Bell, but he was walking away with something even better: Chestnut's snowball cake.

He caught me staring at the cake carrier and shrugged sheepishly. "I'm taking it back to the constabulary. It's evidence."

The tastiest evidence ever.

Chapter Eight

Band rehearsal dragged on longer than usual that afternoon. Luther Partridge, our conductor, had trouble maintaining order. Even with a big performance looming, the elves had a hard time concentrating on music when there was so much chaos in Christmastown. Everyone had heard about the cupcake attack at the Silver Bell Bakery.

Between numbers, Bobbin, our piccolo player, kept piping up about all the mayhem, straining Luther's patience. After we had struggled through another run-through of "Danse Macabre," the final piece in our program, he said, "What should we do if ice zombies show up at the fes-tival?"

This was too much. I stepped out from behind my bass drum. "Ice zombies don't exist."

Bobbin blinked. "That's not what Constable Crinkles says."

Good grief. Had Crinkles done anything besides set off a zombie panic today?

"As if worrying about poisoned candy corn wasn't bad enough!" a trombone exclaimed.

"According to Doc Honeytree's nephew, Wink wasn't poisoned," Juniper announced from behind her euphonium. The instrument was almost as big as she was.

The news electrified the room.

"So it's safe to eat candy corn again?" Bobbin asked, hopping to his feet. "Now *everyone* will be trying to buy some."

And that was the end of rehearsal. While Luther called out final instructions for the concert, elves rushed for the door to get to the candy stores before they closed. Even Smudge and Juniper ducked out before I could catch up to them—although I assumed their business had more to do with investigating candy theft than candy buying.

Dark had descended during rehearsal, but the downtown streets were lit up in orange and white, making the city almost as bright as day as I made my way to the sleigh bus that would take me up Sugarplum Mountain to Castle Kringle. On Festival Boulevard, there was the usual business at the Silver Bell Bakery, but I was surprised to see a light on at Chestnut's Cake Emporium across the street. Given that the proprietor had been taken into custody and the only other employee was dead, what could be going on in there? Then my eyes focused on the elf in a red Cake Emporium smock behind the counter. *Sugar?*

What was the only remaining employee of the

Silver Bell Bakery doing in Chestnut's Cake Emporium? I had to find out.

Not much had changed in the shop since this morning, except that there were cupcakes in the glass display cases, Ella Fitzgerald's Christmas album was playing on the speakers, and a murdered elf no longer lay on the floor.

"What are you doing here?" I asked Sugar.

"You saw for yourself what Bell's like. She's so crazy, I didn't feel safe working there anymore. Not if she killed Wink just for leaving."

If Bell was really crazy enough to kill ex-employees, Sugar had just put herself in more danger. I didn't want to alarm her by pointing that out, though.

"I just saw you a few hours ago. How did you get this job with Chestnut in jail?"

"I visited him at the constabulary and offered to help him. He was grateful for the support, so I came right over and made several batches of cupcakes."

Given the number of elves going into the Silver Bell Bakery across the street, I was afraid she'd chosen the better bake shop but the losing team.

She smiled, remembering that in addition to being a busybody, I was also a potential sale. "Can I get you something, Mrs. Claus?"

I was mulling over my selection when the doorbell tinkled, signaling another customer. I wanted to believe it was the influence of seeing Mrs. Claus in the store that had attracted more business, but then Sugar said in an overly bright voice, "Hi, Dandy."

It was impossible to hide my curiosity as I turned

to take in this elf I'd heard so much about. Dandy was not at all the elf femme fatale I'd imagined from talking to Wink's mother. She was round and compact, with a heart-shaped face and blond ringlets springing from beneath her blue and pink checked cap. Her big blue eyes were the kind that probably betrayed every emotion, and right now the primary emotion in them was stress.

What was she doing here, of all places?

She let out a long breath as she steamed toward the counter. "Do you have a cup of eggnog or something?" she asked Sugar. "I was going to buy something at the Silver Bell Bakery, but the cats in the line started making comments. As if I should be shut up and wearing black today—over someone I'm not even dating anymore."

Sugar pushed a mug of eggnog and a pumpkin chocolate cupcake across the counter. "On the house," she said.

Dandy fished into her purse nevertheless, and produced a few coins. "I'm not looking for sympathy. Wink and I broke up months ago. I'm sure *you* know all about that."

"Wink never talked about his private life," Sugar said.

A shadow passed over Dandy's expression. "No, of course not. Even after six years together, I didn't rate that high in his thoughts. Oh, it started out as a romance for the ages, all right, but in the last years baking was all Wink thought about every waking hour. He was an elf obsessed. It figures someone would kill him over that stupid Halloween bake-off." Tears stood in her bright eyes. "Baking junkies are all crazy."

"We don't know that he was killed because of the contest." *It might have been for love*, I was thinking. Or love spurned . . .

"Of course it was—or something to do with baking." Dandy blinked back her tears as she surveyed the shop. "Funny that this is the first time I should be in a place that meant so much to him." She looked across the counter to the stainless-steel worktable where Wink had died. "I guess that's where . . ." She couldn't bring herself to finish her sentence. "Well, he must have died happy, at least." Her voice broke up a little as she said, "His dream had come true."

For a moment I thought she might sob, but then her mouth hardened. "All those years, nothing was what I thought. Even the ring he gave me was false. I thought he bought it for me because it stood for my favorite flower—a garnet carved in the shape of a rose. Wink laughed and told me that he'd picked it out because it reminded him of little cake-decorating rosettes. *That's* the kind of elf Wink Jollyflake was."

Sugar and I exchanged uncomfortable glances.

"He was really good at those rosettes," Sugar said.

Dandy tilted her head at Sugar as if finally putting something together. "I'm surprised to see *you* on this side of the street."

"I left the Silver Bell Bakery today, to help Chestnut. He's in jail, you know."

Dandy's eyes flew wide open. "Was he arrested for killing Wink?"

"For vandalizing the Silver Bell Bakery," I said.

"Oh." Dandy bit her lip, then shrugged. "Well—

it's nothing to me." She downed the last of her eggnog and pushed the mug across the counter. "Thanks, Sugar."

She turned to leave.

"Before you go . . ." I said, stopping her. "When was the last time you spoke with Wink?"

"Not since he moved out. Three weeks ago." She turned on her heel and headed for the door.

"Don't you want your cupcake?" Sugar called after her.

"No thanks." Dandy's lips twisted into a bitter smile. "I've never liked cake."

As the door tinkled behind Dandy's departing figure, I shook my head. "Poor thing," I said. "Half the town suspects she killed Wink, and she's trying so hard not to show what she's feeling that she's probably adding to the gossip."

Sugar's eyes narrowed on me. "So you *believed* that twisted bit of grief theater?"

Heat rose in my cheeks. Now I knew how Constable Crinkles felt. It hadn't occurred to me that her grief was all a song and dance. "Why would she bother making a show of innocence for me?"

"Because you're the one asking questions."

Sugar boxed up Dandy's cupcake and an assortment of all the other cupcakes for me. Even if Felice, Castle Kringle's cook, had already prepared dessert for tonight, I had no worries that the cupcakes would go uneaten. Castle Kringle absorbed baked goods like a gray whale inhaled krill.

I did briefly consider taking the box of goodies to the constabulary and telling Crinkles about this strange encounter with Dandy. In the end, though,

I couldn't quite bring myself to throw suspicion on Dandy. I decided to sleep on it.

Accusing someone without proof is almost as wicked as the murder itself, Bell had said.

I should have paid more attention to that.

It was hard to sleep on a problem if you couldn't sleep. All night I lay sprawled on my side of the huge sleigh bed, blinking into the darkness as some unformed doubt scratched at the back of my mind. I kept replaying that conversation with Dandy. Something she'd said didn't sit right. Something my brain couldn't pin down.

Around three a.m., it came to me. I bolted upright. Dandy had gone out of her way to let Sugar and me know that she'd never been in the store, and yet she'd nodded to the exact spot where Wink had been found.

Next to me, a sigh came out of the darkness. "What's wrong, April?" Nick asked.

"I think I've solved Wink's murder."

He touched the sleeve of my nightgown, and that's all it took for me to snuggle down under the covers next to him. The warmth of him was so reassuring, so irresistible.

"I need to go to the constabulary in the morning," I said.

"You need to get sleep," he said. "It's a busy week, and the festivities haven't even started yet."

Sleep still didn't come easily, though. I found myself wanting to review the details of the investigation with my usual crew. But Jingles had been curiously distracted this week; he hadn't even seemed that interested in my conversation with Dandy. In the past when I'd had a mystery to untangle, I also called on Jake Frost, Santaland's number one private investigator. But Jake was in Oregon visiting my best friend, Claire, who'd met the detective while staying with me last Christmas.

By the time I reached the constabulary the next morning, my certainty that I'd discovered the real killer had started to evaporate like the late dawn fog over Peppermint Pond. Chestnut's shop wasn't *that* big. Maybe Dandy had just guessed where Wink had died from what she'd been told or read in the paper. I could be casting suspicion on her for no reason at all.

And yet, Algid said he'd seen a woman arguing with Wink. Who was a better candidate to be that woman than Dandy?

Except maybe Bell . . .

Still, was it right to leave Chestnut languishing in jail under a cloud of suspicion while Dandy, a possible murderess, wandered free?

Of course, if I were going to languish in jail anywhere in the world, the Christmastown Constabulary would be my incarceration center of choice. The constabulary was housed in a cozy cottage on the outskirts of town. It felt like hobbit jail. I arrived just as breakfast was ending, and the smell of cinnamon and baking dough was a siren song to my stomach. I glanced into the dining room, and with a little cry of panic, Ollie threw a tea towel over something and whisked a plate away to the kitchen.

Crinkles, who still had his breakfast napkin tucked into his uniform collar, explained, "We were going to sample Ollie's recipe for the constabulary's Halloween bake-off entry, but that's confidential, you understand."

For Pete's sake. "That's okay. I'm not hungry."

Crinkles mistook my annoyance. He probably couldn't believe there were beings who didn't crave carbs twenty-four/seven. "Ollie, what else have we got for Mrs. Claus?"

I kept protesting that I wasn't hungry, but before you could say Jack Frost, I was seated at the long dining table, now festively decorated with a pumpkin centerpiece. Ollie, decked out in a frilled apron over his blue wool uniform, placed a cinnamon roll the size of a hubcap before me.

"This wasn't really necessary," I said, just before I tucked into a perfectly warm, chewy, sweet, and cinnamony cloud of goodness. To be honest, I *did* crave carbs twenty-four/ seven. Maybe there was elf hidden somewhere in my DNA.

"Ollie, why don't you bring a dish of that candy corn in here, too?" Crinkles turned to me and explained, "The Santaland Bureau of Licensed Confectionaries left a complimentary box of candy corn on our doorstep this morning."

"I've never heard of the Bureau of Licensed Confectionaries," I said.

"Neither had I, but the candy looks scrumptious." The constable rubbed his hands together in anticipation. "A perfect morning treat."

I almost made a crack about candy corn being the breakfast of champions, but I stopped myself.

My cinnamon roll had enough sugar on it to induce a sugar coma; nutritionally it couldn't be far removed from straight-up candy.

"Where's Chestnut?" I asked.

"He had his breakfast early," Crinkles said. "Now he's taking a nap in his cell. This afternoon we're going to loan him the kitchen if he wants to work on his recipe for the bake-off. We've promised not to look over his shoulder—Ollie doesn't want to be accused of cheating."

You can probably guess that security at the constabulary wasn't the tightest. There were no bars on the windows, and the "jail cell"—actually a cozy bedroom with twin beds—was secured with nothing more than a button lock. Even that wasn't engaged most of the time.

Ollie brought out a ceramic candy dish shaped like a sleigh. The candy corn looked different from the stuff I'd bought from Dash, who surely would be a member of the Santaland Bureau of Licensed Confectionaries. These candies were tricolored, in the traditional triangle shape. The strangest thing about them was that the pieces were all dusted with powdered sugar. An unusual twist.

"Oh goodie." Constable Crinkles grabbed a handful, then tossed a piece in the air to catch in his mouth. In the split second that I watched the sparkly dusted triangle hang suspended over the constable's open maw, a memory flashed through my mind of Dash's presenting his whole-ear candy corn to me with such pride. Would he have wanted to be a part of this gift that didn't even have his own candy included?

And since when did powdered sugar sparkle?

"Stop!" I yelled as Crinkles' lips closed over the kernel. "Spit it out."

In surprise, he inhaled at precisely the wrong moment. I heard a hiccup sound as the kernel lodged in his throat.

"Constable Crinkles—can you speak?"

His eyes bulged, but no words came out. He couldn't move.

"Ollie!" I yelled. "He's choking!"

Ollie streaked in, apron fluttering. "What do we do?"

From the panic in his eyes, I guessed there would be no "we" involved in this rescue. I hadn't performed the Heimlich maneuver since I did Red Cross training as a camp counselor in my teens. Thankfully that early training stuck with me. I got on my knees behind Crinkles, looping my arms around his middle, and with my fists gave his abdomen a sharp squeeze. With an audible pop, the candy corn dislodged and arced through the air, hitting a Currier and Ives print over the mantelpiece.

Crinkles sucked in a breath, and his cheeks slowly turned from blue to their usual red.

"Call Doc Honeytree's house," I told Ollie.

Crinkles shook his head. "No need for that. I'm fine now."

"You might be fine—but that candy corn isn't. When did you say it was delivered?"

"The box was on the porch this morning when I went out to shovel the walkway," Ollie said. "The note said it was from the Santaland Bureau of Licensed Confectionaries. There wasn't a postal mark, so it must've been hand delivered."

I pulled out my phone and searched for the Santaland Bureau of Licensed Confectionaries—and received no results. Then I called Dash myself. He knew nothing about either the bureau or the box of candy corn. I believed him.

I called Doc Honeytree next, and asked him to send Algid over with a microscope.

"I feel fine," Crinkles insisted.

"I don't want him to examine you, I want him to take a look at that candy. I think it's been poisoned."

Reflexively, Crinkles began coughing. He had to retreat to a recliner chair and ottoman to recover from the shock.

While we waited for Algid to arrive, I told them what I knew about Dandy. And as I spoke, I remembered that Wink's mother had said that Dandy worked at the Candy Cane Factory and would know how to prepare candy—even how to slip a little poison in.

"But if Wink wasn't killed by poisoned candy corn," Ollie wondered aloud, "why is someone using poisoned candy corn now?"

"And why poison *me*?" Crinkles said.

"Maybe it was intended for someone else." We all turned toward the door, where Chestnut was standing. One side of his blond locks were smashed lopsidedly from his nap. Even so, he looked much better—and certainly much calmer—than the last time I'd seen him.

He raised a possibility I hadn't considered. After

yesterday, the whole town would know that he was here.

"Do you know anyone who would want to kill you?" I asked.

He shrugged. "Well . . . Bell's pretty angry at me, obviously. And maybe, if it's being spread around town that *I* was responsible for Wink's death, his relations might want to kill me."

He was right about that.

"Where were you during the night Wink was killed?" I asked.

He drew back defensively. "At home."

"Alone?"

"Yes—but *I* didn't kill Wink. Why would I? He was my only employee, and a darned good cake baker. He was irreplaceable."

"And yet not even a day later, you'd replaced him with Sugar."

"Because she offered to help keep the store going while I'm here. I'm not going to look a gift ox in the mouth." He pointed to the sleigh candy dish. "Anyway, you can't accuse me of having done this. It's more likely that I was the intended victim."

Maybe. But whoever sent the candy must have known that Crinkles or Ollie would eat some, too.

When Algid arrived, oozing coolly into the room with his microscope, he confirmed my fear about the candy corn. It had been tampered with. The shock was it hadn't been laced with poison at all.

"Ground glass," he announced. "Finely ground glass."

The constable, deputy, and I stood slack-jawed with disbelief and revulsion. Someone poisoning candy was hard enough to comprehend, but somehow rolling it in powdered glass seemed even more diabolical.

"I read a book once where someone was killed that way," I said. "It was gruesome."

Algid's thin lips twisted into a smile, and he raised a spidery finger. "That's the stuff of bad fiction."

I pointed to the candy bowl. "*That's* not fiction. Crinkle's choking wasn't fiction, either. And if he'd swallowed that glass . . ."

"That's the point, though," Algid said. "He probably *wouldn't* have swallowed it. Teeth are marvelous things—they're very sensitive to texture. Unless the constable had gulped the candy down whole, he would have realized the candy was off as soon as he bit down on it. The likeliest scenario is that he would have spit it out."

Actually, it was very likely that the constable would have hoovered the candy down whole. "What if he *had* swallowed it? In the book I read, the victim bled to death."

Crinkles groaned.

"Again, fiction," Algid said. "Glass ground this fine isn't any more lethal than swallowing sand. I doubt it would kill a grown elf."

I frowned. "So you're saying that whoever sent this candy *wasn't* attempting to kill?"

"Not if they did even the most elementary search for how to lethally tamper with food," Algid said.

"Maybe they didn't, though." Criminals weren't

always masterminds. They just tended to think they were.

"My guess is that the culprit wanted to make a statement more than he wanted to kill someone."

"And why would they want to do that?" I asked.

That answer became clear almost immediately, when word of the ground glass in the constabulary candy corn leaked out. Business at the candy stores dried up immediately, and the bakeries lost their customers, too. Anything made with powdered sugar was now suspect. Who knew whether something was sugary or glassy? My phone filled up with distressed messages from Dash and the other candy store owners, as well as from bakers asking how they were expected to complete their bake-off entries when none of the candy corn at the Santaland candy stores could be trusted.

I explained very patiently that all the candy stores *could* be trusted, but I wasn't sure my words held much weight against the possibility of buying ground glass candy.

Then, as I was headed home, one of the Halloween bake-off judges texted to tell me that he wouldn't be able to judge the candy corn bake-off. **Forgot I had a prior commitment**.

For Santaland, a country fueled by sweets, distrust of candy was tantamount to a national disaster. Especially two days before Halloween.

Chapter Nine

"**I** want to be an ice zombie for Halloween," Christopher declared.

Tiffany sighed in maternal exasperation. "I worked all last week sewing your Dracula cape."

The Clauses of Castle Kringle were all lounging in the main salon, a rare moment when we were all at leisure after dinner. Lucia was sprawled the wrong way in a chair by the fire, long legs dangling over the puffy upholstered arms, feet toasting before the hearth. Quasar crouched next to her, nodding off, his head propped up by his antlers tilting down into the rug. On the sofa next to Tiffany, my mother-in-law, Pamela, sat properly erect, her gray ballerina bun and bifocals making her appear every inch the dowager Mrs. Claus. She was tatting doilies in the shape of spiderwebs for the Halloween carnival's craft booth.

Nick was with us, too, relaxing with the evening

edition of *Christmastown Herald,* in what would probably be the last calm days before nonstop Christmas preparations kicked in. Although the headlines were hardly relaxing these days. The walrus-shaped potato had been pushed off the front page by murder and robbery.

Christopher tossed a floppy brown forelock out of his eyes. "An ice zombie costume won't take long. I can shred some of my clothes and do the rest with makeup."

"Which clothes?" Tiffany asked, alarmed.

"Just some of my normal ones." Before it could register that this assurance hadn't reassured his mother one bit, he went on excitedly, "I can't wait to see everybody's scared faces when me and my friends show up at the Haunted Ice Castle in our costumes. They'll think it's an ice zombie invasion."

"You should leave it to the Haunted Ice Castle to terrify people," Tiffany said.

Christopher rolled his eyes. "Right. Everyone's going to be *so scared* of a headless snowman."

My phone pinged, alerting me to a text. I looked down at my screen and groaned. Another bake-off judge, Nick's cousin Amory, was bugging out. **Sorry, April. I forgot I'm working late at the Candy Cane Factory that night.**

Sure he forgot. No doubt he remembered the moment he heard about the crushed glass candy corn incident. I texted right back, suggesting his wife, Midge, might judge in his place.

Pamela eyed her grandson over the top of her bifocals. "Why don't you be Dracula this time and save the ice zombie idea for next year?"

"Because everyone's talking about ice zombies *now*," he said. "I can be Dracula any old time."

"Christopher and his gang want to get in on the ice zombie ground floor," Lucia deadpanned, unfolding herself from her chair to grab a sugar cookie from the dessert trolley Felice, the cook, was wheeling in. In her white uniform with a chef's cap and white booties, Felice looked none too happy to be serving as wait staff.

I frowned. Jingles and Butterbean usually waited on us after dinner. Where were they?

Next to the decorative plate of cookies was a crystal candy dish that was almost to overflowing with candy corn. It looked like the candy I'd bought at Dash's.

"That candy corn was supposed to be for you to use for the bake-off," I told Pamela.

She gave the dish a dismissive glance. "I know," she said, "but they're oddly shaped."

"Candy corn's not supposed to look like that," Tiffany agreed.

I felt a knee-jerk urge to speak up for my favorite confectioner. "It's full-ear candy corn. Dash is very proud of it—and it tastes great."

"It's peculiar." Pamela kept tatting her spiderweb. "Anyway, Jingles found some normal candy corn that will do very nicely for my cake design."

"Where *is* Jingles?" I asked Felice.

The stout elf planted her hands on her hips. "I've been wondering that myself! He and Butterbean disappeared just after dinner was served. Those two have been as jumpy as snowshoe hares all week."

"Did Jingles tell you where he found the candy corn?" I asked her.

"He said a peddler came to the castle door."

Great. Even Santa's castle was buying black market candy corn now.

I frowned and reached over to scoop up several pieces of candy. It was hard to believe that there could be better tasting candy corn than Dash's. That little hint of cardamom put them over the top for me. As I absently nibbled a piece, wondering where this mysterious peddler had found enough candy corn to take door to door, I looked up and saw the entire room watching me in horror. All except Nick, who was still buried behind his newspaper.

"What?" I asked.

The muscles in Christopher's face had gone slack. "You're *eating* that stuff?"

Quasar had jerked awake, and now his nose was fizzling like a punk sparkler on the Fourth of July. "It c-could be poisoned."

"There's nothing wrong with this candy corn," I insisted. "I bought it myself, from Dash."

My phone pinged. It was a reply from cousin Amory.

Midge has to stay at the lodge on Halloween in case of trick-or-treaters. Sorry.

Of all the lame excuses. Not even the most dedicated trick-or-treater was going to trek all the way to the top of Sugarplum Mountain to Kringle Lodge, where Midge and Amory lived. They were cowards—and I was still without a judge for the candy corn bake-off.

I groaned.

Pamela stared up at me impatiently over her bifocals. "What is the matter, April? You keep groaning."

Christopher laughed. "Maybe *she's* practicing to be a zombie."

"All the judges for the candy corn bake-off are chickening out because of what happened at the constabulary today. I need to scare up someone else to be the judge." I didn't kid myself that I could find another three-person panel of judges. But maybe, I thought, scanning my family's faces, I could strong-arm one person. "Any volunteers?"

It's amazing how quickly those two words can clear a room. My question was like a Chinook that caused my in-laws to melt away. Even Nick hoofed it for the exit, but I managed to catch him by his red velvet sleeve.

"Who better to be the candy corn bake-off judge than Santa himself?" I said.

He looked trapped, both by my words and the firm hold I had on his Santa coat. "Me?"

"You're not afraid, are you?"

"April, I'm not even a fan of candy corn."

"You can be perfectly objective, then." I pulled him toward me, reeling him in. No, I wasn't above using sex if the occasion warranted. We kissed, and he groaned.

"I'm going to agree to this, aren't I?" he asked.

I smiled, lifting to thread my hands around his nape. "I hope so."

"Oh . . . okay."

He kissed me, and as we stood entangled, my

phone rang. I was tempted to ignore it, thinking it was bound to be Mrs. Firlog pestering me to see if I'd found a replacement judge yet, but out of the corner of my eye I saw a name I hadn't been expecting. JUNIPER.

I swiped her name and lifted the phone to my ear. "What's up?"

Nick sighed, took a step back, and watched me curiously.

Juniper's voice was urgent, almost breathless. "Oh April, I wanted to talk to you before I called the constabulary."

My nerves tingled. "What's going on?"

"You'd better come downtown to the SPEX office. Smudge and I have caught the candy corn smugglers."

"That's great—but why should I be there?"

"Well, because you won't be happy when you discover who it is."

But in my heart I already knew.

Chapter Ten

By the time I arrived at the offices of Santaland Postal Express, the standoff with the alleged burglars had grown heated. Juniper, Smudge, and Filbert—SPEX's manager armed with a snow shovel—had Jingles and Butterbean backed up against the wall of the building's half-timbered exterior. I'd convinced Juniper not to call Constable Crinkles till I got there, but obviously she'd felt obliged to inform Filbert.

Jingles nearly went boneless with relief as I approached. "Mrs. Claus, tell them we're innocent!"

"Totally innocent!" Butterbean echoed.

Smudge turned to me and explained, "We discovered Butterbean standing on Jingles's shoulders, trying to break into a window."

Butterbean's hands fluttered frantically. "I was just peeking in because the door was locked."

"Of course the door was locked," Filbert said.

"We were robbed last week. But you two would know all about that, wouldn't you?"

Jingles drew up, bristling. "Certainly not. You think I would stoop to stealing candy?"

"That's right," Butterbean said. "We were only stealing what belonged to us."

Jingles glared at him, then explained to Filbert, "I told you, we just came here to pick up a package."

"That's a logical explanation," he said, "except that there's no package here for either of you."

"It's in Salty's name," Jingles said. "He's the groundskeeper at Castle Kringle and wasn't at the castle this afternoon when you came by—so you left this notice." He held up a yellow slip.

Filbert frowned at the paper. "Why didn't Salty come pick up the package?"

"Because he's in Tinkertown visiting his sick aunt," Jingles explained. "But we know what's in the package, and it's very important that it be delivered to the castle."

Filbert crossed his arms. "I can't have people coming and taking packages that don't belong to them."

"Salty wouldn't have minded," Jingles said. "It was a joint purchase."

"That's right," Butterbean said. "Salty hates computers, so I did the ordering. But we put it in his name because he's going to be caring for it."

Filbert crossed his arms. "All right, then. What was in the box?"

Jingles and Butterbean exchanged anxious glances, then darted a doubtful look at me. "It's a surprise for Mrs. Claus," Jingles said.

Maybe this would explain Jingles's odd behavior this week.

"What is it?" I asked.

Jingles dug a foot in the packed snow and flicked a resentful look at Filbert. "Well, I suppose there's no harm in saying, since the secret's obviously ruined now. It's a—"

"A turkey!" Butterbean blurted, stealing his thunder.

Jingles rounded on him. "*I* was going to tell her."

"A turkey?" I was surprised, all right.

"We're planning a Thanksgiving celebration at the castle for you next month," Jingles said. "We've never done that before in Santaland—and after all your hard work for Halloween, we thought it would be a special treat for you."

Tears welled in my eyes. "That's so sweet," I said. "But Thanksgiving's still weeks away. The turkey could just stay frozen till then."

Jingles and Butterbean blinked. "Frozen?"

Filbert clapped his gloved hands and turned to me. "I know the package they mean now. It's a live bird, ma'am."

"You shipped a live turkey to Santaland?" Turkey wasn't a thing in Santaland. Chicken, yes. Goose and duck, too. Gobblers were practically unheard of here on dinner tables. "Where did you get it?"

Butterbean bobbed proudly. "WorldofTurkeys dot com—'The plumpest turkeys shipped directly from Farley's Turkey Farm in Arkansas.'" He pronounced the state's name phonetically.

Filbert finally lowered his snow shovel. "You didn't

have to break in, you know. The bird is fine—I saw to that before I went home."

Jingles protested. "We didn't break in."

"Yet," Smudge said.

The castle steward looked at me imploringly. "Can we please just collect our bird and go home?"

"It should be up to Filbert to say whether he wants to report this to Constable Crinkles or not," Juniper pointed out.

Filbert sighed. "Well, okay. But if anything else goes missing from the SPEX office, I'm going to send Constable Crinkles straight to your door," he warned Jingles.

"All we want is our turkey," Jingles said.

As we all traipsed inside to look at the box, I asked Juniper how she and Smudge happened to see Jingles and Butterbean peeking through the window.

"We've been staking out the SPEX office," she said.

"In case the thief came back to the scene of the crime," Smudge explained. "We thought for sure we'd caught the right elves when Jingles and Butterbean were about to break in that window."

"That's okay—you couldn't have known what they were really up to." I didn't quite understand it myself. In truth, I wasn't sure which I felt more: gratitude, or anxiety. From Santaland's experiments with Halloween, I'd discovered that introducing new holidays to a country was not without pitfalls.

A strange sound distracted me—a raspy hiss ending in what sounded like a sickly bark. Smudge, Juniper, and I circled around the crate, which had holes cut in the wood on three sides and *LIVE ANIMAL* stamped on it in several places.

"Um . . ." That noise did not sound right to me. "I think you better open that crate."

Jingles tilted an anxious glance my way. "Are you sure? I wouldn't want him to get loose before we get him back to the castle."

Not that I was an expert on turkeys, but . . . "You might have bigger problems than his running away."

Carefully, they pried open the top of the carton. A hulking, hideous bird poked his head up.

"Golly doodle!" Juniper exclaimed.

What on earth? There was no fan of tail plumage, no comical wattle. This bird had dark, oily feathers, and atop his hunched shoulders, from a black-feathered neck, there poked a red head that looked as if it were fashioned from old, cracked vinyl.

Everyone backed up a step.

"Americans *eat* that?" Smudge asked incredulously.

I shook my head, pointing at the blinking bird, who looked just as startled by us as we were by him. "That is not a turkey. That's a vulture."

Jingles rounded on Butterbean. "You puffin-witted fool, you ordered the wrong fowl."

Butterbean's face fell. "Farley at World of Turkeys *swore* that they only shipped turkeys. Free range!"

Ever the librarian, Juniper had already looked up vultures on her phone and flashed a picture of this bird's double at us. "He's a vulture, all right. It says he's native to the United States and Mexico."

"Can you eat them?" Butterbean asked, a flicker of hope in his eyes. "It's about the size of a turkey, isn't it?"

"Nobody puts buzzard on their Thanksgiving menu," I said.

Jingles scowled at his second-in-command. "You'll have to return it. Luckily, we've got plenty of time before Thanksgiving."

The bird hopped and flapped his black wings, causing us all to jump back another step.

"That's one ugly bird," Filbert said. "I'm not keeping that thing in here overnight—especially not now that his crate's been opened."

"That's okay," Butterbean said. "I'll have to go back and fill out the forms to exchange him and print out the return label anyway."

Filbert took pity on Butterbean and helped re-crate the bird, who sounded none too happy to be shut back up again. It hissed and barked the whole time.

I pulled Jingles aside. "I'm so sorry," he said, lowering his voice. "It's that Butterbean. He bungled the whole thing." Never mind that until opening the crate, he'd been touting Butterbean as a genius.

"Forget the vulture," I said. "I wanted to ask you about the candy corn peddler that came by the castle today."

Overhearing us, Juniper and Smudged edged closer.

"Peddler?" Smudge asked.

Jingles nodded. "Mrs. Claus—the dowager Mrs. Claus—complained that the candy you bought from Dash wouldn't work for her at all. So when this old crone came by, I went ahead and paid her for her candy corn, even though she was charging an arm and a leg. I figured if it wasn't from the official stores that had sent the contaminated candy corn to the constabulary, we'd be safe."

I grunted. "Whoever sent the glassy candy corn to the constabulary wanted to make sure elves stopped buying from the big stores so they could drive up the price of the black market."

"And I fell for it. I was a patsy!" Jingles shook his head mournfully. "First the turkey buzzard, and now this."

"It's okay," I said. "You couldn't have known."

"Maybe that old crone was the one who pulled off the candy corn theft," Juniper suggested, piecing it together. "Or else she might know who did."

"I can think of someone else who might know," Smudge said. "I should have thought of him before—Snuffy Greenbottle."

Juniper sucked in a breath of recognition at the name, which meant nothing to me. "Snuffy Greenbottle's Secondhand Store."

"Snuffy sometimes handles items of dubious origin," Smudge explained, noticing my confusion. "The crone might have approached him first to unload her goods—it's a safe bet that Snuffy at least knows who she is."

I bit my lip. "I think we need to talk to this Snuffy."

Smudge looked at me doubtfully. "It might be

best if I did the talking. You're kind of . . . conspicuous."

Unfortunately, this was true. One thing about being Mrs. Claus in Santaland: It was hard to blend into the woodwork. "All right, but I want to go with you."

Smudge and I agreed on a time to meet up in Tinkertown the next morning. Then Jingles, Butterbean, and I loaded the vulture into the sleigh and headed back to Castle Kringle.

"I sure hope we can get our money back on this buzzard," Jingles said.

Chapter Eleven

Smudge had agreed to meet me in Tinkertown the next morning, just down the street from Snuffy Greenbottle's Secondhand Store, half a block away from the Tinkertown Tavern. It was a rough part of town. Half the doors didn't have wreaths, and while I waited in the chilly morning air, a peppermint patty wrapper cartwheeled past like a tumbleweed down the icy street. On the corner by the tavern, a derelict-looking snowman stood with his moth-eaten scarf flapping in the wind, hat askew, singing "Here We Come A-Wassailing" in an off-key warble.

The mean streets of Santaland. Despite the neighborhood, though, and the secondhand seller's unsavory reputation, the shop itself didn't appear too shady to me. It was a two-story brick and timber storefront, with a weathered sign hanging over the door.

I finally spied Smudge approaching, hands buried in his pockets. Even he gave the snowman a wide berth as he passed him. "I swear, Noggs gets worse all the time," he muttered to me in greeting.

"Is he . . . inebriated?" I wasn't even aware that snowmen could drink.

Smudge snorted. "You obviously missed the spectacle he made of himself last New Year's Eve."

"I heard that, Mr. Smudge Pants!" the snowman called out.

Smudge flicked an irritated gaze back at the snowman and we edged a little farther from him and closer to Snuffy Greenbottle's. "I should have worn some sort of disguise," Smudge said.

He had on his usual outfit of black tights, boots, and wool tunic. Even his elf cap was black, with leather strips sewn into the wool and a black lanyard tassel instead of a fuzz ball at the end.

"Does Snuffy know you?" I asked.

"No—I've never met him."

"Then why would you need to dress differently?"

"To make me look disreputable."

I cleared my throat. How to put this diplomatically? "I think you could pass for someone looking to score some black-market candy corn." At his surprised glance, I added, "If you assume the right attitude, I mean."

We were wasting time. Not to mention, snow was starting to come down, blown sideways by a north wind that felt as if it came directly from Mount Myrrh's icy summit. While Smudge was inside, I would be out here shivering in my wool-lined boots.

"Just see if you can subtly bring Snuffy around to telling you if he knows any contraband candy sellers." I handed him a Santaland gold piece. "Flash this like you might be willing to spend some tall money for information."

Smudge took the coin, tossed it in the air, classic film gangster style, as if it were a trick he'd been practicing his whole life. "It'll be easier than slipping off an ice floe," he said.

With the coin in his hand and a strut in his step, he disappeared inside Snuffy Greenbottle's.

While I waited, I tried to shut out Noggs's warbling and ticked off my mental to-do list. I'd informed Mr. Firlog that Nick would be judging the candy corn bake-off, so that was all squared away. I just hoped we had enough entries so that Nick wasn't forced to award the blue ribbon to his own mother. Hopefully Chestnut would be out of jail by tomorrow. No solid evidence backed up Bell's accusation that he'd killed Wink. How long could someone be held for lobbing cupcakes at a store window?

My phone pinged, and I glanced at the screen, dreading a text from the mayor or Mrs. Firlog about carnival business. Instead, it was Jingles.

Have you seen Grimstock?

Frowning, I tapped on my screen. **Who?**

Butterbean's vulture. Salty named him Grimstock, but he broke out of his cage this morning. There's no sign of him here at the castle.

When Butterbean had contacted World of Turkeys about exchanging the vulture for an actual turkey, Farley had replied with a message saying that there was a strict no returns policy.

So apparently we weren't just stuck with a buzzard, Santaland now had a buzzard on the loose.

After I'd sent a message promising Jingles to keep an eye out for Grimstock, Smudge emerged from the shop at a fast clip. "What did you find out?" I asked.

"Snuffy's staying mum on the subject of candy corn," he said. "But do you think Juniper would like a ring with a ruby in the shape of a rose?"

Evidently he'd gotten distracted in the shop. Now I was distracted, too. Smudge wanted to give Juniper a ring? "A ruby?" I asked.

"Well, I think it's a ruby. It's red. And shaped like a little flower."

I gasped in recognition. *He was really good at those rosettes,* Sugar had said of Wink when Dandy told us about her ring.

"That's Dandy's garnet ring, I bet." A whole scenario played through my mind. What if Dandy and Wink had argued over that ring? Maybe that had been the cause of the middle-of-the-night argument Algid had overheard. Dandy must have lied about the last time she'd seen Wink. . . .

"Come on," I said, hurrying toward the second-hand store's entrance.

Smudge scrambled after me. "Wait—you said you're too conspicuous to go undercover."

"I don't want to go undercover now." *Au contraire.* I wanted to be intimidating. I strode into Greenbottle's, and in straightening to my full height as I crossed the threshold, I clunked my forehead on a ceiling beam.

"Ow."

So much for being intimidating.

An old elf in a purple-and-red motley cap stood behind the counter, a lit pipe protruding from his lips. "Watch your head," he said.

A little late for that warning.

"What can I do for you today, Mrs. Claus?" the proprietor asked, puffing away on his pipe.

"You have a garnet ring," I said. "I'd like to see it, please."

Not that I doubted for an instant that it was the ring Dandy had spoken of. How many red rosette rings could there be in Santaland? I was already reaching into my pocketbook to see how much money I had on me, so I could take it with me.

"I can give you a good price." Snuffy extracted it from the velvet display.

Smudge practically threw himself between me and the old wood-and-glass case where the jewelry was displayed. "That's *my* ring. I was going to get it for Juniper."

I wasn't even sure if she'd welcome a romantic gesture from Smudge. It was true that they seemed to be getting on better, but just two days ago Juniper had been checking out Algid Honeytree. Algid might have scared Juniper into appreciating Smudge a little more, but was "better than Algid" a good basis for a relationship?

I felt the need to warn him about the ring, at least. "Believe me, Juniper wouldn't want this."

"It's a nice piece," Snuffy said, contradicting me. "Heirloom quality."

I shot Smudge a look and lowered my voice. "It might have bad connotations. Unless I miss my guess, it's going to be evidence in a murder case."

Over the counter, Snuffy's wiry brows arched up. I hadn't lowered my voice enough. "Well then . . ." A plume of blue smoke floated over us as he considered this new wrinkle. "I might need to set a slightly higher price on it."

"For Pete's sake," I said. "It's just a garnet."

The old elf's eyes twinkled with dollar signs. "A *notorious* garnet."

"I should never have mentioned it," Smudge said mournfully.

"I'm glad you did. It might be the evidence that catches a killer." I looked down at Snuffy. "When exactly did Dandy bring this ring in?"

"Nobody named Dandy sold this ring to me," Snuffy said gruffly. "It was Wink Jollyflake who sold it."

I stood gaping at the delicate rosette shape, momentarily confused. *Wink?* How could that be?

"And you didn't alert Constable Crinkles when you heard that Wink was killed just a day after he sold this ring to you?"

The old elf laughed. "You've got yourself the wrong end of the candy cane, Mrs. C. It's been a month now since Wink Jollyflake came in here with this ring. That's why I didn't realize that it had any significance. But now . . ."

Now I had to pay through the nose to get it. I even had to borrow my gold piece back from Smudge.

For a completely innocent elf, Dandy seemed awfully nervous. As soon as she opened her cottage door, she gazed wide-eyed up at me and Smudge, as welcoming as she would have been to two polar bears standing on her porch.

It took me a few minutes to talk my way inside the Redball house, a narrow elf cottage that reminded me of the Jollyflake home. The air was warm and smelled of sugar. "Are you making something?" I asked after we were all seated in her front room.

She hesitated. "Candy apples," she blurted out. "For trick-or-treat tomorrow night."

I'd never been a fan of candy apples, which were so hard to eat that they never seemed worth the effort.

A pot clattered from the kitchen, causing Dandy to jump. Smudge and I craned our heads toward the door dividing the two rooms, but it was closed.

"My brother," Dandy explained. "We've lived here together since our parents died."

"Even when you were engaged to Wink Jollyflake?"

Smudge stood up again. "I need some fresh air," he said to me. "I'll wait for you outside."

That was weird. It *was* warm in the house, but I hadn't noticed him looking sickly.

When he was gone, I reached into my pocket and snapped open the ring box I'd brought with me from the secondhand store, revealing the garnet rosette on its small velvet cushion. "Is this yours?"

She flinched only slightly. "Not anymore."

"But it *is* the one that Wink gave you."

She dragged her gaze from the ring up to meet my eyes. "Did you find it with his effects?"

"Actually, it was at Snuffy Greenbottles'."

She bit her lip. "I should've guessed. Wink told me he wanted to sell it. Selfish elf!"

"But you were probably going to give it back anyway, since you broke up."

She blinked at me. "On no. This was *before* I called off our engagement. In fact, his asking for it was the reason I left him."

"If you were still together, why did he want to hock your engagement ring?"

"Why else?" Her face tensed into a scowl. "So he could invest in Chestnut's store. He said Chestnut would make him a partner if Wink could raise enough money."

That news caught me by surprise. Chestnut hadn't mentioned that Wink had invested in his shop. "Do you know if he actually became a partner?"

She folded her arms. "I assume so, but I'm just guessing. Like I said, we broke up. And once I was gone, I was completely out of his life."

How strange. Chestnut had only spoken about Wink's being a valued employee. Never had he mentioned making Wink his partner.

This information changed everything. It gave Chestnut a motive for murder. Now that Wink was gone, Chestnut had his store without the impediment of a partner at all. He even had another solid employee in Sugar, whom he'd lured away from the Silver Bell Bakery. It was a sweet deal for him . . . except for the fact that he was in jail.

If my hunch was correct, he would be in jail for a long time, if not exiled to the Farthest Frozen Reaches.

It was good to have the murder figured out, although I felt a little silly now for having called

Constable Crinkles about the garnet ring. I was so sure it implicated Dandy.

A commotion of male voices yelling outside made us turn. Recognizing one of the voices as Smudge's, I jumped to my feet. From the back of the house, a door slammed. Dandy and I both hurried toward the kitchen door. We were halfway there, when it swung open, and a burly ox of an elf in a plaid jacket and a dark stocking cap came out, dragging Smudge by his collar. Behind him was a redheaded elf I recognized: Chuckle Jollyflake. I deduced that the elf in the plaid jacket was Dandy's brother, Fir.

"What's going on?" Dandy asked.

"I found this elf picking through our trash cans," Fir said. "Probably looking for gruesome souvenirs because of your connection to Wink."

"Put him down." Dandy scowled at her brother. "He came here with Mrs. Claus."

Fir unhanded Smudge, but he remained menacingly close behind him. "Why was he foraging through our garbage?"

I was curious about that myself. "What were you doing?" I asked Smudge.

"I thought something strange was going on here the moment we walked in," he said. "They weren't making candy apples—there's no cinnamon smell."

Alarmed glances ricocheted between Dandy, Fir, and Chuckle, but they recovered quickly.

Smudge sneered. "That kitchen is full of candy corn. To sell when they've peddled all the stuff they stole."

The shock in Dandy's expression and the dismay in the two other elves' faces was all the confirmation I needed.

"What of it?" Fir lifted his chin. "There's no law against making candy corn."

Smudge laughed. "There are several vats on your stove in there. My guess was that you were the makers of the street corn being peddled around town by an old crone. In fact, I'll bet when Constable Crinkles searches this house, he'll find the crone costume hidden somewhere."

"Constable Crinkles has no call to search our house," Dandy said defiantly. "You can't prove we've done anything."

I was sure Smudge had sized up this situation correctly. It even made sense now why Chuckle didn't want suspicion in Wink's death to be thrown on Dandy. He'd wanted to keep Crinkles away from her on the off chance that the constable would be able to suss out their illegal activity.

Unfortunately I was equally certain that Smudge was correct and that we would never be able to prove what they had been up to.

And then Smudge reached into his pocket and pulled out a large, crumpled plastic bag with an American candy logo on it. "The constable will be *very* interested in why I found this in your garbage," he said. "And so will Filbert from the SPEX office, where you stole it and other wrappers like it that I saw in your garbage can."

I was stunned—and not just because this provided solid proof that Dandy, her brother, and Chuckle had stolen candy corn. The bigger shock was that Smudge had been correct: He *had* been able to solve the candy corn heist.

Fir puffed up. "Anyone could have put those wrappers there. It doesn't prove anything."

"It might prove something when Constable Crinkles and Ollie have a look around and find evidence of ground glass," I said. "That's not just theft, either—it could be attempted murder."

The three of them exchanged panicked looks, and then, like a school of fish evading a shark, they pivoted as one and darted for the door. Dandy, small and agile, actually reached it first. She threw it open and the three of them skidded to a stop, piling into each other. Standing on the other side of the door was Constable Crinkles.

Chapter Twelve

The jail at the Christmastown Constabulary had never been so crowded. Fir and Chuckle were in the cell with Chestnut. Dandy was squeezed into the small spare bedroom that was currently being used as a storeroom. It made for quite a crush, and knowing that Ollie would be busy putting the finishing touches on his bake-off entry, I took it upon myself to carry a pot of stew down from the castle on my way to the Halloween carnival.

The constabulary had been transformed. White, gauzy webbing stretched across doorways, and a stuffed spider with pipe cleaner legs hung from the ceiling. Orange and black candles glowed everywhere, including from a carved pumpkin on the mantel. At the dining table, which was covered in several layers of old newspapers, Dandy, Fir, and Chuckle leaned over pumpkins in various stages of having their entrails scooped out and faces carved into their flesh. The newest prisoners were so busy, they almost didn't notice me. It was understandable. I'd frozen at the sight of the elves I'd helped collar just yesterday wielding very lethal-looking carving knives.

Dandy caught sight of me first. "Looking for Crinkles?"

I nodded.

A round figure in a red wool jacket, black jodhpurs, and a brown felt hat bustled toward me. Crinkles in a Canadian Mountie costume. He looked like a shrunken, apple-shaped Dudley Do-Right. "I hope you haven't brought me any more prisoners." He chuckled. "We're all full up."

"I can see that. You're looking snappy, by the way." I couldn't snark too much over how goofy he looked, given that I was dressed in my band uniform, complete with braided wool jacket with ridiculously large brass buttons and a plumed shako hat.

He rocked back on his heels. "I decided to get in the spirit of the holiday, since we've got so much company here right now. Ollie and I spent most of last night decorating and planning activities for everybody. We're going to be decorating sugar cookies to look like ghosts later. You're welcome to join us."

Only the Christmastown Constabulary would worry about prisoners needing holiday-appropriate activities.

"Thanks, but I just brought some stew from the castle for everyone. Felice sent over a couple of bread loaves, too."

Crinkles beamed. "Gee wiggles, that was nice of her. Let me take that off your hands."

He took the covered dish and led me into the kitchen. I couldn't help pausing as I caught another glimpse of a butcher knife flashing in the pumpkin lights Crinkles and Ollie had strung around the chandelier.

"Where's Ollie?" I asked.

"He's delivering his candy corn pie to the bake-off booth."

"Candy corn pie?"

"Don't they make that where you come from?"

"Uh, no." *Poor Nick*, I thought.

He looked puzzled. "That surprises me—it's awfully good. But between you and me, I think Chestnut's candy corn cake would be a shoo-in. Look here . . ."

He removed aluminum foil from a platter containing a large cake in the triangular shape of a humongous candy corn niblet. The icing was perfectly colored and smooth like glass.

"Wow," I said.

"It's got a little marzipan layer between the icing and the cake." Crinkles lowered his voice. "Ollie's going to ask if Chestnut's cake is eligible even if he's in jail. Winning that blue ribbon might lift his spirits. Chestnut's sulking in his room right now. He still denies having anything to do with Wink's death."

I frowned. "It seems odd that he never mentioned Wink was his partner, then."

"He says he didn't think it was relevant."

I wasn't an expert in murder investigations, but

"Who benefits?" is always a good question to ask. So far, I couldn't see anyone else besides Chestnut who benefited from Wink's death.

"I hate to think that anyone I know would commit a murder." Crinkles shook his head.

It had been a disillusioning two days for the constable. Dandy, Fir, and Chuckle swore that they hadn't meant any real harm to anyone at the constabulary when they delivered the glass-covered candy corn. Their goal had been to stop people buying the candy from the big stores, so that people desperate for candy corn would turn to their black-market product. The fastest way they could think of to have word spread that candy stores weren't safe to buy from was by sending the tainted candy to somewhere public, like the constabulary. Chuckle said they'd even considered sending a batch to the castle.

Later, as I was having a coffee at We Three Beans with Juniper, before heading to the bandstand to play our part in the Halloween festivities, I felt my own spirits flagging. Just as the last few days had upset Crinkles, they had made me doubt my instincts. "I misjudged everything," I confessed to Juniper. "I trusted Chestnut *and* Dandy."

"Dandy didn't kill anyone, though."

Not technically, maybe. "I'm not as inclined to give those three the benefit of a doubt when they say that the glass-covered candy corn was just sent to the constabulary as a warning."

Juniper finished her eggnog latte. "I'm just glad that the culprits are all in jail—and in time for the Halloween carnival."

I hoped they were all the right culprits.

"Speaking of the Halloween carnival." She stood up and secured the chin strap under her ridiculous hat—the same drum majorette monstrosity that I was wearing. "We'd better get going. I told Smudge I'd meet him at the band shell."

Interesting. Maybe "better than Algid" wasn't such a bad starting point for a relationship after all.

We bussed our coffee cups and then headed toward the park. On Festival Boulevard, a cluster of elves had gathered. Everyone was looking up.

"What *is* that?" an elf dressed as a devil asked, pointing his plastic pitchfork at the rooftop directly above us.

Juniper and I craned to see an outline of a large bird crouched on the eave.

"Isn't that Butterbean's vulture?" Juniper asked.

"Grimstock," I said.

At least we knew where he was. I wasn't sure if it would be possible to coax him back to the castle—or why we'd want to. Still, I whipped out my phone and took a picture so I could at least provide evidence that I'd seen him here.

As Juniper and I were starting off again, someone let out a startled cry.

"Mrs. Claus—watch out!"

Thinking fast, Juniper grabbed my arm and tugged us both out of the way just as a chunk of ice the size of a microwave oven crashed to the sidewalk next to us, shattering a jack-o'-lantern.

"Golly doodle!" Juniper cried, staring at the mess on the sidewalk. "That thing could have killed us."

I looked at the ice chunk, then at the top of the building overhead. The roofs of tall buildings in Santaland mostly had ice guards—spikes that kept ice from slipping down. Occasionally, though, spikes bent or ice built up and slid off roofs despite the best precautions.

"Are you okay?" Juniper asked me.

"Fine," I lied. The near miss had not only rattled my nerves, it had rattled something in my brain. *Ice.*

"You go ahead," I told Juniper. "I'm going to text Jingles and Butterbean that I've found Grimstock."

She sent me a worried look, but relented. "I'll see you at the band shell. Don't be late."

After she was gone, I looked around for a warm place to duck into to text Jingles and Butterbean. The lights were on in Chestnut's Cake Emporium, so I went inside.

When the tinkle bell above the door heralded my entrance, Sugar moved from one of the back worktables to the customer counter, where a few racks of cupcakes stood. Thin inventory, but Sugar probably wasn't expecting many customers. Most of the foot traffic this evening would be around Peppermint Pond.

She cradled a large bowl of red icing she'd been stirring. "Can I get you something, Mrs. Claus?"

"A glass of water?" My pulse was still racing from my near miss. "I just barely escaped getting crushed by falling ice."

She hurried to pour me some water. "Was it this building?"

"Next door, but it's left a big chunk of ice on the

sidewalk." I tilted my head. "Do you have anything to clear that up with?"

"I do, as a matter of fact." She disappeared briefly into the back and returned wielding a large pair of ice tongs. It looked like the kind of implement that in the old days the iceman would use when delivering ice for primitive refrigerators.

"That's right, I saw you hefting ice with that at Peppermint Pond a few days ago. The day before—"

I shut my mouth abruptly. *The day before Wink died.*

As the truth clicked into place, I lifted the water glass to my lips to cover my awkwardness. Unfortunately, my hand trembled.

Her eyes narrowed up at me. But she didn't have to look up too far.

She would have been on the tall side, Algid had said. *Tall for an elf.*

"It's cold out there," I said, trying to hide my discomfort.

Her lips thinned into a tight smile. "Sure you don't want some hot tea, or warm eggnog?"

My stomach turned at that last suggestion—and not just because I didn't like eggnog. I was starting to feel queasy, period. "I'm thawing out now." *Thawing like a chunk of ice that's just been used as a murder weapon.* All Sugar had had to do was whack Wink on the back of the head with a solid chunk of ice, then leave it on the floor. By the time he was discovered, the murder weapon would have melted away into a puzzling pool of water.

I looked down at my phone again. "I'll just send this message to the castle and be on my way."

I texted Jingles the picture of Grimstock. Then, trying to keep my hands steady, I typed out, **Ice was the murder weapon. The murderer was**

Before I could finish, Sugar's hand clamped down on mine.

My thumb hit the Send button and the phone let out a little mechanical burp. Not that it would help me. There wasn't enough information there to alert Jingles that I was in danger.

Nothing to do now but to try to brazen this out. "Something wrong?" I asked.

Sugar let go of my hand and marched to the front door. She flipped the lock. The sound of that deadbolt shot a cold arrow of fear through me. Her pulling down the shade over the window was even worse.

"Closing up already?" I asked, feigning obliviousness to the peril I was in. "Maybe you're going to the carnival, too. I'm due on the bandstand now. I'll be missed if I'm not there on the downbeat."

She snorted. "I've heard you play with the Santaland Concert Band. You won't be missed."

I bristled. But this was not the time to argue over my percussion skills. "Look, I just want to be on my way."

"On your way to the constabulary to snitch to Constable Crinkles?"

My trill of laughter was a shade too bright. "I don't know what you're talking about."

She snatched the phone out of my hand and snapped it open. My text to Jingles would still be on the screen. She scanned the text bubbles and then glanced up at me. " 'The murderer was—'?"

Smiling, she typed, hit Send, and faced the screen to me. **Chestnut.**

My sense of justice couldn't let that pass. "Chestnut didn't kill Wink. He valued Wink's skill."

Her face turned the color of a red velvet cake. "Have you *ever* heard anyone with a functioning taste bud in their head praise anything Wink Jollyflake baked?"

Come to think of it, I hadn't. Except for Chestnut, who needed his money, and Wink's mother, who doted on him.

Her hands fisted at her sides. "Wink could barely crack an egg when he started working at the Silver Bell Bakery. *I* was Chestnut's right hand for years. Years! We worked side by side." Though the shade was closed, she nodded at the window, toward the bakery across the street. "Together we kept that place solvent—Chestnut and *me*. When Chestnut used to tell me his dreams of opening his own cake shop, it was always understood that I'd go with him."

Understood by her, maybe. That word Algid had overheard—*cheated*. It hadn't referred to a love affair, as I assumed. Sugar must have been referring to what she perceived as Chestnut's betrayal of her. "Why didn't you?"

"Because Wink weaseled his way in—and he had the money. Who knows where it came from."

I thought of Dandy's ring. How much else had he hocked or cashed in to raise money? I was willing to bet that Mrs. Jollyflake chipped in something, too.

"If you let Chestnut go to jail for killing Wink, your dream of sharing this shop with him will fizzle," I pointed out. "He'll be baking cakes over campfires in the Farthest Frozen Reaches."

"Not if I tell Constable Crinkles that I was with him the night Wink died."

"Chestnut will know that's a lie."

She laughed. "Do you think he'll care? I've talked to him in that jail cell. All he wants to do is return here. He'd sell his soul for this place."

I didn't know about Chestnut's soul, but clearly Sugar's was already bought and paid for—in blood. All it had cost her was the life of one elf who stood in her way.

Correction: one elf's life—and mine. My life wasn't worth a bag of peppermints now. Sugar couldn't let me walk out of here now that she'd confessed.

"You might be able to get away with killing a lone baker," I warned, "but my death will pose a lot more problems. I'm Mrs. Claus. I'll be missed."

"During the Halloween carnival? Everyone's at Peppermint Pond, or headed that way. Distractions galore."

"But they *will* come looking for me."

"Here? Why?"

I struggled to find a good answer. "I texted Jingles."

Her lips turned up in a smirk. "I don't think some moose-brained theory about melting ice is going to bring the authorities rushing over. Besides, I'll have moved you by then."

Cold fear grabbed me. "Where?" I assumed I would be dead, but I still was curious about which frozen corner of my adopted homeland I would end up in.

"Don't get your stockings in a twist about that. In Santaland, there are places remote enough that a body could be buried in snow for decades without anyone finding them."

Buried in snow. I really didn't deal well with cold. I turned and made a dash for the door. I had desperation on my side, and longer legs. But Sugar was both muscular and agile. She caught me by my uniform's sash belt and dragged me toward the back. I wasn't going down without a fight, though. I twisted and yanked off her chef cap and pulled at her hair. With a roar, she grabbed the heavy ceramic mixing bowl off the counter and brained me with it.

I stumbled to one knee. Mercilessly, she whacked me over the head again. Red splattered everywhere. As I collapsed onto all fours I thought it was probably my own blood, but when I fell onto my side I realized it was too sticky and bright red even for blood. I'd been attacked with cake icing.

I lay on the floor, looking at those blobs of red, barely conscious as hands grabbed hold of my ankles. Grunting and swearing, Sugar dragged me across the floor toward the back of the store. I let myself go limp and heavy, trying to think, hoping to buy time.

Finally we stopped and she let go of my ankles. Startlingly, she loomed over my face and lifted one of my eyelids. It took every ounce of control I had left to remain still.

"Hmph—not quite dead yet."

She pushed back to her feet. What did she have up her sleeve now? This was a kitchen. Even bakers used sharp utensils. When I heard her walk a few steps away, I tried to gather my forces to make an escape.

But I waited too long. Sugar didn't grab a knife, she just pulled a lever. At the strange metallic sound, I looked up into the maw of the door of one of the massive hoppers overhead opening up. Before I could react, an avalanche of icing sugar fell on me, burying me alive in deadly powdery sweetness.

Chapter Thirteen

Sugar had chosen her weapon well. The fine, sweet powder smothered me in an instant. I attempted to gulp in air, but inhaled only sugar. It shot into my nostrils, throat, and bronchial passages, stinging like acid. I coughed, but there was no give to the prison of powdered sugar all around me. It might as well have been cement. My instinct was to try to take another breath and start the cycle of pain all over again. Luckily, some corner of my brain told me to hold my breath.

Footsteps receded, and then the store's bell rang. The front door shut and locked.

I'd read about people trapped in avalanches, and how air pockets in the snow kept them alive. But that was snow, not sugar. And had the accounts told how to create an air pocket if you didn't already have one? I tried turning my head—but it was stuck. Reflexively, my legs began to kick. Here,

I had more luck. I bent my knees and tried to push with my heels. Once my legs had kicked away enough of the sugar around them, I was able to push with my legs and wriggle free.

I finally rolled onto my hands and knees and coughed what I could out of my lungs. Sugar had overestimated how weak I was—but she'd known I wasn't dead yet. Why would she leave me on the floor, even buried beneath a hundred pounds of confectioners' sugar? I didn't kid myself that she was through with me.

I needed my phone . . . but I didn't see it. Sugar must've taken it.

Lurching to my feet, I weaved toward the door. Something on the floor made me stumble. Red cake icing. I slipped and fell, smearing more of the sticky frosting on my hands. I tried to wipe it off, but my clothes were also covered with powdered sugar. Rubbing my hands on my uniform or face just created more gooey mess.

As I stumbled out the store's entrance, the electric sleigh delivery wagon belonging to Chestnut's Cake Emporium was backing into the shop's loading area. To load *me*, I realized. With all the goings on with the carnival around Peppermint Pond, Festival Boulevard was mostly deserted at the moment—a perfect time to haul away a body.

Sugar hopped off the sleigh. Her eyes flew open with shock when she spotted me.

At the same moment, Fancy from Fancy's Wigs and Hats next door was coming out to lock up for the day and head for the festivities. A cat mask was pulled up at the top of her head like a pair of sunglasses. When she took in first Sugar, then me, her mittened hand flew to her mouth as if to cover a scream.

I pointed at Sugar. "Call the constable! She's a killer!" The words issued from my sweetener-clogged throat in a hoarse rasp.

Sugar jumped back on her sleigh wagon. Fancy, still gaping at me in what I realized was stark fear, turned and ran shrieking in the other direction.

"Wait!" I called after her. But Fancy didn't stop.

Sugar, too, buzzed away. What could I do? Distant strains of "Funeral March of a Marionette" floated over from the park. The Santaland Concert Band's opening number. Had Juniper tried to text or call me? Did anyone realize I was missing?

I ran toward the park, slipping and stumbling. Outside Hollywell's Christmastown Cornucopia, our largest grocery, I nearly collided with an elf mother exiting with two children in costume carrying plastic pumpkin pails. One was a witch, the other a tiny snow monster. The threesome goggled at me with a fear I was beginning to be very familiar with.

The snow monster pointed his little faux fur paw at me. "Ice zombie!"

His voicing the word seemed to terrify them all even more. The two children let out shrill screams. The mother dropped her paper bag of groceries, grabbed her tiny trick-or-treaters one by each hand, and fled. The children, I noticed, did *not* drop their candy.

I turned and stared at my reflection in the Cornucopia's plate glass window. I nearly screamed, too. My face was ghostly white, but smeared with red that looked like gore. I moved to run into the store to see if I could use their washroom to clean up, but before I could reach the door, a terrified store employee drew the shade and flipped the store's sign to Closed.

I was about to pound on the door when I heard something overhead. Whoops of glee and delirious fright emanated from a sleigh pulled by a single fizzle-nosed reindeer. Quasar's Runaway Sleigh Ride. Jubilant, I ran out into the center of Festival Boulevard and waved my arms to flag it down. Then I put my fingers to my lips and let out the most ear-piercing whistle I could manage.

Quasar looked down, and the sleigh dipped. Lucia, who was at the reins wearing a Bride of Frankenstein wig and makeup, saw me and brought the sleigh to a quick stop in the middle of the wide street. The four young elves in the back of the sleigh, in various costumes ranging from a demented reindeer to a garden variety ghost, all took one look at me, screamed in terror, and scattered.

Lucia watched them go in disgust. "Kids these days—little snowflakes!"

In their defense, I admitted, "I've been scaring adults, too."

She gave me another once-over, her black-lipsticked mouth turning down. "And to think you told Christopher to come as Dracula."

"This isn't a costume," I said impatiently, "it was attempted murder." There was no time to stand here sniping with my sister-in-law. I hopped inside the sleigh and explained what had happened as succinctly as I could. "We need to catch up to Sugar—she's in the Chesnut's Cake Emporium delivery sleigh. It's red and white."

Lucia wasted no time taking up the reins again, and Quasar was soon galumphing down the street to gain momentum for takeoff.

If you've never experienced sleigh flight, it's like taking off in the world's flimsiest airliner. Think of riding a roller coaster in freezing cold with no seat guard. As Quasar lifted the sleigh off the ground, my stomach lurched, but I was almost used to that now. The worst thing about taking off in the center of Festival Boulevard was that we were so close to buildings. One strong gust of wind could have bashed us against a rooftop.

How did Nick manage to fly around the world like this every year?

As Quasar looped around Christmastown, Lucia and I hung over the side of the sleigh, scanning the streets below for the red and white delivery sleigh. I'd never flown over the town when it was decorated for Halloween, with orange lights outlining the buildings and cottages, and the lights of jack-o'-lanterns winking on every stoop. In the park, the band shell was lit up, and I could make out my Santaland Concert Band cohorts playing our instrumental version of "Monster Mash," the elves' favorite. Around the band shell and the bake-off pavilion, elves in costume were dancing. And, most gloriously of all, the haunted ice castle was lit in orange from within, with white and orange lights outside beaming up at its glassy exterior, making the ice exterior glow orange.

As a crowning touch, on the crenellated right tower, above an ice gargoyle, perched Grimstock.

Finally, Lucia spotted the red and white vehicle.

"There! I see her. She's on the other side of the park!"

I'd assumed Sugar would head out of town, or to Tinkertown. Instead, she'd apparently decided that losing herself in a crowd would be better strategy. I couldn't say she was wrong. I didn't see how we would ever catch her in that press of elves and people at the carnival. Having Quasar's runaway sleigh overhead didn't help matters. As elves saw the sleigh shave close to the trees and rooftops and head right for the park, pandemonium broke out. At least a quarter of the crowd started to panic and run.

The chaos made it all the harder to track Sugar's movements, like trying to find one ant in a mound boiling with activity. We made Quasar keep circling until I finally picked her out again, running. "I see her!" She was heading toward the haunted ice castle.

Lucia saw her, too. "Bring us down, Quasar."

"W-where?" he called back at us, perplexed.

There wasn't much room. Luckily, though Quasar wasn't the most agile of reindeer on dry land, he was a solid flyer. He picked out a strip of unpopulated area next to Peppermint Pond and landed the sleigh in a way that reminded me of a plane coming to a quick stop on an aircraft carrier. We careened to a halt inches short of a fir tree.

I half jumped, half tumbled out of the sleigh and sprinted toward the haunted ice castle.

Soon Lucia was running next to me, but it didn't make sense for both of us to be pursuing Sugar.

"Go find Crinkles," I said. "Or better yet, find

Nick. He'll be at the bake-off pavilion set up by the band shell."

"Good idea." She was about to peel off to the left when she turned back to me, jogging in place as she called out, "Be careful!"

I expected to have a hard time pushing my way through the crowd, but as I ran, the crowd spread away from me, like unzipping a zipper. Most people were reacting to the horror effect of the sugar and icing on my face, although some might have taken note of my look of desperation. I spotted Sugar up ahead in her white baker's tunic and red Chestnut's Cake Emporium apron, as she sprinted through the haunted ice castle's vaulted entrance.

It seemed an odd choice, but I chugged after her. Near the fake drawbridge leading to the door, I had to skirt around Durdles—or, at least, Durdles's bowler-topped head, which was on the ground two feet from the rest of him.

"She went thataway!" the head called out, nearly causing me to jump out of my skin.

Christopher was wrong; that headless snowman *was* creepy. Trying not to let it break my stride, I yelled my thanks and charged through the door.

My momentum came to a screeching stop when I entered the ice castle's main hall. Though the castle's walls were ice, the floors were wood plank covered in orange-and-black sawdust. "Monster Mash" was being piped inside at extremely loud volume. Every few feet there was a different activity underway: bobbing-for-apple barrels; a fortune-telling crone in a booth; an entrance to the actual haunted house part of the haunted house, from where spooky sound effects echoed; a snowball toss to dunk Deputy Ollie in what looked like a vat of tomato juice, which I assumed was supposed to be blood. Deputy Ollie was wearing a bathing cap that couldn't quite cover his large, Spock-like ears, and a long wool bathing costume that probably hadn't been in style since 1902.

He caught sight of me, but instead of reacting to my beckoning gesture, he pointed at me, wild eyed. "Ice zombie!"

Elves turned, and some shrieked and ran. Others laughed at their scaredy-cat cohort. At that moment an elf got lucky and Ollie dropped into the tomato juice.

I didn't have time to wait for him. I glanced around for Sugar. Overhead, netting had been stretched and covered in gauze to simulate a spiderweb, and from a high platform, elves were jumping onto the webbing into some kind of tag game involving keeping away from an elf in a spider suit.

And then I spotted Sugar—she was jogging up the wooden staircase to the catwalk platform over the netting. I took off after her, but as soon as my footsteps started clattering up the stairs, she looked down. It took her a moment to recognize me, but when she did, she put on the steam and hurried up the rest of the steps.

Where was she going?

I tackled the stairs two at a time to try to catch up. When I finally reached the catwalk, my appearance sent little costumed elves jumping in fear down to the spiderweb below. Sugar ran around the catwalk, away from me. I didn't understand where she thought she could hide.

Then she disappeared.

I frowned as I edged more slowly around the catwalk. There was just one makeshift wood railing to hold on to. Heights didn't agree with me, even if there was a spider web to catch my fall.

I finally came to the opening in the ice through which Sugar must have disappeared. It led out to one of the two towers. I wriggled through, realizing too late that I'd be completely vulnerable to attack when I poked myself through to the outside. What made me realize this was Sugar grabbing my shoulders and yanking me out. She was shorter than I was, but muscular, and surer footed on the ice. That's all that was around us now: ice under our feet and waist-high ice walls with even shorter, square crenellations. There was literally nothing to grab on to as she shoved me toward one of these indentations at the tower's edge. I cast a frightened glance over the side, but I was blinded by the floodlights aimed at the castle walls.

"Why didn't you leave me alone?" Sugar asked.

Was she serious? "You tried to kill me!"

"Only when it became clear that you intended to accuse me of being a murderess. . . ."

"You *are* a murderess."

"So *you* say. But now you're going to jump, and you'll take your secrets about my involvement to the grave."

I attempted an insouciant laugh. "I'm not the only one who knows what you did, Sugar. I've told—"

My mouth clamped shut. Say I did fall from this tower and break my neck. Who would this maniac go after next? I shouldn't give her names.

She unsheathed a knife, backing me up to the tower's edge. "Who else did you tell?"

I shook my head. "No one. I was lying. Trying to save my own skin."

"You don't have to worry about your skin." She laughed. "Just your brains splattered all over the packed snow below."

I hazarded a glance down. Big mistake. It seemed like an impossibly long fall.

"You might have gotten away with Wink's murder," I said, "but if you kill me now, here, you'll have hundreds of witnesses."

"Witnesses to my trying to save you?"

I snorted. "That reindeer won't fly."

"Shut up!" She grew more agitated, thrusting the knife at me again.

My stomach lurched, and I shut up. I had to do something. I focused on the knife, making a show of my fear. It wasn't very hard.

"Maybe you're not so stupid, after all," she said.

"And maybe you're not so clever."

Before she could react, I reached out and karate chopped the wrist of her weapon hand. The knife flew to the tower's ice brick flooring. I gave Sugar a sharp kick in the shin, expecting her to bend in pain so I could throw her to the ground. Instead, she locked onto me. At first I thought she was trying to steady herself. But no—we started wrestling. I twisted so my back was no longer to the edge of the tower opening, but then I slipped. Just as I scrambled to grab the knife from the ground, she swooped down on it.

"Get up!"

"No thanks." I felt safer on the ground, certain she couldn't lift me like a sack of potatoes and toss me off the tower. "I like the view from here. Nice for watching the Northern Lights."

She growled in irritation and lifted my foot by the boot. "Get up or I'll put my knife through your foot."

Reflexively, I kicked out. She jerked backward, just catching herself before she could fall off. In anger, she lifted the knife.

I gritted my teeth, preparing myself for the pain she was about to inflict when that knife plunged into my foot.

Before she could follow through, however, a dark shadow passed over us and then a hulking bird crouched on the tower's edge, flapping its wings in Sugar's face. As Sugar took in the hideous red face, she shouted in alarm. And then she tumbled backward, over the edge.

An eternity seemed to pass between her falling and my hearing the collective yell of dismay that went up once she landed.

I tried to scramble to my feet. I made it to my hands and knees. When I finally peeked over the edge, a crowd had swarmed around the fallen, awkwardly splayed body below.

What had I done? I felt sick. Not that I liked Sugar or wanted her to go free. I'd just never been this responsible for someone's death.

And yet I'd never felt so thankful to be alive. *Saved by the buzzard.*

I looked gratefully at the unlovely creature. "Thank you, Grimstock."

Nick burst through the opening leading from inside the castle out onto the tower. "April—are you all right?" He lifted me up.

I threw my arms around him. "I'm fine now."

I was so happy to see him. The way Nick held me made me feel even better, although I wasn't sure I deserved it.

"I didn't mean to kill her," I said.

Nick pulled back. "You didn't. She's alive."

I frowned. "How can that be?"

"Durdles broke her fall," Nick said. "His body, not his head. Of course, he'll have to be re-rolled, but he'll be as good as new in no time."

As I felt myself quivering on rubbery legs, I wished getting myself back together were that easy. I'd probably be having flashbacks to this Halloween for a long time to come.

Chapter Fourteen

The bake-off pavilion's long table sagged under the weight of baked goods: platters of cookies sprinkled with candy corn, as well as bars, brownies, blondies. Puffy's candy corn donuts had won the second-place red ribbon. Ollie's candy corn meringue pie was the only pie, but there were a dozen varieties of cakes: Cupcakes and cupcake towers in pyramids resembling candy corn. Chocolate bundt cake crusted with crushed candy corn, tricolored bundt cakes and layer cakes, and Pamela Claus's magnificent three-tiered cake, with the layers separated by columns of chocolate. My mother-in-law never baked anything ordinary, and for her pains this time her entry bore an honorable mention badge.

The blue ribbon had been awarded to Chestnut's cake. As soon as Sugar had been taken into custody, Chestnut had been freed to attend the bake-off judging. Now he stood on the dais next to a proud Puffy, a somewhat satisfied Pamela, and a sour-looking Bell, whose cupcake tower placed second. The agony of defeat was written all over her expression.

In the center of them all stood Nick, green faced. I wanted to believe that his pallor had something to do with my brush with death. But I think it was mostly due to the bake-off theme ingredient.

It would be decades before another kernel of candy corn passed his lips.

I'd managed to clean myself up, and now stood at the back with Juniper, Smudge, Quasar, Jingles, and Butterbean. "I think everyone had fun, don't you?" Juniper asked. Her nature bent toward the positive.

"Aside from a murder, attempted murder, and April almost falling to her doom?" Smudge shrugged. "It was great."

She gave him a playful swat. "You can't blame a holiday for one crazy person's actions."

"In this case, it seems more apt than chirping about everybody having fun."

I wanted to clunk him on the head. Just yesterday he'd been thinking of giving her a ring—a murder victim's ring, it was true. But that was preferable to sniping at her for being cheerful.

I made myself hold my tongue. Getting mixed up in Juniper's romantic life could be a friendship ender.

"M-my runaway sleigh ride was a success," Quasar observed.

"Not to mention, you helped catch a killer." I laughed. "You and Grimstock saved the day."

Grimstock was still perched high above us all, surveying the park from one of the haunted ice castle's towers. His arrival in Santaland might have been a mistake, but I would always be grateful to him. A crime-fighting buzzard wasn't a bad thing to have around.

"By next Halloween," Jingles said, "everyone will have forgotten all about the little glitches in this year's celebration. So much will happen between now and then."

"Like next month's Thanksgiving celebration," Butterbean reminded us.

"Butterbean's finally got hold of another company that will express deliver a turkey," Jingles told us.

Butterbean bobbed with excitement. "From My-Turkey. com. We even got to pick the profile of the turkey we wanted. Salty and I chose Gobbles148."

I frowned. "He has a name?"

"Of course," Butterbean said. "We have a whole profile on Gobbles. He should be arriving in a few days. Salty's building a pen."

Juniper smiled. "Thanksgiving. I like the sound of that!"

"The more holidays the better," Jingles said.

I agreed. Sure, it had never been celebrated here, but a big dinner, gratitude, the Claus family and friends gathered all together . . . what could go wrong?

Outside the pavilion, the last act of the evening, the Groovin' Ghoulies, broke into their version of

"Monster Mash." Excitedly, all the elves in the tent dashed out to sing along and dance in the snow under the lights of the haunted ice castle.

Nick appeared at my side. "Care to dance?"

I laughed. Dancing with a guy in a Santa suit to "Monster Mash"? "Of course."

How could I resist?

A TRIPLE LAYER HALLOWEEN MURDER

Carol J. Perry

Chapter One

The entire month of October is notoriously nutty in my hometown of Salem, Massachusetts—culminating in the Witch City's favorite holiday, Halloween. Think Mardi Gras, times ten. Think congestion, traffic jams, gridlock, costumed revelers partying day and night, pumpkins grinning from every available flat surface. Some locals who can afford it actually move out of town for the whole month; some entrepreneurial types turn their spare rooms into high-priced B and Bs. The famed Hawthorne Hotel is booked solid a year or more in advance. Those of us, like me, who have jobs need to figure out a way to get around the cars, scooters, bicycles, golf carts, motorcycles, tour buses and wandering pedestrians in order to arrive at work on time.

I'm Lee Barrett, née Maralee Kowalski, thirty-four, red-haired, Salem born, orphaned early, married once and widowed young. I live with my Aunt Ibby Russell in the old family home on Winter Street, along with our gentleman cat, O'Ryan. I work as program director and occasional field reporter at Salem's cable television station, WICH-TV. Winter Street is just across the Salem Common from the station's Derby Street harborside location, so I'm one of the lucky ones who can walk to my job.

One pretty early October morning—yes, Halloween-Salem is totally nutty but can be quite lovely at the same time—with fall leaves at their red and gold glory and the deep blue water of the harbor shimmering in the sunshine, I climbed the marble front steps, crossed the black-and-white tiled floor, and rode the ancient elevator—we call it "Old Clunky"—up to the second floor. I greeted Rhonda, the WICH-TV receptionist. "Good morning. Anything interesting going on?"

She put down her copy of *Cosmo* and held up one hand, ticking off items on fingertips capped with long, red-polished nails. "Scotty's out doing a report for the noon news about some missing rich businessman. Howie's down at Christopher's Castle interviewing Chris Rich about what's hot and what's not in this year's Halloween costumes."

Scott Palmer isn't one of my favorite people, but he's a pretty good reporter. He gets most of the assignments I used to have before Howie—that's Howard Templeton, the station manager's wife Buffy's nephew—arrived fresh out of broadcasting school and got handed *my* field reporter's slot, earning me my so-called "promotion" to program director. Don't get me wrong. I like my new job.

The hours are way better and it came with a little pay raise, but sometimes I miss the edge-of-your-seat, race-out-the-door, day and night excitement of being in the middle of the action.

"Anything for me?" I asked.

"Yep. Doan wants to see you in his office."

Bruce Doan is the station manager. An early morning summons to his office can mean anything—a plum assignment or a royal chewing out for some real or perceived screwup. I knocked on his office door and responded to a bellowed, "It's open."

"Good morning, Mr. Doan. You wanted to see me?"

"Right. How does your day look, Ms. Barrett? Everything set to go off on schedule?"

It's my job to make sure each of the shows under my direction is adequately staffed with sets and props in place, wardrobe clean, pressed and appropriate, scripts up to date, talent prepared, lighting and sound tested, camera(s) in place and everything ready on time. I did a quick mental rundown on the day's programing. I'd seen Ranger Rob's Ford Bronco in the parking lot so I was confident that he and Katie the Clown were already on set, preparing for the morning kiddie show—*Ranger Rob's Rodeo*. Most of the *Shopping Salem* show had been prerecorded so all the host had to do was introduce the various segments. "Piece of cake," as camerawoman Marty McCarthy was fond of saying. The only other production scheduled for the day was a tour of the Old Burying Point Cemetery—a Halloween special narrated by one of Salem's ghost tour hosts. The half hour show had been carefully rehearsed and the videographer was tops in her field, so I was confident it would be fine.

"Barring anything strange, sir," I said, "everything is under control for today."

"Good," he said. "Scott and Howie are both out at the same time, so I need you to put on your field reporter hat and stand by in case anything interesting happens out there."

"Glad to help out," I said, meaning it. "Who's my videographer?"

"You get Old Jim. Okay?"

"That's fine with me," I told him. Meaning that too. Old Jim is officially retired, but he still fills in sometimes when all the other mobile camera people are busy. He's a real pro, with eyes that often see things the newer photogs miss. "Do we get the VW?" I asked.

Mr. Doan shrugged. "Sure. She's still running just fine." The converted VW bus was WICH-TV's third-string mobile unit. Fair enough, since Old Jim and I were the station's third-string field-reporting team.

"Okay. I'll be in my office whenever you need me," I promised. One of the perks of the program director's job is the fact that for the first time I have my own office—my own little hideaway. Well, not exactly a hideaway since it's an all-glass cubicle backed up to the newsroom and I'm kind of on display all the time, but I like it anyway. I told Rhonda where I'd be if she needed me, and headed through the metal door and down the steep corridor to the WICH-TV news department.

I unlocked my door, passed the file cabinet and

approached the desk, first taking a quick look at the vari-colored sticky reminder notes I'd stuck to the glass wall behind my chair. I took off my red cardigan sweater and pulled a green WICH-TV jacket from a narrow locker so I could look professional if the call came. I had plenty to do, whether or not Mr. Doan came up with a field assignment. I pulled down a random hot-pink square and read it aloud. "Order b-day cake for Buck Covington."

The station works with a fairly small staff, so we're sort of "family" to one another and we try hard not to miss anyone's special day. We have an old-fashioned "sunshine fund" that everybody chips in to and this year I somehow got elected to manage it. Buck is our drop-dead gorgeous nighttime news anchor and his birthday was the following day. He's also my BFF River North's main man.

I realized right away that I might be facing a problem with the ordering and the delivery of this particular cake. It wasn't just the gigantic holiday traffic jam facing delivery vehicles of any kind, but—maybe even worse than that—I wasn't sure that the Pretty Party Bakery would be open. The "missing rich businessman" Rhonda had referenced was the founder and owner of the popular bakery chain, Patrick "Pat" Duncan, who'd gone missing a day earlier. The police hadn't yet termed his disappearance "suspicious," but the term "unusual circumstances" was enough to get Scott Palmer into investigative mode. My police detective beau Pete Mondello hadn't said anything about it, but that's not unusual. We rarely discuss police business. Pete and I had a date for dinner that evening and I was pretty sure the missing man wouldn't be mentioned. I tapped the Pretty Party Bakery number into my phone, crossing my fingers that someone would answer. They did.

"Good morning. It's a pretty day for a party. May I tempt you with one of our giant triple-layer cupcakes? Dark chocolate, French vanilla and orange cream layers with an orange marmalade filling make it perfect for Halloween." It was a familiar kind of greeting, but delivered without the usual cheery lilt.

"Good morning. This is Lee from the TV station. That sounds delicious, but today I'd like to order our regular birthday cake and the name on top is Buck." In the interest of equity everybody at the station gets exactly the same cake. A two-layer vanilla cake with vanilla cream filling and vanilla buttercream frosting. Nothing fancy, but everybody likes it. First name only, on top in seasonal color frosting. No candles—because not everybody wants their age known. "I know things must be upset over there right now," I said, "but can you possibly deliver it by tomorrow afternoon?"

"I'm not sure, Lee. Want to speak to Tommy?"

"Yes, please." I knew Tommy LaGrange, the Pretty Party Bakery's super-efficient, nice-guy general manager. If anybody could make sure that Buck's birthday cake would be presented to him on the air, exactly as scheduled, the following night—it was Tommy.

"Hi, Lee," he said. "No problem with the cake. Our kitchen is closed today, but we always have those plain vanilla cakes in the freezer and lettering the short name is easy. The delivery might be a

problem though. We're understaffed like everybody else and with the traffic—and well, you know
about Mr. Duncan. Everybody here is worried."

"I understand," I told him. "You're not far from
the station. How about if I walk over there on my
lunch hour tomorrow and pick it up? Will that
work?"

"Perfect. It'll be ready for you at noon tomorrow. I'm guessing it's for Buck Covington—the
news guy, right?" There was a smile in his voice.
"He's a favorite around here. Glad to do it."

"Right," I agreed. I knew that everybody at the
Pretty Party Bakery must be worried and stressed
about their missing boss if they'd even closed the
kitchen. I was glad if making a cake for Buck
brought some kind of cheer. I said goodbye, omit-
ting the usual "have a nice day," and wrote myself
another sticky note. "Pick up Buck's cake at noon."
I stuck it onto the glass and pulled down another
one—this time in blue.

"Requisition slip for new quartz crystal cluster
for *Tarot Time* set." I'm not responsible for directing River's late-night show—*Tarot Time with River
North*. She and Marty McCarthy take full care of
the production where, during breaks in a scary
movie, River takes calls from random viewers and
reads the beautiful cards for them. I help out with
decor for the set. I pulled the pad of slips from my
top drawer, filled one out and proceeded to attend
to the various tasks indicated on the other colorful
reminders. It was nearly eleven thirty as I was
squirting blue glass cleaner on my almost sticker-
free wall to wash away the gummy residue when the

intercom buzzed. Rhonda announced that Howie was on his way back to the station and I could forget about the mobile unit thing.

Somewhat regretfully, I took off my imaginary field reporter hat, picked up River's crystal requisition slip and started for the door when my phone chimed. Caller ID showed my Aunt Ibby's name and number. My sixty-something reference librarian aunt was my mother's only sister and she'd raised me since both of my parents had died in a plane crash when I was only five years old. I have my own apartment on the top floor of the lovely old house, and she's careful to respect my independence and I respect hers. She rarely calls me at work. "Hi, Aunt Ibby," I said. "What's up?"

"It's the strangest thing, Maralee," she said. "O'Ryan has been pacing back and forth in the front hall all morning. He finally went out the cat door and he's been sitting under that big old oak tree in front of the house yowling his head off at something up in the branches. I went out to look and I can't see anything up there, but it sounds like there's another cat crying little soft "meows" like a kitten would sound. I can't get O'Ryan to come inside and he won't stop his noise. I'm afraid the neighbors will start complaining if he doesn't quit it."

"A cat stuck in the oak tree?" I asked. "Is this a case where we're supposed to call the fire department or don't people do that anymore?"

"I already did that," she reported. "There's too much going on in Salem for cat rescuing right now. They suggested that I put out some smelly cat food to coax it down. It hasn't worked. The poor thing just cries more pitifully and O'Ryan keeps up that awful caterwauling. Do you think you can run home for a bit and get him to stop?"

Why would she think I could somehow influence a cat's behavior? This particular cat and I had a past. When I first came to WICH-TV I was hired as a hurry-up replacement for the late-night movie show host, Ariel Constellation, when her body was found in the harbor behind the station. Ariel had hosted *Nightshades* in the same time slot *Tarot Time with River North* has now, and she was billed as a "call-in psychic." It turned out that Ariel was a practicing witch and had a yellow cat she claimed was her "familiar." She'd called him Orion—like the constellation. Along with the show, I inherited the cat. I called him O'Ryan—like the Irish name. I turned out to be a terrible call-in psychic but a good cat mom. River took over the late show, I became a field reporter, and O'Ryan came to live in the Winter Street house with Aunt Ibby and me. In Salem a witch's familiar is often feared and always respected. O'Ryan and I had developed a special, if hard to explain, understanding. There was a good chance I'd be able to find out what the commotion was all about. It was close to lunchtime anyway, so I told my aunt I'd be home soon. I locked the office, dropped off the requisition slip with Rhonda and tapped on Mr. Doan's door to tell him I needed to go home to help my aunt out with a little problem.

"Is your aunt okay?" he asked.

"She's fine. Just a bit of a noise concern." I smiled and gave him a quick rundown on the crying cats situation.

"Wait a minute." He held up one finger. "Is Old Jim still in the building?"

"Yes. I just saw him in the newsroom helping set up for the noon news. Do you want me to tell him we're off duty?"

He shook his head. "No. It occurs to me we haven't done one of those short "human-interest" pieces for a while. The audience just eats that stuff up. You know. A little kid's first day in kindergarten. The cute dogs you can get from the pet shelter. A cat-in-a-tree rescue would be a good one. Can you get the cat to cooperate?"

He didn't wait for an answer. He buzzed Rhonda. "Tell Old Jim he and Ms. Barrett are going to rescue a cat in a tree." He paused. "Better tell Jim to grab a ladder out of the prop room."

I told Jim what was going on, buttoned myself into the green jacket, and within minutes we were in the VW mobile unit, lights and camera equipment stashed in the back, along with a brand new eight-foot ladder an advertiser had used in a house paint commercial. I was sure the eight-foot ladder would be of little use against an eighty-foot tree, but hey—if the boss says bring a ladder we bring a ladder, and this was the only one we had. Before long Jim was at the wheel, slowly, carefully, wending our way along the few blocks to Winter Street. I pulled down the visor mirror for a quick check of hair and makeup.

Not a good move.

Only a few people know a secret about me—just Aunt Ibby, Pete and River. I discovered not too long ago that I am a *scryer*. That's a person who sometimes sees things in reflective surfaces—visions that other people cannot see. River calls me a "gazer" and says it is a special gift. I don't think of it as a gift at all. Most everything it has ever shown me has had something to do with death.

As usual, the vision started with flashing lights and swirling colors. As usual I didn't want to see what would come next. As usual I couldn't look away. The swirling colors dissolved and something began to take shape. I squinted and leaned closer to the mirror.

As visions go, this wasn't a bad one. It was a woodsy scene, lots of trees, and in the distance, a small house. Somebody's cabin in the woods? In a blink, the picture was gone and the image of a startled looking redhead looked back at me.

I pushed the visor back up into place, trying hard to shake the memory of the vision away, just as Jim pulled onto Winter Street and steered the VW into place right beside the towering oak tree. I heard the yowling before I'd even opened the door. O'Ryan sat on the brick sidewalk, looking up into the branches. Aunt Ibby sat on the front steps, looking embarrassed by the whole situation.

I stopped to speak to the cat, who acknowledged my presence with a quick ankle rub. "I'm going to need your help on this one, big boy," I told him. He resumed the noisemaking. I helped Jim unload our equipment, then joined my aunt on the steps. "Mr. Doan thinks this will make a human-interest spot," I told her. "I hope we can get the poor kitty down somehow. Have you been able to get a look at it yet?"

She shook her head. "It's about halfway up the tree, I think. At least I saw the branches shaking."

She pointed toward Jim, who had set the ladder next to the base of the oak. "I put a bowl of food on the ground over there." She whispered, "I don't think that little ladder will help much."

"I know. Just following Mr. Doan's orders." I clipped my mike to the lapel of the green jacket and took my position a few feet away from tree and howling cat. We ran through a brief sound check. I waited for Jim's countdown and, smiling into the handheld camera, I began my intro. "Good morning, ladies and gentlemen. I'm Lee Barrett reporting to you from Winter Street, just a short distance from the Salem Common. The sound you hear is coming from a large yellow cat." Jim focused on O'Ryan, who immediately stopped crying or screaming or whatever that was and widened his golden eyes, looking directly into the camera. What a ham. "There seems to be another cat—or maybe a kitten—in the upper branches of this fine old oak tree. Our mission? Rescue the kitty. So here goes."

I picked up the dish of cat food and moved close to the tree. "The fire department suggested that we might tempt the cat in the tree with some nice smelly food." I sniffed at the bowl. "This should do the trick." O'Ryan moved closer to me, silent now. "Those of you who are regular viewers may remember this cat. He once belonged to the late Ariel Constellation. She called him Orion." The cat in question put his front paws on the first rung of the ladder, while I held the bowl of cat food up over my head. Feeling silly, I sing-songed the familiar falsetto, "Here, kitty kitty kitty."

O'Ryan took a tentative move up the ladder—hind feet on the lower rung, forefeet on the next one up. I kitty-kittyed while the cat moved up the ladder. There was an answering plaintive "meow" from above. Jim aimed the camera up into the branches. I looked up too, didn't see any cat, and—thankfully—resumed my normal voice. "We can hear the cat up there. Perhaps you can see it on your screen at home." O'Ryan had reached the rung just under the fold-out platform below the top of the ladder—the part where they put the paint can in the house paint commercial. He gave one more commanding howl, and with a rustle of leaves and a plaintive squeal, a small calico cat dropped from the tree directly onto that broad oblong paint can shelf.

"Oh, my goodness," I heard my aunt cry out—obviously forgetting that we were filming. "That's Mr. Duncan's cat! I just saw her picture on the noon news. That's Cupcake. She's missing too."

Chapter Two

Standing on tiptoes, I reached up onto the ladder's platform for the frightened cat. Not a kitten, I realized, but a small girl cat. Holding her against my shoulder—but away from the mic—I looked into Jim's camera. "Our treed cat story has a happy ending. She's safe and sound. I believe this sweet kitty is a calico cat. See? She has spots of three different colors—black, white, and orange."

O'Ryan had turned himself around and landed back on the ground. He sat next to the ladder, quiet now, watching my every move. I looked down at the calico. "Kitty, you must be grateful to O'Ryan. I guess he told you when it was safe for you to come down." She'd stopped shivering and seemed to relax against my green jacket. "I've heard that these are sometimes called "money cats," I informed my audience, "and that they bring good luck. I've also heard that this one may fit the description of a missing Salem calico cat named Cupcake. Stay tuned to WICH-TV for more information about this cute saved-from-the-oak-tree kitty. I'm Lee Barrett reporting live, under an old oak tree on Winter Street." Jim moved in for a close-up. I lifted the cat's paw gently and made her wave to the viewers, knowing that O'Ryan would disapprove. He hates it when anyone does that to him. Jim gave me the "cut" signal and lowered the camera. Gingerly, I lifted the little cat from my shoulder, and put her on the ground beside the smelly pet food. Sticking a petite pink nose right into the dish, she proceeded to enjoy her lunch, purring and eating at the same time.

Aunt Ibby hurried to join me beside the tree. "She's adorable, isn't she? I'm sure this is the cat who's gone missing from the bakery. I think I should call and tell them that Cupcake is perfectly safe here with us. I know Mrs. Duncan. Sweet woman. She must be absolutely distraught, not knowing where her husband is."

"Yes, you should," I agreed. "They won't see the shoot we just did until Jim does some editing. These human-interest stories aren't scheduled for any special time. They run them when they need a filler in the regular newscasts."

"I have a feeling this one might be different." She stroked the cat's soft back, with its random patches of black, white and orange fur. "Cupcake isn't just any old treed cat."

"If she *is* actually Mr. Duncan's pet," I said. "After all, she can't be the only wandering calico in Salem."

"True," she said. "But O'Ryan clearly thinks she's

important somehow or he wouldn't have been so intent on helping her."

I nodded agreement. "It seems as if he was warning her not to try to come down until we were here to help, doesn't it?"

Cupcake, if it was Cupcake, finished her lunch and proceeded to lick her front paws, one at a time. "I'll take her into the house," Aunt Ibby declared. "She'll be safe here until her rightful owners are found—and I'm betting it'll be the Duncan family." She picked up the cat and walked back toward the house, O'Ryan trotting along beside her. I was helping Old Jim fold the ladder when my aunt called my name. "Maralee, come and look at this!"

She stood on the front steps, holding the cat toward me. "What do you suppose this is on her paws? I thought at first it was just part of her coloring, but it seems to be coming off."

I peered at the dainty paws. All four were rusty colored, just like many of the patches of color common to calicos. I reached out and touched one forepaw. The texture of the fur there was different from her back and tummy. It was stiff and sticky from her tiny toes to her ankles—if cats have ankles—and my fingertip was smeared with a rusty spot. I sniffed at it. "It smells like oranges," I said. "She must have walked in something orange—and sticky."

"I'll take her inside and give her a nice bath," my aunt declared, cuddling the kitty close to her shoulder, exactly the way I had earlier. "I wouldn't want her tracking up the rugs."

"Maybe we should wait on that," I warned. "If

this *is* Cupcake, Mr. Duncan's cat, and he's missing, it's possible that whatever she walked in might be important somehow."

"All right. If you think so. I'll just keep her in the kitchen on the tile floor. Are you going to ask Pete about this? I mean are you going to ask him if a treed cat's footprints are important? After all, it's Halloween season. There's trick-or-treat candy being handed out free all over Salem. Or maybe she stepped on a melted Popsicle."

"Maybe," I agreed. "You're probably right. But I'll call Pete on my way back to the station anyway." Jim was already in the VW, engine running. I bid my aunt and O'Ryan and the calico goodbye and climbed into the passenger seat. "My aunt is going to call Mrs. Duncan," I told Jim. "She's convinced that the cat belongs to them."

"Could be," he said. "I felt sorry for the poor little critter, up in those branches. With those patchy colors on her it's no wonder nobody could see her. She blended right in with the fall leaves. I wonder how long she'd been there before O'Ryan found her."

"I'm going to call Pete and tell him about her. I know the department is searching for Pat Duncan. Maybe the cat is a clue." I almost bit my tongue when I said the word "clue." Pete calls me Nancy Drew whenever I say it. I couldn't help smiling. Would Nancy call this *The Clue in the Old Oak Tree?* I tapped in Pete's number.

He answered right away. "Hi, babe. I was just thinking about you."

"That's nice," I said. "What were you thinking?"

"That instead of us trying to drive anywhere for

dinner tonight in all this craziness, maybe I could pick up some takeout and bring it to your place," he said. "What do you think? Chinese or Italian?"

"Either one is fine," I told him. We do takeout a lot, since I'm not much of a cook. "Listen, I just did a stand-up on Winter Street about a treed cat. We got her down and Aunt Ibby is convinced it's a cat named Cupcake that belongs to that missing baker—Pat Duncan. I thought you might want to know about it—in case it *is* his cat."

"A female calico cat?" He used his cop voice. "Small, with different colored patches?"

"Yep."

"Where is the cat now? Do you have her?"

"Jim and I are on our way back to the station. The kitty is safe with Aunt Ibby," I told him. "She's going to call Mrs. Duncan."

"You found the cat on Winter Street?" Still in cop-voice mode. "Up in a tree?"

"Yes. The big oak in front of our house. Is it important? Do you think the cat is Cupcake?"

"Probably. Look, babe. I'm going to send someone over to your aunt's place to pick it up. I'll see you tonight."

"One more thing," I said. "Tell them to bring a carrier. She's got some kind of orange goo all over her feet. The chief won't like it if she tracks up the upholstery in a cruiser."

"Orange goo? No kidding. I'm going to head over there right now and pick her up myself. Thanks for the tip, Lee." The hang-up was abrupt—convincing me that the treed cat was undoubtedly, definitely and for sure—a *clue!*

Old Jim pulled the VW up beside the side entrance to the station and we retrieved the equipment we'd used. I carried the light stand with the LED lamps and Jim handled his camera and the shotgun mic along with the ladder. I tapped my code into the keypad with my free hand and we stepped into the cool, quiet darkness of the empty studio. In the early afternoon there's usually no live programing going on, so we walked quickly and silently past the various sets—some of them draped with sheets to keep the dust off. It's really kind of creepy in the long, black-walled room when there's nothing going on in there. Jim dropped the ladder off in the prop locker and headed for the editing room while I continued up the metal stairs to the news department's supply room, returned the lighting equipment, and continued up the stairs to the reception area.

"We're back," I announced to Rhonda. "I'm going to run across the street to the Friendly Tavern and grab a burger. I'm starving. Can I get you anything?" The Friendly is handy, the food is good and the staff knows all of us at the station.

"No thanks. I was over there earlier. I thought maybe you'd already eaten. That looks like spaghetti on your jacket," she said, peering closely at me.

I looked down at the orange smudge on the green lapel. I explained the cat print, and hoping the stain hadn't shown up on the video, I shrugged off the jacket, tossed it over one arm, took the stairs down to my office and changed back into my sweater, planning to stop at the dry cleaners on my way home.

I hadn't been kidding about being hungry. At

the Friendly I'd just begun to attack a cheese-burger and a Pepsi with an eye on the TV set over the bar when I heard my own voice. "The fire department suggested that we might be able to coax the cat down with some smelly cat food."

"Hey, that's you, Lee," the bartender called. "I heard about you rescuing a cat. I guess it has something to do with the guy that went missing from his kitchen. Weird, huh? The baker taking off like that, without his phone or his wallet or anything."

I focused on the screen, watching as O'Ryan began climbing the ladder, then cringing at the sound of my own high-pitched "here kitty, kitty," while admiring Jim's shot of the interior branches of the oak. "I didn't expect the station would run this so soon," I said, pleased that the jacket lapel looked okay. Maybe Jim had Photoshopped it somehow. "I didn't know Mr. Duncan had left his wallet and phone behind. Where did you hear that?"

"Gee, don't you watch your own station? It was all over the noon news. Scotty Palmer even had a picture of the messed-up bakery kitchen. They figure the Duncan guy took off from there in a big hurry yesterday before sunup. He even left some cakes burning in the oven—smoked the whole place up."

So that's why the Pretty Party Bakery kitchen is closed today!

"I didn't see the news," I admitted. "I was busy trying to save the cat. Do they have any idea where he went?"

"I don't know. The cops must be looking into it though. I passed by there this morning on the way to work and there were flashing lights all over the place." He leaned across the counter toward me and dropped his voice. "Ordinarily, I'd think he'd taken off on a gambling junket to Atlantic City or Biloxi or even Las Vegas, but he always takes the cute young wife with him on those trips."

"A gambler, huh?"

"Big time, I've heard. High stakes poker, the dogs and the ponies. He drops in here mostly during football season because we have all the sports channels. On the phone with his bookie the whole time."

"If he didn't take his phone or his wallet with him," I reasoned, "it must be something else."

"Guess so," he said. "Enjoy your lunch." The regular programing had resumed, and I concentrated on my cheeseburger, envying Scott Palmer's job. I'd spent my morning filling out requisition slips and ordering birthday cake and trying to talk a cat out of a tree while he'd lucked into a missing person case that already had the police involved and would probably land him the feature spot on Buck Covington's nightly newscast. Shoot. Howie Templeton's day had probably been more interesting than mine had and he was just doing a Halloween costume report.

Before long I learned that I was right about that too.

Chapter Three

The afternoon was ordinary. No more surprise assignments, but I had a chance to take a quick look at the video of Scott Palmer's noon report on my monitor, realizing once again how much I missed my old job. To make it worse, because of my desk being backed up to the window overlooking the newsroom, Scott, seated in his own desk chair, had a clear view of me watching his account of the morning's happenings at the bakery. He tapped on the window and made the phone hand signal with forefinger and pinkie and mouthed the words "Call me."

I pretended I couldn't see him. That didn't work. He tapped again. I wanted to ignore him—I knew he'd be gloating—but on the other hand, I wanted details. I picked up my desk phone and hit his name. "What's up?" I asked—as if I didn't know.

"So, you're watching me again?" he asked, grinning.

"To tell you the truth," I said, "I didn't see it the first time. I was busy with—um—something else. I just heard about it over at the restaurant. It sounded kind of interesting so I thought I'd take a look."

"Yeah, well, I wanted to ask you about that cat thing you and Old Jim did this morning."

He wants to ask me *about* my *morning?* "You do?" I tried to keep the astonishment out of my voice. "What would you like to know?"

"The cat. You really think it's Cupcake? The Duncans' missing cat? The one in the picture frame in the kitchen?" He leaned forward, closer to the glass separating us, his expression intent. "Did you talk to your cop boyfriend about it? What does he think? Do you know where the cat is now?"

"That's three questions at once, Scott." I laughed. "One at a time. Yes, I think there's a good chance she's the one. She's at my Aunt Ibby's house and Pete is going to pick her up from there."

He leaned back in his chair. "I figure the cat was there in the bakery kitchen when Duncan took off. Mrs. Duncan thinks so too. It looked like cat footprints in some spilled orange stuff on the floor."

"Yep," I agreed. "The calico had some orange goo on her feet. Does Mrs. Duncan think her husband just 'took off'? Is he in the habit of doing that?"

He shrugged. "I don't know. She seemed pretty calm. Actually, it was the burned cupcakes that made her file a missing person report with the cops in the first place. She said he always timed them exactly. The reason he was up baking in the middle of the night all alone in the building was because he's so fussy about those cupcakes. He likes to make them himself and always does it at night. She says he likes to keep the daytimes free for other things."

"Something must have happened to make him leave with the cakes still baking." I said, almost talking to myself. "I wonder what it was."

"Makes you curious, doesn't it? Like I said on the report, when the first shop help arrived in the morning, they smelled the burned cake and heard the oven timer buzzing. Somebody went in and shut off the stove and called Dolores, Mrs. Duncan."

"The cat must have followed him outside when he left the kitchen," I said, "if all the rest of the place was locked up."

"Probably. Dolores—Mrs. Duncan—said he really loves that cat. When he invented their giant three-layer cupcakes he named the cat Cupcake after them—because of the calico colors in the layers." He grinned again. "She said they'd be running short on those cupcakes today because of the ones that got burned up. They had to close the kitchen because of the smoky smell. I was lucky to get a shot of the place through the glass pane on the door. I guess you saw it. A tipped over chair and a big aluminum bowl on its side with a huge puddle of that orange stuff on the floor."

I'd run Scott's video through so fast I'd missed that shot. I didn't admit it and told myself to watch it again later when I could pay close attention to such important details. "Well, it was a really good report," I told him truthfully. "I'm thinking you'll get a feature on Buck Covington's news show tonight."

"You're right," he said, "and I'm thinking about using a couple of clips from your cat rescue since everybody agrees that you rescued the right kitty. Buck wants to know if you'd agree to come on the show with me tonight."

I managed about a two-second thoughtful pause before I said, "Yes, Scott, sure, I'd be glad to." It meant I'd have to cut dinner with Pete short. Buck's show runs from eleven to midnight when River's *Tarot Time* show begins. I knew Pete would understand. We were each used to making last-minute adjustments to accommodate the other's job.

"Great," he said. "Buck says for you to be there about fifteen minutes before eleven for makeup and light checks and—but, hey, you know the drill. I guess you've had a couple of night news features yourself, haven't you?"

A lot more than a couple, buddy, and you know it.

I didn't say it aloud though. No point in one-upping him when he was handing me my first feature appearance in a long time. What was I going to wear? There wasn't time to get the goo-smeared jacket cleaned. I ran a mental check on the contents of my closet. Being program director was a more-or-less jeans and T-shirt job, since I didn't have to be on camera, and I never had to wear heels to work anymore. It looked as though getting wardrobe, makeup, and hair presentable might take some time. It was a good thing Pete was taking care of dinner.

I'd better call him and find out what time he plans to come over to my place.

I hit his number and he answered on the first ring. "Lee, hi! I picked up that cat. It was good that you told me about it before somebody gave her a bath. The mess on her feet led us straight to the Duncans' bakery kitchen."

I didn't mention that Aunt Ibby had had every intention of washing Cupcake immediately. "I guess you would have figured out who she was anyway. A lot of Pretty Party customers recognized her right away from Scott's news report. So the orange goo was definitely from the bakery?"

"Orange marmalade," he said. "Mrs. Duncan gave me quite a lesson on the construction of triple-layer cupcakes when I returned her cat. Orange marmalade is what they glue the layers together with. Sticky, sugary and delicious."

"So Cupcake is home safely. I'm glad," I said. "The poor woman must be frantic about her missing husband by now. Did Mrs. Duncan have any idea how the cat wound up in that tree on Winter Street?"

"Nope. We're trying to figure that out. But you called me. What's going on?"

I explained about my sudden invitation to do a spot on the nightly news. "I just wondered what time you'll be over so I can figure out how to get to the station tonight on time. I'll leave here at five and I have to stop at the dry cleaners to drop off a jacket."

"No problem. I'll get out of here sometime before six. I'll phone the dinner order in to Bertini's first, then whip over to Canal Street to pick it up and come straight to your place. Do you feel like lasagna or pizza?"

"Pizza, please, and thanks for understanding about tonight. Scott says I should be in the studio at about quarter to eleven."

"I know you've been walking to work. You're certainly not thinking of walking on the common at that time of night," he said in cop voice. "I'll drive you there and back."

"I've got tomorrow morning off," I told him. "But you have to work, don't you?"

"Actually, no. I've got afternoon desk duty tomorrow. No problem."

That was a relief. He was right, of course. Salem during "Haunted Happenings" is bizarre enough in the daytime, let alone walking around alone after dark among hundreds of costumed bar-hopping revelers. "Thank you, Pete," I said. "It won't take long. They'll be showing a few of the clips of the cat coming down from the tree and Buck might ask me to comment. That's all."

"That'll be fine," he said. "If you get home before I get there, will you ask your aunt to check her security cameras for any unusual action near the oak tree lately?"

"I will," I promised. "I guess the bakery must have some good security film too."

"I'm afraid not. Mrs. Duncan says the cameras have been out all over the building for over a week. She didn't have any idea why," he said. "We're looking into it."

"The man has only been missing for a day, Pete. Does the department always get involved so quickly?"

"The first forty-eight hours are the most important in a case like this, Lee," he explained. "Pat Duncan regularly worked alone in the building at night, baking and assembling those three-layer cupcakes he invented. The regular cooks don't usually arrive until around six or so. The store manager was the first person to arrive in the morning. He heard the oven buzzer going off and smelled the cakes burning, shut off the stove, opened the back door to let the smoke out and called Mrs. Duncan right away."

"And she called the police?"

"Sure. It wasn't like Pat to let those cakes burn. Chief sent a team over. It didn't look right so they sealed the room off until we get a chance to thoroughly check the place out."

"Checking for evidence," I offered. "Fingerprints and things that don't belong there. The tipped-over chair and that spilled orange cupcake filling."

"You caught that in the video Scott Palmer shot." *Not until Scott pointed it out.* "Did I ever tell you you'd make a good cop?"

"Only about a hundred times," I said. "No thanks. I'm much better at directing kiddie shows and making the occasional cat rescue. I'll see you at around six. Love you."

"I love you back. 'Bye."

I looked at my watch. It was only four o'clock. It occurred to me that Mr. Doan might allow me to clock out early, since I'd be working later tonight. I headed back up to the second-floor reception area. "Oh, hi, Lee," Rhonda greeted me. "I was about to call you. Doan has left for the day. He's gone home to help Buffy with the plans for her big Halloween party. There's no reason you can't leave early too. Besides that, he says since you're working so late tonight you don't have to come in until noon tomorrow." She pointed to the white-board where daily duties were posted. "Nothing for you until tonight at eleven. Your first gig on the late news in a long time, huh?"

"Right. I can use the extra time to get myself ready—mentally and physically." Rhonda assured me that I'd be great, that doing the late news was like riding a bicycle—you never forget how to do it. I didn't quite get the analogy, but I hurried back to my office, grabbed the green jacket, then rode Old Clunky down to the first-floor lobby and stepped out onto Derby Street. The dry cleaner's shop on Hawthorne Boulevard was about halfway to the common. I'd be able to pick up my jacket the following afternoon. Perfect.

Cool, crisp October weather makes for pleasant walking. Passing the occasional green-faced witch or flying monkey or fairy princess made it enter-taining too. Costumed performers are an everyday sight year-round on Salem's downtown streets, but in October they're literally everywhere.

O'Ryan was waiting at the front door when I got home, his fuzzy face greeting me from the tall win-dow next to the door. I stooped to tap on the glass. Boom. Flashing lights and swirling colors and the cabin in the woods was back.

Chapter Four

The vision cleared away faster than most of them do. The cabin was gone and O'Ryan, leaving nose prints on the window, his golden eyes focused on my green ones, put one paw up against the window. I took it as a "calm down" gesture from my wise cat. Shaking away the recent image, I stood, took a deep breath, pulled my keys from my purse and opened the door.

"Aunt Ibby. It's me." Stepping into the foyer, I gave the usual call. The stairs leading up to my own third-floor apartment were in front of me, the arched doorway to my aunt's formal living room to my left. O'Ryan did a couple of figure eights around my ankles and headed through the living room toward her kitchen. I followed the cat, the sound of Elvis singing "Blue Hawaii," and the smell of something wonderful cooking.

"I'm in the kitchen," she answered. "You're home

early." She appeared in the doorway, a red-and-white checked bib apron lettered with "Kiss the Cook" in black script protecting her trim-fitting gray denim pant suit. "I'm making a lovely beef burgundy. Can you stay for dinner?"

"Pete's bringing takeout," I told her. "He says he picked up the cat."

"Good thing he did. It wouldn't have taken me long to fall in love with the dear little thing. Come, sit down and visit with me." She turned down the radio and pointed to a captain's chair beside the round oak table. "I expect that Mrs. Duncan was thrilled to have her back."

"She must have been. She told Scott that her husband really loves the cat and the cat loves him. It follows him everywhere. He named her after those fancy three-layer cupcakes because of her three-colored fur."

"Did Pete find out what the orange stuff staining her paws is?"

"Orange marmalade. It's the filling between the cupcake layers. Maybe I'll find out some more about it tonight," I said. "I've been invited to be on the late news. Buck Covington invited Scott and they want to show some of the footage Jim and I got of Cupcake coming down from the tree."

"How exciting. It's been a while since you've been on that show."

"Tell me about it," I said. "I need to get upstairs and figure out what to wear and what to do with my hair."

"I'm sure you'll be just fine," she told me—just as she'd told me so many times since I was five. I told her about Pete's request that she check the videos from the surveillance cameras for anything unusual going on near the oak tree. She promised to do it as soon as the beef burgundy was done. I kissed her on the cheek and climbed the two flights of stairs to my apartment, O'Ryan tagging along behind me. I turned my kitchen TV on to the WICH-TV evening news. I do that automatically after work, mostly listening rather than watching as the daytime news anchor Phil Archer catches me up on what's happening in Salem and the world.

I ducked into the bedroom and spread several outfits onto the top of my king-sized bed. After trying out several combinations, decided on my best designer jeans and a tailored pink silk shirt. Aunt Ibby had long ago convinced me that the "old wives' tale" that redheads should never wear pink was actually a "*jealous* old wives'" tale and that we look absolutely fine in pink. The jeans would be okay too because my bottom half would be behind the news desk. I dressed, fluffed out my hair, and took my time doing camera-ready makeup.

It was exactly six o'clock when I heard Pete's key turn in the lock on my back door. I covered my blouse and jeans with one of Aunt Ibby's long bib aprons, hurried to the kitchen, where we shared the kind of kiss that threatened to delay dinner long enough for the pizza to get cold. Resisting that temptation, Pete opened a cold bottle of Pepsi while I set the table with plates and glasses. I didn't even attempt to hide my curiosity about Pat Duncan's disappearance. "So, did your team find anything important in the kitchen at the bakery?"

"You're not going to be talking about anything except the cat on the news show, are you?" he wanted to know.

"Just about rescuing Cupcake," I said. "Everybody already knows she's the Duncans' cat."

"I guess it'll be all right for you to say the cat's footprints were on the kitchen floor at the bakery."

"In the orange marmalade," I said. "Anything else?"

"Nothing that has to do with the cat." Cop face.

"Off the record then, what about other footprints? Like people, not cats?" Pete knows when I say "off the record" I mean it.

"It's a busy kitchen, Lee. But there were some other footprints with traces of the orange goo on them. Pat Duncan's of course, and the guy who came in and turned the oven off and opened the door . . ." He paused. "There's one more set we haven't identified. They could be from some kind of rain boots."

"That's odd. It hasn't rained here in over a week." I took a big bite of my pizza. My favorite—with sausage, mushrooms, green pepper and extra cheese—waiting to see if he'd continue and offer something else new. Nothing. I took a sip of Pepsi and pushed my luck. "I was at the Friendly Tavern today and there was some talk about Pat being quite a gambler. They thought at first he might be off on a junket to Atlantic City or Biloxi. Did you hear anything like that?"

"Good observation, Lee. I'll make a cop out of you yet." Big smile. "Nobody actually *said* anything about it, but the kitchen wastebasket gave up quite a lot of information about our friendly neighborhood cupcake baker."

"For instance?" I prompted.

"In among some eggshells and empty cardboard coffee cups we turned up a handful of torn-in-half Keno cards, about a hundred used lottery scratch-off cards, another fifty Lotto and Powerball tickets and yesterday's copy of *Vegas Insider.*" He shook his head. "Yes, ma'am. I'd say old Pat has a gambling problem. That was just yesterday's trash. He must place bets on anything and everything everywhere he goes during the day."

"Didn't Mrs. Duncan—Dolores—say anything about it?" I wondered aloud. "The guys at the Friendly say she goes with him on the out-of-town casino trips."

"She didn't comment about it one way or the other," he said. "She was mostly concerned about getting the kitchen back in order so they can start pumping out those cupcakes again. She seemed confident that her husband is okay—wherever he is—and he'll want her to keep the place operational."

"And *is* the kitchen back to normal?" I asked. "I have to pick up a birthday cake there tomorrow."

"They'll have to clean the oven, scrub the place down, but yes, it's useable." He refilled his glass. "We still need to talk to a few people. Somebody must have an idea of where he is. And naturally, we're requesting home surveillance tapes from all of the surrounding area. Did you ask your aunt to check hers?"

"I sure did. She said she'd do it as soon as the beef burgundy was done."

He put another slice of pizza onto his plate. "Beef burgundy? Maybe we should have invited ourselves downstairs for dinner."

"I'm sure there'll be leftovers. Maybe when we get back from the station if she's still up we can grab a bowlful while you take a look at her videos," I suggested. "Is the department still calling his disappearance 'under unusual circumstances' or does it rate 'suspicious' by now?"

"It rates suspicious," he said. "That's partly because his wallet and phone are still in his room at home, but mostly because of the burned cakes. Everybody agrees that he would never let that happen if he could help it."

From the TV I heard Howard Templeton's voice. He was using what I call his big network voice—deeper than normal and sort of excited sounding. "Oh, there's Howie. This must be his report on what's hot and what's not in this year's Halloween costumes. Want to watch?"

"Sure. Why not?" he said. And we each turned in our chairs to face the set. Howie stood in the foreground of the shot, facing Chris Rich, the owner of Christopher's Castle. Behind the two, an enormous revolving clothes rack turned slowly, displaying what must have been many hundreds of colorful costumes. One at a time, Chris removed a garment from the display and described it for the audience, while Howie asked a few—probably rehearsed—questions. The display began with the always popular superheroes, with Chris confiding that Batman is still the most popular superhero of all. A muscular male model displayed a Spiderman outfit, accompanied by a glamorous Black Widow. Chris Rich is good at getting all the free advertising he can and he made the most of Howie's field report. Costumes from Marvel's Wolverine to Disney's Mickey Mouse flashed by with rapid-fire commentary.

"Chris, what costume do you expect to sell the most of this Halloween?" Howie asked breathlessly.

Chris laughed. "Truthfully, I believe it will be an inexpensive astronaut costume."

Howie made a surprised face. "An astronaut? I thought for sure you'd say Spiderman."

Chris tried to look sad. "Here is the year's biggest bargain—just twenty dollars in men's sizes and ten dollars in boys' sizes." A model appeared in full silver-colored space gear, from face-covering bubble helmet to silver boots.

"Looks good," Howie said. "That's a huge bargain this close to Halloween."

"Don't I know it." Chris spoke directly to the audience. "Here's how it happened. I ordered a gross of men's and boys' assorted costumes. Somehow my abbreviation for 'assorted' got read as 'astronaut.' I wound up with twelve dozen of these. That's one hundred and forty-four. They're from China. Too late to send them back. My mistake. You get the bargain! I've already sold over a dozen, so hurry in to Christopher's Castle today to get yours!"

"Wow," Howie marveled. "I guess we'll be seeing lots of people in space suits this year then."

"I sincerely hope so," Chris agreed, with a big wink. With that, Howie signed off.

Pete and I both laughed. "That's funny," Pete said. "Imagine getting stuck with all those identical costumes. Poor Chris."

"The price is right though," I said. "I'll bet he sells every single one of them."

"Really? You know more about that stuff than I do. We have plenty of time to go downstairs now. Let's see if your aunt has had a chance to check her cameras."

I removed the apron, put the two remaining slices of pizza into the refrigerator, put our plates into the dishwasher, dumped the paper containers and the empty Pepsi bottle into recycling bags, turned off the TV and headed downstairs, with O'Ryan following us once again.

Aunt Ibby indeed had plenty of her sumptuous stew left over and Pete enjoyed a bowlful while we watched the small surveillance screen on her home office desk. "The nighttime film is sort of dark, but by early morning everything is nice and clear." She pointed to the screen. "See? There's the lady next door walking her poodles. Look. One of them lifted his leg at the base of the oak tree. The time stamp says it was shortly after midnight last night. Then here comes the girl from the other side of this house just getting home from a date in that nice white car." After the white car pulled away from the curb, we saw several other vehicles go by—no foot traffic except for one more dog walker, who did not clean up after his fox terrier. All three of us commented on his bad behavior, then remained silently focused on the screen.

"Here we go," Aunt Ibby announced. "The only interesting part will come up in a minute. Watch for it."

A man walked into the frame, leaned against the oak tree, and every few seconds, moved to the curb and appeared to be looking for something. It was hard to tell exactly which way he was looking because of the bubble helmet obscuring his face. "Astronauts," Pete declared.

"A hundred and forty-four of them," I agreed.

Aunt Ibby looked from one of us to the other, clearly confused. "See? It's a person in a spaceman Halloween costume waiting for a taxi. There he goes, climbing into the cab. A hundred and forty-four of what?"

Pete and I both started to explain at once the costume kerfuffle at Chris Rich's store. She held up both of her hands. "One at a time, please!" Laughing at the confusion, I stopped speaking, listening while Pete told her what we'd heard on the news, and watched O'Ryan as he stretched, then stood up in the chair where he'd been quietly observing the small screen. He surprised me when he hopped up onto the desk, getting as close to the picture as he could. "Mrrup," he said, touching the screen with a soft paw. "Mrrup!"

He was clearly trying to show me something. I leaned in, watching that paw as it traced the edges of the brick sidewalk as the cab pulled away onto Winter Street. At first I thought what he was watching so intently was a cluster of leaves, tumbling in the morning breeze. Then headlights caught two bright spots at the foot of the oak tree. A small cat's eyes.

"Cupcake!" I yelled. "Look!" Pete and my aunt returned their attention to the screen just as that fox terrier reappeared and the cat named Cupcake scooted up into the tree.

"Can you rewind that please, Ibby?" Pete's cop voice was back. "Back to where the costumed man appeared."

We three, along with O'Ryan, watched as the figure looked up and down the street and finally climbed into a cab. I saw Pete scribble the cab's license plate number onto the edge of a handy desk calendar. My aunt slowed the video down and we saw the now easily identifiable calico cat running along the brick sidewalk, only reaching the base of the tree as the cab pulled away.

"Cupcake was chasing that man," I declared. "No doubt about it."

"It appears that way," my aunt agreed. "Doesn't it, Pete?"

"Maybe." The reply was hesitant. "Do cats do that?"

"I've read about cats finding their way home from many miles away," Aunt Ibby declared firmly.

"That's different," Pete said. "That's homing instinct. Cupcake never lived on Winter Street that we know of."

"O'Ryan could do it if he wanted to. If somebody hurt me he'd chase them." I was sure of it.

"Maybe," Pete said again. "I'm going to phone that cab number in to the chief, then let's take another look at that astronaut." He stepped out of the office while my aunt rewound the tape and then slowed it where the costumed man leaned against the oak tree. In what seemed like seconds, Pete was back.

"Like this?" Aunt Ibby asked him.

"Perfect." He moved closer to the screen. "Lee, would you say those spaceman boots look a little bit like fancy rain boots?"

I knew he was right. "You're thinking of the other footprints in the kitchen. The ones in the orange marmalade."

Chapter Five

Pete looked up at the kitchen clock. "It's almost nine. Do you think Christopher's Castle is still open? I'd like to get one of those space suits. We need to examine the boots."

"I'll call Chris," I offered. Chris Rich is a major advertiser on WICH-TV, so I have his number in my phone.

"Hello, Lee. Don't tell me you're still working at this time of night," he said.

"Not exactly," I told him. "The station just ran that interview you did with Howard Templeton, and Pete and I were wondering if you're still open. We're interested in buying one of your astronaut costumes."

"We close at nine," he said. "I'm just getting ready to lock up. I'll put one aside for you. You can pick it up tomorrow if you want to. Is it for Pete?"

"Not exactly," I said again. "If you'll still be there

for a little while we can come right over and pick it up tonight."

"An early party going on? Sure, I'll be here. I appreciate the publicity you guys give me. I missed seeing the interview. Did everything look good?"

"Everything looked really good," I said. "You have a great selection and I'm sure you'll get rid of all those space suits pretty fast."

"I hope so. It's kind of funny, isn't it? Picturing a hundred and forty-four astronauts wandering around Salem at the same time?" He chuckled. "Say, that might be worth another feature."

"Could be," I said. "I'm doing a bit with Scott Palmer tonight on Buck's show at eleven, so if we come right now that would be perfect. Okay?"

"No kidding. Boy, it's been a long time since you've done one of those, hasn't it? I'll be here for another fifteen minutes or so. Come right on over."

Reminded once again how few and far between my TV appearances had been lately, I told Chris we'd be right along.

"We should go right now," I told Pete. "There'll be lots of traffic to contend with."

He grinned. "That's what lights and sirens are for, sweetheart. Let's go."

Pete thanked Aunt Ibby for sharing the video and I gave O'Ryan a kiss on the head and a whispered, "You are the smartest cat in the world." He acknowledged the compliment by giving me a pink-tongued lick on the chin.

It turned out that we didn't need lights and sirens to get us to Christopher's Castle in the allotted fifteen minutes. Pete's a good driver and because of his job he knows his way around every inch of street, avenue, way, lane and boulevard in Salem. We traveled what seemed to me to be a strangely circuitous route and somehow wound up in the parking lot right behind Christopher's Castle in ten minutes flat. Chris, wearing a magician's outfit, complete with top hat and monocle, greeted us at the door.

"Welcome to my castle," he intoned, "where wonders await you."

"Thanks for letting us in, Chris," I said. "I know this is a busy time for you."

"Glad to help a friend," he said. "Are we looking for the astronaut suit to fit you, Pete?"

"Sure. Why not? I might get invited to a Halloween party. Can I ask what size the space boots are that come with it?"

"Sure. Size eleven medium."

"Close enough," Pete said. "I wear a ten."

"Do you want to try the whole outfit on?" Chris asked. "No returns at this price."

"No problem. We'll take it as is." He handed Chris his credit card and pocketed the receipt. "You mentioned to Templeton that you'd sold a dozen or so of these costumes. Do you happen to have the names of the people who bought them?"

Chris looked thoughtful. "A few of them are regular customers, so I know them," he said, "and most people used credit cards, so I could look them up. Some paid cash though. Is it important?"

"It might be," Pete told him.

"I'll try to make a list for you as soon as I can find time to do it," Chris promised. "This is my high season, you know."

"I understand. Thanks for staying open for us. We have to get going. Lee has a news show to do."

"Sure thing. Break a leg, Lee," he said. "Ask Doan about a feature on the hundred and forty-four astronauts, okay?"

"I will," I promised, thinking that one of those anonymous astronauts might show up on a crime show before long.

The ride to WICH-TV took a little longer to negotiate, but we were still in plenty of time for Buck's program. We left the wrapped space suit in the backseat of Pete's car, and I tapped my code into the keypad beside the studio door. The long room was mostly in darkness, but I could see from the doorway that River's *Tarot Time* set was brightly illuminated.

"I'd like to drop by and tell River we're here," I suggested. "I haven't had a chance to talk to her in a couple of days. There's something I wanted to ask her about." I've always hesitated to call her on the days she worked. I used to work that midnight-to-two-in-the-morning slot myself, so I knew that River needed her daytime sleep. I really wanted to talk to somebody besides Pete about the cabin in the woods vision though, and River could often make some sense out of things when I couldn't. She said it was something like dream analyzing.

"You go ahead," Pete said. "I'm going to see if I can track Scott down. I'd like to get a close-up look at that shot he took through the window of the bakery kitchen. I'll see you in the newsroom."

I hurried down the wide aisle to the set with its blue nighttime sky backdrop, replete with sparkling stars and moon. River, gorgeous in a red satin gown with a large rhinestone spider pin on one shoulder, silver stars braided into her long black hair, sat in her big fan-back wicker chair facing the round table where candles, crystal clusters and amethyst geodes shared space with the beautiful tarot deck.

Camerawoman Marty McCarthy stood nearby, her head beneath the covering hood of a wheeled studio camera focused on what appeared to be a large greeting card with an illustration of angels on it. River is fond of ethereal images on screen while her theme music "Danse Macabre" introduces the show. She jumped up to greet me with a patchouli-scented hug.

"Oh, Lee, I haven't seen you in days. I miss you."

"Miss you too." I dropped my voice, which seemed to echo in the long, silent room. "I have so much I want to talk to you about."

She reached for the tarot deck. "Do you think we have time for a quick reading? I know you're doing Buck's show tonight."

"I'm afraid not," I said. "But something has happened today. I'd like to know what you think it might mean." I looked toward the camerawoman. "It's kind of personal."

Marty poked her head out from behind the camera. "I'm heading for the break room anyway. I'll leave you two to talk."

I hadn't meant to scare Marty away, but I was glad to be alone with my friend. "I had a vision today. Actually, I've seen it twice. I'd like to know what you think it means."

"A vision is different from a dream, you know, but the symbols may tell the same stories." She gestured toward a chair on the opposite side of the table. "The symbols may refer to things happening in the present, the past or the future. But you already know that. Have a seat and tell me about it."

"It's not an unpleasant scene," I recalled. "It's just a cabin in the woods."

"Do you recognize the place, Lee? Maybe a cabin you visited or stayed in when you were a child?" she asked.

"I don't think so. It's just a cabin." I closed my eyes. "It has a chimney on one end, and several windows. There's a small porch."

"It's an unknown place to you then. Is it a place you want to explore?"

"I think so. Yes."

"In the dream world," River said, "this can be a place of danger. Or refuge. Or a chance for adventure. Some readers compare it to the Little Red Riding Hood myth."

"Not very specific."

"In a way it is. I'd guess it's a calling from the unconscious relating to an outside threat that you don't fully understand yet." She paused. "In your case, considering some of your other visions, it could be a real place. A real cabin in real woods."

"And if it is?"

"You've had the same vision twice. If—or when—it comes again, try to move closer. You say there are windows. Try to look inside."

"I will," I promised. "And I hope the big bad wolf isn't in there."

"Have you told Pete about the cabin?"

"No. You know he doesn't like to talk about

these things." It was true. He loves River, but calls what she does "River's hocus-pocus."

"Maybe you should mention it. What if you find it by yourself and it really *is* a place of danger?"

"Thanks, River," I said. "I'd better get up to the newsroom now. I'll think about all you've said. I love you." I stood and stepped back into the aisle.

"Love you too, Little Red Riding Hood. Be careful."

I hurried through the darkness toward the metal door leading to the news department, glad when I reached the brightly lighted corridor beside the glass wall where the hustle of a lively news team was already visible. It takes quite a few people to make a live newscast happen. Wanda the weather girl was already in position in front of the green screen, and the producer, the news editor, a sound engineer, camera crew and several technicians were all busily occupied. Buck Covington was seated at the anchor desk while makeup woman Dolly dusted a bit of bronzer onto his already handsome face. Across the room I saw Scott at his desk in his usual corner. Pete was alone in the section reserved for guests, looking at his phone. I held up my station ID card and entered the roomful of activity, thinking again about how much I like being part of this team.

Pete saw me right away and started across the room in my direction. I met him halfway and asked, "Did you find anything new in that kitchen shot?"

"Maybe. I'm not exactly sure. Did River answer the question you had?"

"Maybe," I echoed. "I'm not exactly sure."

"You look beautiful," he said. "Break a leg."

Apparently, my makeup job wasn't too bad. Dolly added a bit of blush and did something with a comb and hairspray to tame my curls and adjusted the clip mic on my shirt. During a commercial break after some national news and a promo about the Haunted Happenings marketplace, I took my seat beside Scott—who was seated next to Buck. Third seat on the nightly news was a lot better than no seat at all.

Buck started the segment with a clip from Scott's original coverage of Pat Duncan's disappearance. "You were one of the first on the scene, Scott," he said. "How did you find out about it?"

Scott did one of his trademark long stares into the camera. "To tell the truth, Buck," he said, "it was just a case of dumb luck. I've been walking to work because of all the traffic you know, and I picked up the habit of stopping every morning at the Pretty Party for coffee and a couple of doughnuts to go. There were a few police cars out front. Dolores—that's Mrs. Duncan—was working the front counter and I asked her what was going on. I didn't have any crew with me. Those shots you just aired were from my phone camera. I was lucky to get the picture of the kitchen through the window. Mrs. Duncan told me about how her husband always baked the cupcakes at night—and how he'd never leave them to burn. There was a picture of the cat he named Cupcake on the wall of the shop and I got a shot of that too."

"That brings us to our other guest, Lee Barrett, a familiar name and face to regular viewers of WICH-TV." He smiled in my direction. "Lee, you had more than a picture of little Cupcake, the calico cat. You got to meet her firsthand with a daring tree rescue. We'll give our audience a look at what happened when you decided to help a treed cat. Tell us about it."

"I was there because our station manager, Bruce Doan, thought helping a cat in trouble would tell a story people would like to see," I told him. "We had no idea that the sad kitty crying in the branches of a huge oak tree on Winter Street would turn out to be connected to a current missing person case being investigated by the police. The tree happened to be close to my home, and my cat—his name is O'Ryan—was the one who let us know about poor Cupcake being stranded up there."

"O'Ryan may be familiar to WICH-TV viewers," Buck put in. "He once belonged to Ariel Constellation, who many remember as the host of the late show *Nightshades.* Now he lives with you, is that right, Lee?"

"He lives with my aunt and me. If it wasn't for O'Ryan's yowling to get our attention we might not have been able to save the cat in the tree." I watched on the monitor as Cupcake dropped from the branches and landed on the ladder's platform. Talk about dumb luck! "Cupcake is happily at home with Mrs. Duncan now. I'm glad we could help."

"We are too, Scott and Lee. Thanks for sharing your stories with us. Salem police are asking for the community's help in locating the missing bakery owner, Patrick Duncan." A picture of the missing man flashed onto the screen. "If you have any knowledge of where he might be, please call the number at the bottom of your screen. Now, let's hear about the weather from our meteorologist, Wanda."

Scott and I were ushered off the set while Wanda took over from in front of the green screen. "Good job, Lee," Scott said. "We should work together more often. Thank O'Ryan for me and—by the way—see if he has any ideas about where Pat Duncan is hiding out."

"I'll do that," I said, as we walked together toward the edge of the glassed-in room to where Pete waited.

"You might ask Pete too."

I didn't bother to answer that one. "Good night, Scott. See you tomorrow."

Pete and I left the building quietly via the studio door with River's theme music issuing from the lighted set midway down the long studio. "Want to take a side trip up to Rockport? The chief ran that license number so we know where the cab took our astronaut. I'd like to see just where he went."

"Sure. Why not? We can both sleep in tomorrow. Do you know who called the cab in the first place?"

"We don't know who called. The dispatcher said it sounded like somebody with a bad cold—and the call came from the Pretty Party Bakery."

"No kidding. Do you guess it was somebody disguising their voice? Sounding like they had a cold?"

He held the passenger door open for me. "It's not my job to guess," he said in a very stern cop voice, effectively ending conversation on that topic. I climbed into the passenger seat and figured I might as well change the subject. "How did you like the segment? Scott thinks we should work together more often."

"It looked good. As Scott said, he lucked into the story. O'Ryan helped to put you into the mix."

"Don't I know it. You say you're not sure if Scott's kitchen window picture was helpful or not?"

"That's right. There was something about the orange footprints. Our team found shoe prints from Pat, naturally, and from Tommy LaGrange, the general manager who shut off the oven and took the burned cupcakes out, and there were prints that look like they could be from the space boots, and some from the cat, of course. Tommy, the GM, showed us the shoes he'd worn that morning and Mrs. Duncan said that Pat wears a size nine, so his were easy to identify. The thing is, the prints from Pat's shoes were mostly around the work space. None of them led to the outer door. So how did he get out?"

"Do you think he didn't go outdoors willingly? Do you think somebody might have actually *carried* him out of there?"

He shrugged. "Anything is possible." Pete pulled the cruiser onto Derby Street and before long we were heading north on Route 128. I recognized some landmarks along the way. "I've always liked this ride," I said.

"Me too." Pete smiled. "When I was a kid I went to a Boy Scout camp in the woods just between Rockport and Gloucester."

"I used to go horseback riding around there when *I* was a kid," I remembered. "Boy, could you get lost in those woods."

"I know," he said. "Acres of trees and dirt roads and stone fences and the occasional old run-down cabin." *Old cabin?* Was River right? Was my vision just a recollection of a place I'd seen when I was a preteen?

"I hope you're not planning to get us lost in those creepy woods," I said.

"Absolutely not. Just a drive-by. The cab driver says he dropped off a guy in a space suit at Sam's Super Scoops right at the edge of those woods. I checked it out. They're open until two a.m. You up for some late-night ice cream and maybe a nostalgia trip past Camp Red Arrow?"

I agreed. "I'm always ready for chocolate ice cream, and a ride in the woods is okay as long as I can stay in the car."

"Done," he said as we turned onto a dark and winding road—needed high beams—and located the faded ghost sign that marked the entrance to Camp Red Arrow, not far from the riding stables where I'd fallen in love with a pony named Smoothie. Returning to the main road, I thanked him for the trip down memory lane, but welcomed the cheery, brightly lighted, pink and blue Sam's Super Scoops sign. Inside, the shop was warm and welcoming. We each took a seat at the bright pink counter. The chocolate ice cream—with some hot fudge added—was worth the trip to me.

We were the only customers in the place. Pete questioned the server about the costumed space-man who'd arrived by cab a day earlier. "I just work the night shift," he said. "The daytime crew would have seen him. They work ten to six. I'm here from six to two." He leaned forward, his elbows on the counter. "But I think I might know where that costume is."

"You do? Where?" Pete stood, opened his wallet and showed his badge. "It may be important."

"It's in the Dumpster out back," he said. "At least that round helmet is. I was going to grab it for one of my kids, but there was a bunch of trash on top, coffee grounds, banana peels, dirty paper plates, yucky stuff from the rest rooms. You know. You have to be careful about germs these days."

"Mind if I take a look?" Cop voice.

"Go right ahead. You want some rubber gloves? I have plenty of the food-service kind. I'm telling you, it's pretty gross."

"Thanks," Pete told him. "I have gloves and a flashlight in my car, but I could use a big plastic bag if you have one."

Within minutes, and before I'd had the last spoonful of my ice cream, we were behind Sam's Super Scoops with the Dumpster lid propped up, both of us in police department issued gloves, me with a flashlight in one hand, holding a huge black plastic bag open with the other while Pete dove into the mess and came up with not only the bub-ble helmet, but the silver suit and a pair of boots.

We each cleaned up the best we could in the restrooms, bought a couple of quarts of ice cream to go—vanilla for Pete and chocolate for me—and headed back to Salem with the bag of evidence in the trunk of the cruiser.

It was darned near three a.m. when we reached Winter Street. "I need a shower," he said. "Have you got anything in the apartment for breakfast?" he asked.

"Strawberry Pop-Tarts, cold pizza and coffee," I offered.

"Good deal," he said, and it was mutually agreed that—after we each took showers—he'd stay the night.

Chapter Six

It was eight o'clock and the sun was up when I awoke to the smell of coffee and the sound of country music on the radio. That meant for sure that there'd be a shaved, showered, dressed, good-smelling man in my kitchen. I struggled into robe and slippers and mumbled "good morning" as I passed him on my way to the bathroom while Bobby Joe Bell boomed out "Line Dancing" in the background.

Then, showered for the second time that morning, teeth brushed and hair still looking pretty good, I dressed in jeans and a Boston Celtics T-shirt, returned to the kitchen and gave Pete a proper good-morning kiss. I poured myself a cup of coffee—Pete had already had his—and put two Pop-Tarts into the toaster.

"Do you have any plans for this morning?" Pete asked.

"Nope. I have to pick up Buck's birthday cake from the Pretty Party at noon," I said. "I have no plans until then. What about you?"

"I'm not on the clock until the afternoon shift comes on," he said, "but I want to go in now and get forensics to go over the Dumpster suit. Then I want to do some tests with my own space suit costume. I'll make some plaster cast footprints with the boots on, figure out how well I can see in the dark with that bubble mask over my face, generally try to figure out how the guy your aunt caught on camera felt before the cab picked him up."

"Is there anything I can do to help?" I wondered, channeling my inner Nancy Drew.

"There might be," he said. "I've been wondering about Pat Duncan's gambling habit that you mentioned."

"The people at the Friendly Tavern seem to think it's serious."

"Mrs. Duncan brushed it off as 'Pat's little hobby,'" he said. "But the store manager, Tommy LaGrange, is concerned about it. It seems Pat hasn't been paying his bills. Some vendors have stopped delivery to the store recently, and the security system people aren't monitoring the place anymore because they haven't been paid in months. LaGrange is trying to stall off the creditors the best he can, but the future for the business doesn't look good."

"That's bad news," I said.

"I'm wondering if Pat is in trouble with anybody over a gambling debt. Want to drop by the Friendly and sort of nose around? Those guys stick together.

They're not going to want to talk to a cop, that's for sure."

"I could do that," I said, suddenly feeling like an investigative reporter again.

"I'd appreciate it," he said. "Call me right away if you learn anything."

"I will," I promised. "Will you call me and tell me what you learn from the Dumpster suit?"

"Maybe," he said, gave me a quick kiss and headed out the kitchen door.

I wonder if I should tell him about the vision I've seen twice. I very nearly called him to come back, but no. He had enough on his mind for now, I decided. Maybe if I saw the cabin again, and got a closer look as River suggested, there'd be something useful to report—not just hocus-pocus.

Another beautiful day for walking across the common. I wished a good morning to some of the "regulars," like Stacia, the pigeon lady, and Joe, the popcorn man. Once I got to Hawthorne Boulevard, the costumed people began to show up—even this early in the day. I saw a Green Hornet walking with an angel, complete with real feather wings, and a tiny Scooby-Doo in a stroller being pushed by a Wonder Woman mom. "Chris Rich must be having a blockbuster month," I said to myself, "overstock of astronaut suits or not." I'd already decided that if I was invited to Buffy Doan's annual Halloween party and needed a costume, I'd wear last year's Princess Leia getup. But if Pete decided to actually wear the space suit, maybe I'd see what Chris had in the green alien girl department.

I reached the WICH-TV building and scooted across the street to the Friendly Tavern.

They open officially at noon, but I was pretty sure the "Breakfast Club" would be there, having morning coffee and doughnuts—a few third-watch guys from the coast guard station and the fire department, some eleven to seven shift nurses from Salem Hospital, maybe some guys from the local men's hockey teams who had early ice time. The bell over the door jingled and a few heads turned my way.

"Hey, there's Lee!" came the greeting from bartender Leo. "Saw you on the late news. Rescuing cats these days, huh?"

"Somebody's gotta do it." I took a stool at the bar. "But right now I need a large coffee to go to wake me up. I hardly slept at all last night."

"Late date?" He put the tall coffee cup in front of me.

"Not exactly," I hedged. "I miss getting those late news show gigs, so I was doing a little extra investigating about your friend Pat Duncan's disappearance." I glanced around, hoping some of Pat's gambling buddies might hear me. "After the show last night I took a ride to Rockport. I had a tip from a guy who works up there."

Crickets. No response. I pushed the envelope some more. "I hope Pat's okay—that he might just be ducking out on somebody he owes money to."

There was a thinly disguised snicker from the man beside me. "That'd be quite a list. He still owes me fifty from September's Salem-Masconomet game."

Another grumbling comment came from one of the firemen. "He's always late paying up, but he usually gets around to it eventually."

"Not lately," came another voice. "He hasn't even been in here for a couple of weeks. Not even for the North Carolina NASCAR race."

A white-haired man a few seats over from me spoke. I heard the word "Rockport," and strained to hear the rest of his words. "Excuse me, sir," I said. "What did you say?"

He spoke louder. "I've known Pat since he was a pup. Knew his folks too. They started that bakery you know. Pat was a good kid, but always liked betting on the ponies and such. I heard you say something about Rockport. Pat's folks used to have a summer place on a little lake up that way. Pat used to invite my kids up there for weekends in that cabin sometimes when they were all youngsters." He sighed. "I suppose he's gone and gambled that place away by now too."

Boom! A summer place on a little lake. Was that what I was seeing in my vision? Even if I was wrong, I was sure I'd better tell Pete about it. What if the astronaut who'd stuffed his costume into a Dumpster knows where the cabin is? We might have been within walking distance of it when we were eating ice cream.

I thanked the white-haired gent, finished my coffee, paid the bill and said, "Thanks for watching the great cat rescue, Leo." I dropped my voice and leaned across the counter. "I'm serious about looking into Duncan's disappearance. If you hear anything new I'd appreciate a call." I handed him my card. He tucked it into his shirt pocket and gave me a thumbs-up.

"If it'll help you get some more of those 'late show gigs' I'm all in," he said.

"Thanks, Leo," I said, then gave a wave to the group. "See you all later." As soon as I was outside, I called Pete and told him the whole story about the vision and what River had said about moving closer to the windows and what the man in the tavern had just revealed.

He didn't comment on the vision or River's advice. "You're sure the man said Pat's parents owned it?"

I told him I was sure.

"Thanks, Lee," he said. "If the guy is right, it won't be hard to get an address."

I hadn't had a chance to ask if forensics had finished with the suit, but I was happy to think I'd been helpful. I walked across the street to WICH-TV. As long as I was there, and quite wide awake, going to work wasn't such a bad idea. I opened the lobby door and headed for Old Clunky. The beautiful old brass doors had been polished recently. I saw my reflection in the bright metal. The swirling colors shouldn't have surprised me.

The cabin was there. I felt myself moving—floating really—toward the porch, toward the window. I looked inside.

I felt quite sure that the man lying facedown on the floor must be dead.

The brass door slid open, the vision popped away and I found myself looking straight at Scott Palmer. He squinted, frowned. "You okay, Lee? You don't look too good."

I reached for my most recently used alibi. "I need coffee," I mumbled. "Hardly slept a wink last night."

"Too excited because I got you on the late news, huh?" he said. "Guess it doesn't happen for you that much anymore. Well, there's a fresh pot going in the break room. Have a good day," and he was gone before I had a chance to think of an appropriate comeback.

What a smart-ass.

I took him up on the coffee suggestion though, and headed for the break room. I knew I needed to call Pete about the new vision right away. There was a dead man in a cabin somewhere. I was positive about that. Who he was, and where the cabin was, would be up to the police to figure out. I didn't even say hello when he answered. "Pete. Listen. There's a man on the floor of that house in the woods. I think he's dead."

"You saw it?" Cop voice.

"I saw it clearly. He's facedown on the floor."

"We have the address of the Duncans' old summer place in Rockport," he said. "Your source at the Friendly Tavern was right. I was about to send a man over there to check it out." He paused. "I'll get out of desk duty and go there myself. I can't very well tell my officer to expect to find a body that my girlfriend saw in a vision, can I? But, hey. It's still a missing person case. We're still looking for Pat Duncan. Let's just hope that's not him on the floor."

"Be careful, Pete," I warned. "If it is Pat, and if he is dead, what if whoever is responsible is still there in the cabin?"

"I'm always careful, my love. I'll call you later."

"Be careful," I said again, finished off my third cup of morning coffee and, now wide awake, headed for the reception desk to see if there was anything interesting for me on Rhonda's whiteboard.

"Hi, Lee. I didn't expect you until noon," Rhonda greeted me. "I watched you on the news last night. Good job. And you look great in pink."

"Thanks," I said. "I couldn't sleep, so I thought I might as well come in." I pointed to the whiteboard. "If there's nothing special for me today, I guess I'll do some catching up in my office."

"Scott's on his way to the police station to cover a statement from Chief Whaley about the missing baker," she recited, "and Howie's here on standby, so you're probably safe from assignments today."

"Well, if anything turns up before noon, I'm available." I sighed. "I'll go downstairs and order oats for Ranger Rob's horse Prince Valiant, and treats for Paco the Wonder Dog. I suppose Scott's report will be live?"

"Sure. Everybody in Salem is looking for Pat," she said. "Maybe the chief has something new to report. Scott told me that Pat's wife has put up a ten-thousand-dollar reward for information about where he is. Maybe that's what the chief is going to announce."

Ten thousand dollars, and they aren't paying their bills?

Chapter Seven

As soon as I closed my glass door I turned on the TV. I didn't want to miss a word of the chief's update on the missing man while I hurriedly ordered oats and treats online. Within minutes, the "Breaking News" banner flashed and a shot of the Salem Police Station came into view. Scott did a voice-over while the camera focused on an empty lectern on the podium in front of the building that the chief always uses for these events.

Scott used his hushed announcer voice. "Good morning, ladies and gentlemen. We're awaiting the arrival of Police Chief Whaley, who will make an announcement regarding the disappearance of Patrick Duncan, known to many as the owner of the Pretty Party Bakery, long a family-owned Salem landmark business. Mr. Duncan was last known to be in the bakery's kitchen during the early morning hours two days ago."

The chief approached the lectern, resplendent in full uniform complete with medals. He dislikes doing these appearances and I was sure it would be a brief statement, with as little time for questions as he could manage. "Here's Chief Whaley," Scott announced. "Let's hear what he has to say."

Chief Whaley, looking uncomfortable, rustled the papers on the lectern and looked into the cameras. "Good morning. Patrick Duncan went missing from his bakery the day before yesterday under unusual circumstances during the early morning hours. We are requesting the public's assistance in searching for this man." He held up a large photo. Scott's camera zoomed in on it. Pat was a pleasant-looking man—graying hair, blue eyes, a slim, athletic build. I'd seen him at the bakery many times. I remembered hearing that he worked out regularly at a local gym. He knew me by name, but we'd never had any social connections. "He is fifty years old, five feet, nine inches tall, about a hundred and sixty pounds, light complexion, blue eyes, gray hair," the chief intoned. "In hopes that it will encourage citizen cooperation in the hunt for her husband, Dolores Duncan is offering a ten-thousand-dollar reward for any information leading to his safe return to his family. Mr. Duncan did not take his automobile, his wallet, his watch or his phone with him. It has not been determined whether he left the premises willingly or unwillingly. We're asking people in the vicinity of the Pretty Party Bakery who have security cameras to check their footage for possible sightings of Mr. Duncan. A person of interest in

this matter is a man or woman wearing an astronaut costume, last seen in the vicinity of Winter
Street yesterday morning. People in the Winter
Street area are asked to check their security cameras for footage of this person." The chief shuffled
the papers again. I couldn't help smiling at the description of the "person of interest." If Chris's costume sales promotion worked out, before long
there could be 140 people walking around in
Salem who'd fit that description. He gave a special
hotline telephone number where people could
call with information. The number flashed at the
bottom of the screen.

I hoped that when the chief asked for questions,
Scott would pick up on that "willingly or unwillingly" line and ask for some clarification. For instance, is the department thinking of kidnapping
as a possibility? Has there been a ransom note? I
know *I'd* have some questions about it if I were behind the mic.

The question period came and went. Most of
the questions were about the reward money. If several people came up with the same information,
who would get the money? What if somebody has
him tied up somewhere and they bring him in? Do
they get the reward anyway?

Chief Whaley said that the first caller with good
information gets the reward. As to the other un-
likely event, Mrs. Duncan would have to make the
reward decision, but the captor would face criminal charges. After that question was answered, Scott,
to his credit, *did* ask if there was any indication
of this being a kidnapping situation. The chief

answered that all aspects of Pat Duncan's disappearance were being considered and investigated—
then hurriedly said "thank you," and practically ran
back into the building. He really hates doing these
things. A picture of the missing man and the telephone number for information came up on the
screen—good fast work by the WICH-TV graphics
crew.

Pete hadn't said a word about this being a kidnapping, but my inner Nancy Drew had kicked in.
What if there had been a ransom note? What if Dolores Duncan had agreed to pay it? And if she had,
where was the money coming from?

Scott signed off and the station returned to regular programing—in this case, a documentary on
whale watching. I'd already seen it, so I turned off
the set and tried to get my mind to focus on my
job. But, between the disturbing vision of a seem-
ingly dead man on a nondescript floor in an old
cabin in some woods, and the increasingly interesting search for the local cupcake baker, it wasn't
easy to concentrate on groceries for dog and
horse. I couldn't help looking at my watch every few
minutes. It was still much too early to start my walk
over to the Pretty Party to pick up Buck's birthday
cake. Maybe while I was there though, I'd be able
to pick up some more information about Pat Duncan to share with Pete. He'd been right about the
guys at the Friendly being willing to talk to me
about things they wouldn't tell a cop. It only made
sense that the same might be true at the bakery.

By 11:15 I couldn't wait any longer. I told Rhonda
I'd be out for an hour, avoided Old Clunky and

that polished door, and walked downstairs and out onto Derby Street. The bakery is a few blocks away, located among other attractive shops on Salem's downtown pedestrian mall. I could smell cinnamon buns while I was still five or six storefronts away. Very tempting. I'd probably return to the station with more than Buck's cake. The mall was busy, with costumed people moving among the shoppers in a sort of good-natured ballet. I stopped to let a clown who was having trouble walking with his giant shoes get ahead of me in the short line in front of the bakery. "You here for the giant cupcakes?" he asked. "Everybody seems to want them because of the Halloween colors." He winked. "Or maybe we're all just nosy because of the missing man."

"Just picking up a birthday cake," I said, telling myself I wasn't being nosy—only curious.

"You know what I heard?" he whispered. He didn't wait for an answer. "I heard that Pat owes everybody in town and he's run out on his creditors. I wouldn't be surprised, would you?"

I was surprised by the question. "I didn't really know him," I stammered, realizing immediately that I'd used the past tense—that I knew in my heart that Pat was dead.

"Well, thanks for letting me cut in line," he said. "I'm having a problem with the shoes. I should have worn my own shoes inside these so they wouldn't be so floppy."

I'd stayed a few steps behind him, anticipating possible shoe-related collisions ahead. "No problem," I mumbled as he entered the store. Then I quickly stepped out of the line and called Pete. "Have you turned the Dumpster suit over to forensics yet?" I almost shouted.

"I just left there," he said. "They were in no hurry to touch the thing. What a smelly mess. Why? What's going on."

"I know why Pat's footprints didn't lead out the door. It was definitely Pat Duncan in the costume—not some mysterious kidnapper looking for ransom. He put the space boots on over his own size-nine shoes," I announced. "I'll bet they'll find the orange goo inside the Dumpster boots."

Short pause before the cop voice. "I'll bet you're exactly right," he said. "Did I ever tell you you'd make . . ."

"Yes, you did," I said. "No thanks. Let me know what you find out. I have to go pick up a birthday cake now."

Within a minute or so I was inside the bakery where it was good to see that the famed triple-layer cupcakes were back in the display case alongside the cinnamon buns. It was a surprise though, to see a smiling Dolores Duncan behind the counter, serving customers. She caught my eye. "Hello there, Lee! We have Buck's cake all ready for you. It's in the refrigerator case out back. Wait a sec. I'll get it." Stripping off disposable gloves, she pushed open the windowed door to the kitchen. I recognized it because of Scott's photo. "Will there be anything else, Lee?" asked another of the familiar pink-smocked counterwomen.

I ordered a dozen of the cinnamon buns for the break room. "It looks as if everything is moving smoothly," I said. "I'm sure this is a difficult time for you all."

"It is," she agreed, "but Dolores keeps us all going. Such a strong person. And Tommy—you know Tommy? He's the manager. He's doing his best to keep everything moving along as usual. He even got hold of the secret triple-layer cupcakes recipe somehow and showed us how to make them. He's keeping Dolores encouraged. She's positive that Pat will be back with us soon and she was absolutely thrilled that you saved his little cat. I'm sure she'll thank you herself."

She was right. Dolores reappeared with a square, white, pink-ribbon-tied cake box, came around the counter and gave me a hug. "How can I ever thank you enough for saving little Cupcake," she said. "I cried happy tears when I saw how you held her and how she snuggled against your shoulder. I know Pat is grateful too."

I held back my own tears, sure that her happiness was misplaced, and returned her hug. "She's a dear little cat and I'm so glad she's safe at home again." I used the company credit card, picked up my purchases and hurried away, beginning to feel somewhat underdressed among the many creatively costumed pedestrians. I'd developed the habit of watching for astronauts in particular among the superheroes, sexy nurses and green-faced witches. During the short walk back to Derby Street, I spotted two space-suited men and one boy, and wondered if any of them had been reported so far on the chief's special hotline.

Back at the station I put the boxed cake into the

break room refrigerator with a sticky note warning "Do Not Touch," and left the bag of cinnamon rolls on the table with a "Help Yourself" note. There was still nothing for me on Rhonda's whiteboard, so I retreated to my cozy glass cage, knowing I should be doing some prep work for the upcoming week's programs. Ranger Rob and Katie the Clown needed some new "knock-knock" jokes to share with their little buckaroos on *Ranger Rob's Rodeo* and I needed to get the Halloween book list from the Wicked Good Books bookstore for *Shopping Salem.* I kept looking through the glass wall at the news studio clock. How long could it take for the forensic people to clean up a messy space boot and check inside for orange marmalade?

It turned out that it didn't take long at all. Pete sounded excited, in a cop-voiced sort of way. "You called it, babe," he said. "Pat Duncan walked out of the bakery via the back door wearing an astronaut costume. He made it as far as Winter Street where the cab picked him up. We've interviewed the driver again. He says the customer told the dispatcher that he'd be wearing an astronaut suit and to watch for him walking from the Hawthorne Boulevard end of the mall toward Bridge Street by way of Winter Street."

"So that's how he happened to turn up under the oak tree in front of our house," I said, "and little Cupcake must have followed him all the way there."

"Seems so," Pete agreed. "And that dog on your aunt's surveillance film chased her up into the tree."

"Cats are amazing creatures," I told him. "You have to admit it."

"Some of them seem to be," he agreed, "including O'Ryan, of course."

"He kept her in the tree until it was safe for her to leave it," I said. "I've got to get back to work now. Let me know if anything else interesting turns up."

"You do the same."

I promised that I would. It was surprising how soon something interesting actually *did* turn up.

Chapter Eight

By four o'clock I'd completed the Halloween book list and, with the aid of a totally silly session with Rhonda, come up with a dozen acceptable knock-knocks for the little kids. It had been long agreed that River would be the one to present Buck with his birthday cake at the end of his news program. I'd already decided to stay awake until midnight to watch it happen.

My phone buzzed. ID showed the Friendly Tavern. "Hi, Lee. This is Leo, your friendly neighborhood bartender here."

"Hello, Leo. What's going on?"

"I told you I'd call if I heard anything interesting about Pat. The darnedest thing just happened. If I hadn't seen it with my own eyes, heard it with my own ears . . ."

"Leo. What is it?" I interrupted. "What happened?"

"You're not going to believe this, Lee, but Pat Duncan is alive and well and filthy rich. I'm not kidding. Dolores—that's Pat's cute young wife—came marching in here half an hour ago with one of those big green plastic bank envelopes jammed full of cash—all in hundreds. She sat down at the end of the bar and said, 'Anybody Pat owes money to because of his betting, just tell me how much he owes you. He sent me here to pay his debts.' " Leo laughed aloud. "Honest to God, Lee, that's exactly what she did. Handed out those hundreds like it was Monopoly money. She even gave me one even though he was only into me for around fifty, 'cause I know better than to bet with him."

"Did Dolores say that Pat is alive? That he'd come home with all that money?" Maybe I'd been wrong about the body in my vision. Maybe Pat Duncan was okay. I hoped so.

"Um—now that you mention it, she didn't exactly say that he was home. She said that he'd sent her money though. Maybe he's someplace else, but anyway—wherever old Pat is, he must have struck it rich." Leo chuckled. "Some of the guys think he might have hit the Lotto or the Power-ball. The word around town is that *somebody* from Salem won a big prize, but they worked it so the money went to some kind of trust they'd set up so no one would know who the winner was. Not a bad idea. You know how long-lost friends and relatives come out of the woodwork when there's a big win."

Has Dolores reported her sudden wealth to the police? "Thanks so much for this, Leo. I'll get right on it!" I told him.

"You go, girl," he said. "I'll look for you on the nightly news again soon!"

I called Pete immediately. "Is it true that Pat Duncan is back with a pile of money?"

"It's true that his wife has come into a pile of money," he said. "She insists that Pat sent it to her and will be home soon. Unfortunately, we have good reason to believe that's not the case."

"You think Pat's dead," I said. It was a statement, not a question.

Cop voice. "The identification isn't official yet. But, yes, your vision was correct. There is a dead man in a cabin owned by the Duncan family. The man is recently deceased."

"Deceased how?" I wanted to know. "How did he die?"

"We don't have the coroner's report yet. There are no outward signs of violence."

Pete had said "recently." The man has been missing for several days. In police parlance a three-day-old body doesn't classify as "recently deceased." So I asked, "How recently?"

"Eight, ten hours maybe. Very recently. Rigor hadn't passed yet."

River has always told me that the visions, like dreams, can show the past, the present or the future. In this case, my vision of the dead man on the floor had shown me the future and I'd mistakenly thought about it as being in the present. If only we had acted sooner, perhaps we could have saved him. Pat must have been alive in that cabin when Pete and I were eating ice cream at Sam's Super Scoops.

Another question popped into my head. "Who

gave Dolores the money that is supposed to have come from Pat?"

"So far, she's refusing to tell us. She insists that Pat wants her to pay his local gambling debts with it. That he's not going to gamble anymore, so he doesn't want to go to any of the places that might tempt him, and that they're going on a nice vacation when he gets home. She's given out most of what he sent her, she says, to his bookie and some of his gambling friends, but she still has a few thousand to buy some nice vacation clothes."

"Where does she think they're going?"

"Belize, apparently."

"Wow," I said. "I've heard it's really nice there. They have beautiful beaches."

"They also have some very nice offshore bank accounts," Pete said.

"I guess that's a good thing too, if they've really come into money lately. Presuming that the body in the cabin *is* Pat Duncan," I said, "who is going to tell Dolores? Somebody is going to have to take charge of the business, make final arrangements. She's going to be devastated. Right now she's all happy, planning a vacation—and poof! She's going to be planning a funeral. The poor woman!"

"I know." I heard the sympathy in his voice. "I've noticed that in the few times I've met with Mrs. Duncan, she seems to rely quite a lot on the store manager—Tommy LaGrange. Maybe we'll arrange for him to be present when we notify her officially. He seems like a levelheaded person. According to the staff, he's put a lot of effort into keeping the business afloat in spite of Pat's gambling problem."

"I've heard that too," I said. "Has anybody mentioned to you the possibility that Pat might have won a big prize from Lotto or Powerball? The guys at the Friendly mentioned it. It seems that one of the big winning numbers was sold in Salem, but the person who won kept their name secret by putting it into some kind of trust. Is there some way you can find out who the winner is?"

Cop voice was back. "It can be done. I'll see about it. It might take a while. By the looks of his wastebasket at the restaurant, he must have stopped every day at darned near every place in Salem that sells lottery tickets."

"It's true, isn't it," I mused, "that gambling is just as much an addiction as drugs or alcohol?"

"Sad, but true," Pete agreed. "In Pat's case, his gambling has affected not only himself and Dolores, but the entire business his family spent years building. There's a possibility that the Pretty Party Bakery doors might close forever."

"That's so sad," I said. "I remember my childhood birthday cakes coming from there—and so many of my friends' wedding cakes too. I hope there'll be some way to save the place. I'll bet there are still people standing in line right now to buy the triple-layer cupcakes."

"If somebody can figure out a way to pay off the creditors and if there isn't a gambler or a thief hiding in the wings—I guess it could be done."

"If Pat actually *did* win a big lottery prize, that would take care of everything, wouldn't it?" I was hopeful.

"It seems that way to me. We'll get started today on tracing the recent big winners who put their winnings in trusts. Want to do something tonight after I get out of here?"

"What do you have in mind?" I asked, knowing that whatever it was, I'd like the idea.

"How about fried clams and a walk on the beach?"

"Perfect," I said. "Let me know when."

It was nearly five o'clock—my regular time to leave work. I straightened out my desktop—having glass walls encourages neatness—and e-mailed the knock-knocks to Ranger Rob. I sent River a reminder to get the cake from the break room before Buck's news show. Feeling virtuous about the day's accomplishments, I checked out with Rhonda and headed downstairs.

I stopped, as I'd planned, at the dry cleaners to pick up my jacket. The counterman showed it to me before sliding it into a plastic bag. "See? That little stain came out clean as a whistle. Was it orange marmalade, by any chance?"

"That's exactly what it was," I admitted.

"Yep. I recognized it by the smell. My grandma used to make it." He handed me the wrapped jacket. "If it happens again, tell whoever cleans it that it's an orange stain. If you leave it on too long the citric acid can bleach the fabric."

"I'll remember that," I promised.

I hurried across the common. I didn't know what time Pete might be ready for our date, but I wanted to be prepared for fairly short notice. October evenings can be cool in Salem, so jeans and a sweatshirt would be in order for beach walking— New England fried clams go with everything.

O'Ryan, as usual, waited for me beside the front door, his nose pressed against the long side window. As soon as I was inside, I patted his fuzzy head and draped the jacket carefully over the newel post at the foot of the front stairs. "Aunt Ibby, it's me," I called, and started through the living room toward the kitchen, O'Ryan bounding ahead of me like a frisky tiger cub. I nearly tripped over him when he stopped short, directly in front of the closed door of my aunt's small, first-floor bathroom.

"Whoa, boy," I complained. "Watch where you're going."

Aunt Ibby poked her head around the corner. "What's going on? Are you all right, Maralee?'

"I'm fine, no thanks to him." I pointed to O'Ryan, who stood in my way, legs braced, pit-bull fashion, looking up at me, daring me to pass. "He darned near made me fall."

"Oh, dear." She flapped her hands at the cat. "Naughty boy. Shoo!"

O'Ryan backed up, turned and scratched at the bathroom door and meowed loudly.

"Looks like he's trying to tell us something." I reached for the doorknob. "You want us to go in here?" He stood aside, waiting for me to turn it. As soon as I did, he ran into the tidy, square room.

"What on earth would he want in here?" my aunt wondered aloud. "He doesn't do things like this unless there's a reason."

She was right. Many times, since the witch's cat had come to live with us, he'd led us to answers, solutions, results we'd never have found without him. I didn't even pretend to understand how or why he did it, but I knew better than to ignore him.

"He's trying hard to tell us something." I stooped and picked him up. "What do you want us to see?" There wasn't much to look at. A stall shower, a pedestal sink, a toilet, a towel rack, a recessed open cabinet holding towels and tissues, soaps and shampoos. There was a photo of Niagara Falls on one wall and a mirrored medicine cabinet over the sink. I turned slowly, giving him a good look at everything in the room. I pushed the shower curtain aside so he could see behind it. I lifted a pink towel from the rack so that he could see under it. We faced the mirror. I pointed. "See us?"

He meowed again. Loudly. Gave me a soft tap on the nose with his paw. "He wants to see inside," I announced. "Is that right, O'Ryan?" I braced him against my shoulder with one hand and pulled the cabinet door open with the other. A long, loud purr told me I was right. But what did it mean? The three shelves held the usual bathroom necessities—bandages, toothpaste, rubbing alcohol, ointments, face creams. The top shelf held an assortment of medicine bottles and boxes.

I held the cat close to the cabinet. He reached out a front paw and gently tapped the top shelf. "Pills," I said. "What kind of pills do you keep in here, Aunt Ibby?"

"Oh, the usual." She shrugged. "Blood pressure

medicine, aspirin, a bunch of vitamins, some prescription stuff for coughs and colds, some pain pills. You know, the usual things everybody has."

That seemed about right to me. I moved O'Ryan closer to the shelf. He tapped a bottle. I recognized it as an over-the-counter headache remedy. I picked it up. "This one?" I asked. He reached out again, this time tapping the plastic container behind the headache pills. It bore the label common to prescriptions. "This one?"

"Mmruppp." That had a positive sound to it.

I put the cat down and held the bottle out so that my aunt could read the label. "Oh, yes," she said. "This was the medicine the doctor prescribed when I broke my wrist. It's very effective for pain. I saved it in case I ever break anything else."

I recognized the name of the drug. It was a name that often showed up in reports of overdose deaths. "I'm pretty sure you're not supposed to save this kind of medication," I said. "If it fell into the wrong hands it could hurt somebody. Might even kill somebody. The pharmacist will tell you how to get rid of it."

It might kill somebody and leave no sign of violence.

My aunt covered her mouth with her hands. "Oh, dear. I'll get rid of it. Is that why O'Ryan pointed it out to us?'

"Maybe. But maybe he's showing us what happened to Pat Duncan."

"What happened to Pat? Do you mean he's dead?"

"I just found out myself. It'll probably be on the news pretty soon. He was found dead on the floor of an old cabin his family owned up in Rockport—

and, Aunt Ibby, I know you don't like to hear about the . . . um . . . the things I see sometimes—but that scene of the man on the floor was in a vision I've had three times recently."

"I'm so sorry." She reached for my hand and held it tight. "What did he die from? He wasn't that old."

"The M.E. hasn't given a cause—but maybe from what O'Ryan just showed us, I'm betting it had something to do with pills."

Chapter Nine

Pete doesn't like talking about the visions any more than Aunt Ibby does. He calls it "seeing things." He's not crazy about discussing the strange things O'Ryan can do either, but I knew that I'd better tell him what the cat had just shown us. I picked up the green jacket, climbed the stairs to my apartment, and called him. As soon as he answered I skipped the preliminaries and jumped right in.

"Was it oxycodone?"

"Yes." He dropped his voice to a whisper. "Another vision?"

"No. It was the cat this time. An overdose?"

Cop voice. "The cat. Of course. Yes. An overdose."

"Intentional?" It was my turn to whisper.

"Very doubtful, but someone went to a lot of

trouble to make it look that way. We'll talk later, okay?"

"Okay. Later. Fried clams and beach walk."

"Seven o'clock?"

"Perfect," I said.

I began watching the kitchen clock the second I hung up. It's a vintage Kit-Cat Klock and the googly eyes and the swinging tail mark the passing seconds with a tick-tock sound. Would seven o'clock never come? Who was the someone who tried to make Pat Duncan's death look intentional? I checked my watch while I changed into jeans and a purple Emerson College sweatshirt, then ran back to the kitchen to watch Kit-Cat some more. I turned on the WICH-TV evening news. There was no mention of Pat Duncan at all, so the news of his recent demise must not have yet been shared.

Seven o'clock did eventually arrive along with my right-on-time date. O'Ryan had already gone downstairs to Aunt Ibby's place and I was ready to toss my hobo bag over my shoulder, climb into Pete's car, and get straight to the promised "we'll talk later" part of the evening. As soon as we'd pulled away from the curb, I began the conversation.

"So tell me everything. Who tried to make Duncan's death look like suicide?"

"Later," he said again. "First, what's all this about the cat telling you about oxycodone? Exactly how does that work? I mean, how come he never says anything smart when I'm around?"

"He doesn't *talk*," I insisted. "That would be silly."

"But he communicates somehow, right?"

"You know he does. How many times have I told you about the wonderful things he can do? Don't ask me how he does it. I guess being a witch's familiar has something to do with it."

"A witch's familiar? Sure." He tried to smother a laugh. "Seriously, Lee. How do you know about the pills?"

"Aunt Ibby had an old prescription for them in her medicine cabinet. There were still pills in the bottle. O'Ryan was insistent that we open the cabinet," I told him. "Then he simply tapped on the bottle with his paw. Easy peasy."

"Too easy." He sounded disappointed. "That's not exactly something that would stand up in court. Something I could tell the chief."

"Like what?"

"Oh, I don't know. Like you'd seen Pat gulping down pills once."

"According to the guys at the Friendly Tavern, he was a total health nut. If he gulped down anything I'll bet it would be vitamins."

"So a half-full bottle of oxycodone pills on his coffee table doesn't fit the picture?"

"Not in the slightest. What does his wife say?"

"As a matter of fact, Pat's name is on the prescription bottle. Seems he had an old knee injury from when he played baseball in college. It kicks up once in a while and he takes the oxy. Otherwise she says he maintains a strictly healthy diet. He rarely even ate any sweets from the bakery—including the famous cupcakes."

"But the M.E. found it in his system," I said.

"How did it get there? They aren't suspecting suicide, are they?"

"Somebody is hoping we think that, but no, we think your guess about vitamins is right on," he told me. "If Pat was experiencing knee pain he might have taken a couple of pain pills but certainly nowhere near the amount the M.E. found in his system. The M.E. also found significant traces of . . ." He pulled a scrap of paper from his pocket. "Hydroxypropyl methylcellulose," he read aloud, syllable by syllable. "Also known as HPMC."

"What does it mean?" I prodded.

"It's what some medical capsules are made from."

I began to understand. "Like vitamin capsules."

"Exactly like vitamin capsules—like the ones we found in his bathroom."

"But the oxycodone wasn't in capsules," I said.

"Right again," he said. "Plain old white pills." We pulled into the nearly full parking lot behind Dube's Restaurant, justly famous for their fried clams. "It looks like a full house," he said. "We'll talk some more later." I understood what he meant. The tables at Dube's are pretty close together and a conversation about a recent murder wasn't something we'd want nearby diners to overhear. I resigned myself to waiting for the promised walk on the beach to learn more about Pat Duncan's demise.

It was a short ride over to Marblehead's Deveraux Beach and, as though by mutual consent, we waited until we arrived there before we resumed the conversation. I began it.

"So somebody dumped out the vitamins that were in the capsules," I suggested, "and filled them up with the drug."

"Looks that way," he agreed. "The capsules themselves are vegetarian based. They don't contain any preservatives or sugar or anything else except water. They're easy to swallow and tasteless. He wouldn't have had a clue that they weren't his regular vitamins."

"So somebody mashed up the pain pills and filled the empty capsules. What a dirty trick." I was angry at the thought. "Who would do such a thing?"

He was quiet for a moment. There was no one else in sight on the beach and the sound of the waves lapping up onto the shore was so peaceful it seemed far removed from talk of murder.

"Off the record?" he asked.

"Of course."

"Somebody knew exactly how many vitamin capsules Pat took every day—and they knew too, how much oxycodone it would take to kill him, and how fast it might work. Somebody waited until they were sure he was dead, and planted the oxy bottle on the coffee table. We figure that Pat ingested the equivalent of at least one hundred sixty milligrams of crushed immediate release pills—probably more. Enough to kill the proverbial moose."

"But why?" was all I could think of to say.

"The chief always says there are only three reasons for murder." Pete used his cop voice.

"Really? Only three? What are they?" I wondered aloud.

Pete held up his hand. Counted on three fingers. "Money, love and revenge."

"So if Pat Duncan is dead because of one of those it has to be money," I reasoned. "He owed so much of it."

"Probably so," Pete agreed, "but what if Dolores and Tommy have a thing going on? And what if one or the other of them thought Pat was in the way of their love?"

It was a surprising new idea. I frowned. "I don't think so, but I guess it's possible. Does revenge have a place in this picture?"

"Sure. What if Pat did something to make someone angry enough to pay him back by killing him?"

"Triple-layer reasons for murder," I realized, "and Pat could be the victim of any one of them."

"Or more than one of them," Pete said. "Remember the tip you gave me? The one about the possibility that he might have won something big in the lottery?"

"Sure. The guys at the Friendly said somebody had put the winnings into some kind of trust so people wouldn't be hounding them for money," I recalled. "You were going to check that story out."

"We checked it. It took a while to cut through the red tape, but we found a solid connection to Pat Duncan in the result."

"So he was rich after all? The money he sent to Dolores is legit? And there's millions more behind it?" I was happy for her. Even without Pat at her side, she'd be able to hold on to the bakery.

"Not exactly," Pete said. "There was a wining ten-million-dollar ticket sold on an instant ticket game in Salem about two weeks ago. The store that sold it doesn't know who bought it. Their surveillance video shows a man who looks somewhat like Pat, but his collar was turned up, covering the lower half of his face. Besides that, Pat didn't sign it. Somebody else did."

"No!" I couldn't believe it. "The first thing they always tell you is to sign your ticket."

"That's right. But apparently Pat was so far in debt, he didn't want to risk having anyone know that he was suddenly a millionaire."

I thought about that for a moment while we walked along the hard-packed sand at the water's edge. "That makes a certain amount of sense, I suppose," I admitted, "but how else could he collect his ten million dollars?"

"If the winner wants to take his prize in cash, after all the taxes he only gets six million, five hundred thousand," Pete explained. "He arranged for someone else to form a blind trust and to sign for the money."

"That's a pretty big 'only,'" I said. "So who picked up the cash for Pat? Was it Dolores?"

"Strictly off the record for now," Pete said, "Tommy LaGrange picked up the cash."

"Oh, good," I said. "Tommy has certainly been a trusted friend of the family for a long time. So where is the money now?"

Pete shrugged his shoulders as we turned and headed back toward the car. "We don't know for sure. Besides that, we don't know where Tommy LaGrange is either."

I stopped short, looking up at Pete. "You don't

think something bad has happened to Tommy too, do you?"

Long pause. Cop voice. "Define bad," he said.

I didn't know how to answer that right away. I had to think about it for a minute. My voice, when it came, sounded squeaky. Unsure. "Are you thinking maybe Tommy *did* something bad—not that something bad could have happened to him?"

"We believe it's a possibility. The money is gone and so is Tommy."

"That makes me so sad," I said, hoping that what I was thinking wasn't true. "Tommy is—was—Pat's best friend. What does Dolores think about it?"

"I don't know," he said. "She doesn't want to talk about it and we can't force her to. She's justifiably upset about Pat's death, but she refuses to speak about it to anybody. She hasn't even talked to her workers about it. Maybe she hasn't accepted the fact that he's gone. The poor woman is trying hard to keep the business running—a big enough job as it is, especially during the busy Halloween season. She's been throwing herself into the work. The staff says she barely takes time to sleep or eat. But without either Pat or Tommy around to help—and with Tommy possibly being dishonest or even worse . . . ?" He spread his hands in a helpless gesture. "She's between a rock and a hard place for sure."

"I wonder if there's anything I can do—or the station can do—to help her. I know what it is to lose your husband. Maybe I can get Mr. Doan to comp some ads for the cupcakes, or maybe Aunt Ibby could round up a few of her girlfriends to volunteer to help out in the bakery, or maybe she needs a go-fund-me page for the funeral expenses." I was sad and angry at the same time. "The whole community loves that little shop, cupcakes and all. It just wouldn't be right for Dolores to lose the business when none of this is her fault. Maybe Tommy will show up with the missing winnings and help her make sense of it all."

"Maybe," Pete said as we reached the car. He didn't really sound convinced.

The ride back to Winter Street was quiet—not in a bad way—sometimes we can ride along in silence for quite a while, each of us absorbed in our own thoughts. Pete was first to speak. "You said you'd like to help Dolores, maybe through WICH-TV somehow."

"Yes," I agreed. "I would. Can you think of a way I can help without seeming to be nosy? Without intruding on her misery? She's just lost her husband and now a trusted friend might turn out to be a crook—or worse."

"Can you think of a good reason to visit the bakery tomorrow morning?"

"I don't have to think of one. There was a message in my in-box to get some more cinnamon rolls. The first dozen only lasted in the break room for about an hour. I was planning to stop at the bakery on my way to work."

"That's good. Tell her you'd like to help, that you understand about her loss. You can share with her about losing Johnny if you want to." He reached across the console and patted my hand. "Only if you want to. It looks as though Pat trusted Tommy to go and collect the money for him. There was probably an arrangement to give Tommy some of the winnings too. All three names are on the trust. She refuses to talk to us about it. If Tommy LaGrange has grabbed the millions and run, she may never see a penny of it. That's not what Pat would have wanted."

"So you think I can get her to talk about something she clearly doesn't want to talk about?" I was doubtful about my chance of success if a professional police detective couldn't break her silence.

"The gamblers at the Friendly Tavern told you things they didn't tell me," he pointed out. "That was a big help. We *need* to find Tommy. Maybe he's perfectly honest. Maybe he knows something about Pat's death and he's hiding from a killer. Either way, he's the key to the whole mystery."

As soon as Pete said "mystery," my inner Nancy kicked in. Could I help get us to the end of *The Clue in the Old Oak Tree*? I decided instantly that I'd do my best to help Dolores Duncan in any way I could—and at the same time to help Pete solve that mystery!

Chapter Ten

It was a little past ten thirty when we arrived back at Winter Street. "We're in plenty of time to catch the late news and see Buck get his birthday cake," I said. "Do you think they'll have released the news about Pat Duncan's death by now? I watched the five o'clock broadcast and they didn't have anything yet."

"Chief didn't want to release anything before the M.E.'s report was in. I'm sure that by now your friend Scott Palmer is all over it," he said. "A detailed report was scheduled to go out earlier this evening." I fought against a moment of envy because *I* could have been the one to "be all over it"—except that everything I knew about Pat's death had been strictly "off the record." If Pete was right, we'd undoubtedly be seeing Scott right beside Buck at the anchor desk. Again.

"This will be bad for Dolores." I felt sympathy for the woman. "She'll have to accept the fact that Pat isn't coming back. That there'll be no vacation in Belize. That maybe there'll even be no bakery."

I didn't see any lights on in Aunt Ibby's part of the house, so Pete parked in the back driveway and we used the back staircase up to my apartment to avoid disturbing her. O'Ryan greeted us at the top of the stairs with a quiet "meow." Somehow, he always knows which entrance we'll use. "By the way," Pete remarked. "You didn't happen to bring home any of those cinnamon rolls, did you?"

"Sorry, no."

"I guess we'll have to go out for breakfast then."

"Guess so. Want to watch in the kitchen? I'll make coffee."

"Got any cookies?"

I checked the Red Riding Hood cookie jar. "You're in luck," I said. "Girl Scout Samoas." I started Mr. Coffee, put a sleeve of cookies onto a plate and turned on the TV, catching the end of a presentation on the restoration of the beautiful 1894 chapel at the Greenlawn Cemetery. The "Breaking News" banner heralded the start of Buck Covington's newscast.

"Good evening, Salem friends," Buck began, eyes downcast, the classically handsome face wearing an expression of sadness. "The body of Patrick Duncan, the local businessman who was reported missing from his downtown Salem bakery two days ago, has been found in a family-owned cottage in a remote area of Cape Ann. Police continue investigating circumstances of his death. Preliminary reports indicate a possible drug overdose. Scott Palmer has the story. Scott?" The camera shifted to Buck's left, and—sure enough—there was Scott, attempting to look sad, but not quite pulling it off.

"Most people in Salem are familiar with the Pretty Party Bakery," Scott began, as a shot of the pink and white facade of the building appeared on screen. "Here, generations of Salem folks have shopped for cakes and cookies, pies and fancy desserts. Most recently, the bakery has made news with the introduction of their latest confection, the triple-layer Halloween cupcake."

We viewed a picture of one of the cupcakes, cut in half to display its colorful layers, so like the coloration of the calico cat posed beside it. "Here's the cake, along with Pat Duncan's much-loved cat, appropriately named Cupcake." Next came the surveillance camera video of Cupcake racing along Winter Street. "We believe that this brave, small cat followed her master to where a taxi picked him up and transported him to a location near Rockport on Cape Ann, where he later died."

Scott gave one of his traditional long looks into the camera, and lowered his voice. "I spoke this afternoon with Dolores Duncan, Pat's bereaved widow. Here's what she told me." Once again, a shot of the bakery.

"Oh, no." I covered my eyes. "Please tell me he didn't get in there and shove a camera into that poor woman's face."

"Looks like he did," Pete said. "There she is."

Pete was right. Dolores, eyes red and swollen, a hair net askew over her pretty blond hair, up to her elbows in flour, blinked and seemed to back away from the camera. "Mrs. Duncan. We're so sorry about your great loss," Scott began. "Have the police told you anything more about how your husband died?"

She wiped a hand across her brow, leaving a white streak of flour. "Pills," she said. "He took some pills."

Scott nodded, trying to look wise. "I see. Was he in the habit of taking pills? Prescription pain pills?"

"What? No. I mean, he took *some* pills." Dolores turned away, looking behind her where pink-smocked employees watched the pair. "Regular pills that are good for him. Oh, I don't know. Please. Please. I don't know. Ask Tommy."

"For God's sake, Scott," I yelled at the TV. "Stop it!"

At this point a large, pink-smocked woman stepped into the frame, one arm protectively around Dolores's shaking shoulders, her finger pointed at Scott. "Get out of here," she shouted, followed by several words that were bleeped out. For a fleeting instant, the screen went black and we were back at the news desk, Buck wide-eyed, Scott undeterred. "There you have it." He smirked into the camera. "Did Pat Duncan have an addiction to prescription pills? Mrs. Duncan and others at the bakery don't seem to want us to know the details of the man's untimely death. We believe that the person named Tommy is Thomas La-Grange, the bakery's general manager. So far, he's not answered our calls. We'll continue to investigate this tragic loss to the community—and we'll get to the whole truth of the matter. Stay tuned to WICH-TV."

Buck, as unflappable as ever, nodded in Scott's direction. "Thank you, Scott Palmer, for that interesting interview. Now let's hear from Wanda, our crack meteorologist, with tomorrow's weather."

"He didn't mention anything about the lottery money," I said. "Or about Tommy LaGrange being missing."

"There's nothing to report. Pat Duncan never signed the ticket and the money is in a blind trust. I doubt that Scott even knows about it. Tommy isn't officially missing, you know. He just hasn't reported for work. He's not going to answer Scott's calls anyway. I tracked his phone and it's still in his apartment here in Salem. He recently renewed his lease and he told the landlord he was looking for a new job. Mrs. Duncan says that Pat sent her cash by mail and that she paid some of his debts with it." Pete scowled. "We don't have the manpower to check every little thing. A man gives his wife money to pay his gambling debts. Nothing wrong with that. Another man is looking for a new job. Was he unhappy at his work? Did he get fired? It's none of our business. There's enough real crime happening around a city this size—especially at Halloween—to keep the department busy."

"But *you're* interested in what's become of the money Pat won," I pointed out. "And *you* want to know where Tommy is. You're interested enough to want me to talk to Dolores, to see if she'll share anything with me that she doesn't want to talk to the police about."

"Yes. I'm interested. I'd like to assign somebody to track Tommy LaGrange—to find out where he's gone and if he has the lottery money. But so far, he hasn't broken any law. He established the trust. He signed the ticket. They gave him the cash. We know Dolores received an amount of cash that she says came from Pat. How much cash did she get? Maybe she has the whole amount. Who knows? There must have been some sort of agreement between the parties about how to share the money. Either way, an agreement between parties can be perfectly legal. The money she gave to the men at the Friendly Tavern wasn't stolen, wasn't counterfeit." Long sigh. "I'm *still* interested. But unless one of the three—Dolores or Tommy or Pat—is guilty of breaking some law, what can I do?"

"It's kind of a triple layer of people, isn't it?" I couldn't help smiling at the idea. "But, seriously, there's a murder involved," I said, "and you're still investigating that."

"True," he agreed, brightening. "And *that*, with a little discreet snooping on your part, might lead us somewhere."

"Count me in," I said, caught up in the moment, and with no idea of what my snooping might lead us to. Wanda, wearing a really cute Pippi Longstocking costume, finished explaining isobars and cumulous clouds. The seat beside Buck was empty—for the moment. "Watch now," I told Pete. "It's time for the birthday cake."

River, resplendent in a long, pale blue, strapless sequined sheath—using an exaggerated tiptoe motion, sneaked up behind Buck, the birthday cake held aloft. On cue, the stage crew, Wanda, Scott and the camera operators burst into an off-key rendition of "Happy Birthday." Finally, with cake admired, cut and shared and with River discreetly kissed on the cheek, Buck resumed the nightly news with a bulletin about off-street parking.

"Are you planning to watch River's show after this?" Pete asked. I told him I might watch for a while, at least up until the late movie. "I guess I'll go along home then," he said. "I'll call you in the morning about breakfast."

"That'll be great," I said. "Good night. Love you."

"Love you too." He let himself out quietly. I turned off the kitchen TV, donned pajamas, turned on the bedroom TV and slipped under the covers of my bed, where a large yellow cat was already sound asleep. Often River makes a few personal comments before she begins to take calls from viewers, and on this night she chose to talk about cake—in particular, birthday cake.

"Those of you who watched the news just before the beginning of tonight's *Tarot Time* saw me present a birthday cake to newsman Buck Covington. Celebrating birthdays with cake is a long-standing tradition all around the world. Where did the custom begin? Most historians agree that the idea began in ancient Greece." She leaned toward the camera, smiling, clearly warming to the subject. "In those days honey cakes or bread were baked for birthday celebrations. Long ago Romans picked up on the idea too, with special food, and fifteenth-century Germans celebrated with a one-layer cake. During the seventeenth century cakes began to come in multiple layers." She held up a small plate, showing the audience her own neat slice of Buck's vanilla cake with vanilla cream filling and butter cream frosting. "Something like this delicious one from Salem's own Pretty Party Bakery."

She lifted a card from the tarot deck, laying it faceup in the center of her table. The overhead camera zoomed in. I recognized the six of pentacles. "Here we see a merchant weighing out gold on a scale so that he can distribute it with equal judgment. To many, this symbol represents casting bread—or even cake—upon the waters of life, knowing that it will come back threefold." She leaned forward, her long black braid over one shoulder, and looked into the camera. "The Pretty Party Bakery isn't a sponsor of this show, but I'd like to remind viewers that this long-established business has recently come upon hard times. As All Hallows' Eve approaches, perhaps you'll celebrate the occasion with a special sweet treat from Pretty Party, knowing that your help to a neighbor may come back to bless you threefold."

With the familiar dazzling smile, she put her right hand over the tarot deck, preparing to deliver a nightly mission statement. "I dedicate this deck to serve others with their spiritual growth, for wisdom, knowledge and to bring healing and peace to all who seek its wisdom."

River's theme music, "Danse Macabre," swelled. "First caller, please," she said.

Whatever you cast upon the water will come back three-fold.

Something like a triple layer?

Chapter Eleven

As he'd promised, Pete called at six thirty in the morning and we agreed to join the breakfast club gang at the Friendly Tavern. Good choice. There we could firm up plans for my proposed talk with Dolores Duncan and at the same time see if the regulars at the bar had come up with any new information about poor Pat or if they had any thoughts on where the elusive Tommy LaGrange might be. I got there first, just in time to see Pete's unmarked car pull up.

I recognized a few familiar faces among the crowd. We ordered coffee and doughnuts—cinnamon-sugar for me and vanilla frosted raisin for Pete. Bartender Leo took our orders. "So they found old Pat dead after all, huh? Pills, I heard. That's bull. He was too much of a health nut to do that crap." He leaned across the bar and spoke softly. "Who do you think offed him?"

I had no answer to that one and of course Pete didn't either. I shrugged. "No clue. What do you think?"

"We all think it's that manager of his. Tommy. Have you talked to him?" The question was directed to Pete.

"No." Serious cop voice.

Leo pressed on. "We heard he's skipped town. Quit his job and took off. Nobody's seen his car around lately."

I knew that the Salem police were looking for that car too, but Pete didn't say anything, so I did. "Any idea where he went?"

The man on my right spoke up. "We've got a pool going on that. Two bucks will get you in. I say the smart money is on Canada."

Pete remained silent. I fished two ones from my purse. "Belize," I said, suddenly confident that I was right. "That's where Dolores was planning to meet Pat."

"Makes sense," the man beside Pete remarked, tossing two dollars onto the bar. "I'll take a piece of that."

Pete wore his raised eyebrow cop face, but didn't comment. I didn't feel that I'd betrayed any of my "off the record" promises. Dolores had freely shared that she was buying clothes to wear in Belize. If Tommy had made the arrangements for the blind trust, it stood to reason that he probably made the travel arrangements too—and I didn't doubt for one second that the grieving Mrs. Duncan knew all about them. I could hardly wait to finish my doughnut and get right over to the Pretty Party and start some serious snooping.

Pete must have sensed my urgency. "Ready to go to work?" he asked, reaching for the check.

"Yep. I'll get the tip." I put a few more bills on the counter. "I'll walk downtown to pick up those cinnamon buns." We said goodbye to the assembled group and headed out onto Derby Street.

"I think you gave them something to think about." Pete unlocked his door. "Good job. They may find Tommy before we do. They have more manpower to spare."

"Between you, me and the Breakfast Club," I said, "along with a very wise cat and a tarot card reader—we'll figure this out."

A slight noncop eye roll and a "we'll see" was his response. I waved goodbye and crossed the street, intending to check in with Rhonda so that my cinnamon bun run would be "on the clock" and the snooping would be included.

I rode Old Clunky up to the second floor. Rhonda was ready with questions. "How did you like Scottie's ambush of the widow? Even Doan thought it was a bit much."

"Awful," I agreed, checking the whiteboard. "I don't see anything here for me. I'm going to run out for some break room snacks. I'll be back ASAP. Need anything downtown?"

"If you have time, you might check in with Chris Rich and see how the space suit sale is going. Doan is thinking of doing a follow-up and you might get the assignment since Scottie is kind of on the you-know-what list."

"Thanks. I'll definitely make time for that. It *is* a funny story, isn't it? I've already seen quite a few astronauts wandering around."

"Me too," she said. "In various sizes. And how about the creepy one that showed up in front of your place?"

Word hadn't reached the general public yet that the creepy astronaut was Pat Duncan and I wasn't about to comment on it. "Yeah, how about that?" I said. "Well, I'm off on a cinnamon bun run and I'll visit Chris Rich too."

Salem's always a good town for walking and the weather was perfect for it too. Anyway, I needed some exercise to work off that morning doughnut and the previous night's fried clams and Girl Scout Cookies, so I quickened my pace on the uphill sprint to the beginning of the pedestrian mall at the head of Essex Street. Once again, I recognized the good smells coming from the bakery even before the pink and white storefront was in sight. It would be a truly sad day in Salem if the place closed its doors forever.

Only a little bit out of breath, I peeked into the window of the bakery before approaching the door, hoping I'd see Dolores Duncan inside. She was there at the front counter, looking as fresh and friendly as she always had—a far cry from the distraught woman she'd appeared to be on the previous night's late news. I pushed the door open and approached the glass case where both the buns and the triple-layer cupcakes were displayed.

"Good morning, Lee," Dolores said. "I hope Buck's cake was satisfactory?"

"It was perfect, as always," I told her. "How are you feeling today?"

"I'm doing well." She smiled, just a tad too broadly. "Thank you for asking."

"Dolores, could you spare a minute to talk to me?" I motioned toward the kitchen door. "It may be important."

"Of course. Is something wrong?" She spoke softly then to one of the pink-smocked women and lifted the hinged counter so that I could enter. I followed her through the windowed door, past more pink-smocked, hair-netted workers into a small cubicle—even smaller than my tiny office. I sat opposite her across a tiny desk in one of the two chairs in the room. "Is something wrong?" she asked again. "Is it about my husband?"

"It's about Tommy," I said, not bothering with any snooping preliminaries. "It's important. Do you know where he is?"

"Is Tommy all right? Has something happened to Tommy too?" She put both hands to her face. Eyes closed.

"I don't know," I admitted. "Did Tommy go to Belize? To the vacation house you and Pat had planned for?"

The blue eyes opened wide. "Yes. That's where he said he was going. But I've called and called and he doesn't answer."

"He didn't take his phone with him," I told her as gently as I could. "The police have checked. That phone is still in his apartment."

She dropped her hands to her lap. "Oh, that phone. I know. He has a new number now, but he isn't answering calls or texts. I'm worried. What if he's . . . ? What if something is wrong with him?"

I slid into full Nancy Drew snoop mode. "So, you're worried about him too," I said. "I have a friend who knows a special way to track phones by their numbers. He could tell us exactly where Tommy's phone is. Then you could find out if he's safe. If you'll give me that number I'll call my friend right away."

"That would be so helpful, Lee. Here. I'll write it down for you." She scribbled on a pink sticky note and handed it to me. "Can you call your friend now?"

"Absolutely," I said, calling Pete's number as I spoke, trying to sound impersonal and business-like. "Hello," I said as soon as he answered. "This is Lee Barrett. If I text you a phone number, can you tell me where the phone is? I'm asking for a friend. You can? Thank you so much. I'll send it right along."

"Listen, Lee." Pete spoke urgently. "One more thing. Chief Whaley's message about calling with information about Pat is paying off. Apparently Pat had a high-stakes poker game going on for a couple of days in that cabin. Two anonymous callers claim they were there when somebody barged in and broke up the game. We'll talk later."

"I hope your friend can find Tommy," Dolores whispered as I texted the number to Pete. "I really need him back here to help me run things. Between Tommy and Pat, I never had to worry about the business end of things. I just supervised most of the baking and made sure everything looked clean and pretty."

"That's quite a lot," I told her. "Nobody can be expected to do everything. I understand how much you must miss your husband."

"So much," she said. "We had such wonderful

plans." Her voice dropped to a whisper. "I don't know if you've heard about it yet, but we are quite rich. Pat won a lot of money on a lottery ticket. He was going to stop gambling and pay all the bills we owe and take me on my dream vacation and we'd never have to work anymore if we didn't want to." Her voice broke. "It could have been perfect. The three of us, Pat and Tommy and I—we'd share the money equally. Tommy fixed it up so the money was safe in a bank far away. But then Pat took his two million out, put on that silly costume and disappeared."

I saw the beginning of tears in the blue eyes. "Pat sent me a lot of money to pay bills, but then Tommy found out that Pat was still gambling. He was in that old summer camp having a poker game. High stakes poker, Tommy called it." Tears spilled over. "Pat had already lost half a million dollars of our money. Tommy was furious. He said he'd put a stop to it." She put her head down on the desk. "I don't know why I'm telling you all this. With Pat and Tommy gone I have no one I can really talk to. I'm so worried about Tommy. What if something bad has happened to him too? What if . . . what if *he* did something bad?"

I didn't know how to respond. Being a snoop can be an unpleasant burden. Pete needed information, but I felt bad about listening when she was at such a vulnerable point. I patted her shoulder and didn't press her—with a fleeting thought of how Scott Palmer would close in on an opportunity like this. She looked up from the desk. "We need to find Tommy. He knows how everything runs here. He knows how to do everybody's job. If he'll come back I can take that vacation by myself. I know Pat wants me to." She brushed away tears. "I'm so tired."

I hardly dared to form the question. "Where will you go?"

"To Belize. We even got our passports and maps and everything. I hope your friend can find Tommy soon. I already bought some cute outfits."

My phone buzzed. "Lee? He's in a motel in Brownsville, Texas, close to the Gateway International Bridge. Looks like you're right. He's headed for Belize. And one more thing—forensics found one nice clear print of Tommy's thumb on the bottom of that vitamin bottle in Pat's medicine cabinet. Chief's working on an arrest warrant."

I snapped out of snooping mode. I'm no Scott Palmer. "Thank you," I told Pete, and hung up.

"My friend has located Tommy in Texas," I told Dolores. "He's in trouble but he's safe. Anytime you need a friend to talk to, I'm a phone call away. If you need any help in the bakery until all this mess gets straightened out, I know where we can find some volunteers." I stood. "You stay strong. You're going to be all right. I've got to go see a man about some Halloween costumes now."

Her expression brightened. "Oh, the astronaut costumes. That was funny, wasn't it? Yes. I'll be okay. Sorry to burden you with my problems."

"Anytime," I said, meaning it. "Anytime." I picked up my cinnamon rolls and started down Essex Street to Christopher's Castle to arrange for my assigned interview with Chris. I called Pete back.

"Dolores knows about the poker game. She says Tommy broke it up."

"Remember the callers I told you about?" Cop voice for sure. "We located one of them. He didn't come forward because he didn't want his wife to know about the game. They knew all about the lottery money. Pat had already gambled away about half a million of it. He says a guy showed up at the door and yelled at Pat—swore at him about gambling everything away. He told the card players to take their winnings and get out, that he was there to help his friend straighten out his life."

I interrupted. "So did he tell you who broke it up? Was it Tommy?"

"Yes, Nancy Drew. It was Tommy for sure. This man identified a picture. Anyway, while they were picking up their winnings and getting ready to leave the place, he heard Tommy telling Pat, very calmly, to go take a shower and shave and put on some clean clothes because he looked like hell after playing poker day and night. He said he was going to go in the kitchen and fix Pat some nice scrambled eggs and toast and orange juice and that he'd brought Pat his vitamin pills."

Things moved fast after that. The fingerprints on the vitamin bottle were Tommy's. The rest of the high rollers were rounded up and identified him. A judge swore out an arrest warrant for Thomas LaGrange. Brownsville authorities were alerted and Tommy was taken into custody within a few hours. Arrangements were hastily made for a team of deputies to fly from Beverly Airport to Browns-ville. There, Tommy in an orange jumpsuit was turned over by Texas marshals and returned to Salem, where he immediately lawyered up. He was, despite the circumstances, a millionaire and his high-priced attorneys prepared to fight the mur-der charge.

Dolores's third of the money, and as Pat's widow, what was left of Pat's third were deposited in an American bank. This made it possible for Dolores to settle with all of the creditors, and to make some needed repairs and improvements to the Pretty Party Bakery. She took a brief vacation in Belize after all and came home still grieving, but tanned, relaxed and ready to work.

Because we already had footage of Pat Duncan in an astronaut costume on Winter Street, the ob-vious tie-in to the murder made my interview with Chris Rich worthy of another late news appear-ance for me.

Thanks to his newfound wealth and the top-flight lawyers he's hired, Tommy LaGrange still hasn't come to trial for killing Pat Duncan, and the case may wind up in the court system for quite a while. Pete is as confident as ever that justice will prevail.

The Pretty Party Bakery has become a regular advertiser on WICH-TV. Cupcake the cat is some-times a guest on *Ranger Rob's Rodeo* and she often appears in the bakery's commercials.

Pete and I decided not to go to Buffy Doan's Halloween party as an astronaut and green alien girl after all. Buffy's parties usually last well into the night and, unlike the real astronaut suits, Chris

Rich's marked-down versions did not have bathroom adjustments. Anyway, Buffy had announced that the theme of this year's party would be "literary characters." Pete went dressed as Sherlock Holmes, complete with deerstalker hat and curved calabash pipe. I, of course, with long, straight skirt, cloche hat and giant magnifying glass, went as vintage Nancy Drew.

Aunt Ibby's Recipe Hack of Pat Duncan's Triple-Layer Halloween Cupcakes

The real recipe is still a secret, so here's Aunt Ibby's quick and easy cake mix version!

1 package of yellow or white cake mix
2 Tbsp. orange marmalade
Two ¼ oz. squares of baking chocolate, melted
1 can of creamy white frosting
Orange and chocolate Reese's Pieces

Prepare cake mix according to directions. Put about one cup of batter into each of two small bowls. In one of them, mix in the orange marmalade. In the other mix in the melted chocolate. Line muffin tin with twelve paper liners. Put a rounded tablespoonful of chocolate batter into each cup. Follow with a spoonful of orange marmalade batter. Finish with plain batter. Cups should be about three quarters full. Bake according to cake mix package directions. Cool cupcakes on wire rack, then frost with creamy vanilla frosting and decorate with Reese's Pieces.

Visit our website at
KensingtonBooks.com
to sign up for our newsletters, read
more from your favorite authors, see
books by series, view reading group
guides, and more!

Become a Part of Our
Between the Chapters Book Club
Community and Join the Conversation